Darkness Falls

Also by John M. Del Vecchio

The 13th Valley

Carry Me Home

For the Sake of All Living Things

John M. Del Vecchio

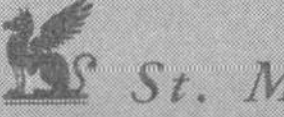 *St. Martin's Griffin* *New York*

This novel is a work of fiction. All of the events, characters, names, and places depicted in this novel are entirely fictitious or are used fictitiously. No representation that any statement made in this novel is true or that any incident depicted in this novel actually occurred is intended or should be inferred by the reader.

Editor: Jim Fitzgerald
Production Editor: Wah-Ming Chang
Copyedited by Pam Loeser
Design by Ellen R. Sasahara

Permission to use portions of "Black Coffee," words by S. Burke and P. F. Webster, is gratefully acknowledged to Sondot Music Corporation.

www.stmartins.com

Library of Congress Cataloging-in-Publication Data

Del Vecchio, John M.
Darkness falls : an American story / by John Del Vecchio.
p. cm.
ISBN 0-312-19216-9 (hc)
ISBN 0-312-26488-7 (pbk)
I. Title.
PS3554.E4327D37 1998
813'.54—dc21 98-23886
CIP

First St. Martin's Griffin Edition: August 2000

10 9 8 7 6 5 4 3 2 1

e pluribus unum

One out of many
Motto of the United States of America

To the public school teachers of America—urban, suburban, and exurban—who, despite ambient stories to the contrary, have made, and are making, our educational systems work.

Acknowledgments

I WOULD LIKE to thank Frank and Filomena Del Vecchio, my parents, for passing on many of the "old stories"; and my aunts, Ann Pavia, Anne Noonan, and Regina and Rosemary Antignani, for adding details. I wish I could have incorporated more, related your stories more accurately; unfortunately many did not fit within the framework of this novel. Perhaps someday, Pop, I'll get to use the story of the Army Air Corps' 1924 flight around the world, and your Waltersville School teacher's reaction.

I would also like to thank: my siblings, Mary-Jo Del Vecchio–Good, Frank A. Del Vecchio, Jr. and Elena Rusnak, for their remembrances; my nephew, Joseph J. Rusnak, for his insights into a contemporary high school; my second cousins Robert J. and John J. Del Vecchio, who helped me learn a portion of the dialect of our grandfathers; Stephen Bachleda, whose very different ethnic background ran so parallel to my own; Heather Biondi-Ratcliffe Strasburger, who researched the domestic internment of Italian-Americans during World War II; George N. Schmidt and the principal, teachers, staff and students of Bowen High School, Chicago, who showed me that the most important elements in education are caring and resolve; General Harry Brooks, who, more than twenty-five years ago, demonstrated the basic dynamics of race relations; the coaches and players (especially Nate, Adam and Cara) of the many teams who have taught me the game of soccer; John Morzenti, Bruce Ratcliffe and Jerry Brooker, who read earlier drafts and offered constructive criticism; and Kate, my wife, who read and corrected *all* versions.

I would like to acknowledge my reliance on three works: Lennie Grimaldi's *Greater Bridgeport—Italian Style,* Harbor Publishing, Bridgeport, CT, 1992; Lawrence Di Stasi's *Mal Occhio [evil eye]: The Underside of Vision,* North Point Press, San Francisco, 1981 (Lenny, I think every Italian-American family had a Zi Carmela—but if they didn't, they should have);

and Carl A. Pescosolido and Pamela Gleason's *The Proud Italians: Our Great Civilizers,* National Italian American Foundation, Washington, D.C., 1995.
Finally, many, many thanks to Michael V. Carlisle, my agent and friend, who has guided me through a minefield.

Author's Note

Language: The endearment Johnny-panni is derived from the Italian *pane* (pah-nay) bread. Johnny-panni is the Italian equivalent of Johnny-cake.

My father's parents came to America from Castelfranco en Miscano, a small town in Italy that straddles the ridge of the Apennines in the wheat-growing region of Benevento Province. My maternal grandmother came from the town of San Felice in Avellino; my maternal grandfather from Sante Croce di Magliano in Campobasso, both northeast of Naples. Various scenes within this story are based upon tales told at the dinner table—however, I have not attempted to tell the story of my own family, and only the most basic elements of the story are Del Vecchio, De Lascio, Antignani or Nittolo.

Originally I had intended to use phrases from the dialects of my grandparents as I recalled them from my childhood. Until I began formal research for this novel, I thought many of these expressions were universal to the area of Italy from Naples to Foggia, from Salerno to Anzio to Termoli. However, in talking to my *piasans*, I found many idioms were not only not universal, but proved to be specific to a single village or to a particular time. Further, I found that my recollection of phrases, and that of my own siblings, differed. Perhaps we had heard or processed them differently as children—many were used infrequently. Within, I have used, in some instances, specific phrases that were brought to America by the Castelfranchese at the turn of the last century; in other cases I have opted to use more modern, and hopefully more recognizable, idioms. Attempting to do otherwise is enough to make one *'ngazzá* (Castelfranchese), or *n'gazz* (nah-gattz: Italian American), or *arrabbiare* (modern Italian), or go mad (English). Antonio Scinto, former mayor of Castelfranco, and John J. Del Vecchio provided and translated a list of *modern* Castelfranchese idioms—of which virtually none were recognizable to the octogenarians at a recent Festa di San Rocco picnic. Languages evolve, *èh?*

Names: I was born in Bridgeport, Connecticut. Many of the surnames used in this novel have been taken from prominent Italian-American families of this area. Bridgeport's Italian-American mayors have included: John Mandanici, Thomas Bucci, Leonard Paoletta, Nicholas Panuzio, Samuel Tedesco and Joseph Ganim (Lebanese-Italian-Syrian). Tedesco, Paoletta and Panuzio are all Castelfranchese, as is the singer Anthony Benedetto (Tony Bennett). In addition, state legislators have included Angelina Scarpetti and Richard Pinto; and Bridgeport's top cop is Anthony Frabrizi.

I have used many of these names to honor our common ancestry. Nothing in this story should be construed to be about these individuals or their families. My desire is to honor them by using these surnames, not to attempt to tell their story.

Locality: There is no such place as Lake Wampahwaug. The communities of Lakeport, East Lake, South Lake Village and all the others do not exist; nor do the high schools, school boards, police departments or other municipal or state institutions; nor do the corporate structures of NSC, ContGenChem or Gallina Books. The people who populate these cities, towns, boardrooms and bedrooms are fictitious. Though they many suffer similar problems: Lakeport is not Bridgeport; East Lake is not suburban or exurban Fairfield County.

Ethnicity: Italian-Americans—the fourth largest ethnic group in North America and one of the major immigrant groups of the mass migration from 1880 to 1923—are said to be the most assimilated ethnic group in America. That is, they have married out of their ethnicity more than any other group, and thus there are few "pure" third- and fourth-generation Italian-American families. Also, it is said that Italian-Americans have adopted American culture more fully than any other immigrant groups—partly because of the denial and/or rejection of overt Italian characteristics resulting from Italy being an enemy nation during World War II.

Still, as a group, the educational and income levels of Italian-Americans are significantly above the national average; entrepreneurship (as measured by business ownership) is 70 percent higher than the national average; and family ties remain very strong—"almost 98 percent of Italian-Americans live in a family situation" (Pescolido). The reader of *Darkness Falls,* a story taking place in the closing years of the twentieth century, should not expect a *Godfather*-like tale. That stereotype is inaccurate and inappropriate in this generation.

The Shovel Man

On the street
Slung on the shoulder is a handle half-way across,
Tied in a big knot on the scoop of cast iron
Are the overalls faded from sun and rain in the ditches;
Spatter of dry clay sticking yellow on his left sleeve
And a flimsy shirt open at the throat,
I know him for a shovel man,
A dago working for a dollar six bits a day
And a dark-eyed woman in the old country dreams of
him for one of the world's ready men with a pair
of fresh lips and a kiss better than all the wild
grapes that ever grew in Tuscany.

Carl Sandburg

The first of Johnny-Panni's last thoughts—6 December

the seed.
the germ.
the beginning . . .
Look.
Look back! to . . .
when . . .
how . . .
the darkness . . .
Who am I? Who am I trying to be?
What made me what I . . .
I hate it. I never hated it before. I can't live it anymore.
Dear God!
Do I go into the storm? Lose myself in the storm?
darkness . . .
Darkness descending since . . .
Since . . .
what seed this darkness?

The Panuzio Home, East Lake, Monday, 19 September, 5:47 A.M.

JOHNNY'S JAW WAS clamped. His molars ground. The muscles of his face were in such spasm his ears hurt. On the trail before him there was an immense stone block. He could not see over it, around it. He pushed. He strained with all his might. He could not budge it. He cursed. He rolled, caught himself, opened his mouth, stretched his jaw. Again he cursed. He brought his arms in tight to his chest, curled, tucked his head. Then he startled, straightened, gasped.

Quietly Johnny Panuzio rolled to the edge of the bed, squinted at the clock. In three minutes the alarm would sound. He glared. He wanted to doze for the last three, wanted to reconstruct, resolve the stone image; but wanted more to catch the alarm before it broke, before it woke Julia. He settled back, took a deep breath. The room was dark; the windows opaque, silver-black, streaked and dotted with rain. He could hear the rhythmic hush of waves from the lake, the drone of cars on Route 86, the creaking of stairs—Jason descending from his attic bed/computer room. Johnny listened as the boy quietly opened the attic door, stepped into the hall, shut and latched the attic, descended toward the kitchen.

Again Johnny rolled. His right shoulder popped, his spine crackled. He closed the alarm button, pushed back the sheet. Behind him Julia moaned. He twisted, looked at her, at her face, her lightened shoulder-length hair on the peach satin pillow. At forty-five there were creases at her eyes, at the corners of her mouth, but instead of detracting from her beauty they added character and power. Panuzio studied her face. He wanted to kiss her but knew she'd grouch; wanted to touch her but dared not. He looked at her form beneath the sheet. To him she was beautiful, still better-looking than any woman he'd ever dated. As if she could feel his eyes she rolled away, grasped the down pillow, clutched it over her head. Quietly Panuzio sighed, dropped his feet to the hardwood floor, stood, wobbled, shuffled to the tiled bath, closed the door.

Johnny Panuzio was approaching fifty yet, like his wife, he looked ten years younger. Or so he told himself. He was of average height, five ten; perhaps a bit stocky, 180 pounds, yet not fat but strong from having lifted weights and having played football in his youth, and from having retrained for fitness in his thirties and throughout his forties. His arms and legs were muscular; his abs hard, defined, though not as supple as they'd once been. He was balding at the temples. If he didn't spread his thick, deep brown curls from center to sides, his hair looked like a Mohawk. He kept his face clean-shaven, sometimes using an electric razor at midday to remove the continuously emerging dark stubble. His most distinguishing characteristic was his eyes, golden-brown, unusually direct. To others they appeared darker, more intense, because of their set beneath a heavy brow, astride a healthy nose. Despite all, he still retained a cherub countenance—a look that, as a toddler, had garnered him the nickname *Gianni-pane* or Johnny-panni, a moniker he'd never fully been able to shake. Little Johnny-Panni. He had been baptized Giovanni Baptiste Michelangelo Panuzio—for his father's father, and for his father's oldest brother (though, in the family, the latter was always referred to as Uncle John).

Panuzio twisted the porcelain and gold shower handles. The old pipes clanked. He flinched, glanced to the door. The water coursing became steady, the spray against the curtain roared, steam billowed. If she'd come to bed at a decent hour . . . he thought, but he knew, as usual, she'd had clients on the West Coast. She did much of her business between noon and eight or nine. Often she read in her office until eleven. How could he expect her to make her schedule coincide with his? Especially with the new uncertainties.

Under the hot water Johnny stretched his back, flexed one knee, the other, felt the grind of arthritic bone, winced. Night thoughts, images, concerns faded. At forty, Johnny had reached his dream. He had a lovely wife, three beautiful children, an interesting and well-paying job, an elegant home on The Point on Lake Shore Drive in the perfect town of East Lake. At almost fifty, he was finding it difficult to maintain his lifestyle, his achievements. His dream seemed to be unraveling. He put his face to the shower spray, let the water beat on his forehead. Perhaps it was not his dream, he thought. Perhaps it was Julia's. He stepped back, shook his head to clear it. He had to plan the day, get everyone going, talk to Mitch, figure out how to handle that pip-squeak Brad Tripps.

JOHNNY TAPPED ON Jenny's door, descended the narrow stairs of the Queen Anne. In the kitchen he nodded to Jason, quietly said, "Good morning."

"What time is it?" Jason stuffed a packet of papers into his physics book, closed it, chomped on a toaster waffle.

"Six thirty-two."

"Damn. I gotta go. Who's coming to Mrs. DeLauro's with me?"

"We haven't talked about it yet."

"I think Mom's got a meeting. Can you make it?"

"Probably. Life skills . . . ?"

"Life Directions Workshop. I gotta go or I'll miss the bus."

"You wouldn't have to rush so much if you hadn't crashed—"

"It wasn't my fault."

"Yeah. That's why the insurance company bumped your premium to twenty-two hundred."

"It still wasn't . . ." Jason turned from his father, flicked his fist in front of his chest, angrily, quietly grunted, turned back. "The workshop?" His tone was demanding, cold. "All juniors and their parents are required—"

"I know. I went with Todd."

"Yeah. Same thing."

"Hey." Johnny wanted to lighten the mood. "Who's this Sanchez girl?"

"Ah . . ." Jason glanced up, away. "They pronounce it *San-shay*. Like in French. House of Saints."

"So."

"Ah . . . her name's Kim."

Johnny smiled. "Mitch says she likes you."

"Dad, I gotta go." Jason did not smile. "I'll miss the bus."

"Did you feed Dog Corleone?"

"Yep."

"Really?"

"*YES!* He's in Grandpa's room. I gotta go."

Johnny spewed questions as if that would keep his son from departing. "Did you look in on your grandfather? Check his dressing?"

"Yeah."

"How's his leg look?"

"Like a pizza."

"I mean better or worse?"

"It always looks better in the morning."

"Did he take his meds?"

"He took em before I went in."

"I hope he took the right ones."

"I don't know. He knows."

"Umm." Johnny paused, rubbed his chin. "Game this afternoon?"

"No." Jason's words were quick, dismissive. "Tomorrow. At Jefferson. The workshop's tonight."

Johnny watched his son rush out, jacket half on, books in one arm, waffle between lips. When the door crashed shut he flinched, gritted his teeth.

Johnny worried about Jason—not the way he'd worried about Todd, Jason's older brother, still worried about Todd, Julia's child, her looks, her mannerisms, floundering as much now, out on his own, as if $19,800 per year tuition were out on his own, as he always had—but different worries. To Johnny, watching Jason was like watching a younger image of himself. He was doing well, had made honors the last two marking periods of his freshman year and throughout his sophomore. And he was a good athlete. In Johnny's mind Jason was one of the better juniors on the high school's soccer team—not flashy, not intense, not much of a scoring threat, not like Aaron, Mitch's son, who was a senior anyway—but a fairly solid defensive player, as quick on the field as he was slow about the house. Like he himself had been, Johnny thought. Except Johnny's game had been football, and he *had* been flashy. To Johnny, Jason and his friends seemed pretty typical of the better element of East Lake's teens, exactly as he and Mitch had been in Lakeport, except . . . Johnny bit his lower lip. Except . . . His head shook imperceptibly. Something's missing. Something we haven't instilled.

His mind skipped. He checked the microwave clock: 6:44. He moved to the hallway, hummed a show tune that he could not identify, checked himself in Julia's full-length mirror, leaned in, searched his face for new wrinkles. Johnny leaned back, adjusted his silk tie, straightened his shoulders. He filled his chest with air, flexed, winked at himself. "Eh, good-lookin." He chuckled. "Not so bad, eh? Not so bad for an old fart. You look good in suits."

Johnny paced to the bottom of the stairs, quietly called up to Jennifer. She didn't need to be up yet, the middle-school bus didn't come until eight-fifteen, but he liked to have her up before he left.

In the hall Johnny paused. He glanced at the family picture wall. In the center, in a heavy gold filigree frame, was a large photograph of his father's father, Giovanni Baptiste Michelangelo Panuzio—*Nonno* or Grandpa to Johnny's generation, *Il Padrone* to his own and to Rocco's. Johnny studied the face, brushed a tiny web from the filigree frame, wiped a finger smudge from the old glass. The photograph of his grandfather had been touched up with pastel chalks. The facial details were clear but the paper, nearly a century old, was fragile, and the edges, even in the heavy frame and under glass, were flaking. For years Johnny had thought he should have it hermetically sealed to stop the deterioration but he'd never gotten around to it. He checked the edge for further deterioration, gritted his teeth, grasped both sides of the frame, leaned in. "Nonno," he whispered, "how would you handle Tripps? With all you faced, where did you find the strength?"

Johnny squeezed his eyes shut, then slowly relaxed, stood perfectly still. His eyelids lay lightly closed, his mind floated back to Nonno, to the house, to his cousins, young, mischievous, to Aunt Tina, glaring, stern . . . Images jumble—dark, precise, random, lucid. They flash, roll forward like a film with all frames shown simultaneously on thousands of screens within the sphere of his mind. He is tiny, minute, at the center of his own screening—seeing, hearing, sensing it all simultaneously, as if it . . . as if he is almost seven and it is the summer of 1954. They are at Nonno's. Sylvia has been taunting him in her shrill singsong.

> Nah nah nah-nah nah.
> Little Johnny-panni.
> Little Johnny-panni.
> Nah nah, *n'gazz.*
> Johnny-panni rots.
> He's so weak, he's a freak . . .

It is as if . . . as if . . . He sees him. He is him. It is more than forty years earlier. It is now. Jumbled. Jumping back and forth. To Johnny, a new sensation—jumping to him, to I, to me, without cognition, to Little Johnny-panni, to then, to now, without reason. *N'gazz.* A thousand simultaneous screens upon which to impose order. *N'gazz.* He is, was, already, a little *n'gazz.*

Darkness. He crouches, places a hand on the butler pantry door. The white enamel paint feels cool. He glances back toward the kitchen expecting Santo or Henry to sneak in with him. Neither appear. He hears Sylvia call out, "Ready or not, here I come."

Sylvia is eight. Normally she would not play with her little brother, or with the cousins his age—seven—but only half the family is at Nonno's. Lena, Connie and Regina, cousins her age, girls, they aren't coming.

Johnny-panni pushes the swinging door, opening it just a crack, just enough to peer into the dining room. The room is dark except for a yellowish glow from one dim sidelight softly swaddling the heavy wood furniture. He listens. There is noise in the kitchen, in the front rooms, in the yard—adult noises, not Santo or Henry or Sylvia. No sound comes from the dining room. He pushes the door another inch, then two, three. Still nothing. The door swings back. He reopens it, four inches, five, six—enough to stick his head through to look. He jerks back. Not from something seen. But . . . but . . . if someone slams it! Shoves it! He shudders, feels his neck, feels the guillotine, feels the snap, the pain. He hears Tessa's scream, sees Rocco's anger.

Again he pushes the door but now he jams his shoulders in, crawls through, carefully lets it close. He scoots beneath the draping tablecloth and into the dark cavern under the dining room table. He is smiling, laughing, a mischievous gleam comes from his face but . . . without an accomplice . . . the smile fades. He creeps to the far end of the cavern where the legs of Nonno's and Nonna's chairs intrude. The wood looks black. Is black. Is gnarled. He runs a hand over one leg. The wood feels warm and smooth until he reaches the foot. He feels the carving, lowers his face to the carpet, lays his head beside the foot of Nonno's chair and sees . . . sees the eyes, the snarling mouth, the horrible nose. I . . . He starts, bangs the back of his head on Nonna's chair, flinches, bangs the side of his head on the table frame. Johnny-panni freezes. His eyes adjust to the dimness. He sees the table legs and the legs of the great chairs and he sees they are all shod with gargoyles and monsters and he slithers from beneath the table and escapes to the edge of the door which leads to the front hall and foyer, to the main staircase to the second floor.

His heart is pounding. Monsters under the table! I . . . He . . . He is scared. He is scared of being scared. He is scared Santo or Henry will tease him. Or Sylvia. She always—

Johnny hears Rocco and Uncle John in the front parlour; Tessa, Nonna, and Aunt Fran in the kitchen. There is noise in the back parlour, adult noise, perhaps Aunt Millie or Aunt Tina or Zi Carmela. Johnny thinks, is sure, Santo and Henry wouldn't hide there, and Sylvia wouldn't seek there. He scrunches beneath the china hutch, feels exposed: feels the heads, the eyes from beneath the table moving, glaring at him. He sidles to the door to the hall. Quickly, quietly, he slips out, rounds the spiral newel, then on all fours scrambles up the stairs to the landing. There he . . . I look into the back of the house, look down the narrow servant stairs, look up into the upper back hall between the room that had been Rocco's and Uncle Carlo's, and the one that had been Aunts Tina's, Sylvia's and Carmela's when they'd all been little.

Johnny-panni sees . . . I . . . I see Sylvia's rump! She is bent, searching under the bed in Rocco's old room. Quickly he retreats, still on all fours, down to the landing, leaping up to the open upper hall between Tina's room, Nonno and Nonna's room, and the upstairs den. He scurries into the den, opens the closet, backs in between hanging garments, pulls the door all but a finger's width shut, smiles. No one will find me here.

He waits motionlessly. I . . . He waits long. He is hot. It is midsummer. The closet is stuffy, smells of old shoes and of an old woman's powders. He does not want to hide anymore. Why, he thinks, isn't Sylvia searching for me? Did she catch Santo? Henry? Henry always gets caught first because he doesn't like to hide because he is afraid. Ha! He's a scaredy-cat. Not like me. I'm going to go to home base, call in Santo and Henry, tell Sylvia we quit so we can play something more fun than hide-'n'-seek where the seeker's a girl who can't find anyone anyway!

I slip from between the smelly garments. My neck is itchy. I sit on the bench in the den, my back to the window, my face to the door, my legs swinging. Ha! Sylvia's so stupid she wouldn't even see me if she walked through the upper hall with her eyes open.

I lean back. I am still thinking I should go . . . I'm going to home base. But I don't want to quit. I don't quit. I'm not a quitter. Not like . . . Ooo! Mama'd spank me if I said who. If I . . . She doesn't spank us. She never spanks me. Sometimes she hits me with her hairbrush. If you cry before she hits, she doesn't hit you. If you cry after she starts, she hits you harder. Johnny, he doesn't want to lose. His neck itches and he pivots his head back and turns it side to side and makes believe he's . . .

On the closet wall, high up, in a heavy gold frame . . . a picture of a man in a blue uniform with gold arm braids; a thin man with a small mustache, high boots, and a sword. A real sword. I stand, step closer to get a better look, but at that angle the glint on the glass blocks the picture. I drag the bench over, stand on it. I know the man in the picture. I've seen him . . . in newsreels, in books . . . but without the sword. The sword is long, curved.

"Ah, Little Johnny-panni! There you are."

Johnny spins.

"Your mother and father have been looking for you." Aunt Tina's voice is high, sharp. "They want to go home."

Johnny doesn't answer her. He glances up at the large photo then jumps from the bench, starts for the door.

"Whoa!" Aunt Tina halts him. He sees her waggle a long, bony finger. "How about the bench?" She begins to move the seat. Johnny helps with the other side. "Do you know who that is?" Aunt Tina asks.

Johnny looks up. Without hesitation, his voice booming, proud, he announces, "Adolf Hitler."

"Adolf Hit . . . ! No-oh!" Aunt Tina's voice cackles. She is a horse neighing. A know-it-all horse. "That's my father."

Johnny doesn't understand.

"That's Nonno," Aunt Tina says. "That's Nonno more than fifty years ago. When he was in the army."

"Granpa?!" He is ashamed. "Granpa had a sword?" He is astounded. He can feel it . . . in my hand.

"Oh. Yes. That was taken in 1900. Maybe 1899. He was drafted into

the cavalry after he had already come to America. He had to go back to Italy. Wasn't he handsome?"

Johnny-panni does not know what to say. Nonno with a sword. Nonno, maybe chopping someone. Nonno looks like Hit . . . With a sword. Like in the movies.

He hears Aunt Tina's voice running on, she seemingly talking to herself or to the photograph, but letting Johnny . . . letting Little Johnny-panni overhear. "It was a mistake. They were supposed to draft his brother, my uncle Nicole, because he wasn't the oldest . . . They never take the first son. But they drafted my father because they didn't have their records straight. When he was let out he went back to his hometown and he told the Scarpettis . . ."

Johnny is lost. It shows on his face. Aunt Tina thinks he is retarded. He can see it on her face. She thinks I'm retarded. Or slow. Slow anyway. She sits on the bench, pulls me toward her like I am a pet, a puppy . . . no . . . a stuffed animal. A lamb. Johnny sits politely. He does not like the way she smells. She looks up at the photograph and her words rise and descend and rise as if an aria. "Mr. Scarpetti—" Johnny can see into her nose; her nostrils are big and he can see up her nose as she gabs at the photo "—was the padrone of the village. He was a very kindly man but to my father, well . . . when my father . . . when he went back to his village before he was put into the army . . . Just like that they order him back from America, snatch him up. Like a slave! Like . . . Ah, but he saw my mother . . . She was so beautiful . . . They called her pacca bel *because . . . Oh, you're too young to know. When you're a man you'll know. But she was so very pretty and Papa told Mr. Scarpetti that he was going to marry his daughter. And Mr. Scarpetti was so angry, he forbade my father from seeing her. And Mrs. Scarpetti, she hit Papa with a pot." Aunt Tina swings her arm. "Bang!" She explodes, laughs, continues.*

"But all the time he was in the army my mother wrote to my father and my father wrote to my mother, and when he came home to his village . . . he was so handsome . . . My father was the most handsome man in the paese*. And the strongest. No matter what they did to him. And Mama, she was almost sixteen . . ."*

Johnny-panni interrupts. He will show her. "Nonna was fifteen!" He doesn't really believe his aunt. She is old. She still lives with her mother and father. She has never married. She is the only woman Johnny knows who is old and who has never married. He has heard his mother whisper that her real name is Santina. To him it sounds like Satan. A girl Satan. That's what his mother means when she whispers, "There's something wrong with that one. It's nothing to do with the family but she . . ."

"Oh, yes." Aunt Tina's enthusiasm speeds her on. "She was fifteen, but almost sixteen."

"But—" Johnny tries to catch her "—you can't get married when you're fifteen."

"Well . . . you . . . can't . . . now." He sees Tina snort, hears her add, "You can't do that today but back then, in Italy, a girl could marry . . . even at fourteen! And my father, he was already a man. He was twenty-two and he had saved his money, so he was of substance." She is rolling again. "But Mr. Scarpetti was going to kill my father. And Mama's brothers were going to kill him, too. And my father said, 'Mr. Scarpetti, if you don't let me marry your daughter, I'm going to steal her and take her to America.' Oh, they had a big fight!"

"Did Grandpa use his sword?"

Aunt Tina's laugh is shrill. "Not a sword fight," she cackles. "But both families, the Panuzios and the Scarpettis, oh, they don't even talk for months. And my mother cried and cried and said to her father that she was going to run away to America, no matter what! So finally Mr. Scarpetti said, 'Okay. You can get married. But only if you marry here. In Italy.' He wasn't going to let his daughter go to America unmarried. Oh, wouldn't that have been a scandal." Again he hears Tina's shrill laugh, and again it is to something he thinks that she thinks Johnny-panni doesn't understand because, he thinks, she thinks I am retarded.

Aunt Tina grabs his hand, leans closer. "That's when Mama and Papa came to America, Papa for the second time. That's how your family came to this country. Mr. and Mrs. Scarpetti, that's my grandfather and grandmother, they never came . . ."

I pull away. "Where's Nonno's sword?"

"Oh! Maybe he gave it to Mr. Scarpetti." Aunt Tina laughs.

"And Nonna's pocketbook?"

"Pocket . . . ? Ah! Pacca bel.*" She holds the side of his face, pinches, laughs at him for being so stupid. "You're too young. Too young. But the padrones . . . You know the padrones?"*

"Like Grandpa?"

"Yes. In the old sense. Not like those here. In Castelfranc they were such gentlemen. Here, nothing but trouble. Oh . . . all the troubles . . . Ah, but look at Papa. Wasn't he handsome?"

Johnny pushed back, released the frame, let his eyes fall upon others. Beside the photo of his grandfather was one of Johnny's father's oldest brother, Giovanni Baptiste II, Uncle John, Johnny's godfather. In the photo Uncle John wore a double-breasted, natural linen suit—the kind of suit he'd worn most of his life, to work at the bank, to go to church on Sundays, even at home. After the death of his father in 1965, and until his own death ten years later, the family title *Il Padrone* passed respectfully, if somewhat whimsically, to Uncle John.

There were separate pictures of Johnny's father, Rocco and Johnny's mother, Tessa, from World War II, both wearing the uniform of the United States Army. Familiar and fluent with the dialects of southern Italy, Tessa Altieri had become an enlisted administrative assistant to General Mark W. Clark, commander of the American 5th Army. For ten months, from the landing at the Gulf of Salerno in September 1943 through the battles of Ponte Bruciato, Monte Cassino and Anzio, Tessa translated for the wild three-star. Someplace, during the cold, muddy, rainy campaign, she'd contracted hepatitis. Rocco had been an infantryman with the 34th Division, had been wounded, shot through the right calf, at Anzio. They'd met in the hospital in June 1944; had been, as far as both their families were concerned, foolishly married after a one-week engagement. In a double frame there were pictures of them cheek to cheek; one, in sepia, in uniform, on their wedding day, the other, in full color, on their fiftieth wedding anniversary.

To one side there was a very small, very old photograph of an uncle of Johnny's grandmother, the playwright, novelist and royal tutor Nicole Del Vecchio, on the day his first film opened in America at the Loew's Poli; to the other, in a matching frame, was a small, dark photo of Nicole Panuzio, Johnny's grandfather's youngest brother, on the day he was disinterned.

There was a very elegant photograph of Julia, on her and Johnny's wedding day, dressed in a flowing satin and lace gown trimmed with minute satin roses. In it she held a bouquet of red and white roses. The picture had been taken at The Bastille Restaurant and Marina in South Lake Village, and Julia's radiant image was surrounded by the blurred blue-green water of Lake Wampahwaug. Their wedding had been traditional, with tens of Barnums and a hundred Panuzios in attendance—perhaps more like the 1926 wedding of Uncle John and Aunt Francesca than the modish sixties and seventies weddings of many of their friends. "This is the woman," Johnny had often laughingly introduced her, "who turned me around. Before we met I was tuning in, turning on, dropping out. She's the best thing that ever happened to me." Difficulties or not—Johnny caught himself grinding his teeth—she still is.

Studding the wall were pictures of siblings and cousins and many, many of the kids—Todd, Jason and Jennifer—on horseback, in soccer uniforms, in canoes with largemouth bass dangling from their lines, Todd's high school graduation photo. Even pictures of Dog Corleone, the family's collie-shepherd mutt. To the far left, almost as an afterthought, there was a cluster of small framed newspaper photographs: one of John Panuzio and Mitch Williams, arms over each other's shoulders, in their Lakeport High School football jerseys, with the cutline **13–13: Scoring Leaders Ready for Turkey**

Day Final; one each of Johnny's cousins Richard and Louis, both in military uniforms, these with the stories folded back under; and one of Johnny's brother Nick, also in uniform, with the cutline **Local Man Wins Bronze Star**. Johnny's eyes lingered. An unpleasant thought shot through his mind. Goddamn militant family.

Johnny moved to the front room. He stood amid Julia's new Chippendale or Louis XIV—or whatever she'd told him it was—furniture, gazed across the road to The Point. In the crook of The Point and the shore, where half a dozen mallards glided effortlessly, large raindrops created expanding, interlocking rings.

Johnny stared at the birds, the water. He felt pulled by the lake, to the lake, his lake, his water. How he'd always loved the lake from childhood, growing up on the other side in the City of Lakeport. How he loved it on the day he and Julia married twenty years earlier, on the day they bought their spacious Queen Anne right there on The Point on Lake Shore Drive in the perfect town of East Lake; loved it every day after work, walking the rocky shoreline before going in; in those early years strolling hand in hand with Julia after dinner, or chasing her, catching her, there, here, on The Point in the dark; or loved it in the light, before leaving for NSC in Lakeport. How he loved this lake, mornings, evenings, summers, winters, fishing, boating, just staring, smelling, listening, breathing.

Johnny closed his eyes, sighed, reopened them. He checked the window thermometer. The temperature was a damp fifty-one. He pursed his lips, thought of the coolness not as normal climatic progression but as the start of the heating season, as fuel-oil bills. He did not want to think about money. He rethought the temperature, thought, If tomorrow it doesn't rise above eighty, perhaps Jason won't embarrass me, embarrass himself, by wilting in the second half. Then he thought he was being unfair, that Jason hadn't wilted against Hayestown but had taken a hard kick to the thigh and had played the last fifteen minutes with his quadriceps in spasm.

Johnny tried to close down his thoughts, to force away the indistinct grating ire oozing from within, to deflect the abrasive yet intangible dissatisfactions which seemed to be coming from all directions. His thoughts tumbled on. Something's missing. Something from his game . . . from his studies . . . from his life . . . good at everything, a natural—not a bad kid, loves, of all things, physics—but . . . it's like he's a passenger on a train . . . something typical of their entire generation, of the entire region . . . like that pip-squeak Tripps . . . enjoying the ride, the view . . . taking whatever they want . . . something typical of this family . . . enjoying the ride but without . . . the entire country . . . without . . . ?

In the kitchen Johnny found Rocco at the Wolfe stove, hunched, concentrating on the dials.

"Hey, Pop." Johnny's voice was loud yet short. He didn't want to disturb Julia. "Pop. You want me to do that?"

The old man raised his eyes askance. Johnny stepped to his side. Rocco looked back to the stove, concentrated on the eggs and milk already in the small frying pan, swirled the mix with a silver fork in Julia's best Teflon-coated omelette cookware. Two shells drooled egg white onto the counter. The butter in its antique milk-glass dish sat on the range top, melting, dripping an oil slick onto the metal surface. Egg drippings were smoking on the hot unit.

"Pop!"

"He can't hear you." Jenny pirouetted into the kitchen. She raised her arms dramatically. "He doesn't have his hearing aids in."

Johnny turned, chuckled. "Good morning, Sunshine."

"Hello, Daddy-oh. Mama's goina like bi-itch about her pan."

Johnny put a finger to his lips. "Don't talk like that, Sweet-ums."

Jenny popped four frozen waffles into the toaster oven, two for herself, two for her father. "You're running late, aren't you?"

He didn't answer but put a hand on Rocco's shoulder. The old man started, rasped, "You want me to make you some? You don't eat enough eggs in this house. Back home we ate eggs two, three times a week."

"No. Thanks. I wanted to know if you wanted me to make em. You shouldn't be standing."

"They're all done. Get a dish. Jenny can eat these. I'll make more."

"No, Pop. No. She doesn't like em. Sit down." He glanced at Jenny. He didn't worry about Jenny. At twelve she was tough, tougher than either of her brothers, maybe tough because of her brothers. She had pizzazz or as she like to call it, "Zazz."

Quickly Johnny slid the eggs from the pan onto a plate. "Jenny, make Grandpa some toast." He served the eggs, cleaned up the shell, sponged the counter and range. He checked the time, knew he didn't have time to wash the pan but didn't want Julia to find it when she came down. He stretched to arm's length, cooled the pan first in hot then cold water, did a perfunctory cleaning, careful not to splatter soap, water or egg on his suit. While he dried he called, "Pop, stay out of the basement today, huh?"

Again the old man did not respond.

"Pop! Stay out of the basement today. It's bad for your leg."

Rocco waved him off with his right hand, uttered harshly, "*Á*." The sound was that of a short, clipped *a*, as in the word *at*, yet it was harder, contemptuous.

"Yer leg ulcer's not goina heal. You gotta keep off it."

"Yer house is falling down. Call Nick. He can help."

Nick! Johnny exhaled forcefully. Nick! Where the hell was he? He could help out more.

"He knows how," Rocco said.

"It's not a matter of knowing how. It's a matter of the edema. You want em to cut off yer foot? Go ahead. Ask Nick. He'll tell ya."

"Daddy-oh," Jenny interrupted, "can I have four dollars for the dance on Friday?"

"What dance?"

"This Friday. At school. The student council dance."

"Did your mother say you could go?"

"Jason could help," Rocco broke in. He had not heard, had not seen, that his son and granddaughter were speaking. "I need to move the chair."

"He can't," Johnny said quickly. To Jenny he said, "See me tonight, Sunshine." Then again to Rocco, "Not with school and practice and games."

"He spends too much time with all these . . ." Rocco could not think of the word. "It's too much. It's no good for kids to do so much. He should spend more time here. I'll teach him how to do foundations."

"He's already made the commitment." Exasperation came through in Johnny's voice. They had had the same exchange a dozen times. Johnny wasn't sure if Rocco was being insistent or if he'd forgotten all the earlier ones.

"Call Nick," Rocco ordered. "He could send his boy."

God, Johnny thought, he's what, ten? Eleven? Don't bust my *coglions*, Pop. He ignored his father's command. "I gotta go pick up Mitch," he said.

"That colored," Rocco said. His voice was thinner, raspier, than usual.

"You know him." Johnny gritted his teeth. "He and I have been friends for over forty years."

"Colored?"

"African," Johnny said. "Or black. I gotta see if he's heard anything more about Tripps. About the reorganization."

"You find my box?" Rocco asked.

"Huh? Oh. You mean from Uncle John's?"

Rocco glared. "I don't want anybody lookin in there."

"Ah . . ." Johnny stumbled. "We won't. It might be in the attic. In Jason's computer room. Or under the eaves. I'll see if I can find it tonight."

"YOU KNOW WHAT that *ciuc* of a brother of mine did?" Johnny raged as soon as Mitch settled himself into the car. Johnny used the dialect form of *ciuco faccia*: face of a donkey; dumb ass.

"Probably nothing as dumb as what Vernon did," Mitch answered.

Panuzio had driven his leased, deep green Infinity Q-45 north on Lake

Shore Drive. He'd left late yet still he'd lingered to gaze at the water, to take strength from the view. The rain had abated; a dreary overcast remained, reducing visibility over the lake to less than five hundred feet. He'd sighed, turned from the water, turned right, onto Third Street, then passed under Route 86, the Lakeport Turnpike, skirted downtown and headed into The Hills. He'd been slowed by a school bus which threw a mud-infested mist onto his windshield; had been grossed out by a fat kid in the rear seat who'd jammed a chubby finger into his nose then withdrawn it and . . . Johnny had lowered the visor so as not to bear witness. Still, in his sour mood, he'd vividly imagined the consummation, felt his stomach churn. At Red Apple Hill Johnny had again turned right, then followed the curving pavement up past the elementary school and down into Cottage Glen. The Glen, once a summer resort area, was now East Lake's shabbiest neighborhood. Under the somber sky, under high, scraggly trees with blotches of dense overhang, the trailers and small dwellings surrounded by dozens of dented and rusting vehicles had increased Johnny's feeling of eeriness, of gloom. He'd checked mailboxes for names: Thompson, Watts, Otto. He'd expected to see Sanchez, hadn't, hadn't dismissed the thought—most of the boxes didn't have names. Quickly he'd pulled back uphill into a newer tract of small, nicely maintained capes.

Along the way he'd turned on the front and rear window defoggers, the intermittent wipers, the surround-sound stereo-radio—Dr. Dave McNichols, WLAK AM & FM; news, weather, commuter reports, light chatter and inflammatory sound bytes. He'd felt irritated, antsy, unfocused, unsettled. His thinking had been continuous yet fragmented: Tripps, Rocco, the kids, Julia, Nick. As he'd pulled up behind Laurie's eleven-year-old Toyota Corolla, he realized he'd driven across town totally unaware of his driving. On the Toyota's bumper he'd spotted a new sticker: **Fight Crime/Shoot Back**. Johnny had chuckled. Aaron! he thought. I wonder if Laurie or Mitch has seen it.

"Nick's a *ciuc*." Johnny momentarily ignored Mitch's opening. "A jerk. He calls me Friday at work. Right in the middle of the afternoon. Tripps is there in my office, sitting on the edge of my desk, and Nick says, 'Hey, Johnny, guess what! Your number hit big. I got five big ones here for you.' I couldn't believe it. Right there. Tripps staring down on me. Lisa—my receptionist . . ."

"Uh-huh." With a handkerchief Mitch wiped raindrops from his smoothly balding pate.

"She hadn't even put the phone down yet. You know the way that keeps the speaker on, right? Christ! In front of little Mr. Moral Majority."

"What'd he say?" Mitch patted his closely cropped, salt-'n'-pepper beard.

"Nothin. You know he wouldn't. But he's like his old man, like a video camera recording everything you say and do. He's sitting there on the corner of my desk, recording me for his old man. You know, he's there in his eight-hundred-dollar suit and his gootsie-bootsie loafers. Mr. Impeccable. Even his nose hairs have been shaved."

"Probably waxed." Mitch chuckled.

"Yeah, probably," Johnny said. "Anyway, goddamn Nick doesn't even ask, you know, 'Hey, gotta minute?' or 'Can you talk?' "

Again Mitch chuckled. "Yeah."

"I'm like this. 'Ooo! Hey! Aaah . . . look, this isn't my phone.' That's what I said. 'This isn't my phone.' With Tripps right there, in *my* office, on *my* desk. I'm fumbling like a jerk. So I hung up on him. Maybe I said something like, 'See me tonight.' "

"Ya hit for five hundred, though, huh?"

Johnny smiled. "Yeah. About time, huh?" Mitch didn't respond. Johnny knew that his friend didn't approve of his gaming, of gaming in general, or of Johnny and Julia's spend-all lifestyle. It was a frequent topic of their commute conversation. After the mortgage, the car leases, the credit card charges, all the insurances and incidentals and dining out, and after Todd's tuition, there was little discretionary capital for a side toot. Johnny switched the topic. "Vernon take your car again?"

"Yeah. Thanks for coming by."

"Ah, no biggie." Johnny chuckled, added, "You can't do it all by yourself and neither can I."

Mitch smiled. "And neither can I," he repeated. It had been their tie, their mantra, their permanent bond for three decades. "You'd think," Mitch said, "Vern'd be able to keep one car running. He got me just before I left. Asked if he could drive me home and use the car for the weekend. I said, 'Vern, where's you car?' He says, 'You don't need one when you live in the city. It's a liability.' That's his way of saying it's out of gas, or's got a flat he hasn't fixed. Or maybe's been towed."

"So what did he need yours for?"

"He wanted to take Elisse to the Indian casino for their anniversary."

"Heartwood?"

"Yeah."

They meandered back toward the highway, stopped at the Shell station to gas up, grab coffee and a *Lakeport Ledger*, and so Johnny could get his daily five Lotto tickets. They continued on, driving to work in a tired, rainy Monday morning funk, talking intermittently about family, friends, the town—everything except the situation at Continental General Chemical—ContGenChem. Blankly Johnny eyed the surrounding traffic. Mitch skimmed the paper.

Route 86 curved to the southwest, skirted the Village of South Lake.

Between elegant homes Johnny caught glimpses of the lake, the posh shoreline restaurants with their private beaches and marinas, the few remaining unexpanded cottages.

"See it?" Mitch asked.

"Ah . . . not yet."

Mitch turned the page, snapped the paper to flatten it, continued reading. Johnny, as was his habit, squinted to find his uncle John and aunt Fran's old home, to see . . . to . . .

"She was another one," Mama says.

Johnny-panni doesn't understand.

"Well," Mama says, "they were the first to leave Lakeport. They moved onto that quiet little street with those expensive shops. That was in forty-six or forty-seven. Just before you were born. So now—" Mama's tone imitates a grande dame "—they are 'Villagers.' " Mama pushes up the tip of her nose with her index finger. "Particularly Francesca," she says. "Of course, they were the oldest and that somewhat justifies their superior airs. But Fran, she looked down on everybody. Especially your father." Mama flutters her hand as if she is shooing away a fly. "Old World," she says. "You know, a cafone. *Rough. Crude." She pronounces it* cah-voh'nn. *"And then because your father was an infantryman in the war. And because he became a contractor. How that hurt your father. You know, to her we were low class. Uncle John knew how she was. He was aloof too but he always respected his brothers. All of his brothers. Just like you do Nicky. John respected them and he protected them and he was kind to them. Especially after* Il Padrone . . . *Nonno, after he died. But John always loved you. You were named after him. He always made sure Ricky and Louis loved you, too. You were their favorite. You were John's first godson. Maybe his only godson. I don't know."*

"Mama!" I am angry. "You don't know!"

Between glances at the roadway, Johnny squinted harder, deeper into the mist. No matter that the day was raw and overcast, to him the lake was warm, inviting. He thought of cars he'd owned before he'd become a successful corporate officer, cars in which the windows would all be open and he'd feel the wind and smell the lake, instead of the perfectly controlled climate within the passenger cell of this Infiniti.

"There." Johnny gestured. He'd spied his uncle's old home; caught a glimpse of a woman descending the porch stairs with a child in hand. A smile came to his face. He thought of a time when he was five or six and he'd spent three nights with cousins Ricky and Louis in their bedroom, and he'd first learned the word *cugino*, cousin. They'd called him *cuginino*, their own word (they could make up their own words!) for little cousin. On the following days they'd collected frogs and turtles, and swum in the lake, three boys together without adults.

Johnny searched the water. The lake was fifteen miles long, five miles at its widest point. Throughout the fifties, sixties, seventies and eighties it had insulated, if not isolated, the Town of East Lake and the Village of South Lake from the urban sprawl and the less desirable elements of the opposite shore. If it were clearer . . . Johnny thought. He did not think in words but sensed, imagined, the far side, The City of Lakeport, the six-lane interstate, the tower of National Solvents and Chemicals (NSC) where he'd worked for the past twelve years. NSC was the region's last major industry, its biggest employer. Rumors had flitted for years that the parent corporation, Bowen and Company, was in financial trouble, but nothing had changed until mid-August. Then in quick succession, Saudi-based Contentinal General Chemical had offered to and then did purchase NSC from Bowen. On Thursday, only five days earlier, the Ledger headline story read:

700 of 4,000 to Lose Jobs

> Continental General Chemical leaked its plan, late last night, to consolidate manufacturing operations in plants in Atlanta, Georgia, and Mexico City. Industry analysts expect the announcement to be made formally later today by ContGenChem's CEO, Nelson Tripps.
>
> If the plan goes into effect, ContGenChem will close part of its Lakeport manufacturing division and move much of its administrative and marketing departments.
>
> News of the "restructuring for increased profitability" sent ContGenChem's stock soaring, as company officials estimated the consolidation will save $47 million per year . . .

Friday morning, Brad Tripps, sitting, as was his habit, on the corner of Johnny Panuzio's desk, had told Panuzio, who had risen to be NSC's director of marketing, to prepare his staff for personnel cuts. At lunch Johnny and Mitch had talked themselves hoarse but to no conclusion. ContGenChem had yet to make an assault on Mitch's engineering department.

Johnny and Mitch continued their drive in. Thoughts, images tumbled in Johnny's mind. They spoke sporadically. Johnny talked about the city, about their old Misty Bottom neighborhood. When he and Mitch had been boys, Lakeport had been a proud industrial city; and East Lake and South Lake Village were just beginning the transition from summer retreats for factory workers and their bosses to year-around exurban living. The term *suburbia* was seldom used—North Lakeport and South Lakeport were outskirts. Images flashed. They talked about the old—now defunct many years—tassel-topped summer ferry which made the cross-lake run four times daily, more on Independence Day; the hot, itchy sensations of riding to "the country" in Rocco's old Ford, dust and wind and heat saturating the backseat, the unpaved roads bouncing them until they were queasy and quiet and praying they'd reach whatever the destination might be before they became overtly sick in the backseat of the old Ford while Rocco sang quietly or talked about the smell of the pines and the purity of the water and of the times when he was a Boy Scout and he'd camped on the beaches, which were now private property.

"You know," Johnny's voice erupted. Mitch closed the paper, glanced over. "I just thought about that Thanksgiving."

Mitch chuckled. "Still bothers ya, huh?"

"It was my grandfather's funeral . . ."

"I know."

"My father made the decision. I would've played."

"I know."

"Or maybe Uncle John. He probably told Rocco. I mean, after Ricky was killed, they were pretty sensitive."

"Still bothers ya," Mitch repeated.

"Not bothers me," Johnny said. "I just flashed on it. Like what would be different? You know, would we be in this mess with Tripps if . . . ?"

"Yeah. Different roads go to different places," Mitch said. Then he added, "Still, sometimes different roads lead to the same place."

"Umm." Johnny paused, then asked, "Forgive me?"

"No." Mitch smiled. "Not in a million years. Nor would my old man. He'd leveraged a hundred dollars into a thousand-dollar bet. He was sure we couldn't lose. That's why I never gamble more than's in my pocket. Usually not even that."

"How bout for not going . . . you know . . . ?"

Mitch guffawed, let Johnny squirm. "Not for that, either," he said. "You should've been there."

"Maybe." Johnny was serious. "Sometimes I think I missed something."

Mitch chuckled, gestured, a flick of his hand—don't mean nothin. Again they rode in silence. Amid heavier traffic they crossed the dam that created Lake Wampahwaug. They entered South Lakeport—now virtually a borough of the city with combined fire, snow and highway departments, and with established student exchange, magnet school and distant learning programs hammered out while the state courts still wrestled with mandated regional solutions. On the left they passed the first high-rise overlooking Route 86 where it merged with the interstate. A minute farther, on the right below the roadway, appeared the puddled, tarred roofs of the first project. A quarter mile farther, a single beam of sunlight split the clouds, glistened on wet concrete, brick and glass.

Johnny scanned the city buildings, the projects, the highway ramp circling the Clara Barton Soup Kitchen, the burned-out and boarded-up homes, entire blocks. He pointed to the old ferry terminal, vacant, covered with grafitti, the piers dilapidated, the pilings askew. "My grandfather," Johnny said self-consciously—he'd said it to Mitch many times before—"worked there as a shovel man for a dollar ten a day." Johnny shook his head. He thought about the old "hood," about its vitality, its "mixed-ethnic" energy, about it today, mostly black and Hispanic, on the front page of the *Lakeport Ledger* virtually every day of the year. They can't do it all . . . he thought. Then he thought about the vibrance and the vitality that he did not feel in his tidy Queen Anne on Lake Shore Drive in serene—insulated if not isolated—East Lake; in his chosen middle-class enclave separated from this landscape of slums, of violence, drugs, crime, hopelessness, despair.

Johnny eased off the gas as a semi squeezed in from the right. Mitch turned up the volume on the radio. Dr. Dave McNichols was yapping about taxes being so high that dollars taken from families had forced both husbands and wives to work outside the home, which in turn had fostered a community of unsupervised kids, which required more tax dollars and more government because the system was failing. "Now they're escalating it again," McNichols blurted. "Telling us only more tax dollars will make it all work!"

Mitch laughed.

"And they're telling us," McNichols scoffed, "the problem is, we don't have enough government! The governor and the courts want to control the racial balance of the entire region. One more socialized master plan drawn up by the elite, by the people who believe they know better than anyone else what's right and what's wrong—then shoved down our throats by their police-state tactics. Hey, I'm sorry! Tell the governor . . . tell the state courts . . . maybe there are inequities. No doubt about it. There ARE imbalances. That's a given. And they DO need correction. That's a given. But governmental tyranny is not the solution. Everything they touch turns to . . ."

Johnny sighed. Traffic slowed, slowed, stopped. Lightly he tapped his wedding ring against the padded steering wheel. "I told Nicky we were buying Lotto tickets," Johnny said.

"You mean you're buyin."

"Yeah. He says, '*Ciuc! Ciuco faccia!* You're nuts!' I said, 'Yeah. Maybe.' He says, 'They don't even have a fifty percent payout. Play the numbers. It's eighty percent.' "

"Is it really?"

"Well, according to Nick. He calls the state Lotto 'legal organized crime.' "

"Seems right to me," Mitch said. "If you or I did it, we'd be thrown in jail. They make it easy, though, don't they?"

"Yeah. Too easy. I gotta stop doin this. I gave Nick that five hundred because I owed him from the casino last month. And I think from one of the card games. You know, Julia spends every penny she makes. Except she throws in a lot for Todd's tuition. But the household bills come out of my salary."

"Sometimes Laurie pisses me off," Mitch said. "You know how frugal she is. But when something like this reorganization hits, I know I'm a lucky man. She always says, 'Don't get us overextended. We don't want to be overextended in unsettled times.' "

"Um. That's what Tessa used to say. Now I got Rocco over my shoulder. 'How much did you spend on this? How much was that?' You know, always with a little smile. A little smirk. Like he's apologizing. 'What's this cost? Is it necessary?' Thing is, it costs to have him in the house, too. I mean, I know he's right. But I resent it. Hell, I'm a nearly fifty-year-old boomer—"

"Boy! You are getting old!"

"Well—" Johnny chuckled "—thank God I'm not as old as you. What's it like actually being fifty?"

"I don't know. I won't know for months."

"That's . . . ah, you mean weeks."

"Six weeks."

"Ha! So you are counting."

"You're not far behind."

"I'm just a baby."

"What do you have, ten weeks?"

"Better than thirteen."

"You better enjoy it. Dagos don't age gracefully."

"Oh, like you boys from southern Italy age better."

They both laughed. Traffic edged forward. The NSC tower, now ContGenChem, came into view. On the radio McNichols was now screaming. "Why don't you all go home? Go home, people! I'm giving everybody the day off. You don't get anything done on Mondays. Tell your boss, 'Doctor Dave says it's okay.' Then we won't have this five-mile-long parking lot. Or why don't you come in when I come in? Road's empty at four-thirty. Even the shooters have gone home. Hey, people! Use your fax machines. Do business by e-mail. Surf the Net. You don't need to be here. Go back to the damn burbs." McNichols tittered. "Watch TV, pay your bills, rake your leaves, go to bed. Say hi to your wife." Again the small, lewd laugh.

"Do things to her. I'm tired of being her entertainment. AND GET THE HELL OUT OF MY CITY!"

"A whole bunch of us are going to get the hell out," Johnny answered the radio. "Just as soon as ContGenChem cans us."

"They won't can us," Mitch said.

"I don't know," Johnny said. "Seems, for most of my life, maybe ever since Ricky's funeral, like I've had this need to self-destruct at critical junctures. Like Friday with Tripps."

"Well you haven't," Mitch said. "Look at us. We're both reasonably successful; both married smart women, got good jobs, nice homes, great kids. We moved away from all that crap McNichols is always babbling about."

"Yeah, but there's always something trying to undermine it. I feel like . . . with Brad Tripps and that *bastone* of an old man of his. It's a family trait. Theirs and mine. And I'm passing mine on. You shoulda seen Jason this morn—"

Mitch shook his head, interrupted. "I don't know, Johnny. I mean, I know what it's like taking two steps forward and being knocked back one. But you . . . you gotta stop living day to day, paycheck to paycheck. Your old man taught me that. That's your real family trait."

"Rocco?"

"Shit, yeah. And Tessa, too. I'll always owe you that."

"Me. You don't owe me any—"

"Sure as hell do!"

"How do you figure?"

"It was that Panuzio attitude that rubbed off."

"What attitude?"

"That you could do anything. Studies. School. That came from me being with you. Not from my family. My folks were great, but I never would have gone on if you hadn't. And I think Tessa would have killed me if I'd failed."

Johnny laughed. "Yeah. Ma always liked you better."

"I'll always owe you that," Mitch repeated. "You and your family. Those traits. That's where Aaron—"

"Yeah," Johnny spurted. "I guess you will, huh? Hey, can I borrow twenty bucks until payday?"

" 'BUT, O, HOW bitter a thing it is to look into happiness through another man's eyes!' "* Miss Radkowski paused. Katie Fitzpatrick, Kim Sanchez, half a dozen other students, sat rapt. Another half dozen listened politely.

As You Like It, Act V, Scene II.

Peter Badoglio and Miro Sarrazin stared, captivated, smitten. A few fidgeted. Jason Panuzio's eyes were cast to the windows. The rain had passed, the sky had cleared to white cotton puffs tumbling on azure silk, but the view of the practice field showed muddy patches before both goals and at the center circle.

" 'But so much the more shall I tomorrow be at the height of heart-heaviness, by how much shall I think my brother happy in having what he wishes for.' " Marcia Radkowski smiled. She stood in the classroom, her long arms wrapped about her, low, one hand on her waist, the other to the opposite elbow. Her shoulders were forward, her head back. She spoke quietly, almost in a whisper. Jason brought his eyes back to her. She was barely five years older than most of her students, only three years older than the one senior taking the course to make up needed credits. "Does it speak to you . . . Jason?"

He had not understood the words, had barely heard her at all. He had been concentrating on her shoulders and neck, thinking she had a great neck, wonderful shoulders and collarbones and . . .

"Jason?"

"Huh?"

"Jason."

"Yeah."

"There's so much remorse." As Miss Radkowski spoke she drew first one hand across in a graceful arc, then the other—an actress', a dancer's, an English teacher's gesturing. "He's so pitiful." Her face fell to frown. "He's so in love with Rosalind." Her arms crossed. She brought them gently to her chest; her delicate fingers touched her collarbones, accentuated her neck. Peter sighed a bit too loudly. Miro stifled a laugh. Marcia spun; her broomstick skirt twirled, hugged her slender frame, then unwound, swished.

"Ah, that's Rosalind's speech, isn't it?"

"No-ooh, Jason. It's Orlando's. Or perhaps it's Jason's. Read the rest of Orlando's part."

"Out loud?!"

"Yes. Aloud. And, umm, Kim, you read Rosalind's. Jason, start with Orlando's last sentence."

Jason blushed, looked down, stared at the page. From next to him Martina Watts sneered, murmured, "Next page. Line forty-eight."

"Thanks," he whispered. Then, stilted: "Ah . . . 'By so much the more . . . shall I tomorrow be, ah . . . at the height of heart-heaviness . . ."

Marcia moved toward him, her hands circling before her, scooping, attempting to draw him out; then cupping up, motioning for him to stand. As he finished the line, her hands rose in a flourish, lifting Kim Sanchez from her seat.

" 'Why, then, tomorrow I cannot serve your turn for Rosalind?' "

Marcia Radkowski returned to Jason. Her hazel eyes dazzled; her deeply tanned skin fairly glowed; her light brown hair, short and flyaway, accentuated her vivaciousness. This was her second year teaching freshman, and now junior, English. In this class alone, Peter Badoglio, Miro Sarrazin and Jeff Kurjiaka had crushes on her; Miro and Jeff often faking swoons at soccer practice, calling her The Dream Goddess, Miss Starry Eyes or Sweet Lips Radko. Even Jason held his breath when she spun or bowed or came to class in one of her sleeveless cotton knit sweaters. Had it not been for Kim Sanchez—in Jason's mind equally beautiful: darker eyes, longer, straighter, darker hair; shorter; bustier—he too would have sat all period in rictal agog infatuation. But he could not do that in front of Kim. Nor could he stare at Kim before Miss Radkowski. "Ah, 'I can live no longer by thinking,' " Jason read flatly.

Without coaxing Kim answered, " 'I will weary you then no longer with idle talking—' "

Amanda Esposito broke in. "Miss Radkowski, isn't it kind of ridiculous that Orlando doesn't recognize her? I mean, *really!* Like at Halloween, just because somebody's in costume doesn't mean you don't know who they are."

Marcia settled back. Jason and Kim remained standing, their books before them, their eyes furtively finding the others. "Do you think disguises are possible?" The teacher raised the question to the entire class.

"That's not the point," Martina Watts injected. She was irritated by the disruption. "Shakespeare say that the way it was. Accept it, girl, and let's get on."

"Martina," Miss Radkowski said gently, "it is a valid question. I'm surprised no one raised it earlier. We're almost at the end of the play."

"This is the part—" Kim paused, cocked her head slightly "—where Rosalind talks with . . . here, 'conversed with a magician, most profound in his art and yet not damnable.' I think she learned the art of disguise."

"I think she a bitch," Martina blurted. She did not look up but spoke as if addressing her desktop. "One connivin bitch. Why can't she be up front wit im? I don't understand why people can't be straight wit each other."

"Hmm." Marcia nodded. "Can anyone defend Rosalind's actions?"

"Like back in Ack Three," Martina spoke out. "Where she talkin to the farm slut. 'He's fallen in love with your foulness . . .' She think she so-ooh good."

"It all turns out," Katie Fitzpatrick said. "I think she was just protecting herself."

"Um-hmm." Marcia nodded again.

No one else offered an opinion. Switching to a businesslike walk, Marcia retreated to her desk. "We have only a few minutes left. Thad, Jeff, sit back. Kim, Jason, you may sit. On the way out I want each of you to pick up a copy of *Call of the Wild*. Read it this week or this weekend."

"We read that in sixth grade," Jeff called out.

"I promise you, then, it will be more meaningful this time," Marcia countered. "There's a sheet with it. 'Endemic to human nature is the carnivorous, lecherous self—' " her words were now quick, louder than during the heart of class discussion, an attempt to hold her students through the period's last minute " '—which must be balanced against our need for meaning.' You'll find this on the bottom of the page. 'Recognizing both the flesh and the soul, the need of the one, the quest of the other . . .' We're going to be talking about this all year in relationship to all the works we read."

The bell rang. Thad Carter and Jeff Kurjiaka sprang from their seats, bolted toward the door. Most of the twenty students reacted more slowly. Danielle Nguyen remained seated, finishing her notes. Kim approached Jason by his desk. She was wearing a white shirt with wide, black pinstripes, a short black, pleated skirt held up by wide black suspenders, black knee socks, black loafers. Jason hefted his books, smiled down to her. At five eleven he towered over her by nearly eight inches. He turned slightly, sighed. It made him giddy to be this close to her in school, and dressed as she was, looking the way she looked, he felt awkward.

"I only have a few seconds," Kim said. Her voice was soft. "My fourth period's over in D-wing."

"I'll walk you."

"No. I want you to do something."

"Sure. Are you okay?"

"I feel a little sick."

Jason reached out, placed the back of his fingers on her cheek. "Maybe you should see the nurse."

"I went after first period." They left the classroom, entered the chaos of the corridor. Several girls near them were pushing each other violently but not maliciously.

"And . . ."

"I told her I felt sick to my stomach." Kim pulled him down so she could talk into his ear. "The first thing she said was, 'Are you pregnant?' " Jason stumbled. Students behind them piled up. "Just because I'm a teenage girl she automatically thinks . . . you know." Kim pulled him along. "It made me so mad."

"You're . . . ah . . ."

"Jason! I told you I'm going to wait. If you're going out with me for—"

"No. No. I mean . . ."

Coyly Kim smiled, cocked her head. "First base is far enough," she whispered.

"I'll . . ." Jason was tongue-tied.

"Listen, you have to do something." Kim was now firm, serious. With her left hand she pushed her dark hair back, curled it around her ear.

"Sure," Jason answered.

"Martina wants to talk to Aaron."

"They broke up again, huh?"

Kim raised her eyes. "Have they?"

"I didn't mean . . . I mean, I don't know."

"Tell him to meet her . . . At the end of next period they could meet outside the library. I'll meet you there, too."

AT THE END of fourth period F.X. McMillian stood by his classroom door, watched his students, his Contemporary Issues: Senior Honors Seminar, retreat, mesh with the mayhem. It had been a good class, an outstanding, lively class, one of the most relevant and most thought-provoking of his twenty-three years teaching.

The hallway was clamorous. Lockers banged, students rushed, meandered, stood in groups, sat shuffling homework, embraced, pummeled one another. East Lake High sprawled across the old pastures southwest of Split Rock Hill like two redbrick octopi—single-storied arms radiating from the high cubic body of the auditorium, intertwining with those from the rectangular box of the gym.

McMillian leaned a shoulder against the cool tile of the walls. He was a slender man, five eight, only 140 pounds. His skin was light, his once red hair thinning, close-cropped, white at the temples, peppered on top. At fifty-one he had the appearance of a worn athlete, the smile of an Irish prankster, the eyes of a doting grandfather. Before him a line of students, as if following an ancient Indian trail, single-filed their way through the flowing forest of standing and crisscrossing groups. Then, as quickly as the onslaught had erupted, it dissolved, and the halls were but dotted with a few stragglers, a few students with passes.

F.X. smiled inwardly. Fifth period was his scheduled prep time—a break to prepare for the next day's classes or to correct papers. Sometimes, during fifth, he'd grab a quick cup of coffee in the History Department's office; other times he'd tutor a student one on one. He straightened, came away from the wall. *Analyze it,* he thought. *Build on it.* It was the system he used with his team—win or lose. *After the game is before the game—after the class is before the class*—after the preliminary oral proposals is before the depth of research, the rounding out, the drafts, the final writing of the senior thesis.

The format was really no different now than it had been twenty-seven years earlier—Lessons Learned Analysis: Here's what we did right; let's build on it. Here are our two biggest mistakes; here's how to correct them. For McMillian the format was the same whether it was classroom, soccer field or infantry company. *After the battle is before the battle.*

McMillian turned to the room, glanced back at the hallway, smiled inwardly. I love this school, he thought. I love it when they're involved; when they make new connections; when they light up like a homecoming bonfire. He entered the deserted classroom. East Lake's students were grossly and subtly different from Lakeport's, where he'd taught for twelve years. In that time he'd tried to gain a soccer coaching position but had first been put on the waiting list; then, for two years, the sport had been suspended over an incident in the stands, and for two more because of a lack of funding. When it was reinstated there were two new teachers with college soccer experience. McMillian came to East Lake primarily because the coaching slot was open. He'd expected the students to be virtually the same, had been surprised at the higher level of reading, writing and computation skills, though not thinking skills, in East Lake; had been disappointed, at first, at the lower level of commitment in the face of obstacles. In Lakeport he'd found his classroom efforts rewarding because of elementary academic breakthroughs; in East Lake, it was more rewarding to make spiritual inroads.

His current students, too, were different from the students of only a few years earlier. If behavioral aberrations had begun in the late sixties and had exploded in the seventies, they had, at least in East Lake, reversed in the late eighties. By the mid-nineties student classroom behavior was generally respectful, reserved, serious. They were concerned about grades, about college acceptance, about the starting salary they'd receive when they began work. They were almost throwbacks to the fifties—except they were smarter, more sophisticated. There were residual problems from the aberration—and there were new problems: AIDs, teen pregnancies, a tendency to react to difficulties with either avoidance or great frustration. The problems coexisted—limited and contained—with academic, social and physical achievements no prior classes had attained.

McMillian's senior seminar was the elite of the elite. These students, not without problems, were the brightest, the most mature, the most political; they were as tenacious as pit bulls and often as contentious. It was a challenge to be as astute, even if they buried their perspicacity within a relaxed teenage lexicon. He saw them as kids, still kids, but also as the rough castings of the region's, the nation's, leadership: six girls, seven boys, six of European genetic heritage, three of African, two Asian, one Hispanic, one Middle Eastern—more a reflection of the nation's diversity than of the town's homogeneity.

F.X. pulled a set of forms from his briefcase, laid them on his desk. They were not papers to be corrected but were his coaching notes: defense, right, slow to shift, cover, take initiative. He read the line, leaned back in his chair, thought instead of Ellen Darsey, Mike Verdeen, Aaron Williams, Rachel Chan, Paul Compari . . . *Analyze it. Build on it.*

". . . thank you, Miss Darsey. I think we have a decent understanding of your proposal: 'Feminism in the Nineties and Beyond.' I like the focus on the broad spectrum of cultural consequences. Rach, you had a comment."

"I'll talk to Ellen after class."

"Good. Get together. Let's see. Mr. Beck."

"I went Friday," a small-framed boy said.

"Um. Right, Ethan. 'Guns, Urban Violence and Gun Control.' How about . . . Paul, let's hear yours."

"Ah, I don't have it finished yet, Coach."

"You have your topic?"

"That's the problem, Coach. I haven't narrowed it down. I can't think of just one issue that really grabs me. Unless I could do it on, maybe, like, you know, professional sports. I don't really want to do it on that public cost of banking scandals."

"How about on the lure of professional sports and the cultural ramifications of the promise . . . umm, high wages to play games . . . umm, on the perspectives and productivity of American youth?"

"Yeah. I thought about that. But I don't think that'd interest me, Coach."

"What would captivate you, Paul? Find a topic."

"Yeah, I will, Coach. Uh, you know that stuff we were talking about—that whole idea whether history should be the study of events, or the study of the evolution of culture . . . how people react to conditions and events created by cultural behaviors and perspectives . . . Uh, I think you called it 'ambient cultural story' . . ."

"That's to be used as the base, the framework, for the issue you're exploring. That's not your contemporary issue."

"Uh . . ."

"Paul." F.X. gestured with a partially opened hand, aiming, jabbing, fixing his student with fingers and thumb. *"Don't get behind!"*

"I won't, Coach. I'm working on it. Really."

"Aaron, is your preliminary ready?"

"Yes, Coach." Aaron Williams had stood, had walked smartly to the front of the class, had flicked his head, tossing dreadlocks from his eyes. "I've titled it—" he checked the sheaf of papers in his hand—" 'The Institutionalization of Politically Correct Racism: Breeding Ground of Poverty

Pockets, Hidden Descent and Covert Intraracial Aggression,' or 'When Atlas Can No Longer Shrug—Welfare, Affirmative Action and the New Slavery.' It's long, but it's only the working title."

McMillian's brow furrowed. "Don't worry about the title. Tell me more. What are you reading? What's your primary focus? How are you relating it to long-term cultural patterns?"

"You've read *Race and Culture,* by Thomas Sowell?" Aaron asked.

"A few years back."

"Some of this comes from that. And from the stuff I got from the state senate this summer. I want to explore the mechanisms of intraracial polarization—between those who have advanced and those who have lagged in ever-deepening squalor. That's the real problem the state faces, isn't it?"

"Umm."

"Why, or how, it happens," Aaron said. "Sowell challenges the fundamental assumptions underlying race and prejudice, and those causing physical and economic segregation."

"Hmm."

"What he shows is that a person's, or a family's, or a race's cultural heritage, their inherited belief systems—like what you label their 'cultural story'—*not* their biological heritage, determines their social status. He emphasizes how laws and government programs designed to integrate races or to . . . umm—" Aaron again checked the papers in his hand "—kind of equalize economic status across races . . . why it hasn't worked."

"You have other sources . . . ?"

Aaron shuffled pages. "I'm getting into some of the stuff by Dr. King, Malcolm X, Eldridge Cleaver, Louis Farrakhan, Jesse Jackson . . ." Aaron paused, tossed his dreadlocks. "Ah . . . Allen Keyes. Cal Thomas. Ah . . . Here. Within the macroscopic African-American community, it is as if there are two completely separate voices; and it leads to two separate yet biologically identical communities."

Aaron flashed a cocky smile at a few of his classmates. Then he added, "I've got lots more, Coach. I've got a lot of this on my computer at home but I haven't printed it out yet. I've been speculating on the effect of ambient cultural story—"

F.X. held up a hand, took a deep breath. Earlier they had discussed Aaron's general themata. "I don't want you to pare it down yet," the teacher advised. "Continue to do your reading but begin to focus on the goal, on that exact spot you want to hit."

"Gotcha," Aaron agreed, then attempted to rush on. "Sowell talks about how multiculturalism and affirmative action aimed at advancing the economic fate of minorities have generally made the targeted group's fate worse."

Lowly, a voice came from within the room, "That's a crock a shit."

"Excuse me?" McMillian looked to the class. He had not been sure if he'd heard the words correctly.

"That's like saying blacks weren't brought here as slaves!" Michael Verdeen scowled. "Like our people weren't, as slaves, coerced into certain attitudes toward work. Like a century and a half of obstacles weren't thrown in our economic paths—" Verdeen's voice broke; he began to shake "—so we wouldn't overcome those attitudes. So we wouldn't develop *white* standards."

"Mike." F.X. McMillian acknowledged Verdeen. "Are you working on a similar topic?"

"I . . ." Verdeen remained seated. He'd transferred from Lakeport to East Lake only at the beginning of the school year. "I . . ." He was visibly shaken, not ready for what he saw as Aaron's attack on African-American culture. "I was going to do it on the constitutionality and long-range effects of the gun searches in the projects. In the name of law and order! But it's . . ." his voice began to fade ". . . like . . ." He became silent, still, his dark eyes seemingly opaque.

"Like . . . ?"

"How come everybody lookin at me?" he blurted. "This goddamn white-bread school . . . Those searches aren't any different than the Nazis even if some a the residents welcome the fascists."

"That's a good point, Mike."

Verdeen broke in, hard, barely controlled, angry. "But I think I might change to 'Regionalism, Racism and Reform.' Why it's needed. Not like what Aaron's saying. Like black people don't have culture!"

"That's not what I said," Aaron snapped.

"It's just denied." Verdeen stared at Aaron. "Denied and continues to be denied. That's why Farrakhan speaks to me en all the brothers in Lakeport."

THE NOISE IN the corridor by the library peaked. Lockers banged shut sealing in pictures of boyfriends or movie stars for another forty-three minutes. Laughs, shouts, phrases burst and died like skyrocket bombs.

"Awesome, man."

"Where's my other pair? Mr. Santoro!"

"I'm not in charge of watching your sneakers, Bill."

"They were my good ones!"

"I thought you liked Andrea."

"In your nut-sack!"

"Whose tag's that on my locker?"

"Must be Carter's. He's off his Ritalin."

Kim Sanchez and Katie Fitzpatrick stood, backs to the wall, books clutched before them with both arms. They scanned the crowd. "Don't you just hate it," Kim was saying to Katie, "the way they make jerks of themselves over Miss Radkowski?"

"I know," Katie answered. "She is pretty, but . . . Even Mr. Bendler does it. And he's married!"

"He does it to all the girls," Kim said. "I can't stand him."

"I know," Katie agreed. She was a sylphic blue-eyed blonde, soft-looking, sensual in a pink cable-knit sweater—a countenance that belied her athleticism, her starting role as a midfielder on the girls' varsity team. Her speech was quick. "You look great today."

"Thanks," Kim said. "You do, too. My mother says wearing black makes my skin look darker, but I like it."

"It looks great on you," Katie said. "You look, like, really exotic. It must drive Jason crazy."

"He's . . . you know . . . I'm really glad Martina set us up."

"He's sweet."

"Uh-huh. He really is," Kim said. "Do you know if he talked to Aaron? Martina should be here n—"

"I don't know. Can you come to the Ice Cream Shoppe tonight?"

"No. My mom hates me hanging around. I can come to your game, though. There they—"

"Oh, good," Katie said. "It should be an easy one. I mean, we tied Kennedy and they're . . ." She hushed when she saw Aaron's face.

"Man! What a fucken hassle." Aaron nudged his way toward the girls. Paul Compari followed at his shoulder. "Verdeen's an asshole. Him and that blacks-as-victims shit. I don't know how he got into the seminar."

"Ah, I don't know, man," Compari muttered. "I don't know how I got in. Hey, I'll see ya at practice."

"Yeah."

Kim bumped Katie with her shoulder, rushed out a few words before Aaron and Paul finished. "There's somebody . . . Jason's friend Ryan Willis. He was on the team last year but didn't play much. He'd like to . . . you know . . . He's got the hots for you."

"Ryan Willis!" Katie giggled. "He's cute."

"Hi, Kim. Katie." Aaron pressed close to them to allow hallway traffic to pass. "Where's Jason? And Martina?"

"Should be here any sec," Kim answered.

"Okay." Aaron smiled. He looked into Katie's eyes, followed the line of her collar-length hair, let his eyes fall to the skin of her neck. Her skin was clear, tanned from many hours on the practice field.

Katie shivered, looked away.

"Hey!" Jason joined them. Kim immediately grabbed his arm. He hugged her. "Boy, did I just hear some sick stuff," Jason said. "You know that educational reform stuff all the towns have to vote on? A group in Wampahwaug is challenging the state's right to require—"

Aaron cut Jason off. "I've just been in it with Verdeen. That guy, man! You know, instead of them attempting to even education levels by busing, if they'd do . . . you know, some color-blind method. There are other ways to achieve the balance they're looking for without, you know, without institutionalizing—"

"That's your new word, isn't it?" Mike Verdeen cupped a hand on Aaron's shoulder. Aaron jerked away, spun. "You know what Baldwin said?" Verdeen was four inches shorter than Aaron, thirty pounds lighter. "He says, 'It is not permissible that the authors of devastation should also be innocent.' "*

"Chill, Mikey boy." Aaron stared down at Verdeen, chuckled sarcastically.

Martina joined them, stood beside Aaron, waiting to catch his attention. They had been *The Item* last spring, *The Couple* of East Lake High.

Aaron did not acknowledge her, focused on Verdeen. "What you jerks imply," he said coldly, "is that skin determines academic achievement. Don't you see that, Mikey boy?"

"Aaron." Martina stepped between the two boys, faced Aaron without turning her back to Mike. "I . . . We . . . need to talk."

"Sure." Still Aaron did not look at her. Jason and Katie stood awkwardly, uncomfortable with the confrontation, the references to race. Kim was less uncomfortable but was upset with Aaron for not responding to Martina. The six of them spanned the spectrum of East Lake's flesh—from Katie, who was now ashen, through Kim who was bronze, to Michael who was almost blue-black.

"You wait, asshole." Verdeen's hands twitched as if he were ready to throw a punch.

"And what?!" Aaron pushed Martina aside, squared off.

"Ah . . ." Jason made a feeble attempt to intervene. Kim squeezed his arm. He let her pull him back.

"You don't know what it's like in the projects." Verdeen stepped back as Aaron stepped forward. "You talk white. You act white. You got no fucken idea."

"Then tell me, Mikey." Aaron feigned a forward lunge. Michael jumped back. "Ha!" Aaron taunted him. "You made it out of Lakeport, but your

*James Baldwin, *The Fire Next Time.*

mind-set, your culture, man . . . You're stuck in the inner city. That's why you're so *special*, Mikey."

"Aaron!" Martina grabbed his wrist. The bell beginning fifth period rang.

"You write that dis shit—" Verdeen seethed; he was now fifteen feet down the corridor "—the boys in the hood know." Verdeen raised his right arm, cocked at the elbow, forearm and hand pointing straight up. He brought his left forearm over and crossed his right, low, by the elbow, making an inverted cross.

In falsetto Aaron taunted, "Oh, I'm scared."

Kim stepped in, pushed Aaron toward Martina. "Talk to her," she ordered.

"I'm going to be late for physics," Jason whispered.

"After eighth," Martina said to Aaron. "Or . . . I can get a pass . . . Can you?"

"Yeah, sure. That guy's a complete dick." Aaron looked at Jason, gestured up the corridor, sneered, called loudly, *"Bastone."* Laughed.

"Not complete," Martina said disdainfully.

"Humph!" Aaron's face scrunched with disgust.

"By the gym," Martina said.

Martina, Katie and Kim walked quickly to the corridor intersection, disappeared. Jason and Aaron headed in the opposite direction. Jason was jittery. He did not fully understand why. Since early August, when Aaron and Martina had introduced him and Kim ("If you ask her, Martina says she'll go out with you"), the four of them had hung together, doubled, even with Aaron and Martina's relationship breaking apart. Jason did not know, did not ask, what was happening between them. And he could not breech the subject of race. "Ah . . ." He stumbled for words.

"Forget it, Jayce," Aaron said. "Some blacks have become so sensitive, they can't step back and see solutions to their own problems."

"Ah . . . he won't, ah . . . you know . . ."

"Him? Naah."

"Ah . . ." Jason changed the subject. "Your pop coming to the game tomorrow?"

"I think so." Aaron's voice returned to normal, his adrenaline ebbed. "He doesn't miss many."

"My fucken legs been killin me. Where I got kicked."

"Yeah. Happens," Aaron said. Then he smiled. "Hey, what's Marcia wearing today?"

"Radkowski?!"

"Yeah."

"You know those like net-weave sleeveless blouse things . . ."

"I could hear Miro groaning all the way to Leahman's room."
"Yeah. If Kim weren't in the class, I'd . . ."

Languidly Julia Barnum-Panuzio stretched, feet together, pointing, touching one post, arms over the headboard, apart, fingers out, gracefully extended. She had heard the door slam and Jason's bus pull away. She had heard Johnny's car start and back down the driveway. An hour later she'd heard Jenny's bus stop, pause, continue on its way. Now the house was quiet, except for the near imperceptible scraping coming from the basement. She stretched again then smirked. A gleam came to her eyes. She smiled. Bastard, she thought. We'll see. Bastard!

Julia rose. Beside the bed she reached her arms toward the ceiling then out, her wrists, hands, fingers flowing, a ballerina's port de bras. She stretched again, arched her back, her neck, twisted slightly to one side, bowed, rose, her arms flowing, her entire body in rhythmic motion. Around again, now stretching her ankles, now reaching very high, her fingers fluttering, then her hands swooping down, ever so slowly, so gently, caressing her hair, her head, to her neck, her shoulders. Lightly she slipped the spaghetti straps of her lacy silk chemise from her shoulders, allowed the lingerie to slide until she caught it with her elbows, teased herself, then raised her arms and wriggled it back on. She beamed, looked out the window, saw the broken clouds, pouted, then tittered. She felt mischievous. "We'll see," she said. "Two can play this game."

Julia Barnum-Panuzio, forty-five, five-feet-eight-and-one-half inches tall, 120 pounds, saw herself as a thoroughly modern woman, a woman of the nineties—lovely, even gorgeous, sensual, in control, driven. Nine years earlier, when Jenny had turned three, she'd returned to the workforce. To her own delight she'd found herself to be strong, smart, organized; an assertive businesswoman with a head for marketing as good as her husband's, maybe better—certainly better for the products bought mostly by women. To the delight of Marvin Meloblatt and Gallina Books, Inc., of South Lakeport, she had found them.

For six months Julia had been the lowly paid secretary to Meloblatt's editor in chief—skinny, weasel-featured Harry Hickel. Steadily she'd moved: lateral advances, zigzagging upward—assistant editor, assistant director of sales, editor, senior editor, senior editor and marketing coordinator—all with small, incremental salary increases. Then, in the mid-nineties, in only her second high-level marketing strategy session, she'd snapped at Meloblatt, Hickel and sales director Rod Nightingale, "We're not after Mrs. Big Stationwagon with three kids and a huge mortgage, saving pennies for college funds. And we shouldn't be. She doesn't buy many books. We're after Miss Minnie Mallrat who Mrs. Stationwagon dumps there with fifty bucks that she'd never spend herself. We're after Tiny Tanya Tenementhouse who's got nothing, who's got no future, who's willing to blow her ADF check, or AFDC check, or whatever it is, on entertainment, because it's the only bright spot in her life. There aren't enough intellectuals in this country to support a pub house. Give em smut. Give em fuck. Give em knock-down-and-dirty pulp. Wrap it nicely, but give em *Entertainment.*"

"Oh, Julia!" Harry Hickel burst out. "And you think of me as a whore!"

Julia sneered. Under her breath she hissed, "Fuck you, *stronzo.*" Asshole.

"Oooo!" Harry chided. He'd heard her. "Is that the way Johnny talks? I love Italian whores . . ."

"God!" Julia exploded. "That's not being a whore, you jerk. It's making money. What good does it do to give Joe Schmuck, who's got ten free minutes and a two-minute attention span, *War and Peace*? Even God knew that. Look at the Bible. Chapter and verse. Average verse, what, four, five, maybe six lines? We've got no time for prologues. No time for development. Catch me with a fifteen-second teaser or you've lost me."

"Julia, I don't think that's necessarily true," Marvin Meloblatt said. "We can do quality books—books for the mind—and still turn a profit."

"Sure we can," Julia agreed. "But only if we're willing to stay a small backwater press; and only if we cover the fiscal losses of mind books with profits from bod books."

"I just love to see her talk," Harry tittered to Rod and Marvin.

Julia ignored him. "Marvin, we're in competition for their time, for God's sake. They can watch TV, go to a movie, catch a game, go to the casino. If they're going to read, for God's sake, there's ten thousand magazines out there. You've got to grab the men by the *coglions* and the women by their hearts . . ."

"Oh, say 'breasts.' " Harry grinned. "Say 'nipple' . . ."

"Harry!" Rod Nightingale stepped between him and Julia.

Julia's tone changed. Sweetly she said, "You're such a jerk, Harry. That's not how you grab a woman. That's two-bit backwater thought." Then, again hard. "Look at the goddamned figures. Who buys? How do they buy? What grabs them?"

"Julia, we do have those figures," Marvin answered coolly. "The average person who enters a bookstore browses for forty minutes, buys three books, one-point-six hardcovers—"

"To us—" Julia's head shook quickly back and forth "—that's irrelevant. That might be important to a big, established house," she insisted, "but not to our niche. Besides, one of those hardbacks, she's seen the star interviewed on TV. That's why she's there. Cut that out and traffic reduces to a trickle.

Marvin, we're entering a new age. We sell product. We sell phenomena. They buy us. If we think we sell books, we don't survive!"

"You mean appeal to the mass market's lowest instincts." Marvin shrugged.

"It's business." Julia nodded. "It's not charity. We can't compete with the big houses. Not yet."

Marvin had turned to Rod Nightingale. "And you agree?"

"It's about what I've been saying," Rod had answered. Being upstaged by Julia was hard on his ego but instead of objecting he'd decided to join forces with her. "That's why I suggested the one percent royalty, after earn-out, to all editors. If they were to bring in something that sold fifty thousand hardcovers, they'd get around a twelve thou bonus. And with a movie, who knows? But with that incentive, I think they'll chase the market."

And Julia had chased the market, had indeed defined it for tiny Gallina Books, and as a bonus had been promoted to executive senior editor. With her rise to power, her ideas and visions transformed the small, conservative (she called it stuffy) and independent house into a new, progressive business entity—Gallina Publishing: A Poly-Media Corporation—an entity that always looked to coventure its properties and products with TV, film and/or electronic product producer/distributors. Over the last two years, new bonuses and rewards had included stock options, personal coventuring and her own imprint—Barnum Books, a Division of Gallina.

Julia showered, shaved her legs, stood naked before her mirror and blow-dried her hair. For today's battle she wanted to look especially enticing. She held her hair back with one hand, dried behind her head with the other. With her arms in that position her breasts pointed up. Lightly, with a forearm, she brushed one nipple, shimmied, giggled, thought of Johnny's puppy-dog eyes. Poor Johnny, she thought. I'm always working. We haven't had sex since . . . I'm either too tired or our schedules don't coincide. She thought of the way he would look at her if he were in the room; how appreciative he would be; how thrilled he would be to see her ass, her skin, her breasts. Such a little boy, she thought. Twenty years of sags, bulges, dimples and stretch marks, and he acts like I'm nineteen. "No, no," she heard herself say. "You can look but you can't touch. I've got two appointments. Maybe Sunday." And he'd gaze, hurt yet loving.

She replaced the dryer, dressed partially, began her makeup routine. Maybe, she thought, maybe there'll be more Sundays. I don't know what to tell him. Those bastards. And that new bimbo. Chief operating officer! Marvin did that to cut me off. To isolate me. Marnie Steiger, M.B.A., C.P.A., B.I.T.C.H.!

"Just to cut me off," Julia mumbled aloud. "Because of that day last May. A year ago, May. Unbelievable."

From the basement she heard a thud. She scowled. She thought of Meloblatt and Hickel. "What a pair," she muttered. *"Pesce-dosc e il stronzo."* Julia pronounced the first word *pee-sha-dosh*, a derivative of either *pisciatoio*, "public urinal" or *pesce*, "fish," slang for penis; prick. She thought of Nightingale, thought, Thank God for Rod.

ROCCO GRASPED THE red brick, rocked it, forced it up, his old fingers momentarily straining then relaxing, straining then relaxing, oscillating the pressure against the crumbling mortar. Then side to side, patiently. Then forward a quarter inch and back, forward five sixteenths and back. Then he rested, withdrew his hand, laid his arm on his chest.

In 1912, the year of Rocco's birth, the house on The Point on Lake Shore Drive in East Lake, which would become Johnny and Julia's dream, was erected by Edward Hancock, owner of Hancock Lumber. The interior wood trim was chestnut and oak; the parquet floors patterned with mahogany, ebony and teak; the interior doors, cherry. Porches were adorned with copings and crowns, corbels and cornices. From top to bottom, but not inclusive, the materials and workmanship were of superior quality. The foundation, however, was brick—red brick and mortar—because Beatrice Hancock had liked the way it looked below the clapboard of a home she'd seen in South Carolina.

"You gotta problem down there." Rocco had pulled Johnny aside on the day he'd moved in. "Johnny, you gotta problem."

"What do you mean, I got a problem, Pop?"

"You gotta problem down there in the foundation."

"What! What are you talking about?"

"Your foundation. It's made of brick."

"Yeah. Yeah, it's made of bricks. A lot of the old Victorians around the lake have brick foundations. That's the old Hancock style."

"It's crumbling."

"It's crumbling?!"

"Yeah." Rocco nodded. "The mortar. It's all dry. Crumbling. Falling apart. Some of the brick, too. Some are broken. Your whole house, the foundation is crumbling."

"Oh, Pop! I'm sure it's fine."

"No. I been down there. With the boxes. You got sand all on the floor. From the mortar. Piles on the floor."

"Yeah. Yeah, I know. I'll get Jason to go down and sweep it up. When I made the workout area a few years back, I swept it all. Again after we had the flooding."

"Umm. Umm. Water leaches out the lime; leaves the sand. I pulled out some bricks. Just like that. Nothing holding em."

Johnny chuckled but he was not happy. "Don't pull em out, Pop. Okay?"

"I'm goina do some work down there."

"Nah. No, Pop. I'll have somebody come in and take care of it."

"No-oh. It's okay. You let me do this. I want to. It'll give me something to do."

"How you goina do that, Pop?"

"Just a little. A little at a time. Todd can help. Jason can help. You get mortar . . . um, maybe ten bags for now . . ."

"You can't do that. Not with your legs."

"I'll just scrape out the loose sand. Nice and clean. Put mortar back in. Reset the brick. Jason can bring the bags down."

"Geez," Johnny'd sighed. "I don't think so."

"Let me do this. I gotta do somethin."

"God, Pop!" Johnny'd said. "Whatever! If that's what you want."

Rocco twisted, reached back in, now with an old screwdriver. He poked, scraped at the dry mortar. He had descended into the basement after watching the morning Roman Catholic mass on Channel 49, on the small TV in his room. Each shuffling step had hurt and with each he'd mumbled, "Be not afraid. I go before you al-ways."* The refrain from the morning hymn.

The pain in his leg flared. He gasped silently, withdrew the screwdriver, sat still. An excruciating stabbing zing shot downward from the wound along his right shin, pierced his ankle, drove to his arch, his toes. He sucked in a shallow gulp of air, held it. "Come fol-low Me, and I will give you rest."

Beneath the pangs there was a constant gnawing ache as if he were being tortured on some malicious medieval leg rack with a clockwork mechanism set as to methodically deliver knifing jabs within the constant pressure. "If you stand be-fore the pow'r of hell and death is at your side—" Rocco did not say the words but thought them, heard them in his head "—know that I am with you through it all." He made the sign of the cross, returned to the tool, squeezed the handle of the screwdriver, turned, stared at the one brick that he'd been attempting to loosen.

Generally the bricks directly below the sill at the top of the foundation, and those at the base of the walls, were in the worst condition—often cracked from the uneven weight they'd borne as the mortar around them had deteriorated. In five and a half months the old man had finished the north and most of the east side of the foundation, shoring the floor joists three at a time, then removing bricks one by one, carefully cleaning and stacking each, until the small section was clear and ready for brick-by-brick reassembly. Biweekly, sometimes more often, sometimes less, Todd (until

---

*"Be Not Afraid": Robert J. Dufford, S.J., and NALR; @ 1975: From the recording, Earthen Vessels.

he returned to school) or Jason raised or lowered or moved the chair and stool upon which Rocco sat and propped his legs as he worked.

Seldom were grandfather and grandsons in the basement together. Seldom did they speak, though when they did it was harmonious.

"I gotta move down two feet."

"Sure, Gramps," Todd would say.

Or "Okay," Jason would answer. "I'll do it in the morning."

"You know where I mean?"

"Yeah."

Todd always spoke quickly to the elder Panuzio as if he were trying to speed up the old man. Jason spoke more deliberately but sometimes in adolescent code. "No problemo! I'll fill the water pail, too. But first I gotta reinstall the 'ware on my fifty-six K, then my RAM-doubler so I can debug my new downloads. You need yer platform dropped, too?"

"Yes." Rocco would nod. "And the step stool. And move your father's weight bench and that bicycle contraption. What's he need that for?"

By early September Jason had begun saying, "I can't believe it! I can't believe you got so much done!"

"We did so much together, eh?" Rocco had beamed. "Little by little."

The pain eased. Again Rocco returned to the wall, pried. The brick tilted. More pressure. Nothing. He brought his arm back to his chest, rested. The trickling of water from Julia's shower in the drainpipes sounded almost like a small brook in summer. Rocco sighed, looked at his bony hands, his flaccid arms. When he'd been thirty-five, he'd weighed 185 pounds; now at eighty-five he was barely 135 pounds. And he'd shrunk from taller than five seven to less than five four. His heart beat erratically—the upper and lower limits were controlled by medication and a pacemaker. His blood pressure, his blood sugar and his prostate gland were under the influence of various extrinsic chemicals. He wore glasses to read, glasses for inside distances, glasses for outside distances—and still he had difficulties with muscle twitching causing double vision. From the open sore on his legs to his eyes, he despised this bodily betrayal.

In each ear he inserted sound amplifiers, clarifiers. Sometimes the hearing aids didn't work; sometimes they became overly sensitive. "For God's sakes," he'd once overheard Julia snap at Johnny. "He's not five years old. He's got to take responsibility for his care, too. You can't do it all."

"So what am I suppose to do?" Johnny'd snapped back. "Tell him not to go down there?"

"Yes. He can't be going up and down those stairs. If he slips and falls and breaks a hip . . . Do you know what it's going to be like caring for him?"

"I know. I know. I already talked to him."

"What did he say?"

"Look, Julie-pie, I'm sure this is going to pass. He's got nothing to do around here. This gives him something. It's the one thing he knows. He's been a builder for sixty years. It's the one thing which keeps his mind off his health. And he's got a bug up his butt about 'Our Foundation.' I'm sure in a few weeks he'll forget all about it."

"If he breaks his hip, I'm not taking care of him. You get somebody else to take care of him. Your brother could help more."

"He's not going to break—"

"Ttaah! Maybe! That's what's keeping those leg ulcers from healing. He's got to take the responsibility for that. It affects all of us. Not just him."

"I know. I know you're right but he'll go stir-crazy sitting with his legs up. He was always so strong. Always a doer. I'd go nuts, too, if I had to be in a chair all day."

"And if he falls down the stairs and breaks his hip, he'll be laid up in a bed for six months. He could go down there after the ulcers heal. At least he could wait until then."

"I'll talk to him. I'll handle it, okay?"

"What if something happens while he's down there and nobody's home?"

Rocco'd heard it all, very clearly, and he'd thought, What if? How long does she think I'm goina last? What if something happens when I'm upstairs and nobody's home? What if? What if I fix your foundation?

"WHERE ARE THOSE guys?" McMillian recounted the players on the practice field—seventeen. Two missing. He gritted his teeth. The team was through warm-ups and stretches, had moved on to 4 v. 2 keep-away in ten-by-twenty grids. Kurjiaka and Bryson were warming each other up in goal, practicing keeper's sideways diving saves. The sky had clouded again, the air—crisp at midday—had become warm, heavy, unsettled. On the nearby game field the Lady Elks were huddled at their bench—the Taftburg Lady Ironworkers had already taken the field. "Drat it," McMillian mumbled.

"Hey, Jayce." Miro Sarrazin held his hand up straight, brought it down pointing right with his entire hand. Jason faked a pass; Joel Meyers foot-swept; Jason pulled the ball back, knocked it to Miro. Miro received it, controlled it with a nonchalance Jason wished he possessed. "I was supposed to tell ya . . ." Miro knocked the ball to Tom Miller at the far end of the grid. "DeLauro was looking for you. You didn't confirm your appointment."

"Damn." Jason received the ball, bobbled it. Meyers blasted it out of bounds.

"Focus," Compari snapped. Panuzio, Sarrazin, Compari and Miller had started the first two games as a diamond defense, with Compari, the only senior, the sweeper and unit leader.

"I am," Jason snapped back. He trotted after the ball, paused to watch the start of the girls' game, noticed that Jennifer Franklin was playing forward instead of Martina. Then he spied Kim on the far side, smiled, gave a brief wave, realized she wasn't watching him. He pulled the ball back with the sole of his left foot, spun left, tapped it forward, chipped it to Compari. Tim London joined them, making it 4 v. 3. The tempo picked up.

"Martina! Come on!" Shouts came from the girls' bench. "Come on!" Martina Watts jogged quickly across the boys' practice field. "Come on! Hurry!"

"Oooo-oooo!" Miro stopped the ball, watched Martina, chuckled. "Look at that jiggle."

"Lookin good, sugar," Compari called to her, then, loud enough for only his group to hear, "Love them thunder thighs."

A little quieter Tom Miller added, "Like to have that dark meat wrapped around your hips, huh?"

Miro, gesticulating, groaned, "Ummm! Like to have it wrapped around my face."

"You guys wouldn't say that if Aaron were here," Jason injected. He felt embarrassed, was sure Martina, maybe Kim could hear.

"Oh, lighten up, Panuzio," Miro scoffed. "Shit. He probably just finished boffing her."

Bip! Bip! Bip! Just loud enough to interrupt them. "Let's go, gentlemen. Bring it in." McMillian stood tight-lipped, stared as the team surrounded him, dropped to one knee. "Where's everybody?" He moved so the players had their backs to the girls' game.

"We're all—"

"Where's Williams? And Burke?"

"Oh, ah . . ." Jason raised his hand as if he were in a classroom. F.X. nodded. "Williams, ah . . . Coach, he's going to be late."

"Paisssh." Compari spit-laughed, then blurted, "He already is."

"No." Jason stammered. "I mean, he had something to do after school. I forget. The media center or something with guidance. Something like that. I forgot to tell . . . Oh, I remember. Something with his Yale application."

"What about Burke?" McMillian dropped his clipboard, dropped to one knee to face the team on the level.

"He's, ah . . ."

"Don't make excuses for em, Panuzio."

"I just meant . . ."

"Chssh!" McMillian hissed crisply. "Listen up! I'm going to skip our standard lessons-learned session. As long as Williams isn't here, I want to address something to some of you guys who are just floating around out there. Panuzio, are you listening?"

"Yeah, sure."

"Yeah, sure?! Yes."

"Yes."

"Yes, Coach."

"Yes, Coach."

"That's better, Panuzio." McMillian blew his breath out between nearly closed lips. In the past decade the lake region had experienced the phenomenon of a sports-identity transition—moving from being primarily a football area to being the state's bastion of soccer. East Lake and Lakeport had become powerhouses. Fall now found the towns and the city seemingly living their rivalries through their boys', and to a lesser extent their girls', high school teams. It was not uncommon for a thousand spectators to come to a midseason Friday night match (the same number attending Saturday football games). At last year's Lake Region Interscholastic Athletic Conference (LRIAC) Soccer Championship, the East Lake Elks versus the Kennedy Kodiaks (JFK was Lakeport's newer and larger high school), a crowd of forty-six hundred had watched the Elks lose in overtime, 3–2. In East Lake expectations were high. The Elks had graduated only three seniors; and in their first matches they had shut out tiny Wampahwaug 5–0, and small Hayestown 4–0. Bumper stickers everywhere sported the F.X. McMillian adage: LIFE IS A CONTACT SPORT: PLAY WITH INTENSITY—ELKS SOCCER. Still, there was a feeling in town that the team had not yet been tested, would not be until they played the bigger schools—Kennedy, Roosevelt, Wilson and Lakeport. Jefferson, though a large school, was not considered a threat.

"Gentlemen," McMillian said, "we've got a problem." He paused, tensed, looked like a compact bomb ready to explode. "If you include the preseason scrimmage, we've scored eleven goals: eight by Williams, two own-goals against Wampahwaug, one fluke by Santarelli. We have a one-man attack. There's got to be an attitude change around here."

McMillian paused, ready to jump on anyone with a stupid comment. The players, too, were ready. At some point during every season McMillian gave *his* speech. The seniors knew it verbatim. "Gentlemen," McMillian said, "there are three elements to this game. To any game. To just about anything in life. Do you follow me?"

Nods. Quiet assents.

McMillian marked the elements by serially extending a thumb and two fingers from a closed fist. "Technical. Tactical. And strategic. In soccer, gentlemen, technical is the skill to handle the ball, your receiving, passing, dribbling, shooting, heading. As a team you've raised your technical abilities fifteen, maybe twenty percent since the scrimmage against Pius XII. And I'm pleased." McMillian looked down, added quietly, intensely, "But that's not enough to win a championship.

"Tactics, gentlemen . . . Tactics are the skills to know when to kick the ball, where to place it, where to move when you don't have it. It's your give 'n' goes, your running off the ball, your moving to space. It's your support of the person with the ball, the angle, distance and direction; your support on defense of the player challenging for the ball; your balancing of the field. It's set plays, and restarts. And I've seen a one-hundred-percent improvement. I'm very pleased."

Younger players glanced to one another, smiled. "But . . . the third element—" McMillian balled his fists, squeezed until they vibrated before his chest "—that most intangible element . . . STINKS!" He stopped, let the word sink in. "Gentlemen, our strategic play is no better now than when you were nine-year-olds playing Park 'n' Rec."

"I . . . ah . . ." Kurjiaka couldn't let it ride. He hesitated, stuttered out, "I don't . . . don't think we're . . ."

McMillian exhaled audibly, eyed him into submission. "Strategically . . . WE STINK!" Again the pause. "We might call this spirit. Or purpose. Or the will to win the game, within the rules. Strategy is exhibited on the field when you're thinking five, ten passes ahead, knowing what each has to be for the sequence to end in a shot on goal. This is NOT run-n-gun bang the ball down the field like a bunch of third graders. Strategy includes that elevation of effort in the red zone, in their box, when you think, Must . . . when you think, ABSOLUTELY *MUST* SCORE. It includes practice. Gentlemen, it includes an attitude of risk, and of patience with yourself. It includes taking the time, and the risks, to learn to do it right, to learn it now for a later payoff. It includes the will to press the attack all the way down the field and put the ball in the back of your opponents' net.

"On Monday it asks the question, 'How are we going to win the game on Friday?' And it answers it. In September it asks, 'How are we going to get to and win the championship game in November?' And it answers it every single day until we hold the trophy. Strategy, gentlemen—It can be summed up as K.W.I.G. 'Quig.' Know Where You're Going. Chase the dream."

McMillian paused. His tone became softer, intimate. "Gentlemen, if any element is missing in soccer, or in life, you will not win. One reason why we play sports is because it simplifies, but mimics, life. Life, gentlemen, is a contact sport. This field is a laboratory and a classroom for life skills. Don't devalue this opportunity. Know your destiny. Refuse to lose."

A burst of applause came from the girls' field. Most of the boys turned, saw the Taftburg players jumping, hugging, slapping high-fives.

"Geez!" Compari blurted. "Taftburg?!"

Bip, bip. McMillian drew them back. "I've got one more thing. I don't want to hear any trash talk. Just don't do it. Talk with your play, not with your mouths."

"Ah, Coach," Dan Crnecki, a left wing, moaned. "You mean that shi . . . that, ah, red card against Hayestown? Those guys started it. They swung first."

"Refs see retaliation."

"He called him a white boy, Coach. They were mouthing off the whole game."

F.X. gritted his teeth. He hated racist comments—and the seeming increase in them—on the field. "I got a call last night from Jefferson's coach. He said he'd heard from Lakeport that we were trash talkers. Said he doesn't allow it, won't play that way. I told him I don't allow it either. Never have. I'm telling you guys right now, any player I hear jabbering out there, I'll pull you. I don't care if the referee hears it or not. And if the comment's racist, you're off the team. Straight and simple. Got it?"

"Aw, Coach." Paul Compari spoke up. "That stuff from Jefferson, that's bull. We're not like that."

"You better not be."

"You know what he's referring to?" Compari stayed on one knee but straightened. "That was that pickup game last month. During captain's practice. One of those jerks from Lakeport—*those* are the guys that do, like immense amounts of trash talk—one of those guys came up and was pushing Aaron around after he scored. They got into a scuffle. We broke it up. We pulled Aaron away. And that stupid son of a bitch, Juarez or something, he ran up behind him and hit him in the back of the head. He was screamin, 'You'll get yours.' Said he wasn't gonna lose to no white-bread team. He was hasslin Aaron, Coach. The whole time. 'Gonna get-chew, man. Gonna—' "

"That's it." McMillian slashed his hand through the air. "I don't want to hear any more. They do it, that's their business. They'll suffer the consequences. You do it, it's my business. Got it?"

"Um." Again, mumbled assent from most of the players.

"Okay. I want to practice our plays against walls. Panuzio, take center half for Williams. Espinoza, take right full."

"Coach?" Jason pointed to himself. "I can't play center mid."

"That's right, Panuzio." McMillian laughed. "And you never will . . . unless you play it."

For thirty minutes the boys practiced set plays; the afternoon became cooler, the clouds thicker, the air mist-filled, the field slippery. Three times they were interrupted by cheers from the girls' field—twice on

Taftburg scores, once when Martina Watts was yellow-carded and given a ten-minute suspension. It gave the boys a sour feeling as they began a 7 v. 7 scrimmage.

McMillian goaded them, forced them to think. "Panuzio? How's your team going to score in the next minute?" "Miller, there's three minutes left, you're down a player, and you hold a one-goal lead. How do you protect it?"

Then, as practice wound down, "Coach! Coach! Mr. McMillian!"

Chris Santarelli stopped in the act of throwing the ball inbounds; Jason Panuzio plopped his hands on his hips. F.X. turned, saw Ellen Darsey running toward him. He froze. His soccer thoughts ground to a halt. "Miss Darsey . . ."

"Oh, Mr. McMillian!" Ellen's face was beet red. "Mr. McMillian." She was nearly hysterical. "Mrs. DeLauro and Mrs. Rosenwald want you to come. There's an emergency."

"Schiatta!" Johnny steamed. "That's what Rocco'd say. *'Che pouzze schiatta.'* Let him burst into pieces." Johnny gripped the steering wheel as if he were about to rip it from the column. "It feels like they're crushing us, doesn't it?"

"One more kick in the ass," Mitch grumbled.

"It's like an avalanche, Mitch. Multibillion-dollar corporations, bank mergers, massive layoffs. They're concentrating all the assets in fewer and fewer hands; all the power—" Johnny snapped a balled hand in the air "—in fewer and fewer iron fists."

"Yeah," Mitch said. "Hard to fight back. The only effective way to fight is to open a competing business but government regulations make it almost impossible to open your own. In the name of protecting the public from unregulated industry, they've created monopolies of quasi-regulated industries."

"Yeah. Well . . . I don't . . . It's just crushing. Information and entertainment mergers concentrate images, thoughts and attitudes in fewer and fewer minds. It's all crushing. Crushing to anyone who's not part of it. It's all a matter of control, Mitch. And of money. The new and seemingly benign dictatorships by the gatekeepers of information and power and money. It's like a giant stone's fallen on us. And we've been part of it! We—" he hit the center of his chest with his fingertips "—nudged it over."

"Aah!" Mitch scowled. "I don't feel like . . . Johnny, we didn't sell anybody out. Besides, nothing definite."

"One more of their fucking manipulative techniques," Johnny said angrily. "Keep em off balance. Protect me, fuck you. Lower people's expectations. Ease em out a few at a time. Let the fear of those that remain quell their indignation."

"Aah—" Mitch turned straight forward, crossed his arms, stared out the windshield "—shit! One more shitty obstacle to overcome, old man. But we'll get through it."

Johnny Panuzio and Mitch Williams had left work ten minutes early in an attempt to avoid the endless questions and pleas from employees in their respective departments—questions and pleas to which they had no answers.

From the moment they'd entered their respective offices that morning, rumors, skirmishes and complications had continuously erupted. At twelve-thirty Mitch had called Johnny. "You know he's a deadbeat," Mitch said. It hurt him to say it, yet it distanced him from the problem. "I can't believe I lent it to him."

"He *is* your brother," Johnny said.

"Umm. He says he parked it on Franklin, between Fifth and Sixth. About a block from his house."

"After dark?"

"Yeah," Mitch lamented, and added, "Even I . . . I wouldn't even walk down there after dark. Sorry to have to impose again."

"No big thing, Mitch. Tripps has canceled my entire interview schedule anyway." Then Johnny cackled. "Geez! Don't ask me why! I'm only the department head!"

"Umm. Well . . . you would've thought Vern would of been more careful. You'd of thought he'd've gotten it back to me without my having to . . ."

"How bad is it?"

"They broke out all the side windows. Took it for a joyride. Took the tires."

"You got it back, though?"

"It's in the shop. Vern says he's goina have it fixed. I'll be without wheels for a few days."

"No biggie," Johnny repeated.

"You'd think he'd want to get the hell out of that place. Get his family out of there. I told him I'd lend him the money. *Á!*" Mitch uttered in disgust. Then, "Hey, Jefferson game's tomorrow? I'm sure I won't have it back . . ."

"I'm drivin."

"I might have it back by Thursday. I'll drive to, ah . . . Hayestown?"

"Plymouth, I think. But I'm goina miss that one. I gotta take Rocco to his doctor."

At 1:43 P.M. the corporate restructuring announcement from ContGenChem's chief executive officer had come, not in person, not verbally, not even over the tower's intercom, nor hand-delivered hard copy to department heads, but high-tech, democratically, simultaneously flashed on every computer screen in the building, from the payroll clerks' to the directors' of marketing and manufacturing. ATTENTION: ALL PERSONNEL. WITH THE START OF BUSINESS TOMORROW . . .

"Like being crushed by an avalanche," Johnny snarled. He glanced at Mitch.

"One of my guys called it 'corporate limbo,' " Mitch said. "Limbo," he repeated. "In both senses. You're not here, you're not there; and individually we're all going to have to slide under that stick. He who falls is out."

A car shifted into the lane before them. Johnny jabbed the brakes, blasted the horn. "Hey! *Stunato!*" Dunderhead. He flipped the driver the bird. "Cocksucker!" he screamed. He bit down hard, huffed, glanced over at Mitch. " 'Total fucking restructuring,' " Johnny snarled. " 'Must justify to the stockholders . . .' " He mimicked the announcement. " 'Every position will be reviewed . . .' Fuck em. Fuck em all."

"At least there weren't any pink slips," Mitch said.

"Yet," Johnny retorted.

Traffic came to a halt. Johnny flicked on the radio, kept the volume low. "You know . . ." He smirked. "Part of me doesn't give a good goddamn."

"Yeah," Mitch acknowledged.

"I mean, what the hell do I do? I make ads. I convince people that without our solvents they live in filth; with em, they're the sexy part of some shining American ideal."

"Glisten'n'Glo." Mitch chuckled.

"Yeah, Mitch. See, half the people will never attain that ideal. That's a problem. I make problems. I make insecurities. That's my job. Advertising is about controlling behavior. That's the bottom line. If I can convince em . . ." Johnny was speaking quickly, his right hand flailing over the steering wheel. "If I can establish a need that only our products can fill, if I can control the image these people have of themselves, force their self-image to have an insufficiency, a need, I can control them. Or if I can convince em they're goina be rich, have a nice car, nice clothes, a nice house. More, really. Make em believe this goddamned unattainable advertised ideal is an inalienable right. Fact is, most people, unless they hit the Lotto, won't even come close. And they don't have to. Who gives a shit?"

"You're putting an awful lot on Glisten'n'Glo, Johnny." Mitch laughed.

"Not just that." Johnny was irritated. He wanted Mitch to agree, to jump in, bolster his argument, be angry with ContGenChem for disrupting his, their lives. "It's like every kid thinks he's going to be a rock star or a movie actor or a pro athlete. Is anybody prepared to be proud of being Joe Jitney Driver in shipping and receiving? 'Gotta have low self-esteem for that.' That's what they're told. But somebody's got to do it. It's a good job. It's got to be done right. It's just not sexy. Not part of Career Night, or Life Directions Workshops. This morning I was reading this thing about education in India; how it's actually reduced productivity because with it came this revulsive attitude toward work—toward doing anything other than bureaucratic desk jobs. It's happening here, too. And I've been part of it. I sell sick attitudes. Sex images tied to toilet cleaners. Did you see that new survey?"

" 'American Sex Attitudes—Two'?"

"Yeah. Big surprise, huh? 'Sex is a prime motivator. Sex appeal's a lure for every product.' Titillating, suggestive, not porn. Get their hormones flowing. And we wonder why kids are fucking their brains out. Why there's an epidemic of teen pregnancies. I sell the big lie."

"G'n'G works," Mitch said. "And the dog collars and wood preservatives are good products. I'm not sure about Shine-in-a-Can."

"Poisons," Johnny said.

"Sexy poisons," Mitch chuckled.

"Especially in my commercials." Johnny shifted, tittered, tried to stifle it, burst into silly laughter over his own tirade.

They laughed together. Mitch gestured toward a blond driver in a BMW slightly ahead of them, then to a brunette in a station wagon with a *Hugs Not Drugs* bumper sticker. They could not see the face of either woman but could see the smooth plane of one's hair, a bare arm and just the line of the cheek of the other. Mitch shimmied in his seat and they laughed again.

Traffic edged forward, stopped, picked up to a steady fifteen miles per hour. For a few minutes they listened to WLAK, to Steve Folders' "The Wide Open Hour." Folders, the political opposite of McNichols and his morning show, was equally obnoxious. Mitch broke their silence. "What would you do if you didn't work for em?"

"I'd . . . I don't know. I was thinking, this morning . . ." Johnny paused. "This review . . . this . . . disruption . . . It's like thoughts are avalanching in on me. Like my head's filled with nonstop conversations. I feel like an old man, Mitch. Like we're entering a new phase. I remembered when Todd was born. It was . . . weird. Weird thoughts. Like an epiphany. Like I understood what sex really meant. But ethereal. Like you can't hang on to that understanding. But it was none of that shit that's in the survey. They didn't ask the right questions. When Jason was born, it was like, now I understand what a family is. Again, none of the images I produce. Then with Jenny it was like, my life's complete. Now Todd's in college, Jason's a junior, Jenny's twelve. And I don't know anything. I don't know where I'm going. In five years they'll all be adults. Rocco'll be ninety. He's going to need more than my care. If he lasts. I've fulfilled my mission. My biological mission. I'm obsolete."

Mitch laughed. "You're letting the bastards get to you."

"You know what I was thinking? Really thinking this morning? I was thinking about . . . You remember the old shuttle ferries?"

"Way back, you mean?"

"Yeah. We used to take em as kids. Look at this damn traffic. McNichols was ranting about regional desegregation, remember? I woke up dreaming this dream. I can't exactly remember. I was going down this trail. Like on one of the hillsides. Going down toward the lake. Beautiful day. The trail's more like a dirt road—deep gullies, exposed rocks. Getting rockier as I descend. Then right in front of me there's this huge stone. I can't see over it, can't go around it. Just completely blocked. Vision, thought, everything. And that was it. I can't remember any more. But I feel like I'm blocked. Like I'm dead. Or should be. At the same time I'm thinking about the shuttle. I think a shuttle service would bring the region closer together than a court order."

"Umm." Mitch nodded. "I don't like the court plan either. I told that to Vernon. He says to me, 'East Lake's eighty-seven percent white, four percent black. Why do you think that is?' He says, 'Average income in Lakeport's about twenty thousand, in East Lake it's over thirty. Why do you think that is?' Then he says, 'Regional income of the bottom twenty percent is only four percent of the top twenty percent. Why do you think that is?' Johnny, I told him I don't have the answers. And I said, 'I'm not sure the figures are relevant.' He said we're denying his kids an equal-opportunity education. He's really into this. I pointed out to him, 'It's got to come from you first. Your attitude as a parent. If your attitude's right, your kids will do well whether they're in Lakeport or East Lake. Lakeport's got good teachers.' He says, 'Don't think of me. Think of a fourteen-year-old mother. Think of her kid. Is she going to have the right attitude? Or do we just abandon her and her kid?' "

"Heavy stuff. I hadn't thought of it from . . ."

"Yeah. Me neither. Aaron got into it with him last week. Did I tell you Aaron's doing his senior thesis on—he sounds like you with your advertising controlling people's behavior by controlling their self-image—on how self-image causes segregation?"

"No. Ha!" Johnny chuckled as if it were an affirmation of his own thoughts. "I'd like to read it," he said. Then, "I . . . Mitch, I envy you. I envy how totally directed Aaron is; how close you two are. You and Laurie did a great job. I just know he's going to get into Yale. I can feel it. If Todd and Jason had half his motivation—"

Mitch cut in. "*Á!* It's not always what it seems."

Johnny glanced over, quickly turned back to the roadway. They were approaching the dam at the south end of the lake. Speeds had increased, were now pulsating between thirty and sixty.

"Sometimes," Mitch said, "his mother and I could kill him. I mean it. I get so pissed at him."

"At Aaron? I love that boy. We love all your kids."

"You don't know . . ." Mitch began, paused, started again. "Johnny, they're different than we were. He's a great kid; but in some ways he's a spoiled brat. You don't know how he stays out all night. About six times this summer. No calls, no excuses. Nothing."

"No, I didn't . . ."

"Again, Friday. I think . . . He wasn't at your house, was he?"

"Ah . . ." Johnny could see that his friend was troubled and he wanted to lessen his burden, and he wanted, too, to cover for Aaron. He was glad that Jason was spending time with him. Still, he could not fib to Mitch. "No, I don't think so," he said. "I think he spent the night a few times during the summer."

"I think he's spending nights with his girlfriend. I don't know how to talk to him about it."

"Safe sex?"

"Any sex. He's old enough to make . . ." Mitch's voice tailed off. Then, "Do you remember when we were in school? You were dating that long-haired brunette, Barbara something?"

"Finch."

"Yeah. And you were so excited about getting a little tit." Johnny smiled. Mitch continued. "Laurie and I were kind of hot and heavy then but we waited until after I was drafted. I mean . . . What I mean is, did you ever talk to Rocco about her? Or about Julia?"

"Of course not."

"Me neither. Not to my father. So how come I'm so upset with Aaron's cattin around? I don't even know anymore with whom."

"Umm. That's like Jason with this Sanchez girl." Johnny used the Spanish pronunciation. "I don't know anything about them. I saw her at the Wampahwaug game. She's a doll. A real sex kitten. How can I object? I sell sex!"

For a few moments they were quiet, listened to the radio. It was nearly five, drizzling. Johnny felt the entire day sitting on him. "I had another dream last night," he began again. "It was kind of like the other one. The trail one. Except . . . it was night. Dark. Rainy. And I was outside looking at something and then I was inside this room behind a window, looking out through a rain-streaked window. And the window's reflecting this vague image. The light in the room maybe. And there's nothing beyond. Just nothing. I can't see through the glass. Mitch, it's like, for the first time in my life I can't project. Right now I'd be happier being Joe Jitney Driver. I'd be . . . My grandfather shoveled coal at the ferry terminal for a buck ten a day. I could be happy shovelin shit."

"Yeah," Mitch said. "But he ended up being the accountant for the entire corporation. And they were just one of his clients."

"Augh. I . . . If I could redesign the world . . ."

"Like—" Mitch chuckled "—controlling everybody's image . . . ?"

"Now, here's a good one!" The voice was loud, harsh, alarming; breaking through a soft song, breaking in upon Johnny and Mitch's conversation. "This just in!" Mitch leaned forward, turned up the radio volume. "Two East Lake High students were killed this afternoon," Steve Folders blared, "in a car crash near The Falls on the Wampahwaug River. No details yet."

"Oh geez!" Johnny blurted.

"At least—" Mitch began.

"There they are," Folders grumbled. "The well-to-do, knockin themselves off."

Mitch continued, "—one of the benefits—"

"Probably sailing high." The disdain was thick in Folders' voice. "Driving Mommy's Jaguar right into a tree. What was that survey last year?"

Mitch finished, "—of their playing soccer is, during practice time, you know where they are."

"Remember?" Folders sneered. "All the high school students in the lake region filled out that questionnaire. And didn't the results show the kids in the well-to-do towns had greater frequencies of drug *usage*?! Don't you like that? When they report on city kids they use the word *abuse*. When they talk about kids from the *burbs* they say 'usage.' They had a higher frequency of abuse than our inner-city youth? But of course! They've got the dough to buy the blow. I mean, just how many pairs of tattered jeans can you spend Daddy's money on? Right?"

"What a fucken jerk." Johnny flipped the bird at the radio. "Listen to this jerk. Two dead kids! It's a fucken avalanche, Mitch."

"Same thing with crime and gangs," Folders shouted. "In the burbs they blame . . ."

"A fucken avalanche," Johnny said.

WORD, ACCURATE OR not, has always spread quickly in small towns, has always permeated to the heart and diffused to the extremities with the speed of a miracle elixir. In the age of electronic information dissemination, word, accurate or not, flashed through East Lake, the lake region, the state, the nation; word of the crash, the accident, the deaths of two, maybe three, East

Lake High students. In town the word was immediately met with shock, horror, denial; in the region, with acknowledgment, relief ("Thank God, this time it wasn't us"), self-justification ("See! They no better than us") and vengeance ("Serve em right, with all their money en fast cars"); in the state and nation, with apathy ("Where the hell is East Lake? Who cares?").

In the school's main office the principal, Charlene Rosenwald, had assembled a crisis intervention team. She was somber, professional, yet her voice wavered. "I have two major concerns," Dr. Rosenwald began. She made brief eye contact with Ciara DeLauro, the guidance counselor, with teachers F.X. McMillian, George Putnam, Phyllis Medina, Jerry Bendler and Deborah Leahman. She avoided Victor Santoro, the vice principal, not because of animosity but because of their previous, complete agreement. "Of course, my first concern is for those students who have been injured. I pray that they fully recover."

The teachers knew sketchy details. Ciara DeLauro had been filled in only slightly more. She had been in the hallway, talking to Marcia Radkowski about cultural diversity—about the rich tapestry of different threads woven together, and the clash of color when threads are separately emphasized—when the first word arrived.

"But my main concern—" Dr. Rosenwald's voice became firm "—is for the image and security of this school. Vice Principal Santoro will head up the task force. Mr. McMillian, I want you to assist Victor in any way he asks."

F.X. nodded. He was still in his coaching shorts and spikes; was still damp from the mist that had turned to drizzle; was uncomfortable but ignored the discomfort as much as possible. He had been the last to join the meeting, had overheard hallway talk of a fatal accident. "Any names . . . ?" he mouthed but was halted by Principal Rosenwald's next words.

"It is imperative that we discover whether these students had consumed any alcoholic beverages; whether they had inhaled or injected any illegal substances."

"Who was involved?" McMillian asked.

Rosenwald continued without acknowledging his question. "If they did," she said coolly, "we must determine if the illegal substances were purchased on school property. Our potential liability is astronomical. The preliminary reports I have received indicate we have two, and perhaps three, students who were killed. There may be more. We're not certain at this point exactly who or exactly how many students were involved. The accident happened on Wampahwaug Road, beyond the town of Wampahwaug, almost to The Falls. The driver has been taken to East Lake Hospital and Medical Center. Others are being taken, as we speak, to St. Luke's Hospital in Lakeport."

Charlene Rosenwald held her hands together as if praying, rocked forward then back, accentuated her words with the beat of her clasped hands. "This is a very serious situation. I cannot emphasize any more greatly the seriousness of this matter; what it can mean to this school. What it can do to this school. What it can cost our entire school system!

"Mr. Santoro will direct the plan of action that we will follow as to official school announcements—to our own students, to the outside community and to the news media. At this point we have few confirmed details; therefore, we have nothing to say.

"Mrs. DeLauro—" the principal turned to Ciara, then back to the table "—will head up the effort to minimize the anguish and to assist the students in expressing their grieving. I have also requested permission from Dr. Schoemer and the board of education to bring in a team of counselors, therapists and psychologists to assist in the intervention process. Dr. Schoemer is in full agreement."

Dr. Rosenwald interlaced her fingers, glanced to the ceiling, back to the table. "At this time I have confirmation of the name of only one student—who has died; that is Katherine Fitzpatrick."

"Katie Fitzpatrick!" The name burst from F.X. McMillian. "That can't be!"

"That's the name I've been given," Charlene Rosenwald said firmly.

"No," McMillian insisted. "She's on the girls' varsity team. They just played Taftburg. This afternoon. I'm sure she played."

"I hope you're right," Dr. Rosenwald said.

"Me too," said Jerry Bendler. "She's really a pretty girl."

"Martina Watts got yellow-carded," F.X. mumbled. "I think Katie went in for her. Then later . . . Martina pulled a hamstring. She's out for at least two weeks. I'm sure Katie went in . . ."

"Frank." Ciara laid a hand on F.X.'s arm. "It was Katie." Ciara's eyes were damp. She wore a hurt smile. "I just spoke . . . just before . . . with her parents."

It was half past one when Julia settled into the beige leather bucket seat of her gold Infiniti Q-45. Earlier the sun had broken through the overcast but clouds remained. They seemed to be winning the battle for the sky. She paid little attention.

Julia had dressed in a classic black silk business suit with pearl buttons with braided gold rims, with an above-the-knee skirt to show off her shapely legs. Her heels were high but not spiked, lifting her to a powerful five feet eleven inches; her stockings were black and sheer. She wore her mother's pearl necklace with matching earrings and bracelet; a black pearl ring in a gold setting which Johnny had found in Venice on one of his sporadic international trips; plus her engagement, wedding and anniversary rings.

She grasped the padded wheel firmly, squeezed it, did an instantaneous review of her appearance, smiled quickly, then started the car, twisted in the seat, held the back twist to release the energy stored in her spine—a movement she'd learned in yoga class—twisted the opposite way, held it, then backed onto Lake Shore Drive. Full-scale war, she thought. And I didn't even know it! If Rod hadn't called . . . bless him . . . hadn't warned me . . . He . . . Johnny still doesn't . . . I should have told him . . . know.

The war had begun, she thought, without her even realizing it; had begun sixteen months earlier, a year ago last May, when she'd barged into Marvin's office through a door that Harry Hickel, Gallina's editor in chief, was supposed to have locked. Her head had been down, her eyes on a manuscript she'd held in her hands.

Even before she looked up, she began. "Marvin! *This is hot!* This is so hot I'll have to cool it down but I'd stake my job and my reputation on it. It's called *God's Country*. Listen to this pass—" At that she sat, looked up, and saw Harry with that ridiculous grin; saw Marvin Meloblatt extracting himself, flustered, zipping, buttoning, closing his belt. At first it didn't register. Then Harry, still bent over the desk, in his high and squeaky voice, and Marvin in his deep, strong bass, spoke at once.

"Jesus! Julia!" Marvin bellowed. "What the hell—" he muffled his voice "—are you doing in here?!"

And Harry in a nasal falsetto, "Don't you at least knock, Julie?! Before you strut in? You *never* know—" straightened up; for all his skinniness, he was hung like a stallion "—what you might see." Slowly, dramatically, in a faux display of modesty, Harry fumbled with his underwear, pulling his pants up under his rigid member, aiming himself directly at her.

Julia froze, stunned, shocked, mouth agape, manuscript limply on her lap. Had she thought about it, she would not have necessarily disapproved, did not disapprove of homosexuality, but to see it, to be confronted by it—not so much by Harry's, which she'd always assumed of the weaselly young man, but by distinguished, fifty-five-year-old Marvin, six feet three inches tall, married to a lovely woman, two adult children, now pale, ashen—confronted with it in the office in midafternoon!

Marvin reacted quickly, grabbed and spun Harry, shook his arm, smacked him on the butt, commanded, "Get out of here!"

Harry still acted the flagrant fop—spastic, fumbling purposefully, displaying himself as long as possible, attempting to appear embarrassed. "Yes, dear," he whined to Marvin.

At that Julia almost burst out laughing, caught herself, covered her smile with one hand, began to rise, to back out.

Yet Marvin took charge. "You saw nothing here," he stated flatly, menacingly.

"I . . . I . . ." Julia stuttered—a total reversal of her emotions, more from fear of Marvin's enraged posture than from the situation. "I saw nothing," she repeated. "There was nothing to see."

"That's right." Marvin's eyes had been hateful.

"I'll come back—"

"No! You stay. That better be one fucking great manuscript."

For months nothing had happened. Julia had thought she'd handled it well. She'd told no one; and Marvin had treated her as respectfully as always. By midsummer she'd put the incident out of mind; had, with Rod Nightingale as her ally and reinforcement, gotten into a bidding war over *God's Country*, a first novel by Justin Robustelli; had bid against three much larger New York houses on the strength of several Hollywood contacts who were "very excited."

Rod, at first, had been skeptical. "Over the transom?" he questioned. "But a middle-aged white guy?"

"It's really well written." Julia looked up, locked eyes with him. "The middle is explosive. The end is poignant. The kind of story that stays with you. That makes you cry and makes you smile."

Rod played devil's advocate. "What's it about?"

"Read it," Julia begged. "Please."

"I've got a pile—"

"It's contemporary. I see it as a miniseries. Two, three nights. His cover letter says it's about the evolution of polarization and the onset of violence in a small town."

"Is this guy a psychiatrist or a professor of philosophy or something?"

"No. He's a plumber—" She wanted Rod's support, was about to say, "but," but he cut her off.

"Then where does he get off using language like that?"

"It doesn't read like that, Rod. It feels very real. Very today. Drugs, crime, government corruption, corporate shenanigans."

"Sounds like the newspapers."

"Exactly. Except personal. You feel every character's pain; you feel their excitement. You feel like you're right in there with them."

"I thought you were the one saying, 'Readers want to escape.' Remember? 'Give em smut. Give em fuck. Give em knock-down-and-dirty pulp'?"

"Yes, Mr. Roderick Nightingale, I remember. I doubt I'll ever live that down. There's enough love and smut and violence and titillation . . . It's just better-crafted than most. And it's actually done in a package that's got meaning. It's not the typical cliché list so it's hard to place."

"General fiction?! Julia! There's no such market anymore. You know that."

"There's a *Romeo and Juliet* subplot. Interracial."

"You mean *Othello*."

"No. They're more like children. Untainted passion. Passion for passion's sake. When they're about to make love for the first time you can feel the steam pouring off the page."

"Ahh! So it is smutty!" Rod grasped his chin, rubbed it, smiled broadly. "I tell you what, Julia. Pick out a dozen good passages, come by the house tonight, and we'll read them together."

That evening, on the way home, she'd stopped at Rod Nightingale's beach home at The Cove in South Lake Village. She sat with him on his deck overlooking a short run of low vegetation, then a man-made beach arcing around a secluded inlet. She had a single glass of J. Lohr chardonnay as Rod read the pages she'd clipped and as she studied him in his baby-blue muscle shirt, black swim trunks and sport sandals. Nightingale was handsome, tall, lean, polished, a thirty-eight-year-old bachelor. His beach home was small, one large room downstairs with a half loft above; elegantly decorated, macho, sporting, yet intellectual—two walls lined with bookshelves, desks and computers.

"Christ! This is hot stuff." Rod looked up to see Julia, the tip of her tongue on the rim of her wineglass, seemingly gazing at his body with appreciation. "Let me help you edit it," he said.

"We've got to buy it first."

"Then let me call L.A. Let me call Zerrelli. I'm with you one hundred percent. Let me lead the pitch to Marv."

By the end of the month Julia had signed Robustelli and had guaranteed him $250,000; with editing, production, marketing and general overhead, she'd committed Gallina Publishing: A Poly-Media Corporation, over Meloblatt's trepidations, to expenditures in excess of one million dollars. All seemed to go well. By November, Julia, with Rod's help, had edited the manuscript and had sent it back to Justin Robustelli for revisions. They'd met four more times at The Cove, each meeting becoming closer, hotter.

"Oh God! You are really an attractive man."

"And you are a lovely woman."

"If I weren't married, Mr. Nightingale . . ."

"Pretend you're not."

"If I weren't, I'd race you up that loft ladder."

"I'll let you win. Ready . . . set . . ."

"But I am married. It may not be perfect, but . . ."

"I know. It's a commitment."

"Yes. It is. Johnny trusts me."

"He's naive."

"Trusting."

"A lucky man."

By December production work on *God's Country* had been under way: galleys had been ordered, advanced blurbs solicited, marketing slots determined. Only the TV sale had yet to be confirmed. Other projects, too, had been producing well. Julia's year-end bonus—paid in April after all accounting was tallied—was nearly half her yearly salary. Then, in May, Marvin Meloblatt had hired the cold and drab Marnie Steiger as chief operating officer. Julia had not seen the significance—had accepted Marnie as a good number-crunching decision maker (something beyond Harry's capabilities)—had not, at first, realized that Marnie Steiger had been brought in as insulation between Marvin and Harry on one side, and Julia on the other.

By early June, Julia's "big project," *God's Country*, had been looking like a blockbuster-in-the-making—editorial excitement, marketing enthusiasm, superb graphics and a two-year option taken by TV miniseries-maker Sam Zerrelli, with details and contingencies yet to be resolved.

Weekly, Julia and Rod had met with Marnie, who then met with Marvin and Harry, to plan Gallina's strategy. Marvin hadn't wanted to jump the gun and had purposely slowed the production schedule, postponed the release date, awaiting final word from Zerrelli. "We've got to hit it just right," Marvin had cautioned. "The right time slot. The right niche. With the money we've got tied up, we've got to work around L.A."

In July Julia had met again with Rod at his home on The Cove. "Julia, I'm really glad you came." Nightingale was again in black swim trunks, now with an open, light cotton shirt that contrasted with his deep tan.

"On a Sunday afternoon, Rod!" She too was dressed casually.

"I just got off the phone with L.A.," Rod told her. "I've been on with Zerrelli's assistant all week."

"And?"

"Come in. Come in. Have a glass of wine. Let me explain what they're thinking."

Julia sat with him, read his notes, had a wine cooler, a second. The day was warm, the summer sun low but still hours from setting. They moved to the deck overlooking the beach and the inlet. "I've wanted to keep this on ice," Rod said. They sat beside each other in lounge chairs; to each side there was a small table. On each table they put their drinks and their cellular phones. "At least until Zerrelli makes his final move."

"Have you pressed him for a time?" Julia asked. "We don't want this going the full two years."

"That's why I wanted you here." Rod touched then squeezed her hand. "I think he'll call back within the hour."

"Oh!" Julia squealed like a schoolgirl. "Oh, Robustelli's going to be ecstatic. He's been wigging out over the delays."

"I wouldn't tell him anything until we have the faxed confirmation. Julia, I just want to hug you. This *is* hot. Zerrelli's talking an all-star cast."

Julia leaned toward Rod, kissed him—just a peck—on the lips. He rolled toward her, put a hand on her far shoulder, gently pulled her closer, kissed her nose. They both laughed and Julia stood and moved to the deck railing. "This is such a lovely spot."

"Thanks."

"That's why the ladies can't resist you, huh?"

"Oh, some do." Again they laughed.

He moved, stood behind her, his right hand gently caressing the small of her back, then slightly lower.

"Don't do that, Rod," she said but there was no conviction in her voice.

"If Zerrelli makes good on his spiel, we stand to have a very good year." As Rod Nightingale spoke he lightly grasped Julia's left wrist with his left hand—just two fingers stroking—and with his right he continued to caress her back and shoulders, then lightly the roundness of her hip, the outside of her right thigh.

She leaned back against him, squirmed. "Oh God!" It had been a long time since she'd felt so turned on. "You know I can't," Julia said.

"Johnny?"

"He's . . . You know his father's moved in with us."

"Umm."

"I don't even feel like it's my house anymore. I . . . Today's Rocco's birthday. They've got a crowd coming . . . I should . . . I should be there."

Ever so lightly Rod brought his hand up her side; ever so gently he touched her breast. She shimmied. He kissed her shoulder. Her stomach tightened, breaths came shallow, more quickly. Rod slid a hand under Julia's shirt, unfastened the front closure of her bra, massaged one breast, the other. Her mouth went slack, her skin tingled. She glanced to the lake. The sun, nearly down, glittered a golden path toward her. She scanned the beach as his hands glided over her body. Her eyes fell to the closed-in shrubbery. She let her left hand drop to his suit, let her fingers brush him.

"Oh Rod," she gasped. "We shouldn't be doing this." She pulled away but he held her. "No, Rod," she said.

He did not hold her tightly, did not use force; he smiled, caressed her face, kissed her forehead. Julia stepped away. "Oh God! Oh God," she said softly. "You could turn on the dead."

He sighed. "You're far from dead. You're . . . This cock-teasing coyness is driving me mad."

She shook her head, backed farther away, turned, snapped her bra closed, sat, finished her wine. Out of nowhere she blurted, "Did you know that Marvin's gay?"

"Huh?" Rod smiled, amused.

"Harry *and* Marvin," Julia said.

"Well, Harry . . . yeah."

"Harry wants me fired. I think. I just thought of that."

Rod cocked his head, befuddled. "Julia, why would he want that?"

"Well," Julia said, "I probably shouldn't tell you this but you probably already know."

"Know what?"

"About Harry and Marvin."

"Oh. You mean . . ."

"Um-hmm. Last year I accidentally walked in on them in the act."

"Where?!" Rod asked. Julia did not notice his skepticism. He refilled her glass.

"In Marvin's office," Julia said. Then conspiratorially, "Marvin was doing it to Harry right there at his desk. From behind. That's why I can't count on Marvin's support or protection."

"Doing it to him?! In his office?! You mean . . ."

"Oh, yes! Marvin was butt-fucking Harry right there. I was so shocked. It was disgusting. I mean, maybe it's not disgusting in private, but in his office! I couldn't speak. I couldn't move. My chin dropped to the floor."

"Julia! What are you saying?!"

"I . . ." She raised a hand to her mouth. "I thought you said you knew."

"Oh, come on, Julia. You don't have to say those things. I know you're angry about Marvin bringing in Marnie, but this . . . You don't have to be vicious. I never thought of you as vicious."

"Wha . . . ! I wouldn't have said . . . You said you knew. You think I'm making it up?"

"Julia!"

"You bastard." She emitted a sharp, short laugh. She had not told Rod the story in spite but as a way of changing the mood.

"You're just angry that Marvin dumped you," Rod said.

"Dumped me?"

"Julia, I'm better than Marvin. I'd be better to you than he was."

"What are you talking about?"

"Oh, come on. Everyone knows you've had a five-year thing with him. Everybody accepted it." Rod snickered. "This 'Johnny trusts me' crap . . . Ha! You know, I really would treat you better than Marv did. Really. I like you more than—"

"What the hell are you . . . I never . . ."

"All those nights?" Rod chuckled. "I mean, it's nothing to me. But all those quick promotions?"

"I never slept with him. I can't believe you thought—"

"Look. Let's just drop it. I'm glad Marvin's back with his wife."

"Drop it!" Now Julia was angry. "Drop it!" Her face was tense, her lips tight. "I never . . . not once . . . with Marvin. That pasty snob. Not once."

"Yeah, right!"

"You think I've been sleeping around . . . ?"

"I'm sorry it came up." Rod stood. He was angry that the situation had soured. "It makes no difference to me at all."

"Well, it makes a big difference to me!" Julia snapped. "God!" She stood, grabbed her phone, tramped to the deck rail, banged a fist on the wood.

"Look," Rod said. He hoped to salvage the evening. "I'm sorry. Really. I . . . Maybe I was fed a line. Someday, Julia . . ." He put his hands together, interlocked his fingers, bit his lip, stood next to her. "Someday, Julia," he said sadly, "we're going to be together."

"Um." Very short. Angry. Then flat. "Maybe."

"I'm sorry," Rod repeated.

"So am I," Julia said. She reached a hand to his face, was about to touch him, when she startled. A couple, not thirty feet away, rose from the shrubs—a young black man, a very pretty white woman. He shook out their blanket. Julia stared. Rod, spying the couple, moved back a few inches. The black man shook his head, his long, distinctive dreadlocks flicked wildly. His entire face was beaming. Then he spotted Julia looking at him. Their eyes locked, his smile contorted. Quickly they both looked away.

"Do you know—" Rod had begun.

"Call me at home if Zerrelli phones," Julia had answered.

But Zerrelli had not phoned that Sunday afternoon in July. Nor had he returned calls during the next week, or the next, or the following month, and when his office did call, they simply said they'd put the project on hold. In early September Julia discovered that Zerrelli's group had a similar project in the works, and Julia had speculated that Zerrelli's option had been designed to keep a competitor from producing *God's Country*, that they had wanted to keep it off the market until their own work had run its course.

Now Julia stood tall before Marnie Steiger's desk, tall, lovely in her classic black silk suit. She faced Steiger, glared down at her. Meloblatt, Hickel and Nightingale were not in the building. Steiger did not make eye contact. "It's quite simple, Julia," the stout, drab number cruncher said. "You've committed us to a deal that's going to break Gallina. We've got to get out of it."

"You, Marnie, are nuts," Julia said sweetly. "All of you around here have gone nuts."

Marnie kept her head down, glanced up through her glasses. "Mr. Meloblatt's orders."

"It's a legal contract. You know that. Robustelli's got—"

"Mr. Meloblatt says to get us out of it before it sinks the company."

"Bring out the book," Julia countered. "Everything's ready. We can have it in distribution in two months. We've already got the market primed. It's expected."

"Mr. Meloblatt said, 'It'll flop.' Without the TV tie-in, it'll flop."

"It's terrific. Get it out now. Before Zerrelli releases his show. Preempt them. Even though we're not the same, we can ride their coattails when they do release the miniseries. This is a better story. All we have to do is get the publicity on the theft. We're golden."

"Ms. Panuzio, at Mr. Meloblatt's insistence, I've been reviewing your employment contract. A million-dollar loss is—"

"You bitch. This has nothing to do with *God's Country*, does it?"

Marnie froze. She cowered behind her files, hunkered down beneath her thick glasses. Still, Julia could see that the COO was enjoying her role.

"Let me speak to Marvin," Julia insisted.

"He's out for the day."

"Harry?" Julia said angrily.

"He's meeting with our attorneys. So's Mr. Nightingale."

"Rod called me this morning. He . . . Good God! He set me up! He—"

"If you would like to resign—" the COO held out a pretyped letter "—instead, Mr. Meloblatt . . ."

Julia stared at Marnie Steiger, but the stout woman's words were no longer reaching her mind. Instead, Julia pictured Marnie as a toad, a blob, something distasteful and insignificant and not worth attacking. "Who needs you jerks?!" Julia swept a ring-adorned hand across Marnie's desk, sending stacks of files splaying across the room. "I built this company from a two-bit press into what it is today. Not you, Marnie. Not Marvin. Not his little boyfriend. Not any of those gutless jerks. I don't need you. I don't need them. I quit."

Marnie Steiger smiled.

JOHNNY DROPPED MITCH at his house, slowly drove away, continued listening to the radio—chatter, ads, something about a gang-related murder in Misty Bottom. There was nothing more on the accident. He meandered, drove toward Hayestown, doubled back, circled St. Paul's Roman Catholic church, worked his way around the construction site of the new apse, looped around the library, drove down Fifth Street, by Adam's Inn and The Bastille, onto Lake Shore Drive. Then, very slowly, Johnny drove toward The Point.

He thought of Atlanta—his department was the one most likely to be consolidated. Would they invite him to transfer? Would he accept? Would they offer him a severance package if he declined? Would Rocco survive the move?

Johnny felt confused, more confused than he'd ever felt. He felt angry, shaken, betrayed. He had served the company for twelve years, twelve faithful years. They'd been good to him; he'd been good to them. It wasn't his fault that NSC had been taken over by ContGenChem or that Mr. Tedesco and the old leadership had been replaced by Nelson and Brad Tripps. *Fancul,* he thought. Fuck em. Robber barons!

Then he thought of Julia, of her probable reaction. Her late night schedule nagged at him but he pushed that from mind. He felt his faith fading, his trust and belief in his own abilities.

Again Johnny thought of Rocco. A year before she died, Johnny's mother, Tessa, had said to Johnny, "If something happens to me, I want to make sure he's not living alone. That he's with family." And Johnny had answered, "Of course, Ma. But nothing's goina happen to you." But it had; and, without even consulting Julia, he'd asked his father to move in. Rocco had agreed, had sold the house-over-the-store where Johnny had grown up, where Rocco had lived for over forty years. Johnny thought about Rocco, about how the old man would know what was going on, about how he wouldn't have it quite straight, and how that wouldn't make any difference. He'd be critical. He'd issue another stern warning. Or he'd say, as if Johnny were fifteen, "If you need money, I've got some. I got the money from the house. Don't get behind."

Johnny's thoughts returned to Julia. No matter what she does, he thought, I will love her. That was the hardest thought of all. He loved her. She pushed him away. He doted on her. She—at least in his perception—rejected him. Perhaps it was exhaustion, perhaps because their lives had taken divergent paths, perhaps because their schedules were so reversed. To him, all that was unimportant. Reason had nothing to do with it. It was a pattern, a diagram wired into him from childhood: Tessa had loved Rocco; Rocco had loved Tessa; his role models from birth. Nonno had loved Nonna; Nonna had loved Nonno; wired in for generations. Now it was his way whether he wanted it to be or not. It could not be otherwise. He had fallen in love with Julia, had made her his wife. He had never fallen out of love.

Johnny sighed, stopped the car by The Point, stared across the water. He felt down, exhausted. He did not want to go home. It's just . . . he could not grasp his own thought. It's . . . just . . . no longer . . . For the first time in his life he said it to himself. It's just no longer fun. It's just . . . Maybe if I'd taken a different road. Like Mitch. Maybe if I'd been a different person. Maybe then the robber barons couldn't . . . couldn't . . . He covered his face with his hands, sniffed. The simultaneous frames, images, screens opened. His arms trembled. He was not at the center of the screening but outside, above, looking down as if from a great height, as if he were a gull circling, watching the sea, hearing, feeling the scenes below.

Johnny-panni is on his mother's lap. Tessa is seated in the backyard, on the bench of the wooden picnic table that Rocco has built from scraps. She is facing away from the table. Johnny looks up, sees past her, sees the intertwining black arms of two great elms. He sees the green umbrella of leaves. He squirms. There is sweat on his forehead, a grimace on his face.

"That's when my father had his first store," Mama is saying to Aunt Sylvia. "I was five. Maybe six. I wasn't as old as Johnny."

Mama is hot. To one side of them there is a tiny patch of grass; to the other, the rough gravel and cinders of the driveway which leads back from the street to the four-bay garage. There are people on the street, sweltering. Their noise ripples like waves in the air and he sees the waves circling the house, coming up the driveway. But in the backyard they are faint, weak, and the shade is comfortable. But Mama's lap is hot. There is no light breeze. Upstairs, inside the flat-over-the-store, the heat is suffocating, the air unbreathable.

"I remember," Mama continues, "the way my mother and father dealt with the gangs. With hoodlums and the robbers."

He . . . I squirm and whine, and Mama rubs my shoulders to calm me.

My sister Sylvia is at Holy Rosary's summer day camp. Nicky is asleep on a blanket on the ground. Little Angie is in a basket. She's just an infant. Tessa bounces me on her knee while Papa's sister, Aunt Sylvia—she's older than Papa just like Sylvia's older than me, and I think my sister Sylvia is named for her—Aunt Sylvia breaks in with her own story, which is a rude thing, but Mama smiles. I think she is happy for the company. Between the heat and looking after us kids, she is not offended by Aunt Sylvia's interruption. Papa is working somewhere. He is always working somewhere. When he comes home he is dirty and tired and it is always late.

"Well, when my father first came to this country—" Aunt Sylvia's voice is like Aunt Tina's, rising and falling, but it is not shrill but sweet and easy to listen to "—there was hope, but there was no money. That's when he worked in the camps for the Italian padrones. Those were terrible times. Those men, who owned the camps, they were robbers. Robber barons. My father couldn't live with my mother because there was no money and for two years he saw her only on Sunday mornings at the house where she did all the chores. She was just a young girl. Mama told us this because Papa was too proud to ever tell. Those were the Padrone Camps where the padrone was

really more like a foreman. No, more like a slave master. Papa built the railroads from Norwalk to Danbury and from New Haven to New London." Aunt Sylvia smiles. Mama smiles too. " 'They paid very well.' That's what Mama would say. She would laugh when she would tell the story. 'They paid him one dollar and thirty-five cents every day, six days a week.' More than he made later as a shovel man. Mama always laughed about that. A dollar thirty-five was a lot of money back then. But they charged the men more than a dollar a day for food, and Papa had to pay for where he slept even if it was in a tent that the men had to move and put up themselves. They lived in the mud beside the construction sites. In horrible squalor. Just horrible. But Papa, he saved some money by not eating every day. And he had money hidden from when he was a soldier in Italy. But it wasn't enough. Those padrones, they weren't like the padrones in Italy. They were mean and cruel and they drove the men like dogs. Sometimes they were called enforcers. They were so hated. Worse than the Wasps or the Irish, because they turned against their own kind and sided with the Wasps or Irish. They charged the Italian men so much that most owed more money than they could ever make. That's how they made them slaves. That's why, when a man calls on Papa today and says, Il Padrone, *he always follows it with the words, 'in the old sense.' You see, Tessa," Aunt Sylvia says, "those were the real hoodlums. They were the first. And it was because of the robber barons that others became hoods. One time I asked Papa about it and he said,* 'E fissaria.' *No big deal. Can you imagine? See, they couldn't make Papa a slave. He was too smart and too strong. He escaped and went to work at the ferry terminal."*

Aunt Sylvia shifts in her seat. Johnny-panni squirms on his mother's lap. It is too hot to sit on Mama's lap and she lets me slide to the dirt where I sit and dig holes that I make believe are craters made by bombs. I make believe I am dropping bombs on the bad men who try to make the Italians into slaves; who make anybody into slaves. I dig more craters and am glad that Aunt Sylvia doesn't make me listen the way Aunt Tina would if she were here telling her stories.

Mama goes in, returns with a pitcher of Kool-Aid and ice. Before she pours the orange liquid into glasses, she helps him . . . me make a circle in the condensation. We add dots for eyes and a big smiling mouth but drops run down making the eyes tear and the smile look angry. Aunt Tina, I think, would never drink Kool-Aid. I'm glad that Aunt Sylvia doesn't hesitate. I get back into the dirt. Now I am making deeper craters and use the debris for bigger bombs which I throw at the old garage where Papa has his cement mixer and tubs, his pipes and lumber.

Mama returns to the story she had begun about her family, the Altieris. "Back then . . . oh, I think I was only six . . . Hmm, let me see. Back in those days there was a terrible gang but it was small. This is, hmm . . . certainly before Donato was born. It was the year that my little sister, bless her, the year Maria was born, that same year she died when she pulled a hot bowl of soup from the table and scalded herself and caught pneumonia . . ." Mama makes the sign of the cross. "I used to take care of her when my mother was working . . ." Tears come to Mama's eyes. I don't know why Mama tells the story if it is going to make her cry. I make believe I don't see. I don't look. I don't want them to see me because there are tears in my eyes and I sniff and wipe my face. "I don't think she was even ten months . . ." I hear Mama say. "She was born in 1920 and this was the end of that year or the beginning of 1921. Who would have thought that a ten-month-old could pull a bowl of soup from the table?!" Mama sighs, pauses, takes a deep breath. Aunt Sylvia consoles her. Nicky flops over but does not wake from his nap. Mama rises, lifts Angie from the basket. She is wet and Mama changes her on the table, but all the time she continues with her story.

"The gangs back then, when Papa had his first store . . . Maybe it was the year before Maria was born so it would have been 1919, when we lived on Catherine Street, over a store there, much smaller than here. We had just a little flat for six of us, and Cara, Catherine and I all slept in the room with Mama and Papa, and Uncle Gus slept on the sofa. Anyway, downstairs there was an Italian grocery that was owned by Mr. Arcudi. I think the name was Arcudi. And Mrs. Arcudi was inside and I was outside on the sidewalk and it was a very nice day. I remember it was a very nice day. The sun was out, nice and warm, like today. And three men went in right past me. All three with hats and suits and ties. That's what men wore then if they weren't manual laborers. Very nicely dressed but not expensive. I remember they kind of pushed in all at once and they must have asked the lady, 'Where's your husband?' because she said, 'He's not here.' She was very loud. She was a big woman and I think she was pregnant. But she always talked loud. Not like my mother who always spoke very politely. The men said something else but I didn't understand, and she yells, ' Va fancul.' "

Mama glances at me, covers her mouth after she says those words. Aunt Sylvia stifles a laugh. I know the words. I've heard them before. I pretend I don't hear because they are bad words. I throw a cluster of crater crud at the garage wall.

"Oh." Mama lowers her voice. "This is not nice at all. I look in and I see one of the men hit the big woman. You know, not punch her, but sideways like he's pushing her to get her out of the way. Right in the stomach. And she makes this noise like an animal and I see that she's been knifed and all three men go to the back room and I don't see this but they kill Mr. Arcudi who is hiding back there."

I . . . I am . . . Johnny . . . Johnny-panni is astounded. My mother . . . when she was just a little girl . . . has seen a woman knifed! Has been only a short distance from a man when he is killed! I . . . He does not really understand but he feels the tension, the monstrosity of the act, feels anger, vengeance.

Johnny is afraid. Johnny-panni is afraid to even show that he has heard anything at all.

"Oh," Mama says, "when my mother heard!" From the corner of my eye I see Mama holding the side of her face with one hand. "I ran upstairs," Mama is saying. "I remember that. I ran and told my mother, and my mother—when my father came home and my mother was so upset and he said it was the Black Hand—and right away she said, 'We're moving. We're moving.' Sure, Cara was four and Catherine was two. I was the oldest. The year Maria died. Oh, that was a tragedy! That was a tragedy. My mother never forgave herself. Benedica! Hot soup. Who would have thought a ten-month-old could pull a bowl of soup off the table? Benedica. Where was I?"

"You ran up to your mother . . ." says Aunt Sylvia.

"Oh, yes," Mama goes on. "When my father came home, my mother said, 'We're moving.' My uncle lived with us, my mother's brother Gus. He was still at work, wherever he worked. The rest of us were kids. My mother said, 'We're moving. We're moving tonight!' And we did. We moved that night. That was the Black Hand. An extortion gang. Not Mafia. That came later. That was Sicilian. The Black Hand, they were napoletano—Naples. But really, they were small. A small group. A reaction to the robber barons, Á! Not like the Mafia. What that became later.

"But later . . ." Mama continued her story to Aunt Sylvia, and . . . he . . . Johnny-panni . . . he listened, but he made noises like a tank squashing the bad guys so Tessa wouldn't know he was listening. "When my father had his store down on Pembroke, in the North End near Misty Bottom, or maybe it was in the Toad's Tail, I'm not sure, this was maybe 1923 after Joey was born—the Black Hand came to my father. He didn't tell us this story but he told it a few years ago one night when all the men got together for cards and I cooked that time for them and they all laughed about it. He said they came and they told him he had to pay protection money to . . . they called it insurance . . . to make sure nothing happened to his store. My father said, 'To who?' And they said, 'To the Black Hand.' And my father said, 'Come back tomorrow.' When they left Papa went next door to Mr. DeMenna, the cobbler, you know, who made shoes. That's right, it was Misty Bottom. Then with my uncle Gus and some other men, my father and Mr. DeMenna went to Mr. Mandanici, the baker. Then they crossed the street and talked to Mr. Sam Jones who was colored. He had a small store that sold kerosene and he delivered coal, and if he was covered with coal dust you couldn't tell. They went up and down the street and my father told everybody the Black Hand *was trying to move in. And other ones said, 'Yeah. They've been here, too.' That night in my father's house, in our little house, they had a secret meeting."*

Johnny is all ears. Tessa's story is as good as a radio show. She is now leaning close to Aunt Sylvia, holding her hand, whispering, but not quietly, a stage whisper. Johnny is on all fours making believe he needs dirt bombs that are closer to the table. He has to pee but he is afraid to interrupt; is afraid to go upstairs by himself, envisions a hand, a black hand, grabbing him in the darkness of the hallway, in the sweltering heat, grabbing him from behind . . .

Mama is saying, "And they said, 'From now on we are the Red Hand. And when they come back we tell them, "I'm sorry. The Red Hand has told us not to pay because this is Red Hand territory." ' Well, they don't tell anybody who is this Red Hand but they all make believe they are more afraid of the Red Hand than the Black Hand. And when the extortionists come back . . . You know what Papa said to the merchants? He said, 'All gangs are the same. Intimidation, extortion. You know the Bible story . . . the man with the camel? The camel wants to put his head in the man's tent. The camel is sin but this is the same. You got to stop them before they start or they'll grow big.' Well, when they come back, the merchants say, 'You gotta take it up with the Red Hand, who is wanting to talk to you. They tell us, "Don't pay you." You talk to them, otherwise the Red Hand says, "There will be a war." ' "

Johnny throws more dirt at the garage. THIS IS WAR, he thinks. He is with his grandfather and his father and they are beating the bad guys who make people slaves or who extort and kill, and Hitler is a jerk and Mussolini bit his weenie, now it doesn't work. Johnny throws the dirt with force.

"My father never did tell me what happened. I don't think they paid. And the Black Hand didn't last long. I don't think. I don't think Pembroke Street paid anybody except maybe the Irish cops and of course the church, but that was for the big festival on the Festa di San Rocco, *which, of course, is who Rocco is named for. San Rocco, he is my favorite saint. He was the patron saint of your father's village."*

Johnny is tired of playing in the dirt. He has to pee but he can't pee in the backyard because Aunt Sylvia is there. Aunt Sylvia is now talking but he is not listening. He is San Rocco, the patron saint, the one his mother loves best. He picks up a rock he has dug out and he heaves it at the garage. It hits with a crash. Tessa startles. "Johnny!" she shouts. He does not look at her but looks at the earth. He is thinking, though not in perfect clarity, if Mama and Papa really really loved me, they would have named me Rocco. I should be someone else . . .

It was after seven when Johnny reached his door. He'd forgotten about the radio, about his own thoughts, was now thinking quickly, putting together an excuse to tell Jason why he'd been so late—*forgot and stopped at the health club, and you know, got sidetracked—no, no—got held up at work, and you know, on the highway tonight, with the drizzle, you know, every time it rains like this* . . . Thinking he'd made Jason late for the Life Directions Workshop, about to blurt out, "Okay. Let's hustle up. Did anyone start dinner?" Thinking, Maybe Jenny—she began dinner at least three nights each week—or perhaps, unlikely as it might be, though her car is in the driveway, Julia. Julia, how to tell her about ContGenChem . . .

Johnny opened the door, leaped in, light, agile. He paused to wipe his feet on the mat, prepared to yell out, "Did anyone start dinner?" but found the house oddly dark, quiet. The flickering of TV light reflected off the windows in the living room.

"Hello. Where's everybody? Jason, what time do we need—"

"In here, Dad. It was canceled."

"Oh, good. I know I'm late—"

"Johnny." The voice was Julia's. "Come in here. You'd better see this, too."

"See what?"

"Shh. There's been a horrible accident. Jason thinks he might know—"

"I know. I know I know em. I know just about everybody in school."

"Oh, I heard something on the radio. There weren't any details."

"Shh. They're coming on again. It's live, team coverage."

Filling the picture of the TV screen in the Panuzio living room was the sheared base of a four-inch tree; then panning forward, there were broken branches, leaves, a mishmash jungle of sticks and greens nearly hiding the rear end of a car, only the reflection of the taillights allowing the viewer to find the spot of focus. The picture changed angle, the same olio except now from the front right of the car. The front of the car was as ripped and shredded as the vegetation; metal twisted and torn, plastic shattered, glass reduced to gravel; the vehicle entangled and wrapped about a scarred trunk. The camera bounced, steadied. The focus zeroed in on a debarked section of cream-colored wood, smeared shiny and dark, reflecting the blip and pulse of emergency lights.

"This mark—" a woman's voice rose above the background noises of police radios, speakers, others talking "—on the trunk of this shattered tree here, we are told, is the blood of Katherine Fitzpatrick, who was a passenger in the front seat of this sedan. Angela, we're all asking ourselves . . ."

Jason did not speak. Johnny eyed his son. Jason's jaw dropped; his eyes froze. He did not move.

". . . could this tragic outcome have been averted if the car were a newer model equipped with airbags? And why wasn't—this is our assumption—why weren't the passengers in this sedan wearing their seat belts?"

The video switched back to the studio in Lakeport, to a demure anchorwoman. "Do you know that they weren't wearing seat belts, Denise?"

"Jerks," Johnny mumbled. "Not wearing—"

Julia tapped his hand to quiet him. She did not look at him but kept her eyes locked to the screen. She did not tell him, did not in that moment think to tell him, that she was no longer employed by Gallina Publishing. That she'd quit. Johnny reached for her hand. "You look super," he whispered.

"Shh," Jenny hissed.

". . . that's the conclusion—" Denise's image, amid the foliage with the car behind her, was inset onto the screen to Angela's right "—a few of the EMTs have drawn. Certainly Katherine Fitzpatrick wouldn't have been found more than forty feet from where the vehicle finally stopped. Some of these EMTs have been volunteering for more than a decade. One told me he's never seen so grisly an accident. 'Gruesome' is the word he used. They weren't even sure if the parts they put into each of the body bags were from just one individual. The impact must have been enormous."

"Thanks, Denise." Angela shook her head appropriately. "Our condolences go out to the grieving families. A terrible tragedy. A shame. Such young, promising lives."

"They must have been doing over ninety when the car left the road," Denise inserted. "That's the conclusion several of the officers have made."

"Ninety?!" Rocco rasped from his overstuffed chair. "She said ninety, eh?"

"Umm," Johnny affirmed.

"Thanks, Denise. Myra Bennett is at St. Luke's in Lakeport. Myra, do you have . . ."

Johnny was about to repeat "ninety," about to repeat "jerks," but he did not want to sound to Jason the way Rocco sounded to him. Again he squeezed Julia's hand. She was trembling. Unfolding before them was every parent's nightmare, this one much too close.

The visual changed to the hospital rooftop. Over the roof's edge the shine and sparkle of a wet city became the backdrop for the dark-haired reporter. "Angela, two of the victims have been brought here to St. Luke's, but the hospital has yet to release their identities, pending, at least for one of the victims, notification of the family. The other, we've been told, a girl, is in very critical condition with massive injuries to her head and spine. We saw her being brought in by St. Luke's Holy Name of Peace helicopter. I think you have that on tape . . ."

"Yes." The anchor's voice. "We've shown the clip. Just terrifying."

"Angela, I've spoken to the brother of that student. He's identified her as Amanda Esposito, a junior at East Lake High . . ."

"Aah . . ." Jason gasped, rocked forward, released a low, pained groan.

"Myra," the anchor broke in, "Let's go back to Denise. We want to hear more from you in a minute. Denise, you have something on the driver?"

"Jason," Julia said softly. "We're so sorry . . ." She swallowed. The trauma was too instantaneous, too quick to comprehend.

"Yeah . . ." Johnny began. "God! The Espositos! Poor . . ." He deferred to the TV.

"Yes, Angela. They've just found him. Evidently he has no serious injuries. They believe he somehow walked away from this terrible accident. Walked perhaps two hundred yards down the—do we have the camera on that?—down by that clump of trees. It's unclear if he passed out or was shaken up or was hiding."

"Oh." Angela was suitably astonished. "This is incredible."

"He may be injured, Angela. But he *is* walking."

"Have they identified him?" Angela asked. "And are they sure he was the driver?"

"No, Angela," Denise answered. "He may have been a passenger. Maybe in the backseat. We don't have his name yet. Police are administering a sobriety test. They're not sure they've found all the bodies, Angela. You can see how dense the vegetation is here. And they don't know how many students were in the car. Both doors on the driver's side were sprung open. They're searching the woods right now . . ."

In the Panuzio living room Jason slowly stood. "I know that car." His head shook back and forth. "That's Willis' car. Ryan Willis. Shit! Oh, shit! That's Willis' . . . That son of a bitch. That *son of a bitch . . . !*"

From the TV, the anchorwoman's voice and ever-changing video images: "More on this tragic accident when we come back. In other news, we'll have an update on the North Lakeport diversity vote along with comments from gang leaders of LASH-OUT, the Lake Area Skinhead Outlaws, and from B-SIN, the Black Street Imperial Nation; plus Don Samuelson with the weather; and Lyn Lancaster with sports."

"You know the driv—?" Johnny started to ask, but his son cut him short.

"Amanda!" Jason's voice was dry. "And . . . That son of a bitch killed Katie?!"

"Jason . . ." Julia stood. There were tears in her eyes. She could see hatred erupting from her son and it frightened her.

Johnny also stood, stepped awkwardly toward his Jason. He could not read the boy's feelings, only wanted to offer his support.

Jason stepped away. "I know who was in there." His voice was loud, firm, angry. "Meade and Bhavsar. God! Willis, Meade and Bhavsar. With Amanda and Katie. I gotta talk to Kim. I gotta go see Kim. She and Katie and Martina were real close. Mom, Dad, I'm outta here."

The second of Johnny-Panni's last thoughts—7 December

the seed.

the germ.

The storm continues.

It is me, but it is not. I don't feel a part of him. I am no longer in that body. In that mind. Good riddance.

The sky and the water meet, mesh in the darkness before him. He feels as if they are one medium, feels as if he's been wrapped in a cold, dark, wet blanket. Oh, I know what he feels. He feels the wrapping like swaddling, over him like a monk's hood, a shroud, completely encapsulating him, yet offering no protection.

Look at him—standing there staring at the water, his mind rigid, his body tense, his legs tight yet trembling. A harsh wind howls across the lake, drives charcoal clouds like tumbleweed, pushes the stone-gray water into swells, whitecaps. And he stares. He sees. He comprehends. He comprehends nothing.

Spindrift and splash coat the shore, freeze, turn the jutting piers into treacherous glass gangplanks. The Point, his point, becomes one contiguous humped and pocked icy undulation.

The wind gusts, relents, surges, presses the cloth of his trousers against the front of his thighs, spurts between buttons of his long coat, ceases, erupts anew. A shiver spreads outward from the center of his back, encircles him: spreads inward, upward from his thighs, engages his very core.

Frenzied gusts sway him. He leans into the wind. The slapping of the waves intensifies. It is dark. Darkness has encapsulated him, has pressed down upon Lake Wampahwaug, upon the entire region, yet he stands there, rigid, picturing the slap, the spray, the thickening ice. He does not see the darkness but I see the darkness. I see the darkness jolted by lights from behind me, from town, I see light chopped and shattered on the lake's surface; I see the darkness contaminated by lights from three miles across, from Lakeport, glowing, glowering on the rumpled speeding bottoms of the clouds.

My fists clench, my arms are so taut they ache. Look at this, he says, thinks. God!! It's not even winter. So damn cold. So damn . . . the fourth storm . . .

A thought erupts. It is me. I am trying to break free, to break out of him, out of his disgust, his cynicism, his hatred, his self-hatred loathing remorse . . . There! A thought. A seed. A kernel of truth. A bridge to salvation, to tomorrow, to . . .

Vanished! Chopped and shattered like light on water.

It is decision time. I am not yet ready to make the decision. I have come here, again . . . again, to see it, view it in black and white. He likes to see in black and white, as if black and white will make it all clear.

The wind surges. Waves dapple a headlight beam as a car swings from Fourth Street to Lake Shore. He hears the car pass behind but he does not turn. Thoughts lurch across the waves of his mind, rise, fall, fragment. Everyone thought so, he thinks. Not a smart aleck, but intelligent. Capable of complex rationality. Creative. Funny. Committed. Caring. Now . . . dumber than Gump. Stupid. Dull. I wouldn't stay with me if I didn't have to. Why should anyone? Why should I?

Why should I? He knows there is no answer. I know . . . Look at him. Sick. Sick to his stomach. In pain. Every joint seemingly inflamed. His mind aching. Out of control, he thinks.

Never in control. Never once in control. Never once, I think. A facade. An illusion. I wanted to do the right thing. Half a century of facades. I am not me but him and he is but a facade, a veneer without substance.

A pain shoots through his arm. If only, he thinks. The pain intensifies. Go down my arm! he thinks. Explode! Then, No! Not yet! Not quite yet.

He stands at the water's edge, stands upon new snow—not nice snow, not fluffy white snow, but heavy gray crud marred with footprints. The temperature has risen to thirty-three—not enough to melt the ice coating the shore but enough for the drizzle to come as a swirling mist instead of flurries; enough to make the ice beneath the crud slick as hot shit.

Johnny senses an odor in the mist, an aroma that seems to hang in the air, seems to him to have hung in the air all fall, grown stronger with each shortened day, an odor of depression, of gloom, of fear; an ambient odor that seems to have permeated the entire region as if the trickle-out effect of the massive layoffs by ContGenChem have caused the lake itself to stink. Or is it only me? Am I the only one to smell the slick spreading, the closing first of only a few small bars and grills near the plant, then a few variety stores in the near suburbs, then exurban stores region-wide that depended upon people's discretionary income? I smell the rotting carcasses of vacant dead businesses, of bankrupt people withdrawing, hiding. I smell the stench, a more horrid smell than that of economic dislocation—the stench of adjunct distrust, hate, violence. The craving for revenge.

A new gust staggers him. He steps back, catches his balance, leans into the wind. He had raised the collar of his long coat as he'd begun his walk but he had not cinched the top button. His fingers tremble, fumble in the attempt. He abandons the task, looks into the wind, thinks he should be able to see from where the wind comes, realizes he cannot see it until it, the wind, is only inches from his face. He hunches, forces his hands to his armpits, squeezes his arms to his chest, turns, glances down, back, thinks he should be able to see to where the wind goes, but behind him the road is dark and the mist conceals his home and the town.

Again he turns toward the lake, the onslaught. Trembling no longer circles him but vibrates his entire being. To see, he thinks. To see from where it all comes, came. How did I get here? To see to where it all goes. Every reaction is preceded by an action; every effect has a cause; every ramification has its precursor. Aaron knew. A baby! Just a baby! But he knew. He wrote. He . . . Violence does not erupt without instigation: depression is not spontaneous self-destruction. Still, his, Johnny's, thoughts crescendo. Does that justify rashness? Does that . . .

A new pain erupts. New fear. New hope. New dread. The pain never comes, never came, when I exercised. It's heartburn. Nothing more. From all the food . . . catered food for the . . . Or from Agita*! Agitation! But soon . . .*

Why Julia? Why Rocco? Nicky? Mitch? Jason? I always tried to be a good husband; son; brother; friend; father. Jason . . . geez! With this weather you'll never get the game . . . The game. The games. Gaming. That bastard Tripps. And Nightingale! And LeRoy.

Rocco . . . it . . . you . . . Tessa . . . the mal occhio*! Ha! Oil and water. Olive oil and water. Envy . . . but if only . . . olive oil and water. If only . . .*

Thoughts ebb, are sucked from him by the wind, are carried, scattered to the far corners . . . One must plan, must project, must make believe he knows where it all goes. All things past are manifest in the present. All growth begins with a seed. All things past . . . Richard, 1955. Maybe '56. At Nonno's. Richard at Nonno's on Christmas day. Of course!

Johnny opens his arms, pats his pockets to insure he has his keys, his wallet. He thinks of his appointment calendar with the next weeks' schedules arranged around the last game, the postponed game because of the storms, the damn storms; around shopping and Christmas and New Year's: his calendar with his goals for the coming year clearly defined—oh, what a good boy am I—

and the steps to reach those goals clearly delineated. Certainly that could be used as evidence.

Then he thinks, worries—Yes, I am worried—perhaps that will not be enough, perhaps he should write letters. I'll write to Zi Carmela. I'll tell her about Rocco, about how he . . . about how Johnny plans to commemorate his father and the entire Panuzio family with a donation to the church, to St. Paul's building fund, so that a stained-glass window in the new apse will bear the inscription "In Memory of Rocco Panuzio." And do you, Zi Carmela, approve? Or should there be two donations? One to St. Paul's in East Lake? One to Holy Rosary in Lakeport? After all, Rocco was baptized in the old marble font at Holy Rosary, has attended mass there for nearly his entire life, only stopped going when he moved in with me . . . What will she think? Is it okay to discuss this with the priest before . . . ? He couldn't write that. What would Zi Carmela think? Maybe that he'd been planning on his father's death? Even if Rocco was eighty-five, that's just something one does not do—except . . . except, of course if one is . . . And if he did not act, someone else might. Someone else might get the window! Then wouldn't it be okay to plan? Wouldn't it? Zi Carmela would know.

The wind surges, ebbs. His teeth chatter, his thoughts run on. Solve it by saying, "A Gift from the Panuzio Family." It doesn't need to be solved! It's just for the letter! Who's got ten grand for a goddamn window?! God bless America! Who's got . . . A letter to Mitch. That's what I'll send. Not a letter, a report. A proposal. For Mitch, left there, on his, on Johnny's desk. Talk about our optimism, about our need to do it together. Yes. Yes.

He is on The Point, his feet at the edge of the waves. Again he thinks about his father. Then about his grandfather, and his godfather and godmother, and his cousins, and again about his father now with his sons. His father had been born in Nonno's house, in the house of Il Padrone in the old sense, in the house on Williams Street between Arctic and Jerome Avenues in Lakeport only a long block from Holy Rosary. He'd been born in 1912 on the Festa di San Rocco and was thusly named for the patron saint of Castelfranco en Miscano, in Benevento province . . . He could have named Todd for his father! Except Julia wouldn't . . . "Rocky! It sounds like a thug. A hoodlum." But at least, perhaps, Jason. Jason could have been Jason Rocco instead of Jason Randolph, Julia's father's name. Todd could have been Todd Giovanni . . . He could have insisted. He could have insisted. He could have . . . Not in America! Not in a thoroughly modern American family. Thoroughly modern American families are dysfunctional. The wives are more interested in their careers than in their husbands and children. The husbands have problems with their own careers and they pay sparse attention to their wives and to their children. Children are raised by the community, which raises them with a different set of values, a commercial set of values, than would a family in the old sense. To the community *a child is a consumer, a future producer, a product of and for community production, a carbon-based unit, a commodity to be educated, to be developed, for the use of Tripps and Meloblatt and the padrones in the new sense.*

Thoughts cascade in, whirl, swish, blow out barely leaving a trace, making no sense, no connections, beginning to end, only middle fragments, shards, like broken ice, shattering, scattering, falling into, through, the veneer of thick crud, soundless, lost, an illusion . . .

Perhaps, he thinks, one cannot see precursors until after the fact, then can only surmise them to have been such, as if they could have been or should have been—that's the worst, the should have been—seen. In Memory of . . .

Dumber than Gump. Look at me, him. His arms are tight, his fists clenched. The wind hitting my face brings snow—the fourth winter storm of the season. Sparse snow, yet driven. My ears, nose, lips, forehead sting. My eyes tear. So cold. So damn cold. So damn cold! And the wind. Freezing. Forcing itself into me. An outside force inside of me. Growing inside of me.

Look at the ice. The piers coated with ice. Slick as shit. And the rocks. I could slip so easily. It is no longer me. I am no longer in that body. That mind. I am detached. I am . . .

East Lake,
Tuesday, 20 September, 6:17 A.M.

"WHAT TIME DID you get home last night?"

"I don't know," Jason answered.

"About?" Johnny stood in the doorway between the kitchen and living room. Jason was sitting on the edge of the sofa watching TV, a toaster waffle in one hand, the TV remote in the other. Dog Corleone lay by Jason's feet, his eyes on Jason's waffle.

"I don't know," Jason repeated. "Three maybe."

"Where were you?" There was no warmth in Johnny's voice. He'd gotten up at four, again at five, to see if Jason was home. He had not checked when he'd risen at five-fifty.

"A lot of us gathered at the site . . ." Jason did not take his eyes from the screen. The volume was low; to Johnny, barely audible. "Then we kept vigil at St. Luke's—"

"In Lakeport?!" Johnny's tone hardened further.

"Yeah."

"Who drove? Not that *Kim* you've been seeing."

"Yeah. What's the matter with that?"

Johnny exhaled heavily—an angry, fearful disapproval—said nothing.

"There were lots of us," Jason defended himself. "Maybe a hundred."

"It's a matter of . . . of responsibility." Johnny was seething, attempting to control it, wanting to let Jason know he was angry yet trying to hide, to mask the most overt manifestations of his inner rage. "I don't want you staying out with that girl to all hours. What kind of parents let a sixteen-year-old girl have their car until five A.M.?"

"It wasn't . . . Dad, this wasn't just a regular time. We weren't out partying." Jason's voice quivered. "It was a vigil. They showed a teaser clip before the commercials. You'll see it. Some of the kids even held candles and prayed." Jason turned from his father. He was on the verge of tears. "What's the matter with that?"

"What's the matter . . ." Johnny turned, looked at the ceiling, gritted his teeth, held his hands as if praying for his son's sanity. He was surprised by Jason's emotions but he could no longer hold back. "What's the matter is you're in an unsafe city at three in the morning! Where you could have been mugged or beaten or killed! That's what's the matter with that." His voice rose. "Jerks! Do you need somebody else killed?! Sometimes you kids are jerks! I don't want this going on."

Johnny stomped to the kitchen. He was angry with himself for letting go yet felt justified because of the perils Lakeport posed after dark, and because Jason had said, "Maybe three," instead of an hour he knew to be more realistic. "Jerks," he sputtered. "I don't know what this world's coming to!"

Jason's eyes darted, a furtive glance to where his father had stood, then an embittered glare from a face that masked its own anger, its own pain. He pumped the remote volume button as the news returned.

"If you've just joined us," Joanne Gilbert, coanchor with Kurt Kleinmahn, began, "in local news we've been following the unfolding story, a tragedy. Two East Lake teens were killed last night, and three were seriously injured, when the car in which they were riding lost control and crashed down a treed hillside above the Town of Wampahwaug.

"Police said the car, driven by Ryan Willis, seventeen, of East Lake, after cresting a rise, apparently misnegotiated a sharp downhill turn, left the road, careened off several large trees before slamming . . ."

Johnny reentered the living room, his hands at his sides as if ready to grapple, his neck, head, thrust forward, his face muscles knotted. "*Èh! Stunat!* Turn the damn thing down! Your mother's still asleep."

The changing video on the TV caught Johnny's eye. The station replayed parts of the previous evening's footage but with new audio. "Willis was slightly injured in the accident which claimed the lives of Katherine Fitzpatrick, sixteen, and Veronica Mayberry, fifteen. Those injured have been identified as Amanda Esposito, sixteen, Christopher Bhavsar, seventeen, and John Meade, eighteen. East Lake superintendent of schools John Schoemer confirmed that all were students at East Lake High."

Jason leaned forward, slid from the sofa to the floor to be nearer the set. Dog Corleone nuzzled in under his arm. Johnny stood where he'd issued the order, wished he could rescind it or at least change its tone. He could barely make out the announcer's words.

"Later in this report we will have a statement from Theodore Willis, father of the driver," the announcer continued. "Bhavsar's condition has been upgraded to serious but stable," she read. "Esposito and Meade are both in critical condition at St. Luke's Hospital in Lakeport, where both students underwent emergency surgery within hours of the crash."

The video showed, with muted sound, a replay of a helicopter landing on the roof of St. Luke's. Then again switched to the accident scene where a reporter held a microphone in the face of a haggard man identified as Eugene Kilty, a Wampahwaug fireman. "There was blood and branches everywhere," the shaken man said. "I was the first one ta arrive. You couldn't really see bodies because of the branches and leaves."

Again a video switch to the anchors, now with Kleinmahn reading, "That wet stretch of rural road was transformed yesterday into a scene of chaos and confusion with sirens, flashing lights and the throbbing of helicopters, as ambulances and emergency crews from Wampahwaug, East Lake, Plymouth and Lakeport converged on the scene at about four-thirty P.M. Apparently the teens were on their way to a popular gathering area known as The Falls."

Johnny stepped closer, sat on the sofa behind Jason, his concentration half on the TV, half on the volume, wondering if, even at this level, it might disturb Julia, then wondering if Rocco was up, if Jason had checked on his grandfather. He decided not to ask.

"It was a total mess." The video was now of a different man. "It was like something out of a war movie . . ."

Another quick video return to Kleinmahn, and a jump to a new clip, this one of Thomas Griffin, Wampahwaug chief of police. "At this time no charges have been filed. The accident is still under investigation. And no, there's no evidence or indication that these teenagers . . . that drugs or alcohol were involved."

Back to Kleinmahn. "Investigators have not yet determined why Willis lost control of his 1984 Oldsmobile Cutlass Supreme. Emergency medical technicians last night speculated that the vehicle was traveling at a very high rate of speed, but investigators say they have not been able to establish evidence of the car's velocity. There were no skid marks on the rain-slickened road, they said, and though the hillside vegetation was dense, it may not have slowed the vehicle as it plunged down the embankment.

"Police found the body of Katherine Fitzpatrick, apparently a front-seat passenger, some forty feet from where the vehicle impacted on a large tree. Veronica Mayberry and John Meade were also found outside the vehicle, apparently having been thrown from a back door which, investigators speculate, sprung open on a careening impact with a tree further up the hillside, before the car's final head-on where it came to rest. Mayberry's body was not found until nearly two hours after the accident because of the dense vegetation."

"Good God." Johnny partly covered his face with one hand. The picture was now of St. Luke's. Julia came in. She had on a light blue satin robe, matching heelless slippers. Quietly she sat beside her husband. "You're up early," Johnny whispered.

"Mrs. DeLauro, the guidance couns—" Johnny nodded recognition and Julia continued. "She called about midnight," Julia said. "Asked if I'd come in and help as part of an intervention team."

"Oh." Johnny said nothing more, motioned to the screen, thought, briefly, the counselor had called her because she knew that Julia's schedule was flexible. Or maybe she was just calling everyone. Julia still had not told Johnny about Gallina. Johnny had not mentioned ContGenChem.

"Parents, friends and classmates of Esposito, Bhavsar and Meade," the first anchor read, "kept a vigil outside the hospital's intensive care unit last night. More than one hundred students from East Lake High held candles and prayed."

"See?" Jason said. He did not turn to his parents.

"Esposito's mother, Mary Van Weyden, of Jefferson, expressed her sorrow for the parents of the two girls who were killed. Bhavsar's father, Ometh, asked for others to 'pray for and forgive' the driver."

Again Kleinmahn took over. "East Lake High School principal Charlene Rosenwald also expressed her sympathy and the 'congregational sympathy of the entire East Lake educational body.' Rosenwald said that there will be a special service in the school gymnasium this morning."

Now the screen filled with Dr. Rosenwald's face. "We will be holding a second gathering after school to help the community deal with this tragedy," the principal said. "Counselors will be available for students or anyone from our extended community. It is our understanding that several of the EMTs had a very difficult time at the scene.

"All of these students," Rosenwald added, "were outstanding academically as well as being just 'good kids.' This is very difficult for all of us to deal with. Myself included."

"A tragedy," Gilbert said as the video returned to the anchors.

"Horrible," Kleinmahn said, then added, "We'll be back in a moment with the results of yesterday's referendum in North Lakeport on the regional Diversity Plan and that town's own nonbinding Affirmative Action Proposal . . ."

"Mom," Jenny called from the kitchen. "It's Mrs. Williams."

"I didn't hear the phone," Johnny said.

"Okay." Julia went to the kitchen. Jenny came into the living room.

"I gotta go," Jason said. "I'm goina miss the bus."

"Do you want a ride—" Johnny began but was interrupted by Jenny.

"When did *you* get in?" she interrogated her brother.

"None of *your* business," Jason snapped back. Then, to Johnny, "No. I want to talk—"

From the kitchen Julia called, "Jason." She stretched the cord through the hallway, stood by the family picture wall, one hand held lightly over the receiver. "It's Laurie Williams. Was Aaron with you last night? Did he stay here?"

"He was . . ." Jason looked at his watch. "I'm not sure. He didn't come home with me."

"Was he at St. Luke's?"

"Probably at his girlfriend's," Johnny muttered lowly.

"Ah . . . I think . . ." Jason mumbled. "Ah . . . I'm not sure. He was probably there all night."

"Geez!" Johnny shook his head, threw an opening hand into the air. *"Fa Napoli!"* he yelled. He gestured repeatedly. "You kids! You kids! *N'gazz!* You kids are jerks!"

"I'm outta here," Jason mumbled.

"Wait a minute!" Johnny stepped toward Jason.

"What?"

"Where's that box I asked you to get?"

"Upstairs. I don't know!"

"Well, is it coming down by itself?"

Jenny yawned. "I'm goin back ta bed. This family's crazy."

"It's coming," Jason rasped.

"So's Christmas," Johnny snapped back.

"There's the bus! I gotta . . ." Jason let the front door crash behind him.

Another crash came from the kitchen.

"Now what?" Johnny muttered.

"Laurie," Julia said quickly into the phone, "I have to get—" Then away from the phone, calling, "Johnny!"

"What?!" He entered the kitchen to see Rocco near frantic.

"Where . . . ?" The older man had his hands on the counter, bracing himself. His head was down, his arms shaking.

Julia glanced at Johnny. "You handle it," she whispered. "I'm going up to shower." Then into the phone, "At the hospital . . . All night . . . Laurie, I'll scold him for you if I see him."

"Pop?" Johnny questioned. This was new, baffling, unexpected.

"Where . . . ?"

"Where what, Pop?"

Rocco looked at his son suspiciously.

"I think you're still asleep, Pop."

The older man raised one shaky hand to his mouth, covered his lips. His jaw quivered; his head hung; his eyes closed. Though he had braced himself against the counter, he was not steady. Johnny cupped a hand under his father's arm. Tears filled the old man's eyes. Gasping shook him, not violently but weakly. There seemed to be so little physically left of him.

"Come on. Sit down, Pop."

Rocco let his son guide him to a chair at the breakfast table. Sitting, he sucked in a breath, exhaled a shallow sigh. "I forgot," he said.

Johnny thought to say, "Forgot what?" but nothing came out.

Rocco's tone changed. "How come you're home? It's not Sunday."

"I'm goina go in late."

"Eh? You can just go in when you want? You're a big boss now?"

"No. No, it's not that. There's been all this . . . It's not that late."

"Help me downstairs."

Johnny shook his head, amazed at the transformation. He ignored Rocco's request. "If Jason plays today, do you want to come to his game? You can sit in the car and see the field at Jefferson."

"Calcio?" Soccer.

"Yeah."

"It's too cold to sit." Rocco's head jerked to the left then, mechanically, back to the right, as if he were searching for something.

"Pop, you want some coffee?"

"Juice. I need juice with this pill. A little milk with this one. Then . . ." He lapsed, fumbled with his morning prescription bottles which Jason had aligned on the table. "Jason wraps my leg too tight."

Johnny brought his father a small glass of orange juice, a second with milk, returned for a coffee mug and the pot to refill his own. "It's gotta be pretty tight. Remember what the doctor said."

"Not that tight!"

"I'll rewrap it. Jason's already gone."

"No." Subdued. "I don't want anything. You go to work."

"Don't do that, Pop. If it needs to be rewrapped—" Johnny was emphatic "—I'll do it. But it can't be too loose."

"I can do it."

Johnny's gaze rose to the ceiling, dropped back. He sighed, said, "Do you want toast and jam? Maybe a banana? If Jenny comes back down, she can make eggs."

"We should move the piano. It's too much weight for that side."

"No. We don't need to touch it."

"The house tilts that way."

"No it doesn't."

"I can see it downstairs. Move it to the other side where the foundation's done."

"Pop! Right now I can't even think about that!"

Rocco hung his head, swung it slowly side to side. "Your foundation . . ."

Johnny grasped the back of his head with one hand, squeezed his eyes shut. "I know, Pop. But not now. I'm not worried about it now. Right now I got other things to worry about."

AT 7:31, NEARLY a half hour late, Mitch Williams opened the door of Johnny's Infiniti and got in. Rain, which had been heavy all night, droned on the roof, hood and trunk. Mitch wiped his forehead with his handkerchief. "Just what we need," he said sarcastically. "More rain. Thanks for picking me . . . Johnny, I'm so damn angry. Aaron still hasn't called. His mother's—"

"Did you try that girlfriend of—"

"The Wattses? I . . . Laurie's going to check with the school first. She feels pretty comfortable with what's-her-name. Sharon someth—"

"Mahoney? The secretary?"

"Yeah. That's her. I don't feel comfortable calling his girlfriends. I still can't believe . . . Augh! Hell with it!" Mitch collapsed back in the seat.

"Jason didn't get in until after five. Maybe we oughta kill em both. That girlfriend of his . . . Kim. She drove—"

"Yeah," Mitch interrupted. "I mentioned her to Laurie. She said they've got a store. Her father's got a Spanish grocery in Lakeport. Maybe two. They don't live far from us. Other side of Red Apple Hill . . ."

"Cottage Glen?"

"No. The opposite direction. In the Rock Hill Court area. They're supposed to be very nice people."

Tersely, *"Á!"* Then, "She's sixteen, Mitch! Out to five . . ."

"You been following the accident?"

"Yeah," Johnny said. "Till about eleven-fifteen." He pulled onto the Route 86 on-ramp. "They're jerks, Mitch. I mean it. These kids!"

"At least yers came home." Mitch shifted uncomfortably in the seat. In the few seconds it had taken him to go from house to car, he'd gotten drenched.

"Um," Johnny grunted. "I guess lots of kids stayed at the hospital with that candlelight vigil."

"Yeah. When did we start staying—"

"It seemed, actually, you know, on TV this morning, kind of . . . nice. I mean. I got pissed, too. Still . . ."

"Yeah. I guess."

"Jason said lots of em went to each other's homes. God! Look at this damn traffic! We're not even to the Village!" Johnny banged the steering wheel. His and Mitch's irritations were feeding each other. He leaned forward, flicked the radio power button. "Let's see if McNichols can tell us if we're going to get in today."

Resignedly Mitch sighed, "Another day, another—"

"Hassle." Johnny finished his friend's sentence. "You know, I'm just not at all excited about going back to ContGenChem. I'm tired, Mitch. My feet hurt. I'm—"

"Your feet?!"

"Yeah. Especially my left foot." Johnny lifted it from the floor, rotated his ankle in the limited space.

"What's the matter with your foot?" Mitch asked.

"I think it's growing," Johnny said. "All my left shoes are tight. They didn't used to be. Really. Can your feet grow at forty-nine?"

Mitch chuckled. "I don't know."

"I think my left foot's growing." Johnny was serious.

"Maybe." Mitch chuckled. "Only thing on me keeps getting bigger is my johnson."

"Yeah, right!" Johnny blurted. "You wish."

They both laughed then grew silent and listened to the radio and glanced into the surrounding cars. The rain, the accident news, their sons' behaviors and the upheavals at ContGenChem had created an underlying somberness that the levity could not dispel.

"Could you imagine," Johnny began again, "being Ryan Willis?"

"Imagine," Mitch responded, "being his father. Imagine if your kid went out and killed two of his classmates. I don't know how you live with that."

"Yeah." Johnny sighed. "Better than having your kid be the . . . ah . . . killee, but . . . Geez!"

"You know his father, don't you?" Mitch asked.

"I don't think so."

"He used to coach peewee baseball."

"Oh . . . Was he . . . ? A big guy? Real tall? Used to hunch over all the time when he was around the kids?"

"Yeah. That's him. He's a good guy. Did you hear his statement this morning?"

"No. They mentioned it but I left . . ."

"He's having a tough time," Mitch said. "He said Ryan'd have a full statement later. Said it was indeed an accident. Tragic. He asked the families of the other students not to judge Ryan until they knew all the facts."

"How do you teach a kid—" Johnny's words were sharp "—to be responsible? To be accountable?"

"Umm." Mitch let out a long breath. "Look at us. Two pissed-off old farts. How's Julia handling it? Laurie's a wreck."

"Augh, you know Julia. She's tough. She's upset, but . . . you know . . . she's cool. She could handle . . ." Johnny snorted. "I bet she could handle . . . She could even handle something on the side."

"Something . . . What?!"

Johnny glanced over, simply nodded.

"No way, Johnny."

Johnny shrugged.

"What are you saying?" Mitch asked.

Johnny shook his head, said nothing.

"No way. I don't think so. Because you aren't getting any? Johnny, she's just as tired as the rest of us. That's the way she handles it."

"She started to say something last night about work. Something about trouble and that fucking faggot she works with. Shit! The entire summer?! Not once does she come to bed." Johnny scowled, added, "Augh, who cares? Who gives a rat's ass? I'm not exactly that excited about getting it anymore, either."

"Bullshit!"

"Á!" The short, staccato colloquialism.

"Yer full a shit," Mitch said decisively.

"She . . ." Johnny hesitated. With everything that had happened in the past twenty-four hours, with all the upset, he seemed willing to say things he'd never said before; willing to express concerns more deeply than ever. "She . . . she doesn't like me anymore. I mean, maybe she likes me. Or tolerates me. But she doesn't love me. I think she still thinks I'm okay but she doesn't really love me. Nor do the kids. I don't think they like me at all anymore. Except Jenny."

"Of course they do," Mitch said.

"Not Julia. She doesn't love me. Maybe she's lovin somebody else."

"Bullshit, Johnny! You're just feeling sorry for yourself."

"Aah . . ."

They rode on in silence. The rain remained heavy, the wind began to gust. Traffic came to a halt before the dam. On the radio Dr. Dave McNichols was ranting about racism, affirmative action and reverse discrimination. Traffic jerked forward. Johnny sighed, tried to find a nice-looking woman in another car on whom to erect a fantasy but rain-fogged windows made vehicular voyeurism nearly impossible. He glanced far to the left, downriver; then to the right, at the lake. Only the lake seemed peaceful. "Someday, Mitch," he began. "Someday, I'm going to look seriously into that shuttle."

"Good. Hey." Mitch tapped his briefcase. "Remind me to make you a copy of Aaron's paper on affirmative action. I'll have my secretary make a copy and send it over."

"I'd like that," Johnny said. "I'd like—" Suddenly they were distracted by a radio teaser.

"We weren't drinking or doing drugs. We were playing hooky from Katie's soccer game and Chris' band practice. Everyone was laughing."

In the car both men focused their attention on the statement. It was eight o'clock, they were barely to South Lakeport. The teaser quote was followed by WLAK's prenews music and credits. Before they finished Mitch said quickly, "Oh. I almost forgot. Vernon's giving me my car back. So I'll drive down to Jefferson."

Johnny nodded assent, didn't comment because the teaser quote was being repeated.

"Those are the words of Ryan Willis," the WLAK's newscaster said. "Willis, as you will recall, was the driver of the car in which two teens were killed yesterday, and three . . ."

"Yeah, yeah, yeah," Johnny snapped. "Get on with it."

". . . Willis read this statement to reporters only minutes ago, from the bedroom of his East Lake home, where he has been since being released from a local hospital and medical complex."

"Everyone was laughing." The technician reversed and replayed those words, then let the tape run. "We weren't going anywhere, just riding around; going up to The Falls because it's such a nice spot. Especially in the rain. I don't know how fast we were going. I don't think it was that fast. But everyone was fooling around and just before the turn somebody in the backseat put their hands over my eyes. They were fooling around. Katie said something. She was sitting next to me and everyone else was in back and I shook my head to get them to let go. Then when they did we were right at the edge of the road, at the edge of the hill. I went to jam on the brakes but we were already off the road and everything was being jarred really hard. That's the last thing I remember."

For a full two seconds the radio was quiet. Mitch's jaw hung. Johnny was momentarily speechless.

"Police investigators speculated that when Willis moved his foot to hit the brakes, the rough jarring on the apron may have caused him to stomp on the accelerator. This, Sergeant Ralston Lord of Wampahwaug speculated, could explain the tremendous force of the impact which sprung the doors and threw Katherine Fitzpatrick through the windshield."

"God." As if for protection, Mitch Williams raised both forearms, fists closed, in front of his face.

"I didn't—" the voice from the speakers was again Ryan Willis'; it was clear that he was now sobbing "—do anything . . ."

———

UNABASHEDLY SHE GREETED student after student with a long embrace. Some spoke, some were without words, some broke down and cried. "It's okay to cry," Ciara DeLauro whispered. "It's okay to be sad, to be frightened. It's even okay to be angry. Or to be relieved and happy you weren't in that car."

Julia Panuzio stood to the side, watched the guidance counselor, admired her ease and amity with the students. Julia felt out of place, useless, unneeded.

Ciara moved from student to student in the school's main lobby, from group to group. Period One had begun but no teacher or administrator enforced class attendance. Half the student body had congregated in the lobby before the gymnasium, and in the adjacent armlike hallways. Period Two was scheduled to be a special assembly, with voluntary attendance—not a memorial service, not yet, but a gathering and sharing of feelings, remembrances and information. In the cafeteria professional counselors, volunteers and student peer facilitators talked with a smattering of teenagers or among themselves. In classrooms, with familiar teachers and friends, many kids unconsciously began the process the professionals called "making meaningful."

A few students used the time to joke, to escape, to procrastinate. "Hey man, you hear that Ronnie was a virgin yesterday morning?"

"Ha! Yeah."

"Then she took a big stick last night. Heeheehee." The laughter mimicked Beavis and Butthead.

And repeated. "Heeheehee. Took the big stick. Heeheehee."

And dumbly, on purpose, "I don't get it." Another commercial aped. More snickers. Some groans. Some smiles on faces that did not mean to smile.

Julia saw Jason enter the lobby, shied back to the cafeteria doors so as not to intrude upon his space, watched, awed; felt as if she were seeing a part of him, learning about a part of him, that she did not know existed.

"Oh, Jason, I'm so glad you're here." Ciara DeLauro held him tightly, hugged him as if she were his mother, held his arm, pushed him back to look up at him, into his eyes. "You were at the hospital last night. Oh, and Kim." Ciara continued to hold Jason's arm with one hand, pulled Kim Sanchez to herself with the other. "I feel like the mother of the loveliest children in the world. I'm so lucky. So lucky . . . I know you were very close to Katie. And to the others."

"I'm sorry I didn't get back to you yesterday . . ." Jason began.

Ciara DeLauro was short, shorter than Kim, and heavy, and older than Julia. She smiled, looked up with her huge brown eyes, sighed. "Don't worry. It's okay. We have time. I do want to show you a catalog . . . for

Lehigh University. They're very strong in science and, of course, engineering. And . . ." She turned to Kim. "There's a program for electrical and computer engineering there that Susan Brannard's in. She graduated when you were a freshman. Do you know her?"

"No," Kim said. "I didn't know many seniors then."

"She'd love to have you come down and stay for a few days. I told her about you."

"Oh! I . . . Thank you."

"I know this isn't the time . . ." Ciara squeezed their arms, slid her hands down to their hands, squeezed them, brought them together, looked at Jason, then Kim, looked down and then departed for several new arrivals.

"I didn't know you were interested in computer engineering," Jason said. He smiled, quietly added, "Chip-head."

"Um-hmm," Kim intoned. They moved to an open section of wall between other couples. Kim leaned into Jason, looked up. They kissed, gently, passionately. "There's lots you don't know about me," she said.

"I'm willing to learn," he whispered.

She snuggled into his chest, pressed one thigh against his, hooked a foot behind his calf, pressed in harder. "I want you to hold me all day," she said.

At the cafeteria Julia slid behind the door, swallowed. She was not used to such public shows of affection. "Mrs. Panuzio, would you be willing to listen to—"

Breathlessly: "Of course. Show me where."

By third period, though grieving and shock remained palpable, most classes returned to a semblance of normal routine. In Marcia Radkowski's junior English section, Kim Sanchez placed a framed eight-by-ten glossy of Katie Fitzpatrick on Katie's desk. She stood next to the desk, facing the picture—Katie's light features and pink sweater contrasting with Kim's darkness, black dress, dark accessories. Amanda Esposito's desk was distinguished by a single red rose, placed there, without others knowing, by Peter Badoglio. He sat in his seat, arms crossed, in no mood to talk or to listen.

Jason Panuzio stared out the window at the soccer fields. The rain was still heavy, the close field flooded. He stifled a yawn.

Martina Watts approached, stood near him. She was dressed in work boots, corduroy pants, a white T-shirt topped with a dark green plaid flannel shirt worn open and out like a jacket. "Looks like shit out there, huh?"

Jason startled, settled as recognition took hold. "Umm," he mumbled. "How's the hamstring?"

"Hurt," Martina said. "Make me feel sick. I sure ain't playin on that shit."

Miss Radkowski cleared her throat. Without a word those standing took their seats. The classroom was lifeless, tired, drained of spirit. Marcia Radkowski was ashen. "Please listen," she said. "Just for a minute." She paused, let her eyes rest on Katie's picture, then on the rose on Amanda's desk. "We're going to get through this," she said. She raised a book before her.

" 'But it was another thought that visited Brother Juniper,' " Marcia read. She held the book with her long delicate fingers. It trembled as she continued. " 'Why did this happen to *those* five? If there were any plan in the universe at all, if there were any pattern in a human life, surely it could be discovered mysteriously latent in those lives so suddenly cut off.' " Miss Radkowski's voice became stronger for emphasis. " 'Either we live by accident and die by accident, or we live by plan and die by plan.' "

Marcia looked up, silent, attempting to infuse the room with meaning. *"The Bridge of San Luis Rey,"* she said. "Thorton Wilder. Copyright 1927. Is there meaning in what we are experiencing? Is it random chaos or divine order?" She took a half step back, felt for the desk, leaned back, sat, her feet together on the floor, her upper body and head slumping. "Don't answer me," she said. "Not yet. I want you to do something. I want each of you to write a short reflection on Katie or Amanda which we . . ." Marcia's voice broke as she pictured the two students who were not there. She inhaled deeply, quivering, then exhaled completely, regained her composure. "Which we will give to Katie's parents; or we'll bring to Amanda in the hospital."

"Do you want us—"

Marcia held up a hand, shook her head. "Whatever you want to do. Anything or nothing. A letter, a poem if you'd like." She cast her eyes to the desk, whispered, "But let's be silent for the next twenty minutes. If you'd like to share with us your feelings or images, we'll do that. But you won't have to."

Some students rose, got paper from a ream on the counter at the back of the room; some took sheets from their notebooks; some sat, did nothing. Only the noise of shifting chairs or desks, of cleared throats or sniffled noses, broke the quiet. After ten minutes Jeff Kurjiaka stood, brought his writings to Miss Radkowski's desk, handed it to her, whispered, "I don't want anyone to see it," then spun and left the classroom. In a few minutes Tara Wallace came forward. Then Thad Carter, Erin O'Malley and Miro Sarrazin.

"I . . ." Kim Sanchez stood. "I'd like to share a poem."

"Please."

"It's called 'Katie.' " Tears welled in Kim's eyes. "I forgot. Yesterday I . . ." Her voice faded. She raised her paper, read:

Katie

Katie: My heart dances with images
of you
of us
And I feel so thrilled to be
your friend
friends
To you I'd give my heart
if your life could beat
could beat again
I cry when I think it was I
was I
I cry
Else you'd not have known he liked you
would not have gone
would not be gone.

When Kim sat she was trembling, crying hard. Jason came to her, took her from the room. He had tears in his eyes for her. "I'm the one—" Kim let Jason lead "—who told her about Ryan."

Inside the classroom, Martina said, "I'll read mine." She did not stand. Instead she sat back in her chair, her legs stretched straight under the desk, her feet apart, her heels digging into the floor tiles.

"Yes," Marcia said. "Go ahead."

"It's a poem, too," Martina said. "About that latent mystery."

the world is run
by cruel and ugly forces
much greater than you or me or family
all people
of all races
succumb to a vicious god

"Bummer, man." Peter Badoglio blew the words out.

Just before the end of the period Ciara DeLauro came in to confer with the class. The picture, the rose, caused her to pause. Marcia Radkowski stood. There were a number of small groups talking quietly, a few students still writing, several just sitting. Ciara made her way to the front, reached out, clasped Marcia Radkowski's slender hands between her plump palms. "Are you doing all right?" she whispered.

Marcia shook her head. "No," she answered.

"It will take some time," Ciara said. "Two students . . ."

"That's not it," Marcia began. The bell rang, students gathered their books, left.

"And it's easy to feel as if you've lost control of your class . . ."

Again Marcia shook her head. "I went, too . . . Read this." She handed the guidance counselor Martina's poem. "I went to give her a hug," Marcia said. "After she read it to the class."

"Umm," Ciara acknowledged.

"She said to me, she said, 'You make me sick.'"

"Marcia. Dear Marcia. She's angry. She's striking out. You just happen to be an easy target."

"She made me feel—" Marcia began to sob "—like I'm . . . like I'm the one responsible . . ."

"Now, Marcia," Ciara said firmly. "Understanding how Martina feels will help you understand—"

"If I were a better person," Marcia Radkowski interrupted Ciara DeLauro, "or if I'd been stronger, been a better influence, maybe all this wouldn't have happened."

AT THE END of Period Four Paul Compari cornered Jason Panuzio in the hallway by the library. "Hey, Jayce! Where the hell's Aaron?"

Jason looked at him quizzically, glanced down the hall to see if Kim was approaching, turned back to Compari. "How the hell should I know?"

"We're still on at Jefferson, aren't we?"

"I haven't heard anything. You were with Coach last period."

"He hasn't heard either. Rosenwald told him it was tentative."

"Okay by me," Jason said. "I'm so fucken tired . . ." Paul raised his chin, gestured behind Jason to Kim. "Ah . . . *Scusa.*"

"Yeah. Jayce, I gotta git. If you hear somethin . . ."

"Yeah. Okay."

"What was that all about?" Kim asked.

"If the Jefferson game's on," Jason said. Then he looked down and with the fingers of his free hand squeezed the bridge of his nose while squinching his eyes shut. "And if . . . Did Martina say anything about seeing Aaron?"

"She didn't mention—"

"I told my folks—"

"There's the bell. Do you have to go to physics?"

"Kim, I told my folks . . . His folks called to find him. I said he was at the vigil last night, but he wasn't there."

"He probably wanted to be alone. He was probably bummed to the max . . ."

"He wasn't at practice either."

"When?"

"Yesterday. I made an excuse for him. He could have . . ."

"Could have . . . what? Oh! You don't think . . ."

"God! I hope not."

"He was coming on to Katie yesterday. Boy, was I mad. That wasn't the first time either."

"God!" Jason repeated. "You don't think like maybe he went with them? Like maybe he hasn't been found yet. Like they didn't find Ronnie for two hours. What if he's up there, like, you know, alive? Like hurt? Like he can't move or talk and bein black and the rain and—"

"But Ryan Willis didn't say anything," Kim said.

"Maybe he thinks . . . Oh God! If he's up there . . . if he's hurt . . . I . . . Go find Martina. I maybe—" Jason slapped a hand to his forehead "—killed . . . I gotta go see Coach."

"MAY I HAVE your attention, please." From speakers throughout the building came the voice of Victor Santoro, the school's vice principal. He repeated his words, then said, "Principal Rosenwald has some news. First, I have a few short announcements. All after-school activities for this afternoon and this evening have been postponed or canceled. Peer facilitators are requested to return to the cafeteria during eighth period. All sports activities scheduled for today have been postponed or canceled. Now Principal Rosenwald."

"Thank you, Victor. I have some additional sad news to report." Charlene Rosenwald's voice was clear, precise. "At eleven forty-eight this morning, John Meade, who was injured in yesterday's accident, died at St. Luke's Hospital."

"JOHNNY, MITCH."

"Hold one, Mitch." Both men were in their offices in the ContGenChem tower. It was late afternoon. They had spoken earlier in the day, and Mitch had sent Johnny a portion of Aaron's preliminary statement on affirmative action. Johnny still had it on his desk. He had read the first four pages, had blocked out several paragraphs, had underlined a few sentences. The concepts had sent his mind racing.

> . . . behavior is consistent with self-image. Self-image is the product of individual and cultural story . . .
>
> . . . I support affirmative action. However, I am opposed to race-

based or gender-based—versus economic-based—affirmative action . . .

. . . I oppose race-based policies because they imply the genetic inferiority of the economically lagging race: as, too, do gender-based policies imply the genetic inferiority of the economically less advantaged gender. The implications tend to instill a self-image of inferiority which, if it becomes internalized, produces specific self-defeating behaviors.

These implications of inferiority are hokum!

Race-based affirmative action is racist. It eventually hurts the very people it is intended to help.

Johnny glanced at his secretary then back at the pages. He'd felt as if Aaron had been talking directly to him. Within two pages, Johnny had decided to ask Mitch and Aaron if he could use Aaron's paper as the basis for an article he intended to write. Johnny had seen how he could adopt the concepts of cultural story and self-image, but change the focus from race policy to advertising. He shuffled files on his desk, scanned another marked block.

Race-based solutions to economic problems are doomed to create worse economic problems for the protected race. It is time to scrap these programs, and to establish economic status-based programs. This will allow race to fall away as a conflict point. If the majority of those assisted are from one race, or one gender, or if they are veterans, is of no concern. The concern is only if they are poor . . .

Discriminatory actions, based on race or gender, even if they are specifically tailored to make up for past discriminatory actions, perpetuate race and gender discrimination . . .

"Hi, Mitch. I just heard from Julia. The game's been canceled. Hold again, okay?" Johnny lowered the receiver, glanced at his secretary, said, "Lisa, can you give me a moment?"

"Certainly, Mr. Panuzio," the young secretary answered. She slipped from the office and closed the door behind her.

"Son of a bitch," Johnny said quietly into the phone to Mitch. "Tripps has been in and out of here all day. I'm only partway through Aaron's—"

"Mr. Impeccable or the old man?" There was no emotion in Mitch's voice.

"Mr. Impeccable. You okay?"

"Yeah. Ah . . . I've got a big problem."

"Vernon?"

"No. Aaron. We're going to report Aaron missing."

"What?!"

"He's not at school. His girlfriend hasn't seen him since they had a fight or something in school yesterday."

"Jason said he was at the hospital last—"

"No. He said a lot of kids were there. He was trying to cover for him."

"That little . . ."

"The police are going to recheck the accident site and there's an investigator going to talk to Ryan Willis. Damn it, Johnny. I'm worried. Nobody's seen a trace of him since yesterday!"

Wednesday, 21 September, 9:10 A.M.

"I MEAN, LIKE DUH! It was scary, man. Like they had pictures of her brains comin out her nose."

"OH! That's gross!"

"Shh!"

"Not me, man. He's the one talkin . . ."

"Shh! If you want to talk like that, don't do it in the funeral parlor."

"It wasn't me. It was them."

McConnell's Funeral Home overflowed with family, teachers, students, friends. Katherine Fitzpatrick's casket was closed—a beautiful walnut box adorned with an arrangement of sixteen red roses. Across First Street, Roselli's Funeral Home was equally packed for the wake of Veronica Mayberry. To Jason and Kim it seemed as if the entire town were present, yet at East Lake High classes had resumed their normal schedule. At the front of the room a priest sat with Katherine's parents, her sister and aunts, uncles and cousins. "She was so bright. So full of energy." Repeated, said by all in varying ways. "So willing to help others."

In back, the conversations Johnny and Julia overheard were less subdued, less refined.

"Hey, I mean, like DUH! You know, they went back up lookin for Williams' body. Him bein black, they figure they might a mistook him for a tree."

"TV said Willis denied he was with em."

"What the fuck does Willis know? He'd say anything to save his butt."

"Shit. Like you wouldn't!"

"Shit. That reminds me. You hear they're going to cancel the prayer service?"

"No way! They're just about to start."

"Yeah way, man! News from the Middle East. On TV this mornin. They found the body."

"Whose?"

"Geez! DUH!"

"DUH yerself!"

Jerry Bendler nudged F.X. McMillian. "This is a really sick bunch," he said. "Listen to em. Have you seen what they do in computer art?"

"I try to ignore it."

"Mangled bodies. Blood. Dismemberment. No wonder they don't see this as reality."

"I hate to make this their lesson," McMillian said.

Blurted, "Not just out her nose, man. Out her mouth, too."

"That's it, gentlemen." F.X. slid in behind the two students. He grabbed their collars, lifted them from their seats. "I believe you've got business outside. Now."

"You can't touch me!"

"We didn't do nothin!"

"Shh! Mr. Bendler will drive you back to school. Now!"

Alone on the porch, with services continuing inside and across the street, McMillian socked his right fist into his left palm. He'd been through it before. Hated it. Again he socked his palm, making it hurt.

"It overshadows everything, doesn't it, Frank?" Ciara DeLauro had quietly slipped out from the service. She put a hand on his arm.

"Yes," McMillian said. "Chi-chi, how many times . . . ?"

"Since we've been here?"

"Yes."

"Twice. I think you had fatalities at Lakeport, too."

"Three . . . Five times in all. Five fatal accidents . . ."

"Do you go to church, Frank?"

"No."

"When I go to church it makes me feel like a good person. And when I feel that I'm a good person, I feel like I'm worth having good things happen to me. Therefore, I don't sabotage my achievements. Or my relationships."

"I know the theory," McMillian said. "I heard this morning that Amanda's spine was severed. That they think she'll be paralyzed from her neck down."

"Yes. I heard. Chris is improving."

"Yes."

"We have lots of work to do."

"I know."

"When the children are damaged," Ciara said, "the whole community hemorrhages."

"I know, Chi-chi. I'm hoping they don't find Aaron . . . He's one of the brightest students I've ever had. And best player. And I was thinking about Ryan Willis. What do you do to someone who causes such tragedy?"

"Confession," Ciara said. It was the beginning of her model for healing. "He's already tried."

"Um. Seemed pretty lame."

"Confession, contrition, restitution, reconciliation. You can't throw him away."

"It's the restitution that he can't . . . How do you . . . The pain he's caused . . ." McMillian stopped. Across the street pallbearers carried the casket of Veronica Mayberry to the waiting hearse.

"Marcia showed me a poem by Martina Watts," Ciara said. "She's very disturbed, Frank. Still, it's a matter of working it through; of working on her global views and her self-image. A disturbed student's problems are always tied to his or her self-image and world view."

"As are the achievements of the best," McMillian said. "What do you do with a Ryan Willis?"

Johnny had emerged from the interior, had moved to sidestep the two teachers on the porch, had overheard their last sentences. F.X. nodded to him. Ciara excused herself, opened the door, disappeared inside. "I've gotta get to work," Johnny explained. "Can't stay."

"Um," F.X. affirmed.

"Terrible thing," Johnny said.

"You're Jason's father?"

"Um-hmm."

"Smart boy."

"Really?"

"Yes."

"He's . . . he's really withdrawn around the house. I'm lucky if I get a grunt out of him."

"It's the age. He's quiet but he's not withdrawn. Especially at practice. Actually—" F.X. smiled "—he talks too much."

"Jason?!" That brought a brief matching smile to Johnny's face. Then, "Ah well." He paused, felt he needed to add a condolence. "A real tragedy here," he said. Then he added, "I heard your comment as I came out. I think they should incarcerate people who cause this."

"Um." McMillian groaned. His eyes were again focused across the street. "Thirty years ago I saw a number of young men killed. I hated it, but not as much as this. At least they died for a cause. Doing something. This is pure waste."

"Yeah. It is. Oh! Oh, you mean . . . Viet-Nam?"

"Yup."

"I . . . I never went. My brother did. And two of my cousins. I expected to be drafted but I was never called. Just lucky, I guess."

"Yeah," F.X. said. "Maybe."

AT 12:36 P.M. the phone in Johnny Panuzio's office buzzed. He glanced up from the personnel files on his desk. Sunshine was strong upon the lake; the day looked crisp. From his office-cell in the tower he could see the far shore, East Lake. He'd almost stayed there this morning; had almost stayed through the full service with Julia; had even thought to go to Mitch's, to stay with him; but Brad Tripps' secretary had called him before they'd left the house, had told Johnny that Brad wanted to talk to him at eleven, that it was important.

"Who is it, Lisa?" Johnny asked his secretary.

"I believe it's Mrs. Panuzio, Mr. Panuzio."

"Could you ask her to hold for two minutes? Or I'll call her back."

"Yes, Mr. Panuzio."

Johnny sat up straight, grasped, kneaded the lip of his desk. He wasn't sure why he'd put Julia on hold, thought, fleetingly, perhaps there are just too many punches coming too fast to be able to parry them all.

At eleven, between radio announcements, Tripps had come in, had sat on Johnny's desk, had chatted inanely for a few moments. Then he had asked for the prioritized list of employees, and then he had said, "John, the company, the new company, is going to sweeten the pot. For those that stay . . . well . . . Let's just say, I've been with ContGenChem for three years and I've seen how they reward their people. We like your work, John. You and your wife—Julia, isn't it?—I'd like to fly you both to Atlanta. Make believe it's Christmas, Johnny. We'll show you around. It's time you moved up."

That had been a flash of light between dark, depressing developments. First had come the radio report: "Police investigators returned this morning to the scene of Monday afternoon's accident in search of additional victims of the crash which has now claimed the lives of three East Lake teenagers." The radio report had recapped the accident, detailed the death of John Meade, expanded to describe the makeshift memorial students from East Lake had built at the edge of the road above the crash site.

Then it continued. "East Lake High soccer star Aaron Williams and classmate Janet Lattini have both been reported missing and last seen Monday, prior to the accident. Police returned to the densely vegetated hillside off Dresser Pond Road with search dogs shortly after sunrise. Parents and friends of the missing teens joined . . ."

There had been a crash in 1965 in which six of Johnny and Mitch's classmates had been killed; four of them had been riding on the hood of a vehicle when the driver lost control, hit a parked car on a narrow city street. They had been hurled more than a hundred feet. Mitch had brought it up when he'd called earlier this morning to tell Johnny that he wasn't going in to work.

"He wouldn't have done that, Mitch," Johnny had assured his friend. "Aaron isn't dumb. Our kids might be jerks but they're not stupid."

After Tripps had departed from Johnny's office, Johnny had caught the updated news. "This just in. On the ongoing search for the two East Lake teens feared to be unfound victims of the hillside crash, one, Janet Lattini, has been found. She called home this morning after hearing her name on WLAK Radio at a friend's home where she had been staying . . ."

Johnny had breathed a sigh of relief, had gone to the outer office to see if others had heard, had heard instead more darkness, had heard his secretary telling one of the computer artists that he, Johnny Panuzio, had become one of them, one of the ContGenChem boys, and that the files of the entire marketing staff had been pulled to determine who got the ax. "Like a Judas goat," Lisa had said.

Johnny had almost interrupted her, had almost blurted, "I'm going to fight for every last man and woman here." But he hadn't. Knew he couldn't; wouldn't.

"Julia."

"Oh God!" Julia was breathless. "You finally picked up."

"I only have a minute," Johnny said. "I'm really swamped here."

"Johnny, you've got to come home right now. They've found Aaron."

TRAFFIC WAS LIGHT.

He drove wildly, without concentration, without awareness, as if he were on autopilot; his mind speeding, spinning, wobbling out of control, a deep-space capsule tumbling into the vortex of an inner darkness. Aaron . . . Judas . . . Christmas . . . swirling . . . The screens, the simultaneous projections exploding, jumbled, juxtaposed . . . a boy . . . a child . . . a . . . searching, purging memory banks, dislodging, disgorging . . . the base . . . the seed . . .

He sees him. He sees Christmas. Christmas is supposed to be fun yet Johnny-panni is miserable.

It started out great. Most of the presents were clothes but under the tree there was a brand-new Flexible Flyer. The image is solid, exact, beautiful. A Flexible Flyer for Johnny-panni and for Sylvia. And for Nicky and Angie, too, except, of course, they are too little. Pop had promised they would all go to the hill over by St. Luke's Hospital after dinner at Il Padrone's*—at Nonno's. A brand-new Flexible Flyer with varnished wood slats and glossy red metal runners. And it is out on the porch!*

He is stuck sitting in the dining room because of Henry, Zi Carmela and Uncle Paul Bragiotti's eldest. And because of Santo, Uncle Sal and Aunt Millie Panuzio's youngest. The three eight-year-olds—in trouble for running up the back stairs and down the front and back up again so fast they didn't hear Nonna yelling, "Slow! You knock someone over. They break their hip." Still running, running into crazy Aunt Tina's room, the sister who has never married, Johnny-panni running into Tina's bathroom to hide, only to find stockings and undergarments hung to dry and Tina flying in after me . . . He sees her, hears the shrill scream, gasp. Sees her finding me instead of Henry or Santo. She is livid, her face red with anger, her words unintelligible . . . Like I knew her disgusting underwear was hanging up in there. Like I was some kind of retard who goes smelling old ladies' underwear! Yuk!

He sees him, sees Johnny-panni, stuck in the dining room, sitting, pouting when his godfather, Uncle John, and his grandfather, Il Padrone, *enter. The men sit at the far end of the main table set for Christmas dinner. They speak without seeing Little Johnny-panni against the far wall at the little side table set for the small boys.*

Johnny sits quietly, his hands together before him on the table's edge. He is thinking about the sled, the hill near St. Luke's. With his father carrying Angie and his mother holding Nicky's hand, and all following Sylvia, he had pulled the sled, the red runners glistening against the new, crisp, sparkling white blanket, pulled it first from their flat-over-the-store to Holy Rosary, where he'd had to leave it in the vestibule during mass, then the additional two blocks to his grandfather's elegant home on Williams Street, where he'd had to leave it on the porch. He sees it sitting on the porch, still on the porch as he sits quietly, angry, pouting, afraid Aunt Tina has told everybody he . . . I . . . I was playing with her underwear. "I was not!" But I don't say it.

"I called San Francisco yesterday," Uncle John says. This catches Johnny's attention. It is a big deal, in 1955, that someone in the family should make a call to such a distance. Johnny moves his left hand to the back of his head, pulls, hunches low to the small table, keeps his eyes up, peers below the chunky wrought-iron chandelier with its thick, barely translucent yellow glass that casts a yellow hue throughout the room. He watches across the main table, through the sparkling china and crystal and colorful platters of anti-pasto. Nonna calls it an-te-pahst. *They are off-limits until the adults sit and pass them around the main table first, then to the side tables. Johnny knows that Henry has been sent to the back parlour by the Christmas tree, that Santo is in the front parlour near the piano. He feels cheated, being stuck in the huge, dim dining room with its heavy, dark furnishings with gargoyle feet*

ready to bite you, bite your ankle if you're bad, and dark, hand-carved wainscoting, and dim yellow lighting, and small, twice-curtained windows that barely let in the sparkle of this perfect winter's day. This perfect Christmas day for sledding.

Nonno does not respond to Uncle John but sits back in his massive chair. To Johnny, the chair—with its immense arms which end under his grandfather's beefy hands in gargoyle heads, and with its massive raised back with inlaid ivory mosaic—is a king's throne. Nonno and the chair block Johnny's view of the ornate fireplace and decorative mantle of the far wall—just as their presence blocks him from sneaking out.

Nonno slowly rocks his large, bald head.

"I wished Zia Lucia Merry Christmas from the whole family," Uncle John says.

Still Nonno does not speak. That, Johnny knows, is his right. The Padrone does not need to answer. How had Rocco explained it? "Padrone di casa is master of the house. But Il Padrone is The Master—The Master of The Family, La Famiglia; or of the Countryside, La Paese, the surrounding neighborhood or community." To eight-year-old Johnny, Il Padrone is ancient. He is very large, very respected. Seldom does he speak English; seldom does he laugh. He is Il Padrone; he is Nonno; he is frightening. Johnnypanni stays hunched.

"Jack and James and their families were coming over for Christmas Eve dinner," Uncle John tells his father. "Then they were all going to go to Jack's for Christmas. They're probably there now."

Giovanni Panuzio speaks to his eldest son in curt Italian. Johnny does not understand the words. He slides lower. He is ashamed that he does not understand.

In the foyer new voices erupt. Johnny hears the deep voice of Uncle Carlo and the frazzled voice of Aunt Kate and the cacophony of their six children, all up from South Lakeport. He can hear them being greeted by his godmother, Aunt Fran, and by cousins Richard and Louis, who, with Uncle John, he has heard his mother say, attended midnight mass at the chapel in South Lake Village and had started their drive over the dam early this morning while it was still snowing. He hears Aunt Sylvia and Uncle Lenny DiMasi and their three arrive. They are not so loud. They've driven all the way up from Jefferson!

Chatting, laughing, giggling fill the house. Except the dining room where Johnny sits at the small boys' table. Johnny pulls at his new sweater. Zi Carmela has knitted it. She has knitted one for each of her own children and one for each cousin. It fits well. Johnny likes the color, a deep blue, and he likes the cable pattern on the front and down the sleeves but it is heavy wool and the house is heating up. He wants to take it off but is *afraid that might hurt Zi Carmela's feelings. He hopes Tessa will see him fussing, tell him to take it off. He knows she'll put it somewhere safe. Then he wouldn't worry about spattering it with sauce, worry about wearing it to school on the first day back in January, worry about his classmates making fun of him.*

Classmates . . . intruding upon the vision . . . flashing forward to here, to now, to anger, to fear, to . . . tumbling back . . . purposefully, protectively . . .

Tessa is not there. He cannot stir for fear of interrupting the men at the far end of the room. He sees him grab at the sweater, pull the front away from his neck, gasp, glance at his grandfather, at his godfather, to the corners of the room. Atop the heavy china hutch, amid decorative plates in display stands, are baskets wrapped in red cellophane. Even in the low light the paper refracts, glints. He sees boxes of Torrone interspersed between the globes of red, orange, yellow and green, and his mouth waters for the nougat candy.

A second side table, a card table, is set for his oldest cousins: Richard, twenty, and Louis, eighteen, Uncle John and Aunt Fran's sons; and Jimmy, eighteen, Carlo and Kate's eldest; and Anthony (Cecilia's twin), seventeen, Sal and Millie's firstborn. There is a third table out the door in the huge butler's pantry for an even dozen middle cousins, from Cecilia at seventeen, to Sylvia and Lena at nineteen, and to little Mary, five, who is always well behaved. There is a high chair behind Tessa's seat for Angie. Erica, Zi Carmela's baby, will sit on her mother's lap. He sees the room, a still frame . . . not yet set in motion.

Uncle John fills Nonno's wineglass with deep, thick, red liquid, pours for himself. They still have not noticed, or at least have not acknowledged, Johnny-panni, who remains scrunched behind the small table, afraid they might say something he is not to hear, afraid they then might think he snuck in when really it had been Tessa, at Tina's insistence, who'd stuck him in the corner and told him to be still.

"Papa." Uncle John raises his glass. Johnny thinks it is funny that Uncle John calls Nonno Papa, as if he, Uncle John, is still a little boy. "To Nicole. To Uncle Nick. May he rest in peace."

Uncle Nick? Johnny thinks. Who's . . . ? But before the thought congeals he hears his mother's call. "Let'sa go, everybody." Through the pantry door he spies Tessa placing a serving dish of pasta with tomato sauce on the middle cousins' table. "Let'sa go, everybody." She is trying to sound like Nonna. "It'sa time to sit. Everybody on the table."

In the dining room, at the far end of the main table, Il Padrone*'s voice is dry. Johnny isn't sure he hears the words correctly. "When I found him . . ." he says. He does not finish the sentence. There are tears in his old eyes, but his face is hard. "Let those bastards who did it to him . . . to Lucia . . . ten* *years . . . it took the government ten years to kill him. Let them . . .* scottatura en infèrno." *Let them burn in hell.*

"Eh! Pop! Merry Christmas. Merry Christmas, John."

"Oh! Merry Christmas, Sal." Uncle John stands, greets his brother.

"I hope we're not interrupting."

"Nah. Of course not."

"Mom thought you two were in the office . . ." Sal begins but before he can finish, Tina, Millie and Kate come in—Millie and Kate kissing Il Padrone *on his bald pate, saying, "Peace be with you," and wishing him a wonderful Christmas Day—while through the pantry door Zi Carmela comes, bestows a deep bowl of pasta with clam sauce on one end of the table, and cousin Cecilia follows her and places another dish with pesto sauce at the opposite end. Johnny openly grasps his sweater at the collar, pulls it away from his skin. He is so hot he . . . I hate being there. I always hated being there. Being tortured. You didn't need to . . . You said we could go sledding. You . . . Papa, you . . .*

Nonna comes in. Her arms, though she still cooks, are no longer strong enough to handle the big platters. She is empty-handed. She plops herself down in the chair Uncle John has vacated, the smaller throne chair next to Il Padrone's. *Aunts, uncles, cousins, even Great-Uncle Lou—Luigi Scarpetti, Nonna's widowed brother—converge. Everyone is noisy.*

A new image . . . complete . . . simultaneous . . . instantaneous. All sitting . . . the table covered with foods . . . except still standing, talking, Aunt Kate holding Millie's hands, laughing. ". . . Oh, the best thing about being married to an Italian man is he's got no memory at all about sex."

Tina, at the end of the table opposite her mother and father, looks up in disgust. She gestures at her brother, Carlo, Kate's husband. "Him?"

Johnny-panni shrinks back against the wainscoting. He is still alone at the small table.

Kate looks past Millie to Tina. "Who else?!" Then quickly to Millie, smiling, "Even after twenty-three years he still thinks it's all brand-new and exciting!"

Millie giggles, glances at Johnny, covers her face in mock embarrassment.

Tina's face turns shrewish. "That's why you've got six—"

"Tina!" Carl snaps. "Cut it out. You can't be nice, even on Christmas?"

"You treat her like a puttana," *Tina sneers. "Like a harlot."*

"Ha!" Millie huffs at her sister-in-law. Kate squeezes by Tina, between the main table and the table for the older cousins, past Rocco, whom she kisses, to her seat next to Carlo. Henry, Santo, Nicky and Anton sit. Millie sits between Great-Uncle Lou and Sal, looks angrily at her husband, at the far end of the table where Tina presides, says to Sal, "Pooh-tanh! *How would she know?"*

"Huh? What?"

Nonno claps his hands twice. "Okay," he announces. "In nòme del padre, del figlio, e dello spirito santo. *Eh . . . Ree-key." He gestures with an open hand. "You say grace."*

At the older cousins' table Richard stands. He is the first grandchild, a junior at Princeton. He bows his head. "Bless us, O Lord," he begins, and everyone chimes in, "and these Thy gifts, which we are about to receive, through Thy bounty, through Christ, our Lord . . ."

"Amen," Johnny sings out before anyone else. He . . . I smile. I look around. Tina glances . . . at . . . at him. He shies back.

"Amen," comes from the others.

But Ricky is not finished. "And dear Lord," he says reverently, "bless the farmers who grew this food for us. And, Lord, Jesus, bless America, our country. Merry Christmas, everyone. Amen."

Again there is a chorus, a cacophony: "Amen," "God bless America," "Merry Christmas." Wineglasses clink. "Salute." *To your health.* "Salute tutti ognuno." *To the health of everyone in the world.* "Mangia." *Eat. Enjoy.*

Johnny looks at the older cousins' table, at his cousin Richard, who is twelve years his senior, already a man, sitting with Louis and Tony and Jimmy, all in serious conversation. "Bless the farmers?" Johnny has never thought about farmers, about blessing them, about this being their food. Johnny thinks that it is odd that Ricky would say that on Christmas Day. Or that he would ask Jesus to bless America. Jesus does not bless countries. Johnny knows this. Jesus does not have a country but could live in any country. Johnny knows this from the nuns because he listens at catechism, and because someday he is going to be a priest. Or an engineer, like Ricky. A second later Henry kicks him under the table and he kicks back and Santo kicks Nicky by mistake. Nicky howls. Johnny sits straight, still, attempting to look like he's done nothing. Everyone is eating and drinking and talking, and Nicky's howl is ignored.

"Do you like it with tomato sauce?" Zi Carmela asks. Henry pokes him. Johnny is hoping Nicky will shut up before they get in deep trouble. He looks up. He kicks Henry under the table. "Tomato sauce o al burro e parmigiano?"

"That one." Johnny points to the noodles in the rich red gravy.

"You too, Nicky?"

He sees Nicky nod.

To Tessa, across the main table, Johnny hears Zi Carmela say, "Tess, you've done a great job with these boys. Henry and Mary will only eat it with butter."

"They like it that way, too," Tessa says. "I want them to try the clam sauce. They never eat it at my mother's."

"Be satisfied," Sylvia says. "Brian and Anton won't try anything. Lena eats everything—calamari, scungilli. Even asparagus."

"That's because she's a girl," Uncle Paul says. He turns, looks directly at Johnny. "Boys gotta eat the pomo d'amore." Uncle Paul laughs, winks. "Right, Johnny-panni?" he calls out.

Johnny doesn't answer. He is embarrassed to be singled out. He does not understand the words.

"You mean pomodoro," Uncle Carl says. "Tomatoes?"

"Well, now. But before they were known as apples of gold," Paul says, "they were apples of love."

Tina drops her fork onto her plate. "You act like a bunch of rabbits."

Carmela is back up with a platter of antipasto. "Shut up," she hisses at her older sister. "Just because you're a witch doesn't mean everyone has to be."

Johnny can't believe it! A witch! But sure! A witch! That explains . . .

"Did anyone—" Uncle John waves from the quieter end of the table. "Did anyone see Babes in Toyland last night? It was on from nine to ten-thirty."

"We watched it," Millie answers. "Even Santo stayed up . . ."

Carl, across the table, startles. "You guys got a TV?!" He turns to Tessa and Rocco. "You?"

"Not yet," Tessa says.

"Admiral's got a new model," Carl says to no one in particular. "Twenty-four inches!! Two hundred and thirty bucks. That's the one I'd like."

"Is that with Flashmatic?" Millie asks.

"With what?" Rocco chuckles. He thinks new devices are frivolous.

"It's a light beam. You can turn the TV on or off right from your chair." Millie aims her fork as though she's aiming the device. "I think you can even change channels."

"I'd rather see that new Sinatra movie," Lenny DiMasi says.

"That should be banned." Tina's voice is flat, authoritative.

"What movie?" Tessa asks.

"The Man with the Golden Arm," Lenny answers.

"I'm ashamed he's Italian," Tina says.

Uncle Lenny's face twists. He shakes his head. "What!" He glances around. "Listen to her! Why?"

"A film like that . . . it encourages people to use narcotics. Can you imagine—"

"That's the point of it," Lenny interrupts. "It's to discourage people. You watch Sinatra go through real torture, real physical and spiritual torture. Who's gonna wanna go through that?"

"I thought you didn't see it," Tina charges.

"I didn't," Lenny parries. "I read about it."

"It promotes narcotics," Tina repeats.

Rocco reaches a hand in front of Tessa to get Kate's and Carl's attention. "I'd rather see Too Bad She's Bad."

"You just like to look at Sophia Loren," Tessa teases.

"I sure do." Rocco raises his wineglass. "And Gina Lollobrigida. We saw her in Frisky. *I'd like to see em both in one movie."*

Johnny-panni is shocked. His father is talking about actresses, about women. He has seen a picture of Sophia Loren with her big . . . It is not the kind of picture a priest would look at. He thinks what his father has just said must hurt his mother.

"Fat chance," Kate says. "They hate each other."

"They do not." Carl defends the starlets.

"Yes they do," Kate insists.

Johnny hopes they do. He hopes, too, that someone brings in Nonna's chicken. She makes the best roast chicken . . . And braciola. *And . . .*

"They just do that for the publicity," Lenny says.

"I like Dave Garroway," Aunt Fran says. "He was in Babes—"

"He's a shrimp!" Zi Carmela's voice is alive, her hands flair. "I like Campanella." She holds the handle of her fork in both hands, the tines sticking up, and waves her arms as if getting ready for a pitch.

"What do you know about baseball?" Carl picks a marinated mushroom from the antipasto, tosses it across Carmela's plate. Carmela swings, misses, laughs. The mushroom drops to the floor, bounces, rolls under the table where Johnny and the little boys sit, watch in astonishment. No one picks it up.

"I know that he's the only player to win MVP three times," Zi Carmela says. "Except for Yogi Berra. And maybe DiMaggio."

"Nice Italian boys," Tessa proudly.

"Campy's a Negro," Richard corrects her from the table behind.

Zi Carmela lurches back. "With a name like Campanella?!" She and Tessa know little about baseball.

"Maybe Negro and Italian," Richard says. He does not want to embarrass his aunts.

"Who would do that?!" Tina grimaces. "Why would any—"

"When I was in Italy, during the war," Tessa says, "some of the Italian girls liked going out with American Negroes."

"Never!" Tina's face reddens with anger. "Christmas Day! The topics you talk!"

"Some of them are beautiful men. Very nice men," Tessa says sadly.

"Auntie Tee," Richard says. "There's nothing wrong with that. I've dated an African girl in New York."

From the other side of Tina, Paul is fascinated. "Really? Tell us . . ."

"Well, not really dated," Richard says. "We all go together in a group."

"How about Italian girls?" Aunt Kate smiles. She is blond and blue-eyed—a Parnell by birth.

"Yes," Rocco toasts. "To Sophia and Gina."

"What girls!" Carl clinks his glass on Rocco's.

"Ah, two wonderful pairs." Rocco snickers pleasantly.

"Va va va voom!" Carl adds.

"Rocco!" Tessa nudges him. "You two have had too much wine."

"Sorry, dear," Rocco says in mock self-reproach. Then he grins evilly, lecherously raises and drops his eyebrows like Groucho Marx. Sylvia and Lenny, Carmela and Sal laugh. Rocco puts his head on Tessa's shoulder, his hand in her lap. He begins to sing, "Love and marriage, Love and marriage, Go together—"

"Ooo-pp!" Tessa jumps. "Stop it!" she chastises, laughs.

"If we had a television," Kate says, "we could all watch Rocky Marciano."

"He beat that Archie Moore." Zi Carmela raises her fists.

"Knocked him out," Lenny says. "He's a Negro."

"Did you see where that guy Griffin—" Aunt Fran begins but is cut off by Uncle John.

"The governor of Georgia. Yeah. Did you read that?! He won't let Georgia Tech play Pitt in the Sugar Bowl because Pitt's got a Negro on their squad. What a stunat!*"*

"Southern schools are like that," Fran says. "Not like Princeton."

"Why shouldn't they be?" Johnny recognizes Aunt Tina's close friend as she enters the dining room through the front hall doorway. He does not know her name but she is always with Tina when Johnny's family comes to Nonno's.

"Elaina Maria Secchia!" Uncle John rises, kisses this woman. "Merry Christmas."

The woman is dressed in a bright red dress, a deep green hat, gloves, sparkling pins. "Merry Christmas, John. Merry Christmas, Padrone. *I'm sorry I'm late." She does not sit by Tina but between Uncle John and his father, and Johnny-panni sees that she is a witch, too! Two witches! They flank the table.*

Johnny sees Richard turning in his seat. Louis and Tony are prodding him. "Aunt Elaina," Richard addresses her, though she is not a blood relative, "they shouldn't be because it is immoral."

Tina snorts and food bits fly from her mouth. Johnny slaps his hands over his face because he is about to burst out laughing. He does not understand the conversation but Aunt Tina's look is hilarious. Except she is vehement.

He hides his face, makes believe he is laughing at something Anton has said. Henry kicks him.

"We don't need to mix with their kind," Elaina Maria says.

Tina emits a rasping sound. "I should hope not."

Il Padrone *clears his throat. The table quiets. In a slow voice he says, "Tina, when I first come here, there is slavery."*

Tina knows what is coming. She is defensive. Everybody knows what is coming. Johnny does not. "It was abolished before you were born," Tina says.

"Noh." In his left hand Nonno holds a piece of bread that is red with gravy. He raises it, gestures at his daughter. "I get one dollar thirty-five a day. Nicole, because he is a little boy, he gets one dollar fifteen. Not enough to put food in our mouths. Or for the tools. Or a bed. But twenty-one May, 1901, the state pass a law that breaks the padrone system. Then we are free. Then the Italiano *are free. Every man has to be free. The Negro too. That is America."*

Ricky stands up, claps. "Well said, Nonno! Very well said."

The pasta is consumed, the dishes cleared, a clean setting is placed all around. Carmela, Tessa, Cecilia and cousin Connie bring out the meat courses—breaded and spiced roast chicken, hot and sweet sausage in tomato sauce, meatballs with raisins and pignoli, and Nonna's speciality and Johnny's favorite, braciola*—rolled flank steak stuffed with prosciutto, cheese and spices, and browned in olive oil and garlic before being simmered in the sauce until it nearly falls apart. Along with the meat come vegetables—spinach in butter and mustard, lima beans in butter and white wine, string beans with dried tomatoes sautéed in oil, steamed broccoli with almond slivers, and three salads.*

Johnny looks at the large platters of meat. The braciola *is cut into inch-thick wheels and the platter is garnished with parsley and fresh* finòcchio*, "fen-nook." Johnny takes two wheels, a chicken leg, two meatballs. He cuts the steak with the side of his fork and crams a piece into his mouth. Then he washes it down with 7-Up, another Christmas treat; and stuffs in another bite, then another. He hears Tina say, "Give him more," and Rocco answer, "If he takes it, he's gotta eat it. That's all. I don't want ta hear . . ."*

About the adult table the conversation is lively, sometimes argumentative. They are solving the problems of the world—the president's heart attack, should Earl Warren run instead, should the vice president be shelved in favor of a more certain vote getter; will the Democrats go with Kefauver, Harriman or Stevenson; the merger of the AFL and the CIO, and what it will mean to the booming economy; the new Russian policy of competitive coexistence. The biggest topic is the crisis in education—does equal education for all mean mediocre education for all?

Johnny, Henry, Santo, Anton and Nicky pay little attention until Johnny-panni hears Rocco and Ricky. "Like you and Aunt Tessa," Ricky says.

"The army?!" Uncle Paul is astounded.

"I think so," Ricky says. "With what the communists are doing."

"What about the Air Force?" Rocco says. "They've got that new F-100 SuperSaber. Can you imagine—" he soars his knife over his plate, up past the chandelier, down between the wineglasses "—shooting through the sky at over eight hundred miles per hour? My feet are still dirty from all the mud in Italy."

"Fight them MIGs up in Alaska," Paul declares.

"Or in Indochina," Ricky says.

"There, too?!"

"One of my professors," Ricky says, "told us that even though the allies are still fighting the communists in the South, the French government's going to recognize Ho Chi Minh. They think if they do that, they'll be able to hold on to some of their commercial interests in the North. It's the capitalists and the communists in cahoots against the democratic aspirations of the people. Greedy French bastards."

"Oooo!" Tina recoils.

"Not unlike in Italy," Tessa says.

Johnny looks at the main table, at his mother. She is smiling. She has a wonderful smile even when the talk is serious. She has beautiful teeth. Her whole face is lit up and Rocco has his hand on her shoulder, is eyeing her, smiling too. Rocco likes to tell everyone that the first time he saw her—it was in the hospital in Italy—he walked without his crutches and didn't even realize it.

"I don't think the Italians—" Louis begins but he is cut off by Tony.

"If they didn't fight us," he says, "they wouldn't have those problems."

Johnny is having trouble following what they are saying. He has eaten both pieces of braciola *and one meatball and he is stuffed. There is still a meatball and the chicken leg and a disgusting heap of spinach which is oozing oily green blood onto the meat. Henry and Nicky have been excused. Santo and Anton are rushing to finish so they can leave. Sylvia and Connie come in and ask if they can go outside and use the sled, and Rocco says, "As long as you don't go into the street."*

"Tony," Johnny hears his mother say, "that's not the way it was." She is very defensive and she is not smiling.

"Well," Tony says, "that's what the kids at school think. That's why Italian tanks have backup lights!" Cousin Tony guffaws but sees that Tessa is upset and adds sheepishly, "That's what the kids at school say. Tommy Carlton and all those kids. 'Wops are chickenshi . . .' Ah . . ."

"They didn't want to fight us," Tessa says. Johnny has never seen his mother so stern, so commanding. "And we didn't fight them. We fought Germans in Italy. Not Italians. Your friends have it wrong."

"I don't think my professor—" Richard starts to say but Tessa is very insistent.

"No, no, no." She shakes her head. "The Italians didn't want to fight. They never wanted to fight. They threw Mussolini out in July, 1943, before the landing at Salerno. And they tried to sign an armistice but they were afraid of German reprisal against Italian civilians. They did sign the armistice on September third. I was with General Clark's staff then. But the Germans immediately attacked the Italians. The Italian warships that were going to surrender in Malta were bombed by the Germans before they got there. The Roma was sunk with fifteen hundred sailors lost. Killed! Where Italian divisions surrendered to the Nazis, the men were made prisoners. Where they fought, like in the Balkans, and were defeated and taken prisoner, the Germans murdered thousands. Then Hitler sent his commandos to the prison where Mussolini was held, and they captured him and made him head of their new Italian Social Republic. But that was just a Nazi front.

"Italy wanted the armistice," Tessa went on. "They signed the armistice. I remember General Clark . . . He . . . Oh, he was a handsome man. But he had a big nose. Bigger than the Italian men. I remember . . . Well, anyway, all the fighting was against the Germans. There were no Italians fighting us. Most of them wanted to fight with us! Most of them would greet us saying, 'God Bless America.' You tell that to your friends. You should be proud of being Italian. And American."

"See, Aunt Tess," Ricky says, "that's why I'm going to join the army. I'm going to serve for three years, see some of the world. The country needs good men. Like me. And when I get out, I'm going to go to law school."

"I thought you were going to be an engineer," Uncle Paul says.

"Good for you," Sal says.

"I'm going to sign up, too," Louis says. "Just like Uncle Rocky and Aunt Tess."

"Over my dead body," Aunt Fran says from the far end of the table. She has been in a different conversation, has just heard her sons talking about joining the service. Near her, too, Il Padrone scowls at the very thought but he says nothing.

Or maybe a soldier, Johnny thinks. A priest or an engineer or a soldier.

Zi Carmela leaves to feed baby Erica and to put her down for a nap. Great-Uncle Luigi Scarpetti leaves for a nap, too. Anton is excused but Tessa says to Johnny, "Eat your spinach first. Then you can go." Aunt Millie goes along and imposes the restriction on Santo, who stares at his string beans, *picks out the dried tomatoes, spreads the beans, knocks a few from his plate, and tucks them under the fluted edge. He is excused.*

Johnny-panni sits alone. He looks up. He has been lost in thought and does not remember the older cousins leaving. From outside he hears Sylvia and Connie and Regina, and he pictures them swooshing and sledding over the snow. The adults are finishing the pastries, drinking Strega *and* anisetta, *talking, leaving, returning. Johnny feels as if he is about to burst. The spinach is sickening. And now it is cold.*

"Eat it and you can go." Elaina Maria smiles down on him. "It's good for you. Popeye would gobble it up."

Johnny looks for his mother. She is in the kitchen washing pans. He hears Zi Carmela talking to her. Rocco has slid down to the far end of the table with Uncles John, Sal and Carl, and their father. Tina, Elaina Maria and Aunt Fran are at the close end of the main table. Tina is rigid, her left hand in her lap, her right delicately poised with a fork, motionless. Her face is taut and the color has gone from it. Johnny is afraid to eat. He is afraid not to eat. He is afraid he will be all alone in the dining room with the witches.

"Tina." Elaina nudges her gently. "Are you okay?"

She does not answer, does not move.

"Tina?" Her friend tries to stir her. Still, she does not move.

"Oh, for cry'n out loud." Fran sighs.

"She does that on purpose," Uncle John says from the other end of the table. "Almost fifty, and she still does that on purpose!"

"Leave her alone," Elaina Maria says. "She'll come out of it when she wants."

"Is she sick?" Kate has come in from the kitchen to clear more plates.

"She used to hold her breath when we were kids," Rocco says. "She just uses it for attention."

"Well, she's not getting any from me." Fran stands, moves down and sits with her husband but the cigar smoke bothers her and she joins the few noncleaning women in the front parlour.

"I tell you," Uncle John is saying, "labor and business are in cahoots. That's why this AFL-CIO isn't backing the Democrats."

"They will," Sal says. "They will."

"Meany's for Eisenhower," Carlo says.

"Well, Reuther's a socialist," John counters. "If we follow him, it'll be like in Russia."

"If we don't," Rocco says, "it'll be like living under the Nazis."

"They're not as bad as the communists," Uncle John insists. "I don't want my sons to have to fight communists."

Il Padrone *spits out a stream of cigar smoke. "Better to fight than be interned."*

From the front parlour comes a flourish of piano music—loud, explosive, lively, then softly, slowly building, flaring, falling, trickling.

"Ah, it's time," Il Padrone *says.*

"Ricky's got the music going," Rocco says. "It's amazing, how he plays that without music."

"His own compositions," Uncle John says. Then he adds, "This has been one hell of a Christmas." He turns, looks for his wife who is not there, says, "It'll be something for Frannie to put in her diary."

Sal smiles. "She doesn't do that, does she?"

"She writes everything down," Uncle John says. He laughs. "Better watch what you say!"

Sal puts his hands on his puffed-out chest, smiles broadly. "Tell her to make me the leading man." He rises. "Hey, Tina. You coming?"

"Come on, Johnny. Don't be shy."

"Hey, Johnny-panni. Little Johnny-panni. Come over here and sit on my lap."

Johnny freezes. His legs won't move. His head is down. He sees a big sauce stain on his sweater where it meets his pants.

"Come on, Johnny," Tina repeats. "Don't be shy. You know my friend Elaina Maria."

Elaina Maria pats her plump lap, inviting him to sit. They are all in the front parlour. Il Padrone *is in the overstuffed chair beside the piano. Nonna is seated on a dining room chair by his side. All the aunts and uncles are seated on the sofas or in other chairs, and all the youngest cousins are in laps. Ricky is at the piano very quietly flicking out a jazzed-up version of Sarah Vaughan's "Black Coffee," singing, "Now a man is born to go a' lovin; A woman's born to weep and fret . . ."*

"Come on, Johnny. You've got to sit somewhere."

Johnny was the last to enter. He has not finished his spinach and is afraid Tessa has saved it for him. He feels everyone's eyes. There seems to be no sound other than the faint sound of the piano and Elaina Maria slapping her plump lap. Johnny drops his head lower but looks up, sees Nicky on his father's lap, Angie on his mother's. Sylvia is sitting on the floor with Lena, Regina and Santo. Johnny wishes to sit on the floor but is frozen by the eyes.

"Hey!" Aunt Fran's voice is gruff. "What's the matter with you?"

"What's the matter, Johnny-panni?" Elaina Maria's voice is sad, terribly sympathetic. She beckons. "Come now. Oh, look. He looks like a deer. Like a little lost fawn."

"What's the matter with him?" Fran says again.

"There's nothing the matter with him." Ricky turns, stares at his mother. "Leave him alone. He's just shy. It's okay to be shy when you're eight."

"Not that shy," Fran says.

"Yeah, it is," Ricky says. "I was shy like that, too. Remember?"

"God bless America!" Sal says in disgust. "It's getting hot in here. Let's get this over with."

Ricky toys with the keys, knocks out a few bars from "Over There," followed by bars from another oldie, then another, and finally singing and playing, "Pack up your troubles in your old kit bag and smile, boys, smile . . ."

"Play something for Christmas," Fran says. "Why do you play—"

"This is for Aunt Tess and Uncle Rocky," Ricky interrupts his mother. Again a flourish, now followed by "I'll Be Home for Christmas."

"Oh . . ." Rocco puts Nicky on the floor. He coughs, sniffs, wipes his face, excuses himself.

"How about 'Rudolph the Red-Nosed Reindeer,' " Tessa suggests.

"How bout the kids line up," Sal says. "It's almost dark out. We're gonna be goin pretty soon. I don't wanta be walking in the dark."

Johnny looks out the window. He did not realize how late it had gotten. He has not even sat on the new Flexible Flyer and it is dark! Now he is torn. He wants to run outside, even for a minute, but he is sixteenth in line. Fifteen cousins are in front of him, the line snaking back upon itself in the front parlour, the youngest at the back. At the front each cousin kisses Nonna and Nonno and receives The Envelope! The Christmas Envelope from Nonno. If it has been a good year—and Johnny has heard that it has, though he really does not understand—there will be a ten-dollar bill in the envelope. But it is getting darker and Aunt Tina has turned on the lamp by her seat, and Louis has turned on the lamp at the piano so Ricky can see, though Ricky plays without music and when he hunches over the keys his eyes are closed.

"Come bel." *Nonna pinches his cheek, pulls him close until he is tripping onto her.* "Come bel." *She kisses him. "You a nice-ah boy, Gianni. A very nice-ah boy."*

Johnny kisses her, is afraid he will hurt her if he doesn't regain his balance. To him, her skin looks like loose, crinkled waxed paper and he does not want to touch it, to kiss it, but it is part of the family ritual—kiss Grandma first, then Grandpa, then get the loot.

*"An, Gianni-*pane*." Nonno does not pinch his cheek but clutches all the skin of the side of his face with his huge hand. "One for Christmas," Nonno says. "And one more." Johnny knows what is coming but he acts surprised. "You have a birthday, eh?"*

"Four days ago," Johnny says.

"Close enough." Nonno laughs. "One for your birthday, too."

Again Johnny kisses his grandfather, thanks his grandfather, is happy when Nonna passes Anton to Nonno and he, Johnny, can escape; is delighted when he opens the second envelope and finds a new, crisp five-dollar bill, enough, he thinks, with his other Christmas money, to buy his own Flexible Flyer.

Rocco sits in a chair at the kitchen table in the flat over the store. Johnny sits on his lap. Tessa has lain down with Angie who has a fever. Nicky and Sylvia have gone to bed. "Who's Uncle Nick?" Johnny asks.

"Uncle Nick?" Rocco says.

"Um-hmm." Johnny is leaning back against his father, pretending to concentrate on a Life *magazine that is open on the table. "Is Nonno mad at him?"*

"Oh! No. No. Uncle Nick? Uncle Nicole you mean. My uncle."

"Um-hmm." Johnny turns, glances at his father, turns back to the table.

"Nicole was my father's brother. His little brother. I don't really know much about him. He came here right after Granpa . . . Ah, well, when I was your age, he lived with us for a few years. Maybe I was younger." Rocco shifts in the chair. "He was going to be a filmmaker. He was . . . at least according to John. My brother John. I was too young."

"But what happened to him?"

"Uncle Nick?"

"Uh-huh," Johnny-panni utters. "That made Nonno mad. Somebody killed him."

"Oh! Oh, now I know what you're . . . Nicole was interned."

Johnny turns again. He does not understand.

"They made him a prisoner."

"Like in jail?"

"Um-hmm."

"Did he shoot somebody?" Johnny asks.

"No." Rocco chuckles. "He didn't do anything like that. It was during the war."

"But they killed him?"

Rocco sighs. He is tired and he does not want to go into a detailed explanation yet he doesn't know how to tell Johnny . . . to tell him . . . me . . . Why did he have trouble telling me?

"Nonno said that when he found him . . . somebody killed him . . ."

"No." Rocco's tone is resigned. "What happened was this. After the Japs bombed Pearl Harbor and got us into World War Two, and after we declared war on Italy, our government was afraid that Italian-Americans would side with Italy and fight Americans right here."

"Did they?" Johnny is shocked.

"No. No. Of course not. But the government didn't know. So in, ah, let me think, ah, February . . . yeah, February 1942, the government arrested thousands of Italian-Americans that were living in coastal areas. Just like they did to the Japs . . . to Japanese-Americans. They thought, maybe the Italians will help enemy soldiers land on our beaches."

"Uh-huh," Johnny . . . I say. I am glad that Papa is talking to me. This is Christmas. Papa never lets me sit on his lap when he is tired from work.

"That's what 'intern' means. Like put in a prisoner-of-war camp."

"They didn't enter Nonno."

"Intern. Not enter. No. There were too many Italians on the East Coast. They did some . . . I mean . . . well, not like out west. Uncle Nick lived in California. One day in that February they came to his house and they took him right out of the house. They searched to see if he had enemy weapons. They came back three times. They took Aunt Lu's radio. They took the books, the Italian books. Oh . . . I . . . Let me see. Uncle Nick, at that time, was an importer. Do you know what that means?"

"Like important?"

"No. He bought things in Italy and had them sent here so he could sell them. Cheese, salamis, olive oil. Foods. Different kinds of foods. So he had lots of contact with the old country. The last time they came, the government men, they made Aunt Lu and my cousins move inland. The government thought Uncle Nick was an enemy alien because he never became an American citizen. But with his business, he didn't . . . he was too busy. Lu was a citizen. And, of course, my cousins were born here. Most of the Italians they arrested were released in a matter of months. You know, six months, maybe. But Uncle Nick, they held him for years."

"And Nonno found him?"

"Nonno tried to buy his freedom. But he couldn't. He would have paid any price. He would have bribed anyone to save Uncle Nick. You know, you try to protect your family. Uncle Nick . . . he had made a mistake. See, before the war, he told a lot of people that he liked Mussolini. Mussolini made the trains run on time. Mussolini made it easy to do business with businesses in Italy. So Uncle Nick liked him. And for that they put Uncle Nick in jail."

"They can do that? Because you like somebody?"

"They're not supposed to."

"Then why didn't somebody stop them?"

"Nonno tried. Sometimes people don't know how to stop the government from doing the wrong thing."

"The bastards!" Johnny sees him blurt; hears him . . . me get the angry intonation just right.

Rocco chuckles to himself. I think he thinks, That's not a good word, but decides I'm right.

"Bastards," I repeat quietly. "They killed him, huh?"

"Not . . . Nonno says the internment killed him but he only died a few years ago. He was released, I think, in forty-four. Nonno says when he found him, Nick wasn't the same."

"He could have moved back to Nonno's."

"He was ashamed. That's what your grandfather says. They shamed him."

"But . . . if he didn't do anything wrong?"

"It was wrong to be Italian. Wrong to be an alien Italian. He didn't know anything about politics. He was just a grocer. But he could never live with himself after that."

"Then why does Ricky ask Jesus to bless America?"

"Because America saved the world from Hitler. And from Mussolini."

"But they killed Uncle Nicole and—"

"Sometimes a country makes mistakes. No matter what they did to Uncle Nick, America is still the best."

"But . . ."

"No. No more 'buts,'" Rocco says. "It's bedtime. If you get up early enough, before I go to work, we'll go sledding."

But Johnny knows . . . he knows . . . he always knew . . . Get up early! Papa leaves before the sun rises.

AGAIN THE SCHOOL-WIDE announcement—all after-school activities canceled. Again the milling in the hallways, students waiting for the final bell, ignoring their last class of the day.

And anger: "Two fucken days! Didn't find him for two fucken days!"

And frustration: "Do you have a hairbrush?"

"Look at my hair! If I had a brush, don't you think I'd do something about it?!"

Kim, Jason and Martina sat on the floor of the corridor outside the library. Jason could barely open his throat to breathe, much less talk. He slammed a heel against the floor. Angry. Angry at himself. They had no details—only the sketchiest report. The body of a black male had been found. " 'Coach.' " The word shot from Jason's mouth. " 'I think he's at guidance.' What a fucken idiot!"

Kim wanted to hold his hand, wanted to comfort him, wanted him to comfort her, still saw herself as responsible for Katie's death; but Jason didn't want to touch, didn't want to be touched.

"I'm a fucken jerk. Just like my old man says. 'Jerk!' " Again he slammed his heel into the floor. Then he turned from the two girls, punched the wall until his fist bled.

"You like these?" Martina asked Kim. She ran a hand over the cornrows of her hair, rubbed the tips of her fingers on the in-set beads.

"Um-hmm," Kim answered. She could not deal with Jason's anger; Martina's question broke her away. "They look great."

"Take too damn long," Martina said. "Ain't worth it."

"You look really very pretty," Kim said.

Martina smiled. She had a beautiful smile. "Yeah. But it take so long. That's why I missed the wake this mornin. I only had em half done."

"Aaron would have loved them," Kim said.

"You think, girl? I think he got too good for me. He'd be lookin at Miss Radkowski instead."

"Martina!" Kim scolded.

AN AVALANCHE BEGINS with a single flake breaking its bond to its neighbor. It begins slowly, gathers speed and mass, until the mass is racing, thunderously, sucking in more and more, digging deeper and deeper, until the entire slope, mountain, region, quakes, is buried.

Mitch Williams was sitting, restlessly, on the sofa in Johnny Panuzio's living room when Kim and Jason entered. Beside him was his wife Laurie. Johnny was standing; Julia was sitting in an overstuffed chair. Jenny was in her room with Aaron's sisters, Whitney and Diana.

"They should stay the night," Julia said.

"Look, let me drive you there," Johnny said. "You shouldn't drive."

"No. No, not this time," Mitch said. "Thanks . . ."

"Hello, Mr. Williams," Jason said. "Mrs. Williams. I . . ." He could not get out any more words. Laurie Williams' face was wet, contorted.

Mitch Williams glanced at Jason, away. He rose. Mrs. Williams pushed herself to the edge of the sofa. She did not look at Jason at all.

"We're so very sorry," Kim said. "Jason wanted me to drive him up to the crash site, but—"

Johnny stepped in. "He wasn't at the crash site." He was terse. "Aaron didn't die in the crash."

The words did not compute in Jason's mind. "Then he's . . ."

"No. I'm about to take Mr. and Mrs. Williams to the morgue. They've been at the police station for the past three hours. Aaron was shot."

"Shot! What do you mean, shot?"

"Aaron was shot and killed. Not at the crash site but off Little Brook Road. At Finnegan's Pond. Two people, fishermen, their dog actually, found him. The police are treating it as a homicide."

"Dad? What are you . . ."

"Don't say anything to anyone. Not until we get back. Kim? Okay?"

"Yes. Okay . . . but . . . why?"

"The police want to follow a few leads. Before everyone knows—"

Mitch interrupted Johnny. Sternly he said, "Jason, you must be honest with me."

"Umm-hmm." Jason nodded.

"Was Aaron buying drugs? Doing anything like that?"

"No, sir. Of course not!"

"You've got to tell us the truth," Mitch chastised him.

"I am."

"Did he say anything . . . perhaps about wanting to buy a pistol?"

"No, sir. No. Of course not. That's the truth, Mr. Williams. Aaron mighta had some faults but nothing big, nothing like that. With Aaron, what you saw was what he was. He didn't hide things."

"What about gangs? Don't cover for him. He had those horrible curls . . . dreadlocks."

"That wasn't gangs. That was his Cobby Jones thing. You know, the national soccer team player."

"Martina liked them," Kim said quietly. "All the girls did. They're very . . . ah . . . virile."

THEY KISSED. THEY hugged. Julia was down in the kitchen. Jenny, Whitney and Diana were in Jenny's room. Mr. and Mrs. Williams and Johnny Panuzio had left in Johnny's car. It was nearly seven-thirty; the sun had set; the temperature, which had reached the low eighties, had settled back to a soothing seventy-five. Jason had locked the door to his room and he and Kim had settled on the bed. At first they'd simply held each other. Gradually their hugs became stronger, their kisses more passionate, their caresses more erotic. Jason unbuttoned the top of Kim's blouse—kissed her neck, her collarbones. Their excitement rose together. She kissed his ears, ran her tongue from his neck up to his chin, across his jaw, back to his ear. He unbuttoned her further. She had never allowed him to go this far but now encouraged him to continue. She pulled at his shirt, felt the sinew of his back, ran her hands to his legs, his ass. They kissed deeper; his hands fumbled with the clasp on her bra. She undid it for him, let him peel away the cups. He kissed her neck, her shoulders. His eyes were wide open. He wanted to move down. She encouraged him. "Gently," she whispered. "My nipples are very sensitive." She gasped. The sensation of his lips ran through her body like warm electricity. Then, panting, she held him still, moved her leg to feel the hardness in his pants, gasped, sighed, held him motionless. "Jason. Oh Jason. Jason, I'm not ready. Not yet. Not for all the way. Oh dear . . . you feel . . ."

For a while they just held each other, then Kim whispered, "What if someone knocks?" She rehooked her bra.

"I know," Jason answered.

"Jason, I want to. But not yet. Not here."

"I'm going to have to change my pants. I can't go downstairs like this."

"I'll use the bathroom and you can change."

Again they kissed. "With all that's happened," Kim said sadly, "I . . . Why wait?"

Thursday, 22 September, 8:23 A.M.

BY THE END of first period everyone at East Lake High knew that Aaron Williams had been murdered, yet the circumstances remained shrouded. Students he barely knew pressed Jason Panuzio for details. Word spread that, because their fathers were old friends, Jason knew the particulars.

"Get the fuck outta here," he snapped at one boy. "I don't know a goddamn thing." Soon he scowled as people approached. Sneered if they attempted to talk to him. He tried, too, to protect Kim, who was receiving similar treatment.

"Mr. Panuzio, shouldn't you be in class?" Jason looked up. He and Kim were pressed into a nook, in an alcove in a dead-end corridor. "Miss Sanchez," Principal Rosenwald said. "You, too."

"Yes, ma'am," Kim answered. "In a minute."

"It's time to get back on schedule." Charlene Rosenwald's demeanor was harsh, yet she turned, left without following through. The school was still in a state of chaos. Class attendance had risen to approximately 65 percent. There were students attending the burials, others at the wake for John Meade, some taking advantage of the confusion to simply skip out, some still wandering the halls or chatting with peer facilitators. Rosenwald was torn. Shock, anger, grief and now fear formed a palpable, morbid mixture of moods. She wanted to force the building and its contents into her image of its proper form, yet she did not want to come off as insensitive in the wake of tragedy.

Jason watched the principal retreat, quietly said to Kim, "I've asked it a thousand times."

Kim had wrapped her arm about his waist. He squeezed her about the shoulders. "Me too," she said.

"Who would do it?"

"Could it have been a random act?" Kim ventured.

"But what was he doing out at Finnegan's Pond?" Jason challenged.

"I don't know. Are they sure that's where it happened?"

"I think. Why would somebody do it?"

"He had a lot of people angry at him." Kim said.

"Verdeen?"

"Maybe. Could . . . could it have been a suicide?"

"No. No. I don't . . . think . . . He was shot more than once. Besides, why would Aaron commit suicide?"

"What about those players from Lakeport? Didn't they say . . ."

"That was a scrimmage. You know how guys shoot off their mouths."

"His dad thought maybe drugs or gangs . . ."

"I think they killed him." Jason's face was hard. "I think because he was . . . The gangs call it 'acting white.' Maybe not Verdeen. But that fucker set Aaron up."

Kim lowered her eyes. She did not like to hear Jason swear; did not like the anger in his voice. "Maybe it was that skinhead group," she whispered. "Remember in the news a couple a weeks ago?"

Jason released her. "That still doesn't explain why he was at Finnegan's Pond. Unless they like grabbed him right out of the parking lot."

"Unless," Kim said, "it didn't happen there."

"Like . . . you think . . . they dumped his body?!"

"No one's saying—" Kim began but she could not finish. She began to tremble. Tears poured from her eyes but she made no sound.

IN THE PANUZIO home Johnny and Julia sat at the kitchen table. Morning sun filtered through yellow country curtains. Jenny, Whitney and Diana were still upstairs. Rocco was in his room listening to the TV mass. Dog Corleone was under the table. "I think—" Johnny did not look at Julia but slowly turned his coffee mug in his hands "—we should discourage this. She's trouble. She'll get him in trouble."

"I think she's lovely," Julia countered. She did not look at Johnny.

"She's a tramp," Johnny said.

"I'm surprised at you." Julia's voice was sharp. "I thought your male pride would be bolstered by your son's exploits."

"What the hell does that mean?"

"I don't want to talk about it." Julia rose, brought her coffee cup to the sink. "I'm going to start putting together my résumé," she announced.

"Huh?!"

"If you haven't noticed—"

Johnny glared at her back. Between the accident, the murder, the downsizing, he did not want to hear about or deal with another crisis.

"—Meloblatt's not following through with my projects."

"So? Geez, you got . . ."

"What?!!" Julia snapped. *"My own imprint!"* She grasped the edge of the sink, stared out the window. "My own imprint," she snickered. "How thrilling! Those . . . *stronzo e piscia-dosc!* How do you say that? It was all just a front. Those queer little men can't pull off the big blockbuster. They sabotage themselves. And me with them."

"*God's Country*?" Johnny did not understand. "I thought it was signed, sealed and—"

"Meloblatt's so afraid to act, he's killing it. That's why we've had all the delays. Poor Robustelli. They're screwing him to the wall." Julia paused. She struggled. She wanted to tell Johnny everything; wanted to tell him she'd quit. Thoughts raced through her mind. Thank God I didn't sleep with Rod. Why did I quit? What am I going to do? That butt-fucking, two-faced . . . what if I had slept with Rod? Would it be different? Would . . . "I'm going to put out word that I'm looking," Julia said.

"What about Atlanta?"

"What about my career?"

"There's probably decent publishers down there."

"They haven't even offered you—"

"He said he wanted to fly us down!"

"What about . . ." Julia did not finish her sentence.

Rocco shuffled in, looked at Johnny then Julia. He was hunched over farther than usual; his face was slack. He stood still. Dog Corleone got up, pushed his head against the old man's hand, nuzzled into his legs. "I'm not going to give you anything more," Rocco said to the dog. "I fed you this morning. Don't knock me down."

"He's getting fat," Julia said to her father-in-law.

"He's lonely," Rocco said. "When everybody goes, he sits. He just sits in the rain and waits."

"He's a dog, Pop." Johnny leaned forward. "How's the leg today?"

"Á!"

"We'll have the doctor look at it tomorrow. With the rest of the stuff."

"Nah." Rocco rested against the counter. Johnny motioned for him to sit but Rocco didn't move toward the table. "I don't want to burden you."

"Pop! We've had this appointment for months."

"I don't want to make the doctor's . . ." The next words escaped him. "I don't want to be a burden."

"That's not the point," Johnny snapped. "You need to go. We're going. It's that simple. Besides, it'd be more of a burden if your condition became worse. Because you didn't go."

Rocco shrugged. He looked at his meager arms as if to say, "It makes no difference." He changed the topic. "Your sisters called."

"Oh? Both?"

"Angie says the kids are good, but Tom, he's losing his job."

"Good God!" Johnny shook his head. "What a week!"

"He's a bum," Rocco said. "Tessa never liked him."

"Mom loved him. He's a good guy."

"He's a bum. Now, Frankie . . . Sylvia married well. What a house they got."

"Um." Johnny bit his lip. He wanted to say, "Enough for you to have an entire wing." "She ever goina come down ta see ya?"

"They're busy." Rocco turned, shuffled toward the basement door.

"Don't go down . . ." Johnny began but he knew Rocco couldn't hear.

"Your brother called, too." Julia came back to the table. "He wants to go to the casino. Next week. Or the week after."

"Ahh . . ." Johnny grinned. "Good. I bet he wants ta see if we can roll that five hundred into something significant."

"Probably wants to see if you can throw it away," Julia countered.

Johnny did not look at her; did not want to fight with her, did not want to raise his voice with the girls upstairs.

"What are you going to do—" Julia look directly at him "—if they ask you to move?"

"I don't . . . Tripps was disgusted when I talked to him this morning."

"He didn't understand . . . Couldn't he understand that you needed to be here for Mitch?"

"The whole thing. Mitch. Aaron. I told him about Rocco's appointment tomorrow. And that I did the report in four sections." Julia shook her head. Johnny let his eyes catch hers. He wished she would smile. He looked away. "Instead of one list," he said. "So they can't just lop off the bottom. I broke it down by job function but I don't think that yuppie jerk understands." Johnny tapped the table with the tips of his fingers. "I've worked with some of those people for twelve years. He wants me to betray them?!"

"But what if they ask us to go?"

"The way I feel right now . . . with that son of a bitch . . . augh . . . Julia, if it weren't for the lake I'd pick up and go in a minute. Why not? I'd go anywhere." Now Johnny held out his left hand, palm up. He slapped an open right hand down on it as if counting. "And we may have to! We've got to think about tuitions. Todd. Jason in less than two years. Jenny in five. Fuck it. They want me to sell poison to people to pay my bills. I'm good at it—why the fuck not?"

"You would."

"I do."

"Humph!"

BY FOURTH PERIOD the pot was boiling.

"I got my topic, Coach."

"Good, Paul." F.X. McMillian looked calm, in control, but inside he was ready to burst. He wanted to run, to be outside. For two days there had been no practices, no games. Now, even with the death of his center midfielder, the powers that be had decided the game against Plymouth should be played. "I think it will help restart this school's engine," Charlene Rosenwald had said to him.

"Teenage depression," Paul Compari said from his seat.

F.X. simply nodded.

Paul stood, lifted his papers, walked to the front of the room. It was an uncharacteristic behavior. To F.X. he seemed to be doing it, emulating Aaron, out of respect. " 'Teenage Depression and Suicide,' " he read. " 'A Proposal for Intervention.' " He turned to McMillian. "In this context I'll explore the cultural forces behind this, ah . . . this condition."

Again McMillian nodded. "Sounds good," he said. He wanted to encourage Compari but there was little enthusiasm in his voice.

"Recent reports tell us—" Paul checked his notes, read "—that forty percent of U.S. teens have seriously contemplated suicide." He paused, looked up, stage-whispered to his classmates, "Peace be with you and bless your buns." Then, again in full voice, "That over twenty percent have purchased drugs in school; that sixteen percent have been pregnant, that . . ."

MARCIA RADKOWSKI SAT in the chair beside Ciara DeLauro's desk. The door of the guidance office was closed. With her long, delicate fingers Marcia opened her copy of *The Bridge of San Luis Rey.* She spoke quietly. "It's an unpardonable sin," she said. "I've always believed that."

"I can see it in your face," Ciara answered.

"To go through life with self-imposed shackles," Marcia said. With one hand she tapped her chest with a closed fist. "Not being really alert." Again the tap. "Not being really awake." Tap. "Not being really alive."

Ciara sat, elbows on her desk, hands clasped together, her chin resting lightly on her hands. She smiled. "It's wonderful to feel like that."

"Let me read this to you."

"I'd like to hear it."

" 'But soon we shall die—' " her throat became tight, her voice barely audible " '—and all memory of those five will have left the earth, and we ourselves shall be loved for a while and forgotten.' " Marcia glanced up, then back to the book. Her eyes barely focused but she did not need to read the passage, for she had committed it to memory. Her voice became stronger. " 'But the love will have been enough; all those impulses of love return to the love that made them. Even memory is not necessary for love. There is a land of the living and a land of the dead and the bridge is love, the only survival, the only meaning.' "

"You're twenty-two with the heart of a poet." Ciara smiled fondly.

"Twenty-three. Ciara, I loved them so."

"I know."

"Even Aaron. Even if he wasn't my student."

Ciara nodded, a positive acknowledgment. She liked Marcia. Marcia reminded her of herself when she had been fresh out of teachers college, half a lifetime ago.

"I grew up . . . Ciara, I never told this to anyone. I grew up in a very prejudiced family. I hated it. I swore I'd never be like that."

"And you're not," Ciara said.

"Once, this summer . . . at the beach—" Marcia stopped. She glanced to the door to ensure it was sealed. "I love the beach. I like to read with just my head in the shade of an umbrella. Usually I go to the beach at The Cove."

"Oh, in South Lake Village."

"Um-hmm."

"I haven't been there in years. It used to be the most romantic spot on the lake."

"Sometimes I go to the East Lake beach."

"It's nice, too."

"I went there because I liked looking . . . at . . . you know."

"A man?"

"Um-hmm. Aaron. He was like Adonis. God, he was beautiful. I . . . just once . . . I kissed him once."

"Marcia!" Ciara smiled but her brow furrowed.

"I wanted . . . you know . . . to see."

"You know you shouldn't . . ."

"Oh! I know! I know. I felt so guilty. If he weren't a student . . . but it was kind of playful. Not passionate or anything. And he *was* eighteen."

"Marcia. I'm sure it was innocent enough, but . . ."

"You won't tell? They could fire—"

"No. Of course not. This week . . . It's been so stressful on all of us."

"Thanks, Ciara. Thank you. I had to tell someone."

BEFORE PERIOD EIGHT ended, additional word, rumor permeated the school.

"Sexually mutilated," one sophomore repeated. "What does that mean?"

"Like DUH!" a second teased him. "It don't mean they cut his nose off."

"I know that, asshole. I—"

"I heard they chopped his dick off and brought it to MacDonald's," a third boy said. "Ground it up and mixed it in with the Big Macs."

"No way, man," the second laughed out.

"Way, dude." The third nodded with his entire body. "Why not?"

"Get outta here," the first boy said.

They were joined by a fourth who'd been listening in. "My old man's a detective in South Lakeport. He said they shot it off."

"Yeah, right!" exclaimed the second. "He's a dick, all right."

"Fuck you," the fourth snapped. "My old man said like maybe they shot it off after he was already dead. But maybe not. They have to wait for the final autopsy."

"Yeah, like your old man would tell you anything." There was suspicious distrust in the second student's tone.

"Well, he did," the fourth asserted. "What he said was like they emptied an entire clip into his crotch."

"Oh, gross, man." The first boy covered up with both hands. "Don't even talk like that. I can't even hardly walk."

"Then what kind of a gun, then, huh?" the second challenged.

"Maybe a nine-millimeter," the fourth answered. "They haven't found the weapon."

AT SIX O'CLOCK Jason Panuzio sat in the lee of the brick wall of the gym. All of his teammates had left. All the spectators had gone home. Even Kim Sanchez. Jason leaned back, stretched his neck, closed his eyes. They'd lost to Plymouth 0–1. They'd lost, not because they couldn't play without Aaron, not because the "pathetic Pilgrims" had overpowered them, but because they could not concentrate. A dozen times in the midst of play Jason had foundered, had stared at an attacker, had not even seen the ball but had been thinking, *Did you do it? Did you kill him just to win this stupid game?*

Friday, 23 September, 6:40 A.M.

JOHNNY PUSHED THE basement door open, stepped up, exhaled forcefully. He'd just spent an hour working out: thirty minutes on his exercise cycle; fifteen with his free weights; fifteen in long, slow yoga stretching. Jason was with the dog on the floor before the TV. Johnny looked at him but did not speak.

Without turning Jason said, "Dog Corleone says he's sorry."

Johnny grunted.

"He didn't mean to knock Grandpa down last night." Jason massaged the dog at the base of his ears.

"He's okay," Johnny said. "I gotta take him to the doctor's anyway."

"Did he find the heating pad?" Jason asked.

"It was in his room."

"It wasn't Dog's fault."

"I know. Did you check on him?"

"He's asleep. I think."

Instantly Johnny's irritation flared. "What do you mean, 'I think'?"

"You know the way he sleeps. You can't even tell if he's breathing."

"Well! Did you check?!"

"He wasn't blue."

"Jason!"

"I'm only kidding, Dad. He moved."

Johnny collapsed on the sofa behind Jason. It had been weeks since he'd worked out. He was exhausted—deeper than just his muscle. He fingered the pulse at his carotid artery, eyed his watch, began counting.

". . . it's why we moved here." Johnny's eyes shifted to the screen. He'd seen the clip at five-thirty. "We had friends here. We moved here to get away from it. Exactly so this kind of thing wouldn't happen."

Johnny and Jason watched without speaking. In his head Johnny calculated his heart rate. Down to 116, he thought. Okay! He focused on the TV. Sandy O'Mera turned from the image of Mitch Williams. "Joanne," she said to the unseen anchor, "that's the feeling of one of the few African-Americans who live in East Lake. He had tried to protect his family from the inner city only to have his son brutally gunned down by unknown assailants."

"Thanks, Sandy," Joanne Gilbert said. The screen switched to her. "We'll be back with more on the East Lake murder, after this."

Jason turned to his father. Johnny was dressed in an old sweatshirt, sweatpants. He hadn't shaved or showered. "You're not going to work?"

"This afternoon," Johnny said. "After I bring yer grandpa back home. He's got a ten-o'clock . . . umm . . . back by noon . . . I'll be in by one. After the game . . . where'd you go last night?"

"Just to the library."

"Till midnight?"

"I walked some. Got a Coke at the Ice Cream Shoppe."

"With Kim?"

"No. She had to go home. Her mother's afraid she might be attacked."

"Might be . . . ?"

"Because her complexion's dark."

"It's not open season—"

"Dad," Jason got up. "I gotta go." His voice seemed to be sagging. "I . . . I'm . . . gonna go check out Finnegan's Pond after practice."

"With who?"

"I'm going to walk."

"Jason! That's seven miles."

"I run that far in every game."

"No. If you want to go out, I'll take you out."

"Maybe I'll get a ride. Compari wants ta go, too."

"What's it to me?" Martina and Kim were outside Marcia Radkowski's classroom. They'd been talking since meeting up at their lockers at the end of second period. Class had already begun.

"Martina," Kim said. "I know you were angry with him but . . . Martina, that's inappropriate. God! He's been murdered!"

"Don't mean nothin to me, girl. I should be the angry one. He gone an stole my virginity. We done it a lot. I didn't ever say no. Then he dumped me. Excep he never come out en say it. I tell Coach McMillian. I tell anybody."

"Martina!"

IN A VACANT corridor: "You motherfucken prick."

"Watch your mouth, white boy."

"Verdeen. I'm goina see you hang."

"Wasn't me, Jay-sanh." Michael Verdeen stretched Panuzio's name. "Wasn't me. Maybe you. You his little honkey fag."

"You fuck—" Jason slammed Verdeen on the shoulders with the heels of both his hands. "They're gonna fry you. You set him up, didn't you?"

Verdeen recovered from the shove. Charged forward. He was shorter and lighter than Panuzio and it stunned Jason when he unloaded with his shoulder, drove with his legs, plowed into Jason's abdomen. Jason latched on, growled. Both boys crashed to the floor. Fists flew, landed.

"Ugly, dickless WASP."

"Little black shit. I heard you say you'd get im."

"En I woulda, hadn't somebody beat me to im."

"Ouch!"

"OOph!"

"WHAT the HELL is this?!" McMillian pounced on both boys.

Panuzio relaxed his grip. Verdeen let a jab fly to Jason's nose. Blood splattered.

"STOP IT!" McMillian erupted.

"He was layin for me. White-bread fuckhead."

Jason jerked away from McMillian, lunged. McMillian caught him, dropped him to the floor. "You!" he barked at Verdeen. "Go into class." McMillian held Panuzio by the hair, his ass on the floor, his head pushed between his knees. "Go!" he ordered Verdeen. Michael backed away.

A crowd had gathered.

"Did you see him?" one boy whispered. "Shit, what do you think he was like thirty years ago?"

"Gung ho, I bet."

"All of you," McMillian ordered loudly, "back to class." The students obeyed. To Jason, as he let him up, harshly, "What was that all about?"

"He . . ." Jason sniffed. His nose was clogged, still bleeding. There was blood on his face, his shirt, his pants, the floor, and on McMillian's arms and hands. "He . . . on Monday. He told Aaron he was going to get him. He—" sniff, shaking "—said he . . . said he'd get the boys from his old hood. Have them fuck Aaron up good."

"So what the hell are you thinking, Panuzio? If it is true, and it's probably not, but if it is, don't you think they'd come after you?"

"I don't care."

"Shit!" McMillian held out his arms. "Shit," he repeated. Panuzio, I sure hope you don't have AIDS."

"RICKY DIED FIRST." Rocco's words interrupted Johnny's thoughts. "That was 1965."

Johnny glanced at his father, back to the road. He'd barely noticed the traffic, barely noticed they'd passed through South Lake Village; had been listening, on and off, to the radio; had been driving by rote, his mind teetering on the edge, about to fall into the darkness, had been thinking about Jason, about yesterday's game, thinking, *You couldn't do it without Aaron any more than Mitch could do it without me.* Rocco's words had burst the fragmented images coalescing in Johnny's mind. The intrusion irritated him.

"Then my father died . . ." Rocco paused, continued, "Later that year . . ." He paused again. "Carlo was first. He was really the first one. My brother Carl." Rocco's voice was frail, hard to hear. Johnny gritted his teeth. "He was killed in 1962 in a car accident. Terrible." Rocco shuddered. His voice became a little stronger. "My father was sick and John—your uncle John—he wouldn't tell Papa. Of course Mama knew. So how could you hide it from Papa? And your aunt Tina . . . and . . ." Rocco's voice faded, his face pursed.

"I remember . . ." Johnny began but did not finish that sentence. "Sometimes when I drive by The Village, sometimes I try to see Uncle John's old house."

"I was the one to tell Papa." Rocco did not respond to Johnny's statement. "A drunk. A drunk crossed into his lane. It had to be a closed coffin. Then Ricky. Then my father. Then Louis. Then Francesca. Then my mother. Then John. After what Fran did . . ." Rocco began sobbing.

Johnny glanced again but they were on the dam and he quickly brought his eyes back to the road. Rocco's tears made him uncomfortable. He didn't know what to say to elevate the mood, wasn't sure it should be elevated, thought perhaps Rocco needed to reminisce even if it was painful, thought further that Rocco's moods were not his responsibility.

The events of the past week were taking their toll. Johnny wished he could talk to his father but found his own irritation blocked him. Yet it wasn't just the past week. It wasn't the time Rocco took him away from his own life; it wasn't the caregiving. It was Rocco correcting him. Rocco advising him. It was control and criticism. It was Johnny being fifteen again, being an adolescent again; needing to rebel, needing to separate as he had more than three decades earlier. And yet Johnny needed to do exactly what he was doing. He needed to care for his father who had cared for him for so long. Much of the irritation was directed inward. He wanted to succeed, to do it right—work, family, community; yet he felt he was failing, doing it all poorly.

"After Ricky and Louis . . ." Rocco was looking out the window at the lake. "How could John . . . He couldn't. He drank. Even though Carlo had been killed by a drunk, John drank and drank. One time I had to go to Philadelphia to get him. He didn't know how he got there. He didn't have shoes. Not even his shoes. Pants, undershirt, socks. That's all. He finally drank himself to death. And then Tina, God bless her. She was such a mess. Thank God my mother and father didn't . . . Thank God they died first. If they had to see her like she got, it would of killed them."

"I remember Grandpa's funeral," Johnny began but Rocco continued as if Johnny weren't there. Johnny let him ramble.

"Sal, Millie. Sal made it to ninety. And then Tessa . . ." The old man's body convulsed. Tears ran from his eyes. He tried to hold back but was unable. His sobs were weak. His nose ran. He pulled a rumpled handkerchief from his belt, wiped his nose, his cheeks, his eyes.

Johnny swallowed. He tried to say something but found his throat too tight to speak. He swallowed again. In the last eight months old age had advanced upon Rocco, not in a straight line but as a series of jagged steps, as if he were descending a mountain then dropping down through a rolling piedmont. One day he'd decline, the next he'd be on a smooth plateau, then he'd rise but not back to the height of the last crest, then descend, fall again, lower, a week of decline, an hour of ascent. Plateau, rise, drop, rise, level, down, level, descending for weeks, for months, for years, until he had reached the point where he could barely turn, barely see the mountain.

"We were married fifty-two years. This would be fifty-three. All of her brothers and sisters are gone except Donato. He's the youngest. Seventy. All the others . . . they're all gone. Husbands and wives. My sister Sylvia. She would be eighty-seven. I'm the last. Except Carmela. Even she's eighty. Eighty-one. I don't understand . . ."

"Hey, Pop," Johnny injected forcefully, "aim for a hundred. Why not aim for a hundred?"

"Á!" Rocco regained control. "I meant about Jason's friends. So young. Those little girls. That big, strong, colored . . . I don't understand. Too young."

"Um." Johnny bit his lip. "I don't understand eith—"

"At fourteen," Rocco interrupted, "John helped me build a radio. You remember my father's house?"

"Uh-huh," Johnny uttered. He could not follow his father's thoughts.

"We stretched the wire from the attic to the garage. The antenna . . ."

Rocco pronounced the last word *ahn-teen-a*, and it took Johnny a moment to recognize it. "That was 1926. John . . . he's your *compare*. Your *goombah*. You remember him? Your godfather."

"Of course. I was just saying—"

"After Fran died . . . he went to Chicago. He wouldn't talk . . ." Rocco stopped talking.

Johnny waited for him to resume but Rocco was finished. Still, Johnny waited. He thought to mention his father's emotional swings to Dr. Katzenbaum; wasn't sure if they were relevant to Rocco's care; wasn't sure how to explain them. "After we see Katzenbaum, you want to drive by the old house?"

Rocco did not respond. Johnny repeated the question, louder. "Move over," Rocco said.

"Huh?"

"Move over. You'll miss the exit."

"We've got two miles."

"Um." Rocco paused. "You gotta be in the right lane."

Johnny sighed, moved into the right lane behind a slow-moving truck. A third time he asked Rocco about going past the old family home. "Or by the church?" he added.

"The bishop closed the school," Rocco said.

"Yeah. I saw that in the paper."

"He says the diocese doesn't have thirty thousand for a roof."

"Yeah."

"But he's got six million for a retirement home on the lake. Six million for a few old priests. On the lake. Up by the islands."

"Yeah. I guess they're going to put in a pool and some golf holes. I think they paid three million for the property."

"One hundred seventy children. Irish!"

"Irish?" Johnny laughed. "What's that got to do with it?"

"He's Irish. The bishop. He knows it's an Italian parish."

"Holy Rosary? Not anymore. It's black and Hispanic. Hasn't been Italian for years."

"To an Irish bishop, it's an Italian parish. That's why he closed the school."

"That doesn't make any sense, Pop."

Rocco shook his head. "I knew him when he was younger than Jenny. To him, Holy Rosary will always be Italian." Rocco motioned suddenly, almost in a panic. "Get off here. Get off. Get off."

"I do this every day, Pop. I know . . ."

They exited onto Center Street, swung up Fifth, past Main, Columbus and Franklin to a right on Glenn Avenue. Making a loop they recrossed

Center, were held up by the light on Fourth. "See that street?" Rocco pointed down Fourth. "I worked on every house on that street. One time or another, I worked on every house. They were all my friends. Roofs. Trim. All kinds of additions. Augusto did my plumbing. Risco did foundations. Antignani, the wiring. Every house. A beautiful city. Even during the depression. Everybody helped each other."

Johnny had heard the stories a thousand times.

AFTER ROCCO HAD peed in a vial, after his blood had been drawn, his pulse and pressure taken, and after Dr. Robert Katzenbaum had completed his initial examination, the doctor's nurse, Donna Seleski, reentered the examination room. She was a lovely woman with dark, curly hair, dark eyes, full lips, a husky voice. "Rocco," she said authoritatively, "you can put your shirt back on. Would you like some help?"

"I'll help him," Johnny said.

"Okay." Donna Seleski smiled. "When he's dressed, Dr. Katz will talk to him in his office." She left.

"Ah. Va va va voom!" Rocco chuckled playfully. "She looks like Tessa when she was twenty. You shoulda let her put on my shirt."

"Pop. Shh!" Johnny laughed. "You can't say that today. She'll think it's sexual harassment. She's a professional nurse."

"She'd be flattered . . ." Rocco smiled. To Johnny he had not looked this lively in months. The nurse returned. "Donna," Rocco said loudly, "you have a wonderful face."

Donna Seleski smiled. "Thank you, Mr. Panuzio. Dr. Katz wanted me to make sure you understand why the leg ulcer is taking so long to heal."

"And a wonderful body." Rocco's face lit, his eyes twinkled. "Va va va VOOM!"

Seleski laughed.

"Is that sexual harassment?" Rocco asked.

"It sure is," Seleski laughed. She leaned forward, kissed Rocco on the forehead.

"See?" Rocco winked to Johnny. "Flattered."

Johnny covered his eyes. "Maybe you should tell me about his legs," he said seriously.

"The wraps not being tight enough are only part of it," the nurse said. "With the water pill, all together, we're trying to control the edema. But that's a symptom, not the root cause."

"Which is . . . ?" Johnny focused on her mouth.

"Your father's heart is weak. Dr. Katz will explain it further but he asked me to make sure you understand. When the heart's not pumping with enough force for the flow to pull fluids from the extremities, the fluids that remain build up. That's the edema. The edema forces the capillaries to constrict, which decreases blood flow to the skin. That's why, if he bumps himself, he bruises, and the skin dies. I can have the Visiting Nurses come out. They'll show you how to set up your house . . . how to pad corners and make sure there are no sharp . . . Mr. Panuzio, what are you looking at?"

"Oh," Johnny said quietly. "Excuse me. I . . . You really do have a lovely face."

"Humph!" She turned. "Dr. Katzenbaum will be with you in a moment."

A few minutes later Bob Katzenbaum looked his patient directly in the eyes. "Quite frankly, Rocco," he said, "I'm a bit shocked. I don't like what I see. You're going downhill. You've always been the guy I tell my other patients about. How they can still be healthy and active at eighty-five. But I'm seeing deterioration. We're going to try some adjustments to your medications . . ."

Johnny reeled. His head clogged . . . *downhill* . . . *deterioration* . . . Katzenbaum, shocked or not, sped on as if this were an everyday report, as if the clock were ticking and he had patients waiting in four other examining rooms. Which he did. Johnny did not know what to ask. Katzenbaum handed him the new perscriptions, dismissed them.

On the drive home Rocco alternated from frantic to nearly catatonic, from totally lucid yet morbid in his lucidity, to befuddled, to regressing to childhood remembrances, speaking in an accent he hadn't had for sixty years, joking, singing songs of the depression, then sobbing.

"Thats'a Giovan. Thats'a 'Gio-van from Lack-a-wan.' " Rocco pronounced the name *Ju-wan*, not *Jo-vanh.*

"Lack-a-wan? I don't know that word."

"Papa taught us. Lack-a-wan." Rocco sang off-key. " 'What'a you do, Gio-van? What'a you do, Gio-van? I push, I push, I push. I push, I push, I . . .' " He stopped, said, "When he worked on the railroad. 'Gio-van from Lack-a-wan.' "

"Oh. Sure. Lackawanna. The railroad. The Erie Lack-a-money. Isn't that what they used to call it?" No answer. Johnny glanced over. Rocco sat slumped in the passenger seat. His face looked gray. "Pop!"

"I need my box."

"Huh?"

"My box. My box. I need—"

"Oh, you mean that one—"

Demanding. "I need things from my box."

"Relax, Pop. I'm sure—"

Fearful. "Jason found it!"

"No. Not yet. He'll find it. I sure he'll find it. Or has and just hasn't brought it down y—"

Frantic. "I need to go through it."

"Yeah. Sure."

"Today."

"Pop! When he—"

"Today! *Capisce?* Don't look in there. It's private. You could get it—"

"Pop! I gotta go back to work. Right now I'm doin all I can. I can't do everything. I don't care about the damn box!"

"YOU KNOW WHY they were fighting—" Kim brushed a hand gently over Jason's cheek. He flinched. "That eye's going to get really dark," she inserted, then finished her earlier sentence, "—don't you?"

"No."

"Why Martina's so . . . cold . . . about this?"

"No," Jason answered. "I don't."

"She was a virgin before him."

"So?"

"So! So that means a lot to a girl."

"He didn't go blabbing about it. He didn't even tell me."

"But he dumped her," Kim said.

"Did he?"

"You know."

"Yeah. I guess."

"Well, she thinks she might be pregnant."

"You mean . . . ?" Jason was stunned. He went to move but the motion made his whole face hurt.

"Yes."

"With Aaron's baby?! Did he know?"

"She said she didn't know until . . . She just bought the pregnancy test."

"Is she sure? She—"

"Don't tell anybody," Kim said. "She made me promise not to tell . . ."

"She should have told Aaron," Jason said. Then he added, "Is she goina keep it?"

"YOU'VE MISSED SOME days here." Brad Tripps sat on the edge of Johnny Panuzio's desk; kicked one foot rhythmically; chuckled. "Have you been working part-time?"

"No. Of course not, Brad," Johnny defended himself. "You mean . . ."

"You have a half dozen late mornings in the past several months. And four or five early departures."

"There's been the funerals. And those days when I've taken my father to his doctor. He's eighty-five and—"

"Can't someone else . . . ?"

"I always make up the work."

"By leaving early . . ."

"Those are my son's soccer games. I bring a lot of paperwork home with me. I've got the cell phone, the fax . . . Brad, if I've missed a few hours here and there, I've far more than made up for it at home. Or on days when I've come in early. Or left late. When Mr. Tedesco was in charge, he didn't mind the flexible hours as long as production was on time and quality was high. You reviewed it yourself. You said you liked it."

"Don't you think a department head needs to be present to lead his—"

"They don't need to be micromanaged," Johnny said sharply. "I'll make other arrangements for my father if you feel I need to be here all—"

"Oh. No. I understand, Johnny." Brad Tripps waved his right hand in a short motion as if he were erasing the previous conversation. "I was just asking . . ."

"THAT'S ABSOLUTELY UNBELIEVABLE," Julia muttered. She was sitting alone on the sofa, watching a local TV affiliate's programs. At sporadic intervals the station had broken in with teasers and "bulletins." First came a report on Ryan Willis, "driver of the vehicle in which three East Lake teens had been killed and two seriously injured": "It appears as though Willis will be charged with vehicular manslaughter. More at six." Then, later, "Police have brought in an East Lake teenager for questioning in the shooting death of East Lake High soccer star Aaron Williams. Police would not release the student's name, but Lake TV reporter Myra Bennett was able to ascertain that the student was an African-American male with an alleged vendetta against . . ."

Julia felt shell-shocked. "Unbelievable!" Handling people, no matter how treacherous, in business situations, was one thing, but this, this violence, this racism, this waste, this vengeance . . . When she'd brought the Williams twins back to their home, Julia had been unable to console Laurie Williams. Elisse, Vernon's wife, and Kanisha, Elisse's daughter, had been sitting with Laurie, talking, and Julia had felt as if she'd been hearing a foreign language. It had been another blow to her ego. She'd returned home, thankful it was empty, had filled a bowl with black cherry ice cream and had plopped down before the TV. But she could not escape. "Unbelievable," she muttered. "What the fuck is happening to this town?"

"MARTINA, PLEASE SIT."

"I like to stand, Ms. DeLauro."

"Then may I stand with you?"

"Suit yerself."

"Martina, sometimes when someone close to us is hurt, or killed, we go into a denial phase. To protect ourselves. Sometimes we strike out at those around us. Maybe without even understanding why."

"This about me tellin Miss Radkowski I think she a meddlin bitch?"

"Yes, and—"

"She won't suppose to show you that poem."

"She did. She's worried about you. She thought if we talked—"

"She tell you . . . about me?"

"She said—"

"You don't need to give me no pep talk, Ms. DeLauro. You're a nice lady. Probably the nicest in this whole school. But you should go help Miss Radkowski. She the one wiggin out. She probably had it more en me."

"Excuse me?"

"Nothin."

THE WALKING WAS endless but Jason barely noticed. He'd showered, left the gym, crossed the practice fields, headed north through pastureland until he reached School House Hill Road. He'd carried his book pack on his back, his team bag with muddy uniforms by canvas loops gripped tightly in one hand. He'd followed the road through the hills until he'd reached the extension of First Street, then crossed into the fields and scant woods leading down to Little Brook Road, which ran on a tangent to the south edge of Finnegan's Pond.

The air was warm, wet, heavy. Though he'd showered Jason was drenched. He barely noticed. It had taken him nearly two hours to reach the pond. The sun had set, dusk had turned to night. He approached the water. It was not a small pond but a small lake, nearly a mile long, half a mile wide; not a developed park like the beaches and waterfront of Lake Wampahwaug, but unmanaged woodland and glades with meandering trails that circled the water and branched into the surrounding hills seemingly without pattern.

He searched. There were no markers, no instant memorial of ribbons and flowers and cards, as there had been for Katie and Ronnie at the site of the crash. He was not sure where Aaron's body had been discovered. For a time he stood by the water's edge, listening, smelling. It was dark. He could not see more than a few yards but he could listen, hear sounds from a dozen miles; and he could sniff, smell odors from a dozen days.

Jason turned right, took a step along the path that lead to the source, the pond head, incoming Little Brook. The path was wet, rocky. He stepped slowly, easily, sliding on the moss, stumbling on unseen roots, but correcting his balance, climbing unidentified obstacles, heading without thought, without plan, feeling his way upstream, up-pond. The tree cover became denser, his vision more limited. Vegetation formed a tunnel, opened, closed, blocked his progress. He burst into a glade, followed the edge. Looking up he could see a slight glow but on the ground all was dark, dank. He felt his way. The fog became warmer, heavier. He paused, listened. At some far distance cars were speeding, chirping tires, squealing brakes. Closer, all about him, he heard the rhythmic trilling of crickets, the buzz of insects. Somewhere water was trickling. He moved on.

He stepped into the stream, was surprised by the coolness of the water, stepped further, was surprised at the depth. Another step and it was to midthigh and he questioned if he should continue yet he pressed on. The water of Little Brook was not moving quickly yet the pressure pushed him to his left, downstream, toward the pond. He slipped on a submerged rock, staggered, caught himself. The water reached his crotch. He raised his team bag to his shoulders, stepped; the water reached his waist. He reached back, pulled his book bag higher, stepped. The water receded.

Jason did not pause on the far bank but slowly continued, feeling his way downstream, down-pond, until the trail reached a small, rocky cove. There he sat on a boulder, pulled his legs to his chest, wrapped his arms about his knees, laid his head, his cheek, on his arms, closed his eyes. Tomorrow, at Mr. Williams' request, he would carry Aaron's coffin: he, Kurjiaka, Sarrazin, Compari, Miller and Crnecki—teammates.

Jason sat motionless. His eyes throbbed from his fight with Verdeen. His nose was swollen, his mouth sore. He ignored it. He wanted to think about Aaron. Mosquitoes lit upon his arms, his face. He did not move, did not whimper, let them feed. He raised his head, rested his chin on his arms, opened his eyes. In the mist, the fog, the vapor, he wanted to sense him, to feel him, to see him. He wanted to hear him, hear him without sound.

What happened? he asked. *Tell me what happened. Show me. Make me see it. Show it to me.*

He stared into the vapor, into the darkness. He wished it. He willed it. *Tell me,* he cried. *Tell me.*

He stared and he saw into the mist, saw in the mist a darkness, a hulking object, a body lurching, stumbling in the vapor, the warm fog, a hallucination, an apparition, trapped, falling, spasmodic, jarred, lurching, falling, again, again, repetitive, freezing, thawing, wet, green, pale brown-gray, vivid red!

Quivering. Still.

Tell me! What are you trying to tell me? What are you telling me to do?

The third of Johnny-Panni's last thoughts—8 December

If I am a man of this world, a man of my time, and the world has gone mad in my time, is that not the seed of my demise?

What a stupid question. He asks stupid questions. He always has.

Has the world gone crazy? Is it necessary for it to have flipped out, or is it simply necessary for me to perceive that it has?

Ha! He thinks he is Raskolnikov! That's who Johnny-panni is. Ha! No. No! He is Willie Loman. Yes. Loman. And Ethan Hawley. Nothing new. He is simply them reincarnate; in a new age, by a new age. In an age when they are not supposed to exist! What do you think, Fyodor? Does he qualify? Ha! He qualifies for borrowing six thousand dollars at 5.9 percent for six months until they jump it to prime plus 7.9.

Through the mail!

I qualify, Arthur. I've already been approved. Through the mail! Just not for enough—the pocket-teasing pricks. What a bunch a fucking jerks. All of em. If they knew . . . If they only knew. And what a fucking jerk, letting it happen. "Fuck em!"

I . . . Johnny-panni startles, turns, glances toward the street, the house. The storm has abated. It is quiet. Still. His voice carries out over the water, echoes back toward town. Fuck em, he thinks. He is afraid to be heard. Fuck em if they can't take a joke.

It has snowed for a day, thawed for a day, refrozen, misted, cleared, become frigid. The night is crystal-clear; becoming crystal-clear. Johnny stares across the lake at the lights of the city, the shadows, the backlit deep gray rectangles and triangles and squares with tiny sequins glittering. Boxes! They annoy the shit outta me. Cages! he thinks. Traps bedecked with red and green. The tallest box is outlined in red and green and it has a gigantic yellow star on top. Christmas as advertisement! As an advertisement vehicle! Fuck you,

ContGenChem! That's what I say. That's what I scream. That's what . . . What if I'd ordered a square?! Ha! That woulda been a hoot! Not a star! A square! The Square of Christmas! Tripps woulda gone bonkers. Bonk . . . Crazy fucker. All the things you've done! I hate you, Tripps.

Tripps: "Johnny, technological changes are accelerating. It used to take an entire generation. Now things change within a five-year cycle. Do you understand?" Of course I understand, you little pip-squeak. *"Unemployment is the best way for the economy to grow."* Then you should fuckin try it. Volunteer, jerk. *"Let me give you an example . . ."* Eat it, Tripps. Eat it. What you've done to us. What you've done to me. What you've made me do to . . . ! I HATE IT. I DON'T WANT TO LIVE IT ANYMORE!

My breaths are short, shallow, quick. I don't know if I've screamed or if I . . . if he has thought the scream, the rage. I would know. He does not want his thoughts to be heard. He does not want me to know. Not before . . . before I . . . I'm taking you down with me, Tripps. I'm goina set it up for you to fall. After I'm gone, everyone'll know. I'll leave the seed that'll topple your stinkin tower. *Va fancul.* Consider it planted! Consider it . . . *How? How can I . . . he . . . What can he do to . . . ?*

I watch Johnny advance to the water's edge. Ice makes the rocks slick. He bends, dislodges a pebble, stands, works the smooth stone with his fingers, flicks it with disgust into the lake. It is quiet. The lake is calm. He hears the plip, thinks, Fuck you. You'll never be seen again. *He snickers quietly, takes a small step forward, just enough for the toes of his shoes to dampen, thinks,* Lucky you.

For some moments I stand, stare, try not to think, think. It is quiet. After all that's happened. This raucous fall. This chaotic, violent, debilitating fall precipitating a frozen, silent winter! I see him think. There are six polarizations that evolve, deepen, lead to violence. *They are the words of Ciara DeLauro, Jason's guidance . . .* Men from women; blacks from whites; cities from towns; the wealthy from the needy from the middle; workers from employers; citizens from their government. *I . . . Johnny shakes his head. A thousand ways, he thinks. A thousand means to separate—gender, race, riches—to diversify, to estrange—location, work, authority, just the tip of the iceberg. What of age? he thinks. She didn't mention age. What of language? What of story? Aaron's word. Aaron's theory. What of world view? What of life directions? Life Directions!* Jason, what direction do you see your life going in? *Jason:* Forward, I guess. *Johnny:* God bless America!

My eyes lock on to the ContGenChem tower. The CuntGenChem tow . . . East Lake fades. I am a terrorist. Carefully I set up my missile. Who will stop me? Who would even know what it is? I'd tell them it was a Christmas tree. A giant aluminum Christmas tree from California. Help me elevate it. Not so much. Not yet. The branches won't be in until tomorrow. Ha! That's it. Let's get the top to point over that way a little. Johnny-panni smiles. His nares widen. He inhales deeply. Everyone goes. Why stay? You can't put the lights on the tree until the arms . . . It is much later. They'll never know. I step aside, ignite the rocket. There is no noise, no light flash, until it is halfway across the lake. Ha! Now he can see the flaming tail on target for the tower. Now—Ka-BOOOM! and the side of ContGenChem bursting . . . and Tripps, inside, working late, porking his secretary, Johnny's secretary, Lisa, porking her on Johnny's desk, them laughing at Little Johnny-panni whose wife doesn't pork him anymore.

I glance back over my shoulder. What if someone is listening to my thoughts, to his fantasies? I have a gun. An Uzi. Maybe. Something powerful, something with the ammo supply of a computer-game spaceship. I hide near the tower, five stories up, shoot. A man falls. My weapon is silent. I shoot, a woman topples. Easy as an arcade game. Shoot. Dead. Shoot. Dead. Ca-ching! *Jackpot. Here's a million dollars. Pay your bills.* Ca-ching! *In the aisle. He is in a supermarket. Boxes of cereal form a wall to his left, boxes and cans form a wall to the right. A woman enters the aisle from the far end. She is youngish, thirties, a mother, not pretty, not ugly, a mother shopping for groceries for her family. I see him fire. The bullet hits her head. She flies back. He flees. The city is terrorized. The nation is terrorized. He has started the revolution because he is angry! Fuck em all! Who killed Aaron? Who did all . . . ? Terrorism, revolution, houses of cards . . . He can see it. The deep gray rectangles and squares with their tiny sequin lights encaging the populace is a house, a city, a nation of cards; vulnerable, teetering structures needing to be ignited, needing to be razed, needing to be rebuilt from the foundation.*

Everything's changed. Everything. I don't know where I am. Megajolts change everything. Megajolts change interactions. This was a good town. The town's people were brought together in tragedy. The town's people were driven into withdrawal by fear. The withdrawal manifested itself as polarizations. It was a good town and it attracted good people—people who earned and spent money. The money attracted more people, some not so good. Good people live in a town responsibly, with the welfare of current and future people in mind. Not-so-good people live in a town with the good intention of getting money for themselves right now, or of controlling others right now. They covet goodness. Can one covet goodness?! This is envy. This is mal occhio. Mal occh!

The more attractive a town is, the more money it attracts, the more eyes it attracts, the more not-so-good people it attracts; and then the town is not so attractive anymore. Good people leave. The town deteriorates. Megajolts, polar-

ization, violence ensue. Schools and high-security devices—metal detectors, surveillance cameras, guards. The good town becomes a concentration camp and the schools become prisons.

If Tina were here . . . Johnny thinks. The witch. Aunt Santina. The female Satan. She taught . . . I remember it said, one Christmas eve, at midnight, Tina the witch and Carmela the saint, taught my sister Sylvia the ritual to destroy the evil eye. Finòcchio, finòcchio, nòn dami il mal occhio . . . *But a child's chant. How is it done? How? No. Not Sylvia. Who?*

I am living a lie. I am a living lie. I am a little dago with a chickenshit veneer and a chickenshit core. I am worth more dead than alive. Four hundred thousand dollars. An annuity. Technology has not made life easier; it has only increased the pace. Nonno, they're still playing "Get the Guinea." Pop, they still play that game. They just can't use the words. It's not PC! Ha! Except in The Village Voice! *Bigots! That which you began nearly a century ago, which you tempered in the struggles of the Padrone Camps, the Depression, the savagery of world wars; that which was amended, ameliorated, advanced at Christmas dinner 1955, even if you didn't know I was listening; which was arrested with Thanksgiving '65, even if we weren't, aren't aware; I am about to abort it all. Ha! Precursors stop here. There is no future.* Fancul. *Tomorrow night I am going in. All I need do is step onto the pier, walk to the end, stand on the floating dock, slip. It couldn't be easier. It couldn't be more efficient. More cost-effective. Fuck* mal occhio!

My . . . his . . . The thoughts stop. Something is wrong. I have written Zi Carmela. I've begun the report, the proposal for Mitch, have titled it: "The Reestablishment of Ferry Service on Lake Wampahwaug." *The preliminary outline has been easy. Who knows more about the lake than Johnny Panuzio? He taught Todd to swim in this lake. He taught Jenny to fish. How many times has he taken Jason and his Cub Scout den camping up by The Islands? Canoeing to the islands that cluster in the narrows at the north end below the mouth of the Wampahwaug River; packing in and packing out every bit of food, gear . . . Or upriver to The Falls, camping at the state park or on water district land . . . Todd, Aaron, Jason—never loved to fish! Never loved the lake like Johnny-panni! Ah, but Jenny and Diana—they have fished almost every day during the summer while other middle schoolers are plunking themselves down before idiot boxes, watching cartoons, filling their heads with aliens and angels and all sort of occult creatures camouflaged in animated comedy or drama, posing real questions, not seeking real answers. No wonder the world has gone mad!* N'gazz!

Hey, Mitch, come on. You can do it. *I don't know.* Sure you can. *What if I can't?* I'll pull you. You can hold my ankles. Last one ta the far side's a rotten egg. THEN: *I can't make it! I can't make it! Johnny!!!* And: Hahahaha. *Johnny!!!* Stand up, Mitch. It's only three feet deep!

Oh, Mitch. My dearest friend. I hurt for you so much. I wish I were you. I wish I could carry your burden. I could have done the things you did. I should have been by your side. You did it without me because I didn't do it. Perhaps had I, things would not be the way they are. Perhaps different roads . . .

Who knows you, my dear beautiful lake, better than I? I could have . . . If I'd set out to learn all there is to know about transportation, about lake shuttle systems . . . Imagine if I'd become a riverboat captain! Wouldn't that have been something?! Something right out of Huckleberry Finn! *Tessa would have had a cow. Or if I'd become a lake guide; maybe had a tackle shop, sold worms. I could have written magazine features on the counter while waiting for my customers to come, to buy, to ask my advice about the lake . . . about . . . Rocco would have scoffed. He would have shrugged his shoulders in embarrassment, said to Uncle John or to Zi Carmela, "Á! Maybe someday he'll find himself."* Á! *Maybe someday I can lose myself!*

Silently he cries, yet he does not know if he cries for the lake or for someone or for himself. And what have I done to you, my poor friend? When we were boys, do you remember how Lincoln River used to change colors with whatever was being discharged? Mitch and I would leave you and go up from Toad's Tail, all along the Lincoln's bank, through Misty Bottom, go up toward Heartwood where NSC had their old plant. We'd watch the colors come out of the pipes and sometimes we'd see if we could light them on fire. It doesn't happen anymore, does it? Not with politicians trumping the card Environmental Laws! *Ah, but, my dear friend, I recall you as being so much more natural when Mitch and I were boys, when East Lake was cabins and campsites and you were never closed to swimming because of coliform bacillus. When Grandpa shoveled coal . . . when he became a porter . . . when he was a steward . . . Mitch says you are cleaner today. Is my memory faulty? Are you really? Or has everyone forgotten you? The way you were? Is the "cleaner" tag just a label, a story, told us by Mr. Tripps? I've always known you to be a scoundrel. Ha! It's taken all my self-control to keep from doing something about it! Or the Lake Region Business and Tourism Association. Ain't no fucken money in tellin people my lovely lake is . . . Covet, my ass!*

God bless America! Have I contributed to destroying you? Destroying the very thing I love more than anything in the world other than my family. Other than my people. People? Yes, "I do love you. Like this lake. All of you, my brothers and sisters in Christ; in the lake of Christ. In . . ." Johnny stands tall. He is now orating to the multitudes. His mouth is full of pebbles yet he can be heard clearly in all tongues, in all communities. "Or in nature, if you find 'in Christ' offensive. It is what I have said in church for fifty years and I do, or do not, believe . . . People of the lake, of the region, of the nation, of earth. Not race, not ethnicity, not nationality. Except, maybe, if you're Italian." Johnny lets them chuckle. They understand the lightheartedness of his words. "I really do love you . . . all . . ."

His breathing quickens. He is no longer orating but thinking only within. Have I destroyed them? Have I made life better for anyone? Are they better off with me gone? I have not fouled their bodies but their minds. I have polluted their thought processes, their stories, their self-images . . . and I have supported the idiot box to sell ideas *that kill you, my dear friend, my dear lake, that allow them to broadcast their camouflaged inanities . . . If only that were all . . . If only . . . If only I could redesign how it all works! Redesign a life . . . redesign the economic and the interracial and the familial . . . so it would all work!*

What has happened to me? Playing by the rules has not saved my job! Johnny-panni brings his hand to his lips, pinches the skin at the corner of his mouth. His hand trembles. How could this have happened . . . to . . . He thinks, I am the brother of everyone. Playing by the rules has not saved my life! What have I done? Where to from here? . . . My wife . . . I know. He stands taller but the thought does not congeal . . . does not congeal here now as I search, as I . . . My soul! Johnny-panni slumps.

A new thought: What elements of my body are good for the lake? Do I harbor trace elements that will pollute? What of my germs? My genes? Viruses? The things I carry? . . . Clothes . . . I should make sure I wear only natural fibers. Cotton. Wool. Yes. I have a pair of leather boots. A leather belt. Yes. Only natural materials. It will look like an accident. They will be supported in the style and the manner to which they've become accustomed. That is their right! Fancul!

The paper will say, "Mr. Panuzio, who was in the habit of walking the waterfront every evening, apparently slipped from an ice-coated pier into the frigid waters of Lake Wampahwaug—they'll never know that we are friends, dear lake, dear water—*was apparently pulled under by the weight of his winter clothing, and drowned. His death came on the day his son, Jason Panuzio, played . . ."*

The gun. The aisle. The woman. The death. Shot in the head. Why? People posing questions without seeking answers: sounding brilliant by spouting platitudes, by playing on the pathos of the poor and pathetic; asking questions in the era of the television-mind—questions without quest*—history as catch points and hangers for monetary scheming, contradicted by the basic strength of a good town, the basic achievements of its good people in science, in art, in literature, in philosophy—this town, its cultural activities and its sports, its modern mix of men/women/children, a lake of friends, of caring* *neighbors, one family. The past wave of economic prosperity and the present trough of economic despair . . . I did it myself. I made it worse . . . The gun. The aisle. The woman. The death. Deaths! Children killing children! Katie! John! Veronica!*

Fleeing. The gun. Aaron! This was not terrorism. They never found the gun.

The Panuzio Home, East Lake, Monday, 17 October, 6:21 A.M.

JOHNNY YAWNED. HE placed his briefcase on a kitchen chair, moved to the stove, turned on a unit. He grabbed the tole teapot that he used to heat water for coffee, slogged to the sink. As the pot filled he looked through the window. It was dark, three quarters of an hour to sunrise. He sighed. The pot felt heavier than usual; he felt worn. It was the twenty-ninth day since the accident; the twenty-sixth since the announcement of the murder of Aaron Williams; three and a half weeks since his last workout.

Through the floor Johnny could hear the sound of Rocco scraping at the old mortar. Earlier he'd heard Jason descend for breakfast. His son had returned to the attic before Johnny had come down. Again Johnny sighed. Even Dog Corleone hadn't risen to greet him, but had remained under the table with his head on the floor. Johnny set the glass coffeepot on a cork trivet, topped it with a plastic funnel, added a paper filter. He dumped in four scoops of grounds, delicately sprinkled in another half for the pot. He did not feel agitated or angry, only tired. He did not want to face the morning traffic; did not want to go in to work at all; did not want to think, yet fragmented thoughts continuously burst into his consciousness. Where's the court come off . . . ? What's ContGenChem putting in the water today? I should be a whistleblo . . . Jason! My dear son. Why can't you see how secluded you're making yourself? If it weren't for your team, you wouldn't talk to anyone at all, would you? Other than that *puttan?* We've gotta talk. Very soon. Very soon we're going to have a man-to-man talk. We could . . . They never found the murder weapon? The state police major crime squad . . . everybody going off in different directions . . . stumped. All that rain that night . . . and not finding him until . . . Couldn't reconstruct the precursors. Couldn't . . . I bet they know but won't say until . . . I should . . . I bet I could . . . Imagine if I were able to figure it . . . Why? Why hasn't East Lake joined Lakeport in the regional trash disposal agreement?

I should get involved. Get on the council. Someday. Someday I'm going to . . . Or maybe on the diversity committee. I could be a real positive force there. Yeah! I could . . .

The water in the metal pot came to a boil. Johnny removed it from the heat, poured it gently over the French Roast grounds, being sure to soak all before pouring more quickly, roiling the grounds, insuring maximum contact to extract maximum flavor. Quickly the dark liquid streamed into the glass pot, obscuring the trivet. " 'I'm feelin mighty lonesome; Haven't slept a wink . . .' " The words popped into his mind, came out quietly, melodically. He hadn't thought about the song in a long time, couldn't formulate all the words but remembered the tune. "Dah dat, dah dah; Dah dat, dah dah . . ." Then, remembering, " 'And in between I drink; Black cof-fee . . . Oh, a man is made to go a'lovin . . .' "

Johnny smiled. It was a pleasant feeling to recall that song, and it got him to thinking about past times, about . . . Geez, I had a lot of friends in high school. I knew everybody. Not knew em, not like Jason knows em, but was friends with em all. Good friends. Like Mitch. A lot of good friends. I still know most of em. Tommy Marusa. He moved to Atlanta. Geez, if we'd gone . . . And Lee . . . in Virginia. Eddie's still in Lakeport. I oughta give im a call. Boy, what a year we had! By this time in October we were six en oh. Eked out that first win over Roosevelt on the last play, then rolled over Wilson. I had two TDs; Mitch had two; Eddie the last one on . . . ? Um . . . ? Six en oh! The *Ledger* callin us a powerhouse. A powerhouse led by the Salt 'n' Pepper Duo, Panuzio and Williams . . . and Butch . . . and Joe . . . and Richie, Bruce, Tommie, Jimmy . . . I wonder what happened to all those . . .

"Hiya, Popsters!" Jenny entered, bounced into the cabinets, the counter, the wall, spun, plopped down by the table and gave the dog a big kiss on the nose.

"Hey, sunshine. Are you up early or am I running late?"

"Little of both."

They both looked at the microwave. "Oh, geez," Johnny blurted. "Would you run up and rattle your brother's cage? He's goina miss the bus."

"Sure thing, Pops." Jenny sprinted from the room.

"Don't wake your mother," he called after her.

"She's up," Jenny called from halfway up the stairs. "Did you forget, she's picking Todd up at the airport?"

"Oh. Yeah."

"And Uncle Nick en his brood are coming to dinner, too."

"Oh, yeah. Right. I gotta pick up . . ." But Jenny was out of sight and Johnny's thoughts returned to Jason. Quietly he muttered, "What the hell's the matter with him? 'You play like shit because your intensity's at the level of your ass instead of the level of your heart.' " Coach Riccio's line, 1965. Johnny trudged to the table, back to the stove, began pouring himself another cup. The phone rang.

In the attic Jenny slipped into the room, stood behind Jason at his desk. "Whatcha doin?" she asked sweetly.

Harshly, "What's it look like?"

Overly sweet, "Like you're going to miss the bus."

Jason glanced at the menu bar on his computer screen. "Shit! I haven't printed it out yet."

"What?"

"None a yer fucken business! Get outta here, and don't come back up."

Jenny drew her arms to her sides. She clenched her fists, stamped.

"Fuck off!" Jason snapped.

"Pop sent me!" she yelled. "You're goina miss—"

"Kim's coming for me. Now get outta here."

Back in the kitchen, Jenny was furious.

"Calm down, Sweet-ums."

"He didn't have to yell at me like that." She began to cry.

Johnny put his arm around her, hugged her. "I'll talk to . . . Maybe his big brother will straighten him out."

Jenny wiggled loose, sniffed, opened the refrigerator, pulled out a waxed cardboard carton of juice. It amazed Johnny how quickly she recovered. "How come we have to have the store brand? It tastes awful."

Johnny smiled wickedly, leaned over; his eyes brightened. "One glass of juice," he sang, "is like another; I don't know why, or who's to blame. I'll drink orange, or grape or banana. It's all the same. IT'S . . . all the same."

"Pop. You're weird."

"Nah. Don't you know that song? It's from *Man of La Mancha.*"

"No, it's not."

"Yeah . . ." Johnny paused, thought, How do I . . . ? Or should I tell . . . ? She could handle it, but . . . "It's about . . ." he stuttered. "Ah, this woman is singing, 'One pair of arms is—' "

"Oh, that! That's the song the whore sings, isn't it?" Jenny said.

"Ah . . . yeah . . ." Johnny's mouth began to sag but Jason tramped in, book bag in one arm, soccer bag in the other, a dour look on his face. Johnny stopped, stared at his son, at his sallow countenance. "Jason."

"Uh." Short. Guttural.

Instantly Johnny blew, both hands, fingers splayed, shooting up. *"Fa Napoli!"* His arms shook. "Can't you ever answer with respect?!"

"What?!" Jason's head whipped to look, snapped away.

Johnny spoke through clenched teeth. "Mr. Willis called."

"This morning?!"

"Five minutes ago." Johnny took a slow breath, continued in a more even tone. "He asked me if you'd be willing to go over and talk to Ryan."

Accusing. Attacking. "What'd you say?"

Johnny's right fist flew back out, index finger extended. "One second!" Slowly he regained control, curled his hand back down. "Let me finish. He said Ryan is depressed. He said Ryan feels so guilty he hasn't come out of his room in over a week. He's sure everybody hates him. He refuses to go back to school. Mr. Willis said if you'd assure Ryan it was an accident and you didn't blame him, he thinks it would help him get over this."

A horn tooted. Jason started for the door. Stopped. Turned. "Are you nuts?! That asshole killed three of my friends! Amanda's still all fucked up. *Fa Nabala* yerself. I'm outta here."

In the basement Rocco had set himself up in the far north corner where he'd begun work on the back wall. With pride he let his eyes slide across the new bricks of the near side and far front walls. He had not wanted to descend the stairs so early, had been dizzy and had been afraid of falling, yet he'd wanted to complete the corner before his grandson Todd came home, before his son Nick and Nick's family came for dinner. He sat, rested his eyes on a completed section ten feet away. The pattern was very exact, very even, but the vertical lines of mortar made the muscles of his right eye twitch and the pattern doubled, overlapped, then blurred. Rocco shut his eyes, shook his head, reopened. For a moment the bricks were clear, then the unfelt twitch and the double image and blurring recurred. He slumped, eyes closed, thought briefly that perhaps Todd knew the whereabouts of his box, then slowly turned, opened, looked at the wall beside him. He was too close for his eyes to focus clearly but at least there was only a single picture. Rocco reached for a brick but could not keep his arm out and brought it back and rested it on his stomach. The chair on the platform, with the footstool, was comfortable. He put his head back, closed his eyes, rested.

He was wandering. It was a dream he'd dreamt a month earlier, a dream that had been repeating itself with greater frequency. He was wandering along a muddy road with brick buildings close on both sides. The brick was stucco-coated but he knew the buildings were brick because many of them had been hit by artillery shells and the walls were shattered, and bricks and stucco were strewn on the road. The rubble made the walking more difficult. He slid his hands to his pants pockets, tapped his breast pockets. All his pockets were empty. He had no papers, no money. He'd lost his papers and that worried him and he had no money and was afraid. He slogged on, pushing himself, though he was tired. Night was approaching. He did not know where his unit had moved; did not know they had moved at all until he'd found himself slogging through the mud, alone, through one vacant village after another, past one destroyed building after another, into a narrowing alley of ruins, both sides blocking his view to the flanks, unable to retreat, slogging forward into the approaching darkness, following the road, following the road, the mud pulling at his boots, his legs so heavy, without papers, without money, slogging toward the end of the line.

A PALL, A dark oppressiveness, hangs in the corridors of East Lake High as if a gas, a pollutant. There is dread. There is anger. There is hurt. There is a new vice principal, Michelle Dutchussy, assistant dean of discipline; and a new system of control. There are guards in the corridors. All doors are locked at 7:37 precisely, two minutes after the start of school, and access or egress is granted only after subservient pleading. All bathrooms are locked. The new Twelve Methods of Discipline program stresses Zero Tolerance. A guardhouse is being constructed at the Hayestown Road entrance to the school's only parking lot. Twenty-nine days after the accident, twenty-seven days after the discovery of Aaron's body, twenty-six after the revelation of murder, there is a proposal before the town council to enact a teen curfew. Shock and mourning have transformed to seclusion, estrangement. Teachers struggle with their reactions to students: Who am I teaching who is about to die? Who will not be here tomorrow?

On another level, everything is the same as it had been. Classes go on; learning continues; game schedules have resumed; the band plays; people joke, the halls are noisy, lockers bang. There is still love and hate, laughter and heartbreak, helpfulness, vengefulness, cooperation, disruption, excitement and acne.

The car Ryan Willis was driving, the car in which Katie, Veronica and John were killed, and Amanda and Chris were injured, has been towed, with the permission of Ryan's father, to the front lawn of the school—a dramatic hammer, Vice Principal Santoro's idea, to beat it into the heads of the students, *This Can Happen!* Amanda is still in the hospital. Christopher Bhavsar is home.

Height, width, depth and time, Jason thought. Plus spatiality which is not height, width or depth. He turned the corner and headed down the near-empty hallway that led to the stairs to the locker room. Or vibrating loops ten to the minus twentieth the size of a proton strung together to form all ten dimensions of reality. As he walked Jason pondered the physics of the Superstring Theory, as Mr. Hawkins had explained it at the end of Period Two; had explained it not to the entire class but to Jason and Albert Thorne, who had finished early and who had cornered the teacher into expounding on an idea he'd simply mentioned during class.

"Then wormholes, parallel universes and time warps really are possible," Thorne had concluded.

"Theoretically," Mr. Hawkins had answered. "At any rate, they're fascinating to think about, aren't they?"

"Cool," Jason had emitted.

"Awesome!" Mr. Hawkins had an easy, almost whimsical manner. Both boys had chuckled at his choice of words. "Truly awe-inspiring, isn't it?"

"But even if the structure of space can bend, or be bent," Jason had questioned, "and time can be slowed or accelerated, isn't time the key? Slowing or accelerating doesn't put you behind or in front, it just makes everything lag in that structure, and anything that's there will experience normal sequentiality?"

"Ummm." Hawkins had grabbed his chin. "Can you imagine a way to transport to and from different universes where the transport mechanism would retain you in first-universe time, even though you've relocated to second?"

"Time travel . . ." Jason had muttered.

Jason continued down the corridor. Mr. Hawkins had given him a pass to third period and he'd decided to forgo the beginning of Marcia Radkowski's class, to make a detour to the juice machine. He made another turn, pushed open one of the double doors, paced quietly toward the dispenser. The corridor was quiet, empty. Light came only through the glass of the double doors. As he descended into the progressive darkening, his mood fell into the abyss of upheaval he'd been experiencing for a month—onto the pendulum, the yo-yo, back forth, high low, in out. He felt eerie. He could not imagine there being no sound from the locker room. The machine took his dollar, loudly plinked a dime change into the return cup. Alternate universe, he thought. He whacked a button at random. If I could get into a parallel universe, something following this one by a month, then I'd know . . . He uncapped the bottle, flicked his hair from his face, drank, tossed the empty in the recycle bin.

He leaned against the wall, imagined himself piloting a time cruiser back one month; back to where he could follow Aaron. He chastised himself for thinking, for obsessing, but he could not stop this thought line any more now than he'd been able to control his thoughts for a month. Nor did he desire to dispel the images, the fantasies, the plans, the outline for his vendetta against Verdeen, against . . . He did not know. Not yet. And not until he understood . . . the circular dimension, the bending process, the warp which he could not clearly conceive but which nonetheless held him . . . not until he knew who else was involved. Not until he could take his revenge against the murderer, and the accomplices; and against cops and guards and all those assholes who couldn't figure it out with all their goddamned resources; against them all.

With the exceptions of physics and Kim, life had turned sour. Soccer sucked. The entire team played like wusses. They'd loss to Plymouth, Wilson and Taftburg; had tied Roosevelt and Lakeport only because half of each of those teams were serving a two-game suspension for brawling. McMillian had moved him to center mid, the main distributor's position, the play maker, the point guard. He could have moved Santarelli or Zinsser, both midfielders; or he could have brought up Burke or Duncan, the backups; but no, he'd decided to make Jason Panuzio, a so-so outside full, into his center mid; like taking a football center and telling him to be quarterback! What was the man thinking?! Everybody knows Panuzio is a suck player, is the doofus behind the losses.

And Kim! Kim! How incredible . . . Dear Lord, give me the love to hate her. If we go all the way . . . if she gets pregnant, I'm dead. My old man would die of a heart attack. Her old man'd probably shoot me. God, I hate this school. I feel so totally fried, I could . . .

"Hey, what are you doin down there?"

"Huh?"

"Get over here!"

"Yeah." Jason looked at the double doors, at a large, burly man standing with one foot planted to keep a door open, his arms across his chest. "I was just getting—"

"There's no smoking in this school!"

"I was getting a juice."

"And I'm the tooth fairy. Com'ere." The man gestured as if he were calling a four-year-old.

"I've got a pass." Jason sneered, flicked the paper from Mr. Hawkins.

"You got nothin sayin you ken be smokin."

"I wasn't . . . Who the hell are you?!"

"Security. Gene Anzo. Mr. Anzo to you, slimeball. Let me see it. Where you comin from? How come yer not in class?"

"From Art. I stopped to get some juice cause I felt dehydrated."

"Bull. This says physics."

Jason whacked his head. "Physics. The schedule changed. I had Art second period last week. We switch back and forth because the easel room's overcrowded and—"

Mr. Anzo snickered, shook his head in obvious disbelief. "You better come with me to Dr. Dutchussy's off—"

"I'm not goin there! I got a pass to—"

"You're in a restricted area. Now, come—"

"Restricted! There's no sign here sayin . . . What the hell's this?"

"Watch it, you little snot."

"Fa Nabala!" Jason blurted in disgust and frustration.

"*Fa* . . . Ha! You dumb guinea." Anzo advanced. *"Fa Napoli!"* As he hissed out the words he seemed to expand. "You don't even know how to be a greasy guinzo." He jerked a balled fist toward the offices. "It's *fa Napoli!* Fuck Naples!"

"Fuck you." As Jason took a step up the corridor toward Marcia Radkowski's third-period English, he smashed the back of his left fist against a locker.

Immediately Gene Anzo's thick arms shot out from his shoulders. In one practiced motion he grabbed Jason's right wrist, pulled and twisted, simultaneously slamming his chest into Jason's back, splatting Jason against the lockers, then wrenching both arms up behind his shoulder blades and cranking handcuffs about his wrists. He pulled Jason back, smashed him into the metal surface, pulled him out, smashed him forward again. "Smoking! Assault! Swearing at a security guard. You goddamn kids don't know when to stop!"

"I'M . . ." MARCIA SAT in a long, loose-fitting, dark purple smock, sat behind her desk, the chair pulled in, her head down, her voice anemic, tenuous, without passion. She no longer dazzled her classes. Students no longer swooned. For Marcia Radkowski, third-period English is now the most difficult time of day. Amanda Esposito's desk is vacant, awaiting her return. Katie Fitzpatrick's desk is vacant, as if she is simply absent. Martina Watts' desk is vacant; she has transferred to Jerry Bendler's class. No one has moved forward, no one has moved across, no one has filled the voids.

"I'm sorry, Kim. What were you saying?"

"I said, I thought we were supposed to be comparing and contrasting the needs of the flesh versus the quest of the soul."

Marcia looked at her blankly. Then she looked down at the book on the desk before her. Kim shifted nervously, glanced to Jason's desk, wondered why he was not in class, feared—sure her fear was foundless—that something had happened to him. She looked back at Miss Radkowski.

Marcia's mind had wandered so far afield she wasn't certain which work they were discussing. "When I was your age . . ." It was the voice of State Police Investigator Tom Hilman resounding in Marcia's ears. Like all teachers and most students, she had been questioned about the events of September 19. "When I was your age," Hilman had lamented, "it wasn't like this."

"How old are you, Captain?" Marcia had not liked his tone, his prying, his switching to a tone of burdened grief.

"Fifty-seven," the man had said. "There was tension, but we believed, all of us, that things were getting better. It's all the damned legislation the liberals passed in the sixties and seventies which's brought on this epidemic of youth violence."

"Maybe it comes from the inequalities and iniquities that weren't corrected by laws that the right wing blocked!" She had not wanted to verbally spar with Hilman, nor had she wanted to listen to his lame social opinions.

"Do you know that the number of juvenile murders tripled between eighty-four and ninety-four?"

"That's not from legisla—"

"One third of black males between twenty and thirty are either in jail, on probation or on parole."

"Not in this community." Marcia tried to stare Hilman down but he avoided eye contact.

"You still have to ask yourself," Hilman continued, "how did we get here? As a society, how did we get so we're so set against each other?"

"That's right, Captain," Marcia blurted. "What did you and your generation do to foster this epidemic?"

"Yes. Yes. That's what I'd like to know. It did start with what we did, didn't it? Tell me again; you had this summer relationship with Aaron Williams . . ."

"I told you. We were friends. He was very bright. We discussed books."

"On the beach?"

"Yes. On the beach."

"Where someone could have seen you?"

"On the public beach."

"Um. And other places."

"Like I've said, at the Ice Cream Shoppe, the beach, the library . . ."

"We believe Aaron was murdered between five and eight P.M. on the nineteenth. We think the murderer may have been a white male who resented seeing him and a white woman together. The increase in hate groups—"

"Stop right there! First of all, we weren't, like, 'together.' Secondly, Aaron had many white friends, male and female, as do most of the minorities in this school. In this town. And are you trying to tell me that that's wrong?! That—"

"No. No. Not at all. We're not questioning that. That's all wonderful. I wish every community in the state were like this town. What I want to know, Miss Radkowski, is who saw you together who might have objected."

"No one!"

"There's no racism in this town?!"

"That's right."

"Um."

Marcia raised her head, again became cognizant of the classroom. She looked at Kim. She tilted her head to one side, placed a hand over her mouth. Her eyes watered.

"Miss Radkowski, are you okay?" Tara Wallace asked.

"Miss Radkowski . . ." Anita Santana, who sat closest to the teacher's desk, rose, placed a tentative hand on Marcia's arm.

"Oh." Marcia's head swiveled to the side, then back, "Yes. Kim, that is what your essay is supposed to address. Sit down, Anita. Excuse me. I think I was . . . Are any of you going to join the Drama Club? As you know, I'm the adviser and—" again her eyes were dazzling, her entire face animated; she rose, her arms moving like the petals of a flower blossoming "—this year we've chosen *Othello*. Kim, you'd be—"

"Othello?!" Jeff Kurjiaka blurted.

"More Shakespeare?" Thad Carter muttered.

Marcia continued as if no one had spoken. "—an excellent Desdemona. And Tara? Anita? Erin? We'll be reading the parts for the next several weeks. We may reverse the entire color scheme. Tara, you'd make a wonderful Desdemona. These are just ideas. No decisions have been made. How about some of you boys? Jeff? Miro? We need a great Iago. You know soccer isn't everything."

"Girl . . ." Martina and Kim were at their lockers. "You believe in ghosts?"

"Well," Kim chuckled, "not the Casper kind."

"What kine, then?"

"I don't know."

"But you believe in that 'Intercession of Saints'?"

"I guess."

"Like good spirits? Angels, maybe?"

"Um-hmm."

"Me too. I believe in wraiths. I believe in evil spirits. This town become infected with evil spirits."

"Oh stop it, Martina! That kind of talk scares me."

"Don't scare me none."

"Well . . ." With her right foot Kim pushed in a pile of books and papers, then she forced her locker closed. "I don't like it."

"Like it or not, you better protect yerself, girl."

"Martina!"

"Fo real. I asked my Ouiji board. Happen this summer. The devil hisself come en visit this town and put a curse on it. That why all these hassles happenin."

"Then maybe we should pray—"

Martina cut her off. "How's my favorite teacher doin?"

"Miss Rad—"

"Yeah. Now I got Bendler, I like it better."

"He's an old lech . . ."

"Least when he lookin at my tits, he don't hide nothin."

"Martina! What's gotten into you?!"

" 'Are not these woods; More free from peril than the envious court?' "

"What?!"

"*As You Like It,* girl. That's one a Aliena's lines. 'Sweet are the uses of adversity.' " Martina laughed mockingly. "I'm inta the way Bendler teaches. And I like Aliena. I like the name. Maybe . . ." She looked around, finished in a whisper, "Maybe I'll call this kid Aliena. That's how I think a her. Like a little alien. A little stranger."

Kim whispered also. "You're going to put on weight, aren't you? You know it's not healthy to—"

"I already have. Bout five pound. Slowin me down."

"You shouldn't still be play—"

"My las game today. I'm goina fake a hamstring pull so then I caint play no more. But I ain't goin tell nobody. Then I'm goin home and learnin ta cook. There ain't . . ." Back to full voice. "There's never been a better athlete in this school than me. Boy or girl. But nobody knows. All you hear is football. I'm sick a that. I might just join Verdeen en his Black Caucus. Make some of em take note."

"Martina, he's a front for B-SIN. That's what I've heard. It's just a front for his gang. Besides—"

"I know what you goina say but he didn't set Aaron up. He wasn't nowhere near where it happen. That's why the police had ta let im go. He had no gang connection till they push him to it."

"Please, Martina. Even Jas—"

"He'll show up, girl. White boys don't disappear."

"I saw him first—"

"Maybe Radkowski got him locked in a closet."

"Martina! How can you . . . ? She was in class. She looks so frail. How can you think . . . ?"

"She got all them boys still ga-ga-eyed?"

"She looks like she's dying. She's lost weight. She's gray. She's—"

"You know why he didn't love me no more? Why . . . why he didn't love me like I loved him? Like I still love him. You know that true, girl.

I spit on him. Him en his eyes. For Katie. For Radkowski. For you, too."

"Me?!"

"Like you don't know that?! How he look at your ass. I swear he drool lookin down your cleavage, girl. You makin believe you so good. Don't you go lettin that Jason boy be dickin you. You end up like me. Then maybe he end up like Aaron."

JOHNNY TOOK A deep breath. The day was crisp, the air clean, the wind from the lake playful amongst the buildings of downtown Lakeport. He walked briskly, head up, eyes open wide. In his new position he had little flexibility, and his lunch hour, half hour, had become a sprint from his cubicle on the sixth floor to any of the dozens of delis, luncheonettes or street vendor carts in the blocks surrounding the ContGenChem tower. It galled him, the machinations of Tripps, father and son, that had brought him to this, but he'd accepted it, believed it was temporary. He was, he'd told himself, actively looking. Nothing by plan. Not yet. He hadn't really started yet. Hell, he reminded himself, he'd expected his career with NSC to end with a gold watch, ContGenChem buyout or not, downsizing or not. He simply had not anticipated Tripps' malefic machinations. Nor had he anticipated Julia's responses.

"Johnny, you missed a couple of days again these past few weeks." Brad Tripps had sat on the corner of Johnny's desk, had pumped his foot, had looked down upon Panuzio with sadness.

"There was Aaron's funeral. Then my father was in the hospital," Johnny had explained. "He thought he was having a heart attack."

"Oh! Is he all right?"

"Yeah. It . . . it really seemed . . . As far as I can tell, it seemed to be more of an anxiety attack. He became scared and called the EMTs. I got the call and I left midafternoon that Wednesday. Then Thursday . . . I was in right after I brought him home Thursday morning. They don't think there was any damage to the heart muscle."

"Well, I'm glad to hear he's all right now."

"Thanks."

"Johnny." Brad Tripps had leaned very far forward, had spoken quietly. "Your position has been determined to be . . . *surplus.*" Brad's tongue had lingered on the word; then in a spurt he'd added, "But we're not letting you go. I don't want you to think that. You're very valuable to us and we want to promote you."

Johnny had listened, deflated, openmouthed, elevated.

"The position we had in mind for you in Atlanta has been filled, too.

Instead, we want you to stay on, here: first as the leader of the transition team for the move south, then as the local coordinator of marketing and media activities." Tripps had leaned back, cleared his throat, smiled pleasantly. "Now, Johnny, I'm not going to kid you. It's not a directorship. You won't have a department, and the local marketing will be outsourced. But we still need someone to coordinate it. What da ya say?"

"What da ya say?" as though they were good buddies. At that moment Johnny had not thought to say: What's the salary? What are my duties, my objectives? What resources will I have at my disposal? To whom do I answer? And since when do you, you spoiled pip-squeak, get off calling me Johnny? Instead he had thought to say, and had said, "I'd like that." And it had been announced.

Only later had he found the job description in the company's new Personnel, Policies and Procedures manual, and only then had he realized he'd agreed to a 43.8 percent cut in pay; and only then had he become irate. He'd thought to quit, to walk up to Nelson Tripps and tell him his son was an asshole, to walk up to Brad Tripps and poke him in the eyes. But he hadn't. Instead he'd rationalized not quitting by telling himself that he'd quit when he lined up something better; that it's better to be working and looking than to be unemployed and looking. "Particularly now," he'd said to Julia. "Particularly with you looking." And Johnny had laughed. "Hell, I can barely get past you to the computer to do my résumé, anyway."

Julia had looked at him but had not laughed. She had not found his melodramatic retreat amusing; had not found anything in the situation funny or desirable. Indeed, she had been disgusted by Johnny's seeming pleasant acquiescence, and although she would not admit it, even to herself, she was frightened, lost.

Johnny had interpreted her sulkiness as rejection, had defended himself to himself, ranting inwardly, accusing her, "You've sent out a hundred résumés. You've flown to Atlanta! You've flown to San Francisco, Chicago and Dallas. You've interviewed in New York and Philadelphia. And you've charged it all. And for what! For gracious, exciting strokes. But not a single solid offer. And with barely talking to me! And you think I made these decisions without you. I didn't even make em. And what the hell am I supposed to do if you do get an offer? What'd you say to me when Atlanta first came up? 'How can you commit to that when *I* don't know where *my* career is going to take me?' Well," Johnny's inner fury ran on, "how can you commit if I don't know where *I'm* going? What are we, anyway, some kind of economic units? Economic units of production-owned . . . like machines? Pick us up. Move us anyplace! Interchangeable parts!"

Johnny continued his lunch-hour game, a new deli, a new cart, every day. He virtually skipped down Center Street past Columbus and up to

Franklin, then across to Fifth. In some ways, the scourge of job insecurity wasn't terrible but was liberating. He no longer felt responsible to ContGenChem; no longer felt he *must* do the right thing. Indeed, it was kind of fun, not giving a shit. He was seeing the city in a whole new light, seeing the vibrancy that he had sensed but had not been inside of, had not been a part of in years. And he was seeing new opportunities. A week earlier Mitch had told Johnny he'd found Aaron's senior thesis—theory and argument—on Aaron's hard drive; had asked Johnny, "You still interested in it?" Johnny had been interested but was not at the moment. He had not wanted to take on another project—even if it was just reading—had not wanted to diffuse his energies. "I . . . I can't read it," Mitch had said. "Not yet. Every time I start . . . I can't concentrate." "Yeah," Johnny had said. "I'd like to see it." What else could he have said? And Mitch had responded, "I'll make you a disk." And he had. And Johnny had seen something . . . had seen a potential . . . an opportunity.

On the west side of Franklin, halfway to Sixth, he spotted a small grocery with a red, white and green sign which he could not read because of the oblique angle. He hopped to the curb. He still could not make out the letters yet the ambience brought back memories of the small Italian grocery Tessa and Rocco had taken him, Sylvia, Nicky and Angie to when they were small. He smiled, headed straight for the door. Memories flooded back. They would go to church, then to the cemetery where they would say prayers at the grave of Roberto and Josephina Altieri, Tessa's parents. Tessa would get down on her knees and pray but she would not let Johnny or Nicky kneel on the grass in their good pants. Rocco would squat, say a quick prayer, clean the flower beds. Then they would leave and go to the bakery for hot loaves, the outside crisp, the insides steaming; and then the last stop would be the Italian grocery where Rocco would attempt to converse in broken Italian with the fat man behind the counter. "*Due—*" he'd hold up two fingers "—pounds of *capidiquill, e un* pound of provolone."

"*Capicole,*" Tessa would correct him. "The Neapolitan spiced ham."

"Slice it thin, Louie," Rocco would add.

Johnny whistled as he reached the door. "This *is* it," he said to himself. "This *is* Scarpet . . ." He looked at the colorful door window, at the sign:

Sanchez Grocery & Deli
Abierto 7 a 7
7 Dias/semana

The store was small, exactly as it had been decades earlier. The aisles were narrow, the shelves high, nearly to the ceiling, and crammed with cans and boxes, bags and cellophane-wrapped packages. There were still wooden barrels at the front end of the center aisle, except they were now filled with beans, black and white and spotted instead of of *baccalà*, dried and salted codfish, or polenta, maize meal, as in the old store. And in the old store the floor had been bare wood and dirty with mud from shoes. It was still wood but now it was sealed and urethaned and squeaky as a gymnasium.

Johnny moseyed down one aisle, pretending to be interested in finding something particular. In his peripheral vision he watched three young men, a black, a Hispanic and a European of some sort, he thought, as they nudged each other, spoke in muffled voices. He reached the back of the store where a modern set of refrigerator cabinets with sliding doors had been installed. He looked at the sodas, juices and milks. Typical convenience-store stocking. He glanced back at the three men, then at the side counter where the cashier chatted in soft Spanish with an old woman. Behind the storekeep was the deli table, the meat and cheese slicers, and meats and cheese perfectly arranged, with trays of vegetables and baskets of rolls. A middle-aged man in a cheap business suit stood behind the woman customer, and behind him two tough-looking punks, maybe fifteen, fidgeted. How come they're not in school? Johnny tensed. His eyes flicked to the three men in the aisle, again to the boys, again to the trio. The men did not look at him but the black man watched the front of the store as if he were a sentry. Johnny took a few steps toward a shelf of canned goods. He picked up a can of Goya *Habas Grandes*, another of *Fríjoles Negros*. The cans felt hard and firm and had a nice heft. He glanced back at the three men in the middle aisle. The woman left. The storekeep turned his attention to the businessman, who bought a sandwich and lottery tickets.

"You got the good stuff?" Johnny overheard the Hispanic man say to the white.

"Yeah, my man," the white answered. "How much you need?"

Johnny tightened his grip on the can in his left hand, placed the one in his right under his left arm, reached into the cooler and grabbed a long-necked bottle with the name Mango Delight painted in fuchsia. The man in the cheap suit exited and the young boys paid for some candy then raced from the store. Johnny paced to the glass counter, checked over his shoulder, placed the bottle and the two cans in the small cleared area between the register and the Plexiglas lotto ticket tower. "These and a Quik Pik." Johnny gestured to the state's daily numbers game.

"Will that be all?" the attendant asked.

Johnny's eyes snapped to the speaker. He was a thin man, perhaps in his late fifties, wrinkled yet impeccable. His voice was clear, strong; his English absolutely accent-free. "Are you Mr. Sanchez?" Johnny used the Spanish pronunciation. "Kim's father?"

"Yes, Emilio," he said. "Or Emil." He pronounced the second name *Aymill.* "Do I know you? You look familiar."

"John Panuzio. Jason's father."

"Oh. Of course." Emil extended his hand but Johnny ignored it.

"Look," Johnny said. He had not been prepared to engage in a conversation with Kim's father. His words flowed without forethought. "Ah, I didn't really come in here to buy anything."

"Oh." Mr. Sanchez smiled.

"This use to be Scarpetti's, wasn't it? When I was a boy we used to come here all the time. My father's mother was a Scarpetti."

"Yes. I bought it from Lou Scarpetti. That's twenty-five years ago. Small world. How about that?"

"Um. Well, really, I just came in . . ." Johnny emitted a small laugh. "I wanted to say . . . Do you think our children . . . ?"

"Jason is a very polite boy," Emil said. "And Kim tells me he's going to be a brilliant physicist."

"Um. I think they see *too* much of each other."

"Oh. Because of what happened to their friends. I think it will settle . . ."

"She's kind of—" Johnny rocked an open hand, palm down, before him; smiled condescendingly "—a *puttan.* You know? Maybe she should stay away."

"*Puttan? Pu . . . Puta!* A whore?!"

Again Johnny smiled, rocked his hand squeamishly. He smirked, nodded.

"You're calling my daughter a whore?!" Emilio's face became a mask of anger.

"A *puttana.* Not quite a—"

"I know what you're saying!" Emilio exploded. "You . . . ! My daughter . . . !"

Reacting to Emilio's anger, Johnny's rage spiked. "YES!" His right hand flew up. "Yes! Keep that . . . that . . . SLUT away from my son."

Emilio began shaking; his hands trembled at his sides as if they would break from his wrists. "Get . . ."

The three men came from the center aisle, stared in disbelief.

"Get out!"

Johnny grasped the bottle of Mango Delight by its long neck, raised it. "You bet your ass I'm outta here," he shouted. "We—"

"If he ever touches her, I'll—"

Johnny brought the bottle down with such force it shattered the safety-glass counter, cracks instantly zinging into a spiderweb. "—protect our families."

"—cut off his cock."

"She can't do that." It was 1:31 P.M., halfway through eighth period, the last period of the day. F.X. McMillian stood in Principal Charlene Rosenwald's office. He had already changed into his coaching clothes—turf shoes, loose cotton pants, a sweatshirt. Still, the office felt cool. "She can't . . ." he muttered to himself.

Rosenwald was on the phone at the counter in the main office. From behind, he watched her writing on a pad beneath her right hand, the phone held to her right ear by her shoulder, her left hand moving back and forth in the new discipline manual. She seemed to be taking forever.

Second Vice Principal Michelle Dutchussy walked past. F.X. followed her with his eyes. She was shapely, smartly dressed, perhaps a bit heavy in the ankles. He looked away, looked at the principal's desk. Rosenwald kept her desk immaculate—not simply uncluttered, but disinfected daily and treated with Glisten'n'Glo. Again he turned, expecting to see Charlene still on the phone. Instead, she was there, three feet away, walking around him toward her chair.

"Victor told you?" Her tone was no-nonsense; her reference was to Victor Santoro, the older, now first, vice principal.

"Yes."

"I'm going to suspend him for three days. It's his first offense."

"You can't do that, Charlene."

"If I could have gotten his parents on the phone, I already would have. Both their work numbers are wrong. You would think we'd be the first ones to whom they'd report a change of employment. I'm not surprised he's getting in trouble."

"The grandfather lives with—"

"He can't hear. I talked to him three times. He's either stone-deaf or he doesn't understand English."

"Look, Charlene. I know this Panuzio kid. You can't suspend him."

"Mr. McMillian." Dr. Rosenwald attempted to freeze him with her glare. "Tobacco is a drug and we will treat all drug abuse equally. Not only is our policy clear but it is state law. There is no smoking in *any* public building. We will follow the law and we will protect the health of our young people."

"He doesn't smoke."

"He was caught in a restricted area by a security guard who knows what smoke smells like."

"Damn it, Charlene. Don't give me that BS. He wasn't caught smoking."

"Not only am I suspending him for three days but policy directs that he will not take part in any extracurricular activity for three weeks. He may not play. He may not practice. He may not even watch."

"This is really good, Charlene. Really good and stupid. Ask yourself—whether it's Panuzio or anybody else—if you restrict their organized activities, are you going to decrease or increase their unwanted behaviors?"

Charlene Rosenwald placed the elbow of her right arm on her desk, aimed and shook an index finger at her subordinate. "Mr. McMillian, let me read to you the state attorney general's opinion. 'It is time that we take a stand. Since we do not want our teenagers using tobacco, we will take all necessary steps to ensure that these products stay out of their hands.' Do you understand that?"

"Dr. Rosenwald," McMillian ranted, "I *more* than understand. I understand that because of the draconian enforcement of this new antitobacco policy, which includes the outdoor stadiums, attendance at games has fallen fifty percent. I understand that our students no longer perceive this school as a friendly or nurturing environment. And I understand that sociologists have concluded that social isolation is more dangerous than smoking. I understand that you've taken Mrs. DeLauro's highly effective restitution model of discipline—which was a perfect learning, discipline, retain-personal-control-and-accountability system, which was a system under which a student retained his or her personal empowerment and was able to retain or rebuild a positive self-image and world view—and you've trashed it in favor of Dr. Dutchussy's expedient, politically correct Twelve Methods Law and Order model rhetoric—"

"Mr. McMillian, be careful what you say."

"—which is a bigger pain in the ass than student misbehavior has ever been. You've got only—"

"I'm warning you!"

"—one motivation and that's administrative expedience. You know it; I know it; the kids know it. You bought in to this bovine excrement because it's received national attention. It sounds good in the papers. Maybe Victor's convinced himself otherwise. This control . . . You're creating worse behaviors than you're stopping. YOU! You and this draconian management system. You're causing withdrawal, alienation, polarization. You're causing a rebellion."

"Are you finished?"

"No. I—"

"Now you listen to me!" Rosenwald stood. "I don't care about your soccer team. My responsibility—"

"Garbage. This isn't about soccer. It's about kids." McMillian planted both hands on Rosenwald's shiny desk. "He doesn't smoke. I know the kid. If you go through with this, I'm going to see that he sues this school, Anzo, you, Dr. Dutchussy, this whole town. Can't you see what you're doing? Give him to me. Let me take care of this. I need him. He needs me. God, I don't even recognize this school anymore."

In a very firm, controlled tone Charlene Rosenwald said, "I am ordering you not to discuss this incident with the student in question. I am ordering you to make no public statements—"

"Damn it! Charlene, I'll stake my career on keeping him clean of—"

Rosenwald cut him off. "This meeting is completed."

In the corridor outside the main office F.X. McMillian was steaming. He did not see Victor Santoro until the vice principal gently grasped his elbow. "Walk with me."

"Ah . . . Oh. Vic—"

"Shh. Just listen."

"What?"

"I want you to know, off the record, I agree with you. Keep walking. I heard what you said in there. I agree completely. But just like you don't want Panuzio going off half-cocked, you can't go off half-cocked for him. You know better than to stage a frontal assault. Let me handle this. He'll have detention tonight. Miss half your practice. But I'll make sure there's no suspension. I smelled his breath when Gene brought him down and I'm certain he wasn't smoking. And I've got a feeling Anzo provoked him into that altercation. As to the restricted-area signs, the kid's right. They haven't been printed yet. Or were misprinted and we haven't . . . Whatever. They're not up. Because of that, we haven't made the announcement restricting that corridor when the gym isn't in use."

McMillian stopped, huffed, faced Santoro. "See, Vic! This whole thing—"

Santoro silenced him, pushed him on. "He should have gone straight to class. He's going to have to sit in detention. But I'll use that as my trading chip to make sure your recommendation that he be turned over to you is followed. And, Frank, do a good job for this kid."

"IF THIS IS your last detention," the teacher said, "turn in your detention form. Otherwise, have it signed and hang on to it." As he spoke most of the students rose. "Sit down!" he ordered. "There's still four minutes." Most of the students plopped into the seats behind the desks; a few stood defiantly. Jason Panuzio had not risen at all. " 'If you do not turn in the form,' " the teacher read from the detention guidebook, " 'you will not get credit for having served this detention and you will be considered to have been truant, which will result in additional detentions or possible suspension.' "

"What's that mean?" a student called out.

"It means . . ." The teacher pondered for a moment. "Ah, make sure I sign any slips you're going to take with you; leave the other ones here if you've completed . . . Dag-nab-it, but they make this complicated."

"See! Even you don't—"

"Don't push it! I'm still going to enforce it. Line up and I'll sign . . ."

Immediately there was a swell of bodies around the desk. Panuzio remained seated. His wrists were sore from where Anzo had cuffed him, his shoulders sore from Anzo twisting his arms. He felt sick, nauseated, pissed. He had already decided to bag practice; had decided there wasn't any reason to go if he was going to miss most of it. Besides, he thought, Compari is becoming a pain in the ass, him and his "Peace be with you and bless your buns" answer to just about anything. One would have thought, Paul being Aaron's closest friend, he'd've been the most adamant about seeking justice. But no! He's the passive little lamb. Revenge is being left to me.

Jason had also decided not to go home. Todd would be there. Then Uncle Nick en brood. Goddamn party right in the middle of the week just because Todd had a break . . . and he . . . Jason . . . he'd be stuck explaining his early arrival. He had not seen Kim since first period, did not know if she'd gone to Martina's game, wasn't sure where they were playing anyway. "This is just fucken great!" he muttered to himself. He looked at the mob about the desk. Just great, he thought. One more incompetent asshole. Like all of em. Sic the cops on me for getting a juice! Can't find a killer! These people don't give a shit. They go through the paces. Protect the fucking juice machine!

He rose but he did not mingle with the swarm, most being what he considered alternative people—what his parents would have called riffraff. Alternative actions came to mind but he did not seriously consider any action. At 3:36 he drifted from the room, meandered to his locker, stuffed a few books into his backpack, exited via the front doors. Dutchussy and Anzo were in the parking lot insuring that no one was in a car smoking. Jason sneered at Anzo, thought to give him, the fat slob, the finger, but was afraid he'd be seen. Instead he moved into the landscaping, skirted the lot, broke out onto Hayestown Road, stuck out his thumb.

"Where ya goin?" The driver was a middle-aged man in a twelve-year-old sedan.

"Ah . . ." Jason did not know the answer. "Lakeport," he blurted.

"Take ya as far as the bus station in South Lakeport," the driver said.

"Good," Jason responded.

"You in school there?" the driver asked.

"Umm," Jason uttered. His was in a black-ass angry mood and he let it show.

"Me too," the man said amiably. "Ah, I mean, I went there when I was a kid."

Jason did not respond, thought, *Lot of good it did you.* His nares flared, contracted. The car smelled, stunk. He wasn't sure of what. He'd noted the man's teeth were bad; the seat was ripped. Jason did not want to talk. He stared at an angle out the windshield, enough to see the man's movements in the corner of his eye without looking at him. The man whistled softly, a song Jason recognized but could not identify.

"Radio don't work," the man said as they hit the Route 86 on-ramp.

Jason grunted. He felt relaxed. Not completely. He felt tense in the presence of this quiet, odd, almost nondescript yet filthy man with less than attentive driving habits—another incompetent; yet he also felt relaxed. Perhaps it was not being at practice, not having to perform, knowing that his performance wasn't up to par. Perhaps, he thought, he would quit. Dutchussy had read him the riot act, had told him she was going to suspend him from all activities for three weeks. She hadn't followed through, but he could. He'd show that bitch! he thought. Show . . .

They passed through South Lake Village, crossed the dam into South Lakeport, were soon passing by the first projects, and suddenly Jason knew why he'd come. He clamped his jaw tight, stared ahead. A gun! For a gun, he thought. He'd come for a gun. He could buy a gun. It was time.

"I'm exiting up there. You want to come down to the station or stay on the highway?"

"The station's fine," Jason said. He could hardly believe that the man was willing to stop *on* the highway. "Yeah. The station . . ."

"You want me to bring you someplace near?"

"No," Jason said quickly. "Where you're going's fine." Where you're going, he thought. Where I'm going. A smirk formed on his face. I know exactly where I'm . . .

"I'm parkin there," the man said. "You want out here on the street?"

"Sure. Thanks." Jason grabbed his book bag, popped from the car, closed the door too hard but did not bend to apologize. About him were hundreds of people, perhaps thousands; a white, exurban teen in an ethnic polyglot, mostly black and Hispanic, moving, hanging out.

He looked down. The sidewalks were wide, double or triple the width of those in East Lake. Looked up. There were no trees, no homes. The street was lined with shops, restaurants, video arcades; above the stores were offices. There was litter in the gutter, papers blowing along the walks. People kept their heads down; squinted to keep dust from blowing into their eyes, or to keep from making eye contact with others marching toward them.

Jason stepped close to the nearest store window, looked in, tried to get his bearings. In the window were hundreds of cameras, phones, calculators, recorders; a few items had price tags that, to him, seemed ridiculously low. Behind him four black teens, his age, his size, passed. He clutched his book bag, decided not to put it on his back but to carry it, swing it. He walked quickly, scanned the opposite side of the street for the sign of a gun store, searched windows on his side, was a little shocked at seeing very lewd posters in one window, a display of Porno for Pyros albums in another. He felt uneasy but felt if he kept moving no one could accost him.

Jason crossed a side street. It hit him: He did not have money for a gun. He dispelled the thought, determined that that would not stop him. Still, he realized, he did not know how to purchase a gun. He went into a coffee shop, sat at the counter, made believe he was looking for someone, looked for Mike Verdeen, actually thought he might see him, didn't. He rose, left, crossed the street, continued on his quest. On one corner there was a brick building painted bright purple. He thought to head down the side street, hesitated. The solid side wall was covered with graffiti, colorful tags. Jason backed to the building on the opposite side. The graffiti, mostly words that he could not read, was so artistically painted, sculpted, it held his eyes, caused him to study the technique. He made out the word NERDOS hidden in a constellation of bursting stars; then the letters B-SIN-K, but with the *K* printed backward. A black teen raced by him. The boy's pants were low on his hips, his plaid boxer shorts worn high, the pant legs cinched at midcalf eight inches above rolled-down black socks and the most bodacious zigzagged green-blue-white high-tops Jason had ever seen. Another black teen, in different dress but with the same plaid boxers showing, ran by. B-SIN, Jason thought. The gang. He knew the acronym from all the speculation about Aaron's murder. Black Street Imperial Nation. The backward *K*, he'd been told, meant kill or killer. The graffiti, therefore, was a rival gang's—killers of B-SIN. A smartly dressed black couple and their three young children walked by. Jason smiled at the little girl and she smiled back. He reviewed his own dress: a "Co-ed Naked" T-shirt, plain black athletic shorts, indoor soccer shoes. A black teen in military camouflage-patterned fatigue pants raced down the sidewalk. It brought him back to his mission. Yet how . . . ? It made him jittery that he did not know the answer. How does one go about buying a gun? How do you meet . . . ?

A cop car stopped at the curb where he was standing. He turned, walked back to the main thoroughfare. What the fuck?! he thought. He felt like they knew what he had in mind; knew why he'd come . . . He stuck out like a sore thumb. No baggy pants down to his ass. No . . . Most people weren't dressed like that, not even most of the teenagers, but were he, he felt, he'd fit in. He wouldn't be—here he was—but he wouldn't be an alternative person. He'd fit.

He passed a dojo, a restaurant, several shoe stores. He walked quickly yet without direction. For one block most of the signs were in Chinese; in the next most were Spanish. He crossed into the tiny Little Italy section, which was, at first glance, as foreign to Jason Panuzio as were the preceding blocks. In bits and pieces he recognized familiar items, mostly food, and familiar faces, though he did not know anyone. He did not understand. He passed into a section so covered with graffiti tags—not in the least artistic—that it seemed to him someone had a pathological need to declare his or her virtual ownership of every visible surface.

Jason stopped. He glared through a store window, refocused, read the arched letters on the glass: **Cutlery**. Displayed in a cluttered window was every kind of knife he'd ever imagined and many more. There were no prices. His mind raced. He entered the small shop: a narrow aisle, display cases and counter to one side, a bare wall with five-foot-high tin wainscoting on the other.

"I help you?" a small man said. There was no one else in the store.

Jason glanced at the man. He did not know but guessed him to be Indian, or Pakistani, perhaps Cambodian. He felt unsettled. "Just looking," Jason said. Urban shopping was somehow different from the anonymity of purchasing in a suburban mall—somehow more up close, personal.

"Yes. Very good." The man smiled.

"I . . ."

"Yes?"

"I was looking for a . . . ah . . . a gift."

"Oh yes. Many nice gifts. This one for your mother, maybe? For the kitchen or for the dinner table?"

"Ah . . . actually . . . ah . . ." What to say? Jason's thoughts were mushrooming. A knife could do . . . a knife instead . . . "For my uncle."

"He is a chef? Or a hunter?"

"Well, ah, actually, he's like a doctor. But he's, ah . . . he's a veteran and . . ."

"Oh! Oh! You want a souvenir?"

"Yes. Do you have something . . . ?"

"From Viet-Nam?"

"Ah . . . shh . . . ure."

"Let me show." From a drawer beneath the display counter the small man produced a highly polished ebony box. "Maybe like," he began as he opened the case, "this. This very fine."

On royal blue velvet Jason saw a dull-finished, twelve-inch-long knife with a slightly triangular blade wired to the case. "What is . . . ?"

"This ChiCom," the man said proudly. "This a ChiCom bayonet. You know ChiCom?"

"No."

"Chinese. Chinese communist. This taken from dead NVA soldier. My brother kill him and take his bayonet. Very good quality. Very nice case."

"How much?"

"Very rare," the small man said. "One hundred dollar."

"Oh." Jason deflated. "I don't have that much."

"Your uncle, he is an American soldier in Viet-Nam?"

"Yes."

"Who was he with?"

"Who . . . ? I don't know."

"What unit? What unit was he with?" The man's accent seemed to melt away. He let his disgust with Jason's lack of knowledge show. "You should know his unit. He is your uncle?"

"Yeah. Ah, I don't . . . like . . . know. He was in the army."

"When did he serve?"

"I don't know."

"How old are you?"

"I'm—" quickly Jason thought that there might be an age restriction on purchasing knives "—eighteen."

"You bring your uncle here, to see me. I'll make for him a special price."

"He's coming to dinner tonight," Jason said. "It's his birthday," he lied. "I wanted to surprise him."

"But you don't know—"

"He's younger than my father. Pop graduated . . . I think Uncle Nick must of graduated high school either in 1968 or 1969. My father went to school but Uncle Nick signed up for the army. So I guess around then."

The man looked Jason up and down. He did not smile. "You have seventy dollars?"

Jason dug into his pocket, pulled out a wallet, counted his money. "I've got . . . forty-three . . . Wait a minute." He opened his backpack, pushed and fumbled, pulled out several bills and a handful of change. "I've got forty-eight sixty-five."

The man shook his head.

"Are you interested in physics? I've got my physics book."

The man beamed.

Jason smiled back.

Johnny stood at the edge of the kitchen doorway; looking through the hall into the living room, eavesdropping. It was a quarter after six; the sun had already set. Jason had come in only a few minutes earlier. "What is it, honey?" Julia's voice was soft, concerned. Johnny thought to join them on the sofa, then thought he should return to his new project: editing Aaron's thesis. He'd printed out some finely written text, some rough notes, nearly twenty-three pages in all. But he did not move.

"I don't know," Johnny heard Jason say. To Johnny his son sounded strange, almost conversational. He decided to listen.

"Your arm . . . ?"

"It's just sore. I landed on it funny at practice."

"You didn't break anything?" Julia caressed Jason's shoulder.

"No. It's just sore, Mom. Maybe I pulled a muscle."

"Your grandfather says the school called."

"I got into . . . a . . . situation. But I didn't do anything wrong."

"Can you tell me about it?"

Johnny leaned toward the living room, craned his neck, cocked his head. He wished he could speak with his son in the tones his wife was using; wished he could be as compassionate as Julia, as his own mother had been with him.

"I was late leaving Mr. Hawkins' class . . ." Jason's voice was flat as he related to his mother the incident of the morning. He told her of the verbal confrontation with the security guard and the accusation of smoking, but left out the physical contact, the handcuffing. As he finished his voice was shaking. "I don't know when they called but Rosenwald and Dutchussy made me sit in this little room, like a supply closet, all day. I thought they'd called you or Dad but I didn't know. All I got was one detention."

Julia cupped a hand over Jason's forearm. "That would have made me very angry," she said.

"I didn't do anything except get a can of orange juice. It just pisses me off. I hate that woman."

"Dr. Rosenwald?"

"Dr. Dutch. She's like a Hitler or something. Everybody hates her."

"Well, I'm glad you told me about it. Is that why you were so late?"

"I missed most of practice—" Jason thought quickly, lied "—so I stayed and ran."

"Umm. If you'd like, I'll talk to Dr. Dutchu—"

"No," Jason interrupted. "Ah . . . probably better not to."

"I don't like this keeping you from class. Over juice?!"

"I even had a pass! From Mr. Hawkins."

"I'm going to talk to her tomorrow."

"Please don't, Mom. Really! I think I've got it all worked out now, and if you go in, it'll just open it all up again."

"Well, I'm going to keep tabs on that school. If there's any . . . Does Mrs. DeLauro know? Did she say anything?"

"I . . . didn't . . . I didn't see her. Please don't say anything."

"What about your father? Did you tell him?"

"No. He . . ."

"He's concerned, you know," Julia said.

"I can't talk to him. He'll just yell. He'd take their side."

From behind them Johnny nearly blurted, "No. I wouldn't." But he bit his lip.

Julia sighed. "He's under a lot of pressure, too," she said.

Jason scoffed. "He doesn't have to take it out on me."

Julia dropped her eyes, shook her head. Then she looked at her son's face. "Can you derive—" she raised a hand to brush back his hair; Jason flicked his head, flicked the locks from his eyes "—some meaning for it? Something . . ."

"Yeah. I suppose. Don't trust those people."

Again Julia shook her head. She checked her watch. "We'll have to discuss it more tomorrow. Todd's going to be back with your grandfather any minute. And your uncle and Aunt Dana will be here in about fifteen."

Johnny retreated before they rose. He slid to the dimly lit back hall that led to Rocco's room. He needed to be alone. Just one minute alone. One quiet minute. His arms were trembling. Beads of sweat broke onto his brow. His mind yawed. He placed a hand on a cabinet to stablize himself, yet inside he felt as if he were falling, dropping, out of control . . .

"I have something to say to you," Tessa says. "Please sit down."

"But Ma! I'm supposed to meet Barbara." Johnny-panni does not want to sit. He does not want to listen to his mother. "We're doing a project with Mitch and, ah, Laurie Robinson. We've got to—"

"No," Tessa says firmly. "I'm afraid you must call the Finches. Or the Williams. This is very important."

"What?" cracks from Johnny's mouth. He is bouncing on the balls of his feet. It is nearly seven o'clock, the fifteenth of March, 1965. He is seventeen years old, a junior at Lakeport High School.

"Un pepe un cul." *Tessa ignores the rudeness of his tone; shakes a hand but not in anger, gently gestures for him to sit beside her. "Sit down. Your father's gone to Uncle John's. Your cousin . . ."*

"Who?" The change in Tessa's voice freezes him, stops him . . . me from bouncing. "What cousin?" He stands flatfooted. Stares. "What cousin?" The question comes out of me like a lightning bolt. I don't know why.

"Captain Richard." Tessa breaks into tears.

"Ricky?!" Suddenly Johnny-panni isn't buying her emotional stuff. But he isn't sure. He glances to the window of their flat; sees the streetlights are on; sees that the night is clear. He wants to meet his girlfriend at the library. Barbara Finch is hot and I'm in hot pursuit. For two weeks we've been rendezvousing at the library, then ducking out, but it has been cold and she's been wrapped in layers. Now winter has broken, perhaps only temporarily,

but it's warm enough to go out without a jacket. Warm enough for me to get my hands on . . .

"Yes," Tessa says. "Uncle John called. Fran is distraught, and of course, John's very upset."

"About what?" Johnny asks. He can't even call Barbara because she will have already left. Maybe she'll rendezvous with someone else! "What happened? I mean, he's . . ."

"Please. Sit down."

Johnny sits on the sofa next to his mother. She cups a hand over his forearm, squeezes, and he knows, he now absolutely knows this is something serious and he will not be meeting Barbara at the library.

"I wish Sylvia were home."

"She works till eight." Johnny is curt. He does not hide his disappointment.

"I wanted to tell you both together. Before I tell Nicky and Angie."

"Well, tell me! How bad can it be?"

"Captain Richard was killed yesterday." Tessa breaks into soft sobs. Her crying makes me . . . Johnny fights back tears. They are not tears for Ricky. They are communal tears, tears for Tessa's pain, for a pain he feels the family will have, does have, whether he has it or not. Their pain is his pain and their pain brings tears to his eyes and he sniffs and Tessa squeezes his arm and he knows that the squeeze, meant to comfort him, comforts her. Still the pain is mixed with confusion. Johnny has not seen Ricky in years; has only kept up with his deeds—mostly words of his promotions—through Tessa and Rocco; does not even know where Ricky is stationed.

"How . . . ?" The word gets stuck in his throat.

"I don't know. I don't understand these things anymore. It's not like when I was in Italy. But call your friends. Tell them you can't go out for a few days. Not until after the funeral."

"Is he still in the army?" Johnny asks. As he asks he thinks that that is a stupid question. "I mean . . ."

"With God's help—" Tessa smooths Johnny's curly hair "—we'll find some meaning in this. We'll all get through . . ."

"Um." Johnny-panni nods. He is searching his mind for context; recalls talk of Ricky being in Asia.

Recalls . . . Screens change. Focus changes. It is a week later and he hears most of the story; it is two weeks later and he recalls how Ricky could play the piano, how Ricky, the oldest of all the cousins, could challenge Aunt Tina, could defend Little Johnny-panni. It is a month later. He is with Barbara Finch. The anger sets in.

Tessa is crying. It is again nearly seven o'clock the fifteenth of March,

1965. Quickly she inhales, gulps air. "Louis is going to bring the body home. I'm sure they'd like you to be a pallbearer."

"WHAT WAS KRISTIN doing?" Jenny was on the phone in the living room, hoping for some privacy. Julia was in the dining room, setting the table; Jason had gone upstairs to his computer/bedroom; Johnny was back in the kitchen cleaning the counters. He was sweating, hoping the work would justify his appearance. He did not want to overhear any more conversations. He heard Jenny's side.

"Why?" Jenny looked over her shoulder to make sure no one was listening.

"Oh." Jenny fidgeted.

"That's so cool," Jenny whispered.

"Well, I can't," Jenny answered. "I told Tara I'd sit with her. Not Diana. Who's sitting with Whitney?"

Johnny poked his head into the living room. "Who you talkin to, sweetums?"

Jenny held up an index finger. Into the receiver she said, "Lena, my daaad's like right here. He's asking me a question." Then to Johnny she said, "Lena."

"Oh. Ah, keep it short, huh? There's still things to do around here."

To Lena, loud enough so her father could hear, Jenny said, "I can only stay on two more minutes." Johnny nodded, went back to the kitchen.

"Her mother won't?!" Jenny's voice exploded with an incredulity only a twelve-year-old girl can express. "So she's . . . Oh, like weird. Like very." Then Jenny added, "That whole family's gotten like weird. Like really weirded out. God! Like it's rubbed off on my brother, too. And my pop."

After a pause, "So who's Diana going to . . .

"She's not my best friend anymore," Jenny said. "And I'm not going to tell Tara . . .

"I'm not going to do that," Jenny insisted. "Besides, I don't want to sit with her. She's like gotten . . . like since her brother was killed . . . like she barely talks. I don't like being with her anymore."

Lena's shrill voice burst from the phone. "Well!" Jenny held the phone a foot from her ear. "Somebody's got to!"

"You could," Jenny said.

"No way," Lena screamed. "I don't . . . like I don't do charity."

"JOHNNY!" THERE WAS urgency in Rocco's voice. It was a quarter to seven. Rocco and Todd had been at the store longer than Johnny had expected. "Do I got a hat on?"

"Huh?"

"Do I got a hat on?" Rocco patted the side, then the top, of his head.

"No, Pop. You don't have a hat on. Did you leave it at the store?"

"Feels like I got a hat on. Feels all tight up there. I put my hand up there, there's no hat. But I feel like I got a hat on."

"Todd." Johnny addressed his eldest son as he entered. "Did your grandfather have his hat on when you went out?"

"Huh?" Todd had a brown paper bag filled with groceries under each arm. Dog Corleone followed him in, nose up, sniffing. "What hat?" He eased one bag, then the other, onto the counter. To the dog he said, "Wait a minute. I got—"

"I thought," Jenny interrupted, "like, you were only getting, like milk."

"Like like," Todd mocked her. "Like Grandpa wanted to get like more stuff."

"Pop," Johnny said, "I don't think you were wearing a hat." Johnny began unpacking the bags. "What are all these cookies?"

"No-oh." Rocco shook his head. "I didn't have my hat. But my head, it feels like I got a hat on." Now he grabbed his scalp with both hands. He tottered, caught his balance, leaned against the counter.

"Pop," Johnny said harshly. "Sit down. Sit down and get your legs up. You shouldn't even of gone."

"Á." Short, harsh.

Johnny huffed, turned his back, gritted his teeth, began to rap his fist down on the counter, jerked it back, glanced to see if anyone noticed.

There was commotion at the back door. Dana burst in followed by Nick, Nick Junior and Robbie. All four had pots, pans, platters or casserole dishes. "*Èh*, Padrone," Dana called as she entered the kitchen. "How are you?" She kissed her father-in-law even before she put the large platter she carried on the counter.

"Good . . ." Rocco began.

"*Èh*, Pop." Nick, holding a big pot to the side, turned, also kissed his father. "Be careful, it's hot." He placed the pot on the stove.

"Ooo! That smells good," Johnny said.

Young Nick, thirteen, whom they called Nicco, and Robbie, nine, put their dishes down, hugged their grandfather, their uncle. Dana kissed Johnny. She hugged Jenny, grasped her gently by the shoulders, held her at arm's length. "My God, you're getting *so* big! So mature-looking. I can't believe you're younger than Nicco."

"Only three months," Jenny said.

"Quite the young lady." Johnny smiled at Jenny but Jenny was already racing Nicco to the back hallway.

Dana turned to Todd. "Oh, my! You get more handsome every time I see you. How's school? How are your classes? It's so good to have you back home. And where's your brother? And your mom?"

"I'm right here," Julia called from the dining room.

She came into the kitchen to see Nick grab Johnny's belly. "You gettin fat, bro."

"Ouch! Boy." Johnny grabbed his own stomach with both hands. "Do I feel out a shape."

"Come downstairs," Rocco said to Nick. "I fix." He beamed proudly. "Johnny's got a problem, but I fix . . ."

"How bout after dinner, Pop?" Johnny suggested. "Show em after—"

"I wanna show him—"

"Sure, we'll look now," Nick said as he edged over toward Julia. "I wanna see how far he's gotten." He put his arms around his sister-in-law, squeezed her. She was wearing a long, flowing, navy-blue dress detailed in silver, cinched at the waist to show her figure, with stockings and heels. "You lookin good, Mama!" Nick fluttered his eyebrows lustfully.

"Nicky," Julia giggled, "you stop that." She pushed him away. "Somebody go up and call Jason." Julia turned to Dana—who was in a simple cotton poplin smock and wore out-of-season fisherman mules with squat heels and lug soles—gave her a most proper hug, smiled, said, "How are you? It seems like we never get together anymore."

"I know. We're all great. Busy, but things couldn't be better. Nicco's applying to the new magnet school—the Science Center."

Johnny overheard Dana, joined in that conversation. "You guys are doing that?"

"Well, he's applying. We don't know if he'll be accepted. But the distance to Kennedy High in Lakeport, you know, isn't much more than to our Roosevelt High in North Lakeport."

"I thought that was all rejected," Johnny said. "By that diversity vote."

"The mandatory realignment part was; not the voluntary—"

"Is that so?! I didn't realize . . ."

"Um-hmm." Dana began removing the foil from a platter. "Besides, the state courts are probably going to force some kind of solution. Oh, ah . . ." She turned. "Julia, do you want the *prosciut* and cantaloupe . . ."

"Come in and see first," Julia said. She led Dana to the dining room.

"Oh!" Dana exclaimed. "Look at . . . ! Oh, how elegant! I always feel so underdressed . . ."

"Don't be silly," Julia said. She turned to the table. "It's Tessa's crystal. I had them professionally cleaned. The jeweler thought it was some of the finest-cut—"

Dana slapped the side of her face. "My kids shouldn't eat at this table," she blurted.

"Oh, nonsense." Julia smirked.

"Ah . . ." Dana squirmed. "This was the set that was Tessa's mom's?"

"Um-hmm. Isn't it gorgeous?"

"Yes, but . . ."

"We can put the melon and ham on the salad plates and—"

"If Robbie knocks one of these stems over, I'll never forgive myself."

"Dana! They're here to be used. Look, you made all the dinner. This is the least I could do."

"Nick made most of it," Dana said. "He's such a good cook. Wait'll you try the *braciola.*" She kissed her fingertips. "His grandmother's recipe. And the vegetables!" Again she kissed her fingertips, but now followed the gesture by tossing her hand in the air, opening it like a flower blooming. "Um-umm!"

In the kitchen Nick turned the heat on under the *pasta e fagiòli,* which they pronounced *pasta fa-zool.* It was his own concoction, still noodle and bean soup with cut vegetables, but unlike the traditional heavy peasant soup, the broth was clear, the various elements cooked separately, combined at the last minute. "I called Sylvia this morning," Nick said to his father.

"How come—" Rocco sat sideways to the kitchen table, his legs braced outward for stability "—she doesn't call? You're all so spread! How can you take care of each other?"

"She and Frank are fine," Nick said. "The kids are well. Everybody's busy. You know how it is. We all take care of ourselves."

"No more are we a fami—" Rocco began but stopped when a soccer ball banged off the side of the house. Johnny started; Nick seemed barely to notice. From outside they heard Jenny's shout, "Not there, turkey breath," followed by Robbie's, "He kicked it. Not me," and Todd's direction to his cousins, "Just move it out farther."

"Sure we are, Pop," Nick said. "But Sylvia's got her practice in Albany, and Angie and Tom—"

"Tom's a bum," Rocco said.

"Naw," Nick countered. "He's got a new job. A big promotion. Of course, it means transferring to Seattle . . . but . . . you know, we talk. I talked to her, to Angie, yesterday." While Nick chatted he stirred the soup, prepared the frying pan for the fresh vegetables. "Angie said she's going to do a *mal occhio* over East Lake to chase away the evil spirits."

"What—" Johnny dipped a crust of bread into the edge of the meat platter "—does she know?"

"I guess it was in the papers out there, about the multiple killings in a small town."

"We didn't have—"

"Á!" Short, dismissive. Nick's gesture identical to his father's. "You know how the papers are."

"There was an auto accident and one—"

Nick cut Johnny off. "I know. Hey, while this is heating, why don't I go down and look at the foundation."

"Sure," Johnny said. Rocco began to rise. "Pop, stay up here. He can see what you've done . . ."

"A good foundation," Rocco said to Nick. "Without a good—"

"We'll be right back up, Pop." Nick tossed a pot holder onto the counter. "I'm just going to take a quick peek."

"If you see my box down there . . ."

"What box?" Nick called from halfway down the steps.

"From Uncle John's," Johnny answered for his father as the two brothers descended into the basement. "Some box he has that came from Uncle John after he died. I think Pop thinks we're hiding it or something. He probably lost it in the move."

In the basement, not only was Nick surprised at the amount of work completed, but Johnny, too, who had been down only a few days earlier, was amazed. Quickly the conversation changed. "He doesn't look so good," Nick said to Johnny. "What's Katzenbaum say?"

"He says, 'He's getting old.' "

"Did he tell you the results of . . . ?"

"Hey. You're the doctor. I don't know what all that stuff means. Why don't you call him?"

"You don't gotta get huffy with me. I just asked . . ."

"Well, damn it, you could do some more . . . I mean, look! I can't be the only one taking him to his doctors. He's like a full-time job. And he's driving me nuts. All I ever hear is, 'Your house is fallin down. Your house could cave in.' He's killin himself down here and I didn't want him doing it in the damn first place. He's gotta put me on a guilt trip. All the time."

"What guilt . . . ?"

"Like yesterday! He says, 'You didn't take me to my meeting.' I said, 'What meeting, Pop?' He says, 'Sons of Italy.' Or maybe Knights of Columbus. I don't remember! He says, 'Columbus Day. It's the first time I missed the meeting in fifty years!' So I said to him, 'How am I supposed to take you to a meeting if I don't even know you've got a meeting?' And he says, 'I don't want you takin me no place. I'll call a cab.' And I say, 'That's not the point!' But he gets . . . like . . . He like withdraws. I feel like I'm his marionette. It's like he's paranoid. Like even with Katzenbaum. He says, 'I don't trust him. Maybe I should find a new doctor.' Which means I'm supposed to go out and find him a new doc—"

"Katz is excellent. I'd go to him myself if I—"

"It's like Pop's angry all the time," Johnny said. "Angry and sad and all alone. But he uses it. He even uses the dog to make me feel—"

"He is," Nick interrupted.

"He is what?"

"Look, I'm an orthopedist, not a shrink. But he is angry and sad and alone. All his friends are dead! His wife of fifty-three years is dead! All his brothers and sisters except Zi Carmela are dead, and she can't hear so he can't even talk to her on the phone. They're the last of a generation."

"Maybe I oughta get Jason to teach them both how to e-mail . . ."

"Hey, ya know, that's actually a good idea. We could get em—"

"He won't."

"I bet he would."

"I'm tellin ya—" Johnny was adamant "—he won't learn how to do it. He . . . All the time, 'It won't be long. It won't be long now.' " As Johnny raised and flipped his hand he let out the familial, sharp, yet this time quiet, *"Á!"*

"Umm." Nick ran a hand over a section of new brick, allowed his fingers to follow the mortar joints. Far more than Johnny, Nick could admire the artistry of the work, for Nick had worked with his father from the time he was discharged from the army until he was twenty-eight—at which time he'd returned to school, finally becoming an orthopedic surgeon at the age of thirty-eight. "He's got to see himself as part of something," Nick said to the wall. "As contributing. This is his contribution. He's got to be part of something bigger. The family. The community. With everybody in his generation gone, that's been taken away from him."

"I suppose," Johnny said.

"What about you?" Nick chuckled. "The firstborn Italian son who can't contradict his father? You look like you should be spending more time down here on your bike."

"Boy! Did I do something stupid today."

"What?"

"I . . . I was in this deli at lunchtime and . . . It was the old Scarpetti grocery. You remember? Nonna's cousin's place. We use ta go Sundays after church."

"Yeah. Down on—"

"Oh shit! Shit, did I do somethin stupid. I swear there was a drug deal goin on right there. I flipped out and banged down a soda bottle on the glass counter and broke it. Then I ran out."

Nick laughed. "You . . . Did they chase you?"

"Nah. But I called the police and told them what I saw happening and what I did and told them to tell the owner I'd pay for the counter. But I can't believe I—"

"Man, I can't believe that either. My own brother! A store trasher!"

"It's not funny."

"Yes, it is."

"No, it's not. I'm really afraid they're goina press charges. Shit! With the cutbacks, with Julia quitting, I'm not makin . . . I can't afford . . ."

"Umm," Nick hummed. He didn't believe his brother.

"Really . . ." Johnny paused, looked down. He did not look at Nick. "I . . . I don't know why I can't keep it together. They're goina throw me in jail. I just know . . ."

"Can't keep what together?!"

"I've always had this problem. Ever since high school. I really screwed up my life."

"Certainly doesn't look that way to somebody on the outside."

"Well, it is."

"You're just havin yer midlife crisis," Nick said dismissively.

"You know why I went into marketing and advertising?" Johnny said. "To be with beautiful women. That's it. You don't have to laugh."

"Everybody does that."

"No, they don't."

"You're a man. You got two heads. They both want to lead. Especially when you're eighteen or—"

Johnny interrupted. "And because it was easy."

"And because you're good at it. And you found a beautiful woman. And you've got three beautiful kids, a beautiful house, two—"

"I could have been an engineer. I could have been a chemist. Maybe I'd have developed something . . . I've been working on this thesis of cultural . . . for Mitch . . . I . . ."

"You could have been a bum. You could have been a druggie."

"I was. Remember? When you were in the army . . . when you came back and worked for Pop . . . I was until Julia forced—"

"But you're not now, and that you were isn't important. We're not that kind. None of us. Geez, Johnny! You were a kid. That's not what our family's about. That comes through. We do the right thing. That's why you called the cops. I think you're a hero."

"I . . . I don't know anymore. We're in financial straits. My mind's . . . like . . ."

"Hey. Come on. You know I still got yer winnings. Let's go out to Heartwood. Saturday. See if we can turn your luck around."

———

In his attic computer room with the door locked, Jason hunched over the ebony box he'd taken from his book bag. There was noise downstairs and out in the yard. Twice someone knocked. "In five minutes," he'd answered the first time. "I'm in the middle of something," he'd answered the second. "I'll be down when I get it done."

Carefully he removed the thick chipboard base wrapped in army-blue velvet to which the NVA bayonet and its metal sheath were attached. He flipped the board, painstakingly untwisted the three bright copper wires holding the knife, slipped the wires from the tiny holes drilled in the muzzle clamp and the edge of the blade, bent back the third from the muzzle ring. The bayonet was free, lying across his hands. In his hand it felt vile; he felt wicked. He smiled; he chuckled. He grasped the hilt with his right hand. The space between muzzle ring and clamp was exactly the width of his closed palm. He squeezed, rotated his wrist, turning the blade, swishing it, getting the heft and balance. The weapon was longer than he'd realized. He measured it: slightly more the twelve inches overall; the blade alone nearly eight and a half inches. Again he grasped the hilt. He stood, silently slashed across before him, stabbed back, slashed up, jabbed down. He changed his grip, lunged, thrust the blade tip into the wall. He withdrew the blade. A chip of plaster fell to the floor. He tried his left hand, tried passing it back and forth, tried concealing it up his shirtsleeve; on his calf; tried quick draws. Again he tested the heft, tested slightly different holds, attempted to find the perfect hold, the perfect balance.

As he swirled his arms Jason thought of revenge, yet he could not imagine a specific target. He thought through, visualized, then practiced specific moves, specific uses, but he could not think of a specific person—not even Michael Verdeen. He still believed Verdeen had set Aaron up; everything pointed to him. But he now also believed Verdeen's alibi, and he believed the police. Yet he also still believed, because they had not identified the killer, that they, the local, regional and state police, were incompetent.

Jason tried punching with the knife grasped perpendicular to his arm, a move he'd seen in movies, but the physics of the force to him didn't seem to make sense. He hit his headboard. The blade barely nicked the wood. He tested the blade on his thumbnail. It was relatively dull. But the point was sharp. With only a modicum of force he plunged the tip into his pillow and was amazed at the depth of the puncture. Clearly, he thought, the weapon was designed more for stabbing than slicing. But sharpened . . .

Jason tried to conjure up an image of Aaron's killer but he could not. Still, he knew that that person would be, had to be his first target. He knew, sooner or later, he would find out; knew, sooner or later, the word would come, and then he would take revenge on the killer, and then and only then on Verdeen and the other accomplices. And he knew, knew the term *premeditated.* But he did not care.

From the other side of the door, "Let's go." It was his father. "Everybody's at the table."

"Half a minute, Pop. Really. I'm just putting it away."

"Of course, I put him down as a reference," Julia said to Nick. "I didn't think . . ." She had already explained much of the turmoil that had led to her "mutual separation" from Gallinas.

"Well, can't you do something?" Dana injected. She'd just returned from the kitchen with a refilled gravy boat. "I mean . . ."

"How come I didn't know this?" Johnny said. He was miffed. "This is the first time I've heard—"

"I told you," Julia said defensively. She and Johnny were at the far end of the table from the kitchen. Rocco was at the head; Dana and Nick next to him on the open side for easy access to the preparation area, then Robbie and Todd. On the window side of the table Nicco sat next to his grandfather, Jason in the middle and Jenny beside her father. The lights were slightly dimmed; music softly filled the background; the two bottles of Valpolicella that had been decanted were mostly empty.

"Can you add a follow-up letter that explains why he's saying all that?" Nick asked.

"This is what he wrote to virtually everyone. A friend at BookMakers sent it to me; but I'm sure he sent it to everyone. It goes something like this." Julia put one hand on her hip, flipped the other open on a limp wrist. " 'We love her dearly,' " she said in falsetto. " 'We found Julia Barnum-Panuzio to be energetic and creative, and truly to be a powerful force within our organization. However, there came a time—' " she flipped her hand over " '—when we questioned her tolerance and her honesty.' My honesty!" Julia's voice dropped two octaves. She thumped her chest with a closed fist. "Mine!" she repeated. "And tolerance! That's the equivalent of calling me a bigot. That's a death knell in publishing."

"Oh!" Nick said. "I see."

"Then explain it to me." Johnny fidgeted. "Homosexual liaison right there in the office," he muttered, shook his head.

"If she says she saw this guy and his assistant doing it," Todd answered his father, "and that's why she was fired, it automatically proves that she's intolerant."

Julia nodded. "That's it exactly. Or I'm lying."

"Maybe we should do this after dinner." Johnny glanced at Jenny, then at Nicco and Robbie.

"They can hear it," Nick said. "Least my—"

"I already know," Jenny said matter-of-factly. She refilled her wineglass with white grape juice. "They taught us about alternate lifestyles in Health."

Johnny closed his eyes, covered them to hide his embarrassment.

"But," Dana said to Julia, "if you were lying about having walked in on them, then you wouldn't have anything to be intolerant about because you wouldn't have seen—"

"That's too logical," Todd said. He was enjoying his new adult status within the family.

"Huh?" Johnny said. The others ignored him. Lightly he grasped the edge of the table; impatiently his right leg bounced, vibrated. He thought to ask Todd about Wisconsin's soccer team but was cut off.

"Preempt it," Nick prescribed. "Withdraw your résumés. Change your cover letter. Explain in it the what and why so you . . . You don't want to work in the same situation again, anyway. Tell them that. All publishers can't be—"

"I don't think any of them are!" The words erupted out of Julia. "Except Gallina! But most will be sensitive to the issue. All the big ones. Tolerance doesn't mean just sexual, but racial, religious, ethnic. Now I'm put in a position where I have to prove . . . It's like . . ." She paused, turned to Johnny. "Stop that!"

"What?"

"That . . . You're making the glasses shake."

"He's *un pepe un cul*." Rocco winked.

"What's that mean?" Jenny asked eagerly.

"He . . ." Rocco paused to think of the translation.

Nick laughed. "I haven't heard that one in a long time." Jenny repeated her question and Nick smiled, said, "Antsy. It means . . ." He laughed.

Jenny leaned across the table to eye him into telling her.

"It means," Nick said, " 'pepper up your butt.' "

"Nick!" Johnny barked. Jenny giggled.

"Á!" Nick flicked his hand.

"You . . ." Johnny eyed his daughter sternly, but he could not hold the sternness and he chuckled, "You're the one who's *un pepe un cul*."

"Anyway—" Julia picked up where she'd left off "—it's like what happened to Jason today."

"Mom!" Jason had been quietly devouring heaps of rice with green peppercorn and sweet Marsala sauce.

Johnny's smile fell away. "What happened?" He did not want another surprise.

"Nothin!" Jason clamped his mouth shut.

"He was accused of smoking when he wasn't," Julia said. "It's really no big deal, except that it makes you angry to be accused of something when you haven't—"

"You don't smoke," Johnny said to Jason.

"I know that!" Jason retorted.

"Then . . ."

"It was just a mistake," Julia said. "Back to Gallina. At least they're—"

"Were you with somebody who was?" Johnny demanded.

Jason stood. "I've got a ton of homework. I'm done. Can I be excused?"

"—finally bringing out Robustelli's book. The one I was working on."

Johnny ignored Julia, shook his head, not denying Jason's request but in woeful frustration. "Maybe you could help clear the table?" he said.

"Pop . . . !"

"Oh, don't have him do that," Dana spoke out. "I'll clear it. I don't mind."

"God's Country," Julia continued. "It should be in the stores this week."

"I'll help." Todd stood, began picking up plates. To Jason he said, "Old man Santoro chew you out?"

"There's new people this year." Jason trudged toward the kitchen. "Real dickheads."

Rocco grabbed Jason's wrist, stopped him. "You do what they say," Rocco said. He did not look up because tilting his head made him dizzy, but he continued to hold his grandson's wrist. "But protect yourself."

"Yeah," Jason mumbled.

"Todd," Nick called to the kitchen, "bring in the Strega and *torrone*, okay?"

"Sure."

"I'm goina give you some advice," Rocco rasped loudly. "I know you don't need advice, but I'm goina say it anyway. We know the kind of people who act like that. Don't be like them."

"Of course not, Grandpa."

"I know what they're like. I remember back to the war in Italy . . . one major . . . I still remember his name, James T. Atkinson. Nice to your face, but . . . behind your backs. Zzzzzst! You know?"

"I guess."

"Take this from an old infantryman. CYA. You know C . . . ?"

"Like Catholic Youth . . . ?"

"No." Rocco shook his head. "Do right; obey rules; but CYA."

"Pop!" Johnny shook his head. "What are you telling him? What's going on at this table tonight?!"

"I'm telling him," Rocco said loudly, "to watch his back. You never learned . . . Tessa and I, we never taught you. Cover your ass."

"Absolutely right," Nick said.

The Point, East Lake,
Tuesday, 18 October, 6:54 A.M.

JOHNNY STEPPED TO the water's edge. The night had been not just cool but downright cold. Between the rounded rocks where water lay still and was only a few inches deep, he could see thin, patterned, crystal-clear sheets of ice. He bent. His left knee buckled and a stabbing pain shot through his thigh. He stood, gasped, exhaled, forced the leg straight, tight, relaxed. Again he bent, knelt. He slipped a hand into the cold water at the edge of the ice, grasped a thin piece, gently broke it from the rocks, lifted it, examined it. As his fingertips melted into the thin sheet, he closed his eyes. He did not say a prayer but in his mind he felt a prayer, felt a communion with *his* lake, *his* holy water. He put the ice against his forehead. The sharp coldness felt wonderful, alleviated the throb of last evening's wine and Strega. He bit the edge. The ice tasted like dirt, like lake water from the shallows. He took another bite, crunched and crushed it between his teeth, then spit it out. The dirt taste was an improvement over the foul feeling in his mouth.

Johnny stayed low, peered into the mist rising from the warmer water away from the shore. He turned, again spit into the sand. He thought about Julia, envisioned Julia watching Meloblatt with Hickel, there, in the office, bent low over the desk.

Again he spit. Though the air was cold and the lake steaming, the sky above was clear, becoming blue as the sun rose behind him. Ten yards from shore a small fleet of mallards circled in the cove. Farther out, at the edge of the rising mist, Johnny spied an otter gliding toward the end of his dock. The animal dove, disappeared. Johnny remained still, vigilant. Images seemed to bang on the inside of his skull—Julia, Emilio Sanchez, the shattering glass, Jason, Julia watching, the cracks in the glass exploding like a spiderweb . . .

Before him, the otter surfaced vertically, seemingly stood on a submerged platform, its head, neck, shoulders and forelegs out of the water. The otter scanned the shore, spotted the man, hissed loudly, splashed over and disappeared. Johnny crept toward the pier. His shoes slid off rocks, wedged between them, scuffed in the sparse sand. His knee twisted, sent pangs stabbing. Still he stayed low until he reached the pier. Then he tiptoed out, dropped to the floating dock at the end, crouched into the edge of the fog, methodically searched for the otter's reemergence. All I've ever wanted . . . he thought. A horn tooted. Damn it, he thought. He squeezed his hands into fists, brought his fists to his temples, pushed on the sides of his head, remained still. Again the horn. He crushed his eyes closed. His arms trembled against his head.

"I TOLD JASON this morning," Johnny said, "that I met Kim's father. Ay-mill. Something like that." Johnny's voice was calm, detached. "I told him that Ay-mill really doesn't like him being with his daughter."

Mitch glanced over, then back to the road. He'd arrived at seven sharp to pick Johnny up: but Johnny hadn't been there. He'd tooted repeatedly, tooted until Todd had come out to tell him that he didn't know where his father was, just as Johnny had shown up looking disheveled. They were ten minutes behind Mitch's schedule. "What'd he say?" Mitch asked gruffly.

"Nothing. Nothing at all. I suspect he knows it but doesn't want to face it."

"Emilio really said . . . ?"

"I think he's got this, ah . . . you know, this Spanish thing . . . like only someone of Spanish heritage is good enough for his daughter."

"I thought it was *you* who didn't like *her*."

"Oh." Johnny sniffed, rubbed his nose. "She's nice. I guess. I mean, you know how pretty she is. But she dresses like, ah . . . what's the word? An odalisque."

"I don't know that."

"Like a concubine. Like she wants to be subservient. You know, fine, kid. Go sow your wild oats. But think twice before you get too serious. She's probably someone else's slave when you're not around. I mean, she could get free condoms right there in school, right?"

Mitch was terse. He made no pretense of agreement. "I think you're making too much of it."

"Um." Johnny shrugged. His head hurt. He did not want to engage in an argument. He wanted to plant a seed, a thought; wanted to try out the idea, the story. Mitch was his test audience. "Maybe," he said.

"They came to Aaron's funeral," Mitch said. "They couldn't have been nicer. The whole family. Especially Kim."

"Augh, maybe I am making too much of it." Johnny gritted his teeth, sighed, added, "But who didn't come? He was a wonderful kid. The whole town came. His thesis is great. I'm . . . finishing it."

"Yeah," Mitch said flatly. "I still can't . . . I haven't read . . ."

"You hear anything more about how . . ."

"I think they mistook him."

"Who?"

"I don't know. I don't know who they thought he was, but it has . . . Hilman, from the major crime squad . . . ? He thinks it has all the elements of a drug-related hit. The more I learn about this goddamn shit, the more pissed I am."

"Understandable."

"Did you read that stuff—drug use amongst teens has better than doubled in the last four years?"

"I knew—"

"Cocaine usage is up one hundred sixty-six percent. Marijuana use is up—"

"They were trying to make a political issue of—"

Mitch did not let Johnny finish his sentence. "Do you know why?"

"A number of reas—"

"Bullshit!" Mitch bullied Johnny into silence. "There's one fucken reason and only one fucken reason. Those cocksuckers at the top of the government . . . those gutless bastards who gutted . . . who absolutely emasculated the War on Drugs. There's a department known as the Office of National Drug Control Policy. Despite the fucking rhetoric, the fucking tears and wails about the tragedy, they chopped that budget by more than seventy-five percent. That's just for starters. Shame on those bastards. What kind of example do they set?"

"Well, they—"

"Bullshit!!" Mitch exploded. He was driving erratically. The car lurched left with each statement, swung right with each pause. "The example they set is tolerance for abuse! Reduced stigma for addiction! They've raised rehabilitation to a glorified seat. It's like it's born-again Christianity! Bullshit! It's not!"

"Whoa!" Johnny reared back as Mitch nearly rammed a car alongside them, the other driver swerving to a safe distance.

Mitch was oblivious. "What the fuck do they think they're goina get?!" His words were fast, hard, angry. "Reduced usage? Assholes. They're all assholes. I fucking hate all them fucking jerks. Like trying it is okay. Like experimenting is okay. Then if you get hooked, like it's a mental disorder. 'We'll pay for your therapy.' Fuck you!"

"Um." Johnny swallowed. His head hurt. His mouth tasted like dirt and dirty socks. What could he say? He had not seen Mitch so angry since Thanksgiving 1965.

"Pricks," Mitch raged. "They killed my son as much as if they pulled the trigger! Fuck em! Fuck loyalty to those scumbags! If I thought I could get away with it, I'd blow away half the motherfuckers—"

"Mitch!" Johnny grabbed the wheel, pulled the car back into their lane.

"Geez H. . . . !" Mitch pushed his hand away. Johnny sat back. In a conciliatory tone he said, "If . . . if you decide to do it . . . I'll go with you. But don't go and do—"

"Fuck you!" Mitch balled his right fist, cocked his arm as if ready to strike. "You skipped out before. You're not going to—"

"I didn't skip out!" The words shot out defensively. "I never got called up."

"Pu-che-ssshh!" Mitch spit in disgust.

For some time they rode on in silence. Johnny wanted to defend himself, almost blurted out, "At least you've still got your job, your salary. At least your wife's not . . ." But he did not, could not. He knew there was no comparison; knew, too, that the spillover of Mitch's anger, not cutbacks or downsizing, was threatening to subvert Mitch's position with Tripps. He did not know how to help appease his friend's anger. He had his own problems. His head throbbed.

He imagined himself being arrested, being escorted from the Tower, maybe in shackles. Then he thought to say, "Ya know, Jason and the team can't do it without Aaron any more than you could do it without me, or I could do it without you," but he knew that that wasn't any good, either. He wanted to empathize with Mitch; he wanted Mitch to get it out, felt he needed to get it out, felt Mitch had held it in too deep, had allowed it to fester too long; but this morning Johnny's head hurt, he didn't want to go in at all, and he wished that Mitch could empathize with him, too.

They crossed the dam, swung north, came to a near standstill in rush-hour congestion. Mitch's deep, slow burn streamed from him like the unstoppable flow of lava. "You may not understand this," he said harshly, "but what we're going through . . . we've gone through . . . a cultural revolution. Nobody calls it that, but America has changed as much in the past thirty or forty years as anything Mao or Pol Pot ever tried. We've changed more without programs of violence than they did with all their revolutionary policies. This is *not* your father's America."

"Yeah," Johnny shot at Mitch. "And it's not my grandfather's or your grandfather's America, either. And I hope some of it's been for the good."

"You think I'm goina say yes because I'm black."

"Yeah. Maybe."

"Fuck it. That change came a hundred . . . two hundred years ago. There's a big lag time from attitude change to full implementation. That's still not here. But the other changes . . . this cultural revolution of the last fifty years . . . it's undermining everything. The ramifications are going to explode on our kids. Those that survive. Aaron . . ."

" 'Atlas Can No Longer Shrug,' " Johnny said.

Mitch snorted, bit his lip, muttered, "That's his paper . . . That . . ." Mitch paused, swallowed. "Is it any good?"

"It's terrific," Johnny answered. "I wanta get it published."

Mitch clamped his jaw shut. Energy seemed to ooze out, to flow from his every pore; he seemed to deflate where he sat behind the steering wheel in the car in the stalled traffic. The skin below his eyes puffed, sagged. His jowls hung. Lifelessly he said, "You've really been going through those files."

"Yep," Johnny said. It was better to talk about Aaron this way.

"He worked on it all summer," Mitch said softly. "I didn't pay any attention." Mitch squeezed the wheel hard, held on. He was on the verge of tears but he held them in. "McMillian . . ." Mitch whispered. Again he swallowed. "Aaron had McMillian . . . had a lot of McMillian's notes. You know McMillian?"

"Umm. Yeah."

"They got pretty close . . . with . . . Aaron doing that legislative internship. McMillian kind of guided him. Kind of was his mentor. Did you know he'd done some pretty extensive writing? Academic stuff. On Viet-Nam. Aaron used McMillian's stuff as his paradigm."

Johnny nodded. His head felt a little better.

JULIA MANEUVERED HER Infiniti south through the heavy traffic on Route 86. She too had a hangover. After the Valpolicella and Strega, they'd made espresso and laced it with Benedictine. Rocco had moved to an overstuffed chair in the living room and had passed into almost catatonic sleep; Robbie and Nicco had joined him on the sofa; Jenny and Jason had gone to their rooms; Todd, now beside her in the passenger seat, had stayed at the table. He too was in pain. They barely spoke.

It was eight-twenty. The sun had been burning the mist from the lake for nearly an hour but had made little progress. At the Village of South Lake Julia glanced across, past Todd, toward the private cove where Rod Nightingale's cottage overlooked the brush and the beach. In their reds, yellows, oranges and many shades of lingering green, trees blocked her view. Yet . . . she felt . . . She wasn't sure. Attraction, revulsion, confusion.

She felt nauseated. "Did your father give you any money?" Julia asked.

"A hundred dollars," Todd answered lethargically. He too was looking out the window toward the lake, the rising mist, the colorful trees.

Again Julia glanced over. What if? she thought. Then she thought of Johnny, of their scene last night. "You didn't tell me," he'd growled. They'd been in bed only a minute and she'd felt amorous. "I'm sure I did," she'd whispered. She'd run her foot over his, a sign of willingness that they'd developed over the years. He hadn't responded but had sneered, "You watched them butt-fuck?!" She'd gotten defensive; he'd gotten angry; finally she'd responded, "What do you fucking want me to say? I saw Marvin with his cock up Harry's ass! Okay? Yes I did! Or that Harry's got the biggest dick I've ever seen! You want more details?!" And she'd told him more; told him things she didn't even realize she'd seen but now became aware of in the retelling.

"Your father," Julia said to Todd, "still thinks that's a lot of money."

"Um," Todd responded. "He said he'd send me some more."

"You'd better take another hundred from my purse. You can't go to St. Louis and then to Madison without anything in your pockets."

"Grandpa gave me some money, too."

"Oh? How much?"

"Twenty."

"That was nice of him."

"Yeah."

"We thought you were going to be home longer. I imagine your grandfather's pretty disappointed."

"I told Eileen I'd come and meet her folks."

"You should have told us before . . ." Julia sighed. "I mean, you didn't have to come home for just one day. We could have waited until Thanksgiving. You could have told us on the phone and then gone straight to St. Louis."

"I wanted to tell you in person. And Eileen wanted to tell her folks."

Julia released the steering wheel with one hand, massaged her forehead. *Tell you in person,* she thought. Shit! If I'd fucked Rod, everything'd be different. Everything. Or if I'd never gotten into that whole mess. The things I've seen! Things I could tell if . . . if . . . Rod and me . . . Our posture wasn't exactly businesslike. Julia felt trapped, felt as if she were seeing the trap more clearly now than ever. They make you feel like a whore, she thought. Why do men always want to make women feel like whores? She thought of a paraphrased adage of General George Patton that she'd seen, she did not know where—"The courageous woman is the woman who forces herself, despite her fears, to carry on." Carry on, she thought. To Todd she said, "And when are we going to meet this Eileen?"

"Maybe we could fly back for Christmas break."

"Umm. That would be nice. Todd? I'm still confused. She goes to school in . . . ?"

"St. Charles. I met her when she came up to visit a friend of hers from high school."

"Aren't there enough girls in Madison? When we visited, I thought the school had the most beautiful—"

"Oh," Todd said, "there's lots of girls. Pretty girls. Neat chicks. But it's really hard to . . . I mean, you've got to follow all these procedures or you'll be charged with sexual harassment and be expelled. There's even a rumor about a secret society that purposely sets guys up to get them expelled."

"Some probably deserve it. Date rape is no—"

"No. No. It's not that. It's not like they target somebody who's done something to one of their friends. It's more like a sport."

"A sport! They can't—"

"Mom, school's different now . . . It's really no different than what you went through at Gallina. With some professors you've even got to be ultra-politically correct just to get a passing grade."

"Politically correct, Todd? You do understand why things need to be politically correct, don't you? That's become something to attack, but really, most of the time, you can drop the 'politically.' When there are abuses . . ."

"It's relativism, Mom. That's what gets me. Anything can be justified if it serves some PC cause. If you can sell it as multicultural, you can lynch people."

"It can't be that bad!"

"Well . . . I . . . Honesty is no longer a concept anyone believes in. There's no such thing as truth."

The view at the dam interrupted the stumbling flow of their conversation. Julia and Todd stared southwest, down the valley of the Wampahwaug River. The river could not be seen; the valley was filled with thick marshmallow-fluff clouds to a level where the vapor spilled over the banks of the ridges; above, the sky was cloudless and the low mist refracted the sun, randomly splashing hundreds of small rainbows into crevices and onto rumples.

"Oh!" Julia exclaimed. "Isn't that wonderful!"

"I wish . . ." Todd began, but he did not finish his sentence aloud.

F.X. MCMILLIAN HELD the paper with both hands, his hands resting on his desk. He'd taken the paper from Michael Verdeen during fourth period, had not looked at it until classes changed. In the middle of the page there was a rumpled human figure in baggy clothes, a cigar in one hand, the head bent at a right angle to the body, a ring in one ear, the entire head in a smudge of graphite—perhaps a cloud. The drawing was not a work of art, not a work of street art, but neither was it childish. If anything, to McMillian, the sketch was raw. Above the figure, in a cartoonlike balloon, was printed, "I'm high like an eagle. Fuck the Bitch ass cop that pull out gloks and kill my people."

McMillian did not know what, or how much, to make of it. He had reported to the police—had seen it as his duty—the argument between Williams and Verdeen, exactly as he'd reported the scuffle between Williams and Juarez from Lakeport, and had told Hilman about the latest fight between Panuzio and Verdeen. Still, McMillian liked Verdeen. Verdeen was smart, not just street-smart but intelligent. He was a good student, an enthusiastic and disciplined researcher, a decent wordsmith. When he wanted to be. To McMillian it was a matter of focus, or misfocus. "Michael," he'd told him, "you can be so much more than this. If all your actions are reactions to things you dislike, the things you dislike control you. Instead of negative reaction, why not positive action?" McMillian saw no impact, yet he'd been teaching long enough to know that words, thoughts, ideas sometimes did not gel, sometimes gelled weeks, months, years later.

A few days after his encouragement, Michael Verdeen had answered him with a quote from James Baldwin's *The Fire Next Time*: " 'This innocent country set you down in a ghetto in which, in fact, it intended that you should perish . . . You were born where you were born and faced the future that you faced because you were black and for no other reason . . . You were born into a society which spelled out with brutal clarity . . . that you were a worthless human being.' "

McMillian had responded, "Are you worthless?"

"As I'm told," Verdeen had countered.

"Your self-image and your world view, Michael, control—"

"Save it for class."

Now McMillian stared at the paper, shook his head ever so slightly. Should he confront Michael? Should he call Hilman, report this new incident? As he stared his hands tightened, crumpled the edges of the page. If Michael did do it . . . McMillian thought. If he had nothing to do with it . . . McMillian did not finish either thought but instead asked himself, How do I help this young man?

Slowly McMillian crushed the page into a ball. He stood, tossed the ball up, played it with the outside of his right foot as if it were a hacky-sack, knocked it into the trash.

JEFF KURJIAKA, THE East Lake keeper, tossed the ball back to Panuzio. Jason flicked it with the outside of his right foot, let it bounce, then volleyed it back at the far post. Kurjiaka dove, snagged it out of the air, landed on his side, smothered the ball against his chest.

On the field other East Lake players were in triangles, knocking the ball around, warming up. Compari, Miller, Sarrazin and Burke were in a defensive diamond, clearing the ball away from imaginary pressure, first from one side, then the other. The Kennedy High Kodiaks had not yet arrived. It was sixty-six degrees; the sun was strong, the sky cloudless; a slight breeze came from the north—an absolutely perfect game day, especially welcomed after the thunderstorms of the previous week which had postponed play and threatened to lengthen the season.

Again Panuzio volleyed the ball back at goal. It sailed high and wide, and Kurjiaka groused, "On goal, man. Start focusing. Concentrate!"

"Sorry," Jason called. Kurjiaka trotted out behind the net to retrieve the ball. *Sorry, motherfucker,* Jason thought. He was not aiming the barb at the keeper but at himself. One sorry fucken jerk, he thought. What is this?! Her old man doesn't like me?! What the fuck? I thought he . . .

"We need—" Jason looked up to see McMillian only a few steps away. "—a strong game from you today, Panuzio."

Jason nodded, did not respond verbally.

"A real strong game," F.X. said. "We tied this team two weeks ago. We're better now. We've made our adjustments. K.W.Y.G. it, Panuzio." He pronounced the acronym "quig."

Again Jason nodded. McMillian moved on toward the goalkeeper. That's the problem, Jason thought. I don't know where I'm going. I don't . . . His thoughts jumped to his brother, Todd, to Todd's comments before Jason left for school this morning. "You're like Dad," Todd had said. "You're the athlete in the family. I could never do that stuff." Like Dad! Jason had never thought of himself as being "like Dad." I'm nothing like . . .

McMillian came back from the goal, heading out toward midfield. It was his habit to talk to each player individually before every game. As he passed Panuzio he looked him in the eyes. Then he motioned him close. Jason approached. "Look at that." McMillian indicated an empty area off the field.

"At what?" Jason didn't see anything unusual.

"Look at the leaves," McMillian said. A few small, brown leaves were being blown by the breeze. "They look like skittish mice tiptoeing across the grass, don't they?"

Before Jason could answer, McMillian walked on. Jason stared at his back, glanced back at the leaves. His brow furrowed in question. Then he chuckled. He turned, saw Kim and Martina at the edge of a group of loitering students; saw Chuck Zinsser's and Tim London's parents; noted that his father was not there; knew that Mr. Williams no longer came.

The Kennedy High bus arrived, the players disembarked, but the Kodiaks did not come to the field, did not begin their warm-ups, did not have a pregame talk. They sat or stood in twos and threes, some near the field, others against the trees that separated the field from the subdivision on Split Rock Hill. McMillian glanced but did not eye them. He knew the coach, Elmer Drapins, did not care for him, for his style. Indeed, McMillian was worried. There was not a white player on Drapins' team—rumor saying Drapins' wouldn't have one. There were no Hispanics, no Native Americans, no Asians. Twice in the past two years Drapins had had games suspended because of racial incidents. His players were known to purposely provoke opponents into trash talk that would get them ejected. Twice in the past seven years his teams had been disqualified and suspended for using illegal players—once for having brought in two college players, posing them as Kennedy High students.

"Bring it in," McMillian called. His own players had warmed up with two slow laps followed by stretches, passing drills, some 3 v. 1 and finally cross-field sprints. "Gentlemen," McMillian said. "We've been here before. We know this team. We know their tactics. They're fast. They're good size. They're physical. We've been known to be physical, too, from what I've heard. That's the refs' problem. Let them handle it.

"Gentlemen," McMillian continued, "we win as a team; we lose as a team. No one individual can win this game by himself. And if anyone makes a mistake, it usually happens because two other mistakes were made before that. Don't get down on your teammates. Know where you're going, gentlemen. Know how you're going to get there. That's always the key. Be thinking three, four, five passes ahead. When you sprint, be absolutely explosive. Everything you have. Right, Miro?"

"Yeah."

"When you jog, jog. Don't confuse the two. Right, Panuzio?"

"Yeah."

Behind the cluster of East Lake Elks, the Kennedy Kodiaks quietly took their positions on the field. In place, as if to music, they began to juke, to dance and bounce, jiving to a beat they alone seemed to hear, juking and leaping in perfect coordination.

"What the hello is that?" Victor Santoro, the vice principal, blurted from behind the Elks' bench. Then, quickly, he covered his mouth. Panuzio and his teammates trotted into position. Santarelli, eyeing the Kodiaks, began to laugh but it was a nervous laugh. Crnecki, Samadhi and London, the Elk forwards, bounced cynically, defiantly, with their opponents. Two referees took their places diagonally—one in each half of the field—using a scholastic system that did not necessitate linesmen.

A whistle started the game. Quickly the Kodiaks were in control, passing back, swinging the ball, then forward, then back, square, then a deep, angular, penetrating ball between and behind Elk defenders Miro Sarrazin and Dan "Bucky" Burke. Both Kodiak wings sprinted toward the space, easily outsprinting all but Paul Compari, the Elk sweeper, who just beat the Kodiak wing and blasted the ball up the touchline, across midfield, toward London, who lined himself up, waited for the projectile, only to have a Kodiak fullback step in front of him, smack the ball in the air with his head, send it diagonally up and across.

"Good ball," Drapins called. "Push up."

McMillian said nothing, as was his habit.

The Kodiaks worked the ball quickly to within twenty yards of the goal, pulled it back, swung it, swung it back. Panuzio sensed the back-swing, stepped in as three Kodiaks converged. He had angle, position, a fraction of a second, but before he could play the ball he felt an incredible, fist-sized stabbing pain in his back, felt all air rush from his lungs. He collapsed. The Kodiak center mid collected the ball on his chest, ran through, forcing it before him. The ball bounced once, the player still coming forward volleyed it hard, low. "Geez!" McMillian shouted to the ref. "You gotta call—"

"KEEP!" Kurjiaka's voice was the loudest on the field. Bucky stabbed to stop the ball, caught just enough to deflect it. Kurjiaka's lightning reflexes were quick enough to get his left-hand fingertips to the sphere, not quick enough to keep it from rippling the net.

"GOAL!" Drapins imitated the Spanish announcers on TV. "GOAL! GOAL!" His arms waved wildly.

"You gotta call that!" McMillian called at the referee. Panuzio still was not up but was in a fetal position, on his knees, his face in the dirt.

"GOAL!" Drapins yelled again; yelled, McMillian was certain, to distract the ref.

Panuzio rose to his elbows, his forehead still on the field. One referee signaled the okay for McMillian to come onto the field to check his player and McMillian jogged out. Panuzio lifted his head a few inches. "Are you okay?" his coach asked. Panuzio did not speak but panted, his breath just returning. "I saw that rabbit punch clear as . . . I can't believe one of these guys didn't call it! Lie down. Just take it easy. Catch your . . ."

Jason pushed his torso up, rose to one knee, took a deep breath. His face was red. Perspiration beaded his forehead. A clump of grass and mud clung to his chin, mouth. He spit, rose. McMillian put his arm around him to help him from the field. On the sideline East Lake spectators applauded. Panuzio pushed McMillian away.

"You sure you're okay?" McMillian asked.

Panuzio grunted. The Elks kicked off. Play resumed.

Ciara DeLauro and Marcia Radkowski crossed the parking lot, came down the hill to the sidelines. Ciara had coerced Marcia into coming to the game, believing that if she saw positive activity it might break her melancholy.

"Hi, Kim. Hi, Martina." Ciara smiled.

"Hi, Mrs. DeLauro." Kim smiled back. "Miss Radkowski."

Martina nodded to Ciara but did not make an utterance, did not acknowledge Marcia Radkowski.

"How's the game going?" Ciara asked.

"We're down one nothing," Kim answered. "They scored in like the third minute. But it's been a lot more even since then. This is kind of a dirty team. First Jason got hurt. Then Masad."

"Umm." Ciara and Marcia walked on, talked to a few other students, to a few parents, found a spot on the sideline down opposite the Kodiak penalty box where they could stand alone and talk quietly. On the field things seemed to be heating up and Ciara heard F.X. McMillian, uncharacteristically, yelling at a referee, saw him, uncharacteristically, fling his clipboard at the bench.

"Maybe this wasn't the best game to come to," Ciara said softly.

"I can't stop thinking about him, Chi-chi. I don't think this is going to make it any better."

"Quite a few of the students here are yours. I know you have Jeff, Miro and Jason. And, of course, Kim. And there's Erin O'Malley and—"

"Did I tell you, she's going to be my Desdemona?"

"No. Ah . . . Marcia, did Charlene okay *Othello*? I'm not sure how appropr—"

"I asked her if we could do a Shakespearean. She was all for it."

"Does she know *Othello*?"

Marcia reared back in dramatic mock surprise. "I couldn't ask her that!" She beamed. "Could I?"

"It's nice to see you smile," Ciara said. "There's so much good here. Even the sun's cooperating today."

"If Aaron were here," Marcia said, "I'd shower him with hugs and kisses. I can't tell you how much I miss him. Especially on days like this. How much I loved him."

"You told me about the kiss," Ciara said. It embarrassed her. She didn't know why.

"I loved him, Chi-chi. I really loved him. That time when we kissed . . . we embraced. I told him, 'Aaron, we can't do this.' I said, 'I'd like to. I really like you.' God, Chi-chi, he was so sexy. But I told him, 'We can't.

Not until you're out of school.' Chi, I had a crush on him. I can't deny that anymore. And he found me sexy, too. I guess we kissed more than once."

"Marcia!"

"I know." Marcia gazed onto the grass of the field before her, saw nothing. She clasped her hands before her almost as if in prayer, quoted, " 'O, banish me, my lord, but kill me not!' " Then she seemed to return to the present. "Chi, I can't watch this."

On the field the game was becoming brutal. Neither referee made any calls, not even signaling "advantage—play on," which would indicate that they'd seen an infraction by a defender but did not want to stop the player with the ball. Shots and punches were being thrown off the ball; swearing could be heard from both sides; precise ball movement gave way to kick and run and smash into whomever was nearby; and that gave way to Panuzio and many of his teammates playing react and chase versus anticipate and position. At midfield Chuck Zinsser tapped the Kodiak player he was marking. The ball was on the far side. The player looked at him, grinned slightly. "I'm not gettin into this," Zinsser said.

"Me neither, man," the player replied.

"Yeah," Zinsser said. "I like playin. Not fightin. That isn't soccer."

"We got three guys get into it ev-rah game," the Kodiak said. "I hate that."

"Yeah," Zinsser agreed. He put out his hand.

Quickly the Kodiak player grabbed it, shook it. "You don't break mah leg, man," he said, "I don't break yours."

The ball came across the field toward them. They banged shoulders, leaped, fair play. Panuzio looped back to cover his teammate. Zinsser knocked the ball with his head toward Samadhi. The Kodiak sweeper, a large man with a thick mustache and goatee, beat the Elk forward, played the ball deep to his right wing, who beat Miller. Compari, the Elk sweeper, was caught too far upfield. Sarrazin and Burke took up chase too late. The Kodiak wing was at full bore, one on one with Kurjiaka. From the opposite side, Panuzio angled in, closed the distance, slid, missed the ball with his foot but caught it with his knee. The wing hit Panuzio, tripped, flew through the air, slammed onto the near-grassless patch before the goal. He stayed down. From the far end, the ref blew his whistle, but the near ref waved it off, indicated a goal kick.

"C'mon, Ref!" Drapins screamed.

"Oooooo!" Long, loud, spewed from spectators.

"You fucken idiot!" A Kodiak player cursed the ref.

"Nice play," Investigator Tom Hilman called. "Good defense." He'd just arrived, had not seen earlier incidents. No one paid him much heed. He'd become a regular; seemed to be a soccer junkie.

The Kodiak wing popped up as Kurjiaka teed up the ball. The referee checked his watch, blew his whistle ending the first half. Drapins cursed.

"Nice play, Jason." McMillian grabbed his shirt at the shoulder, pulled, forced Jason to look at him. "Your back okay?"

"Yeah. Fine."

"Then stop playin stupid! You and Compari get this team out there behind the bench. I got something to say."

The Elks moved to an isolated spot beyond spectator or official hearing. Players grouched openly, loudly, about opponent play, about lack of effort by teammates, mostly about the horrendous and seemingly blind referees. They drank from water bottles, poured water on their heads, spit it on the ground, shoved each other. "Gentlemen," McMillian whispered. Players turned. "Gentlemen," he said even more quietly. Panuzio nudged Burke to pay attention. "Once upon a time—" McMillian's voice was barely audible, forcing players to be silent, still "—I was part of an army that was superior to the opposition. We were superior technically and tactically. We won nearly every encounter, nearly, if you like, every one-on-one contact. Yet our strategy was wrong and, as you know, we lost the game."

Jeff Duncan, a sophomore backup midfielder, guffawed. He was not accustomed to McMillian's convoluted talks, had no idea where he was going or what he was talking about. Compari punched him. He bit his lip.

"It is no different, gentlemen," McMillian continued, "for you, here, today. You are the best athletes. You are stronger, faster and have better technical abilities than any team in the state."

"These guys are pretty fast, Coach," Burke injected.

"Yes, they are," McMillian agreed. "But we're quicker. Still, if we play stupid . . . if we play with poor strategy, if we continuously bang the ball forward, we will lose. A smart team with good strategy will beat a strong team of better athletes with poor strategy every time. No one, however, beats the team with the best athletes, the best technical abilities, the best tactics AND the best strategy. That combination always wins. We must put ourselves first in a position where we are beyond losing; then into a position to win. Panuzio, *capisce?*"

"Yeah."

"Paul? Everybody?"

"Yeah."

"All right, here's what we're going to do . . ."

Just before the Elks took the field for the second half, McMillian pulled Panuzio aside. "I need you to take charge," he said. "You understand what we want?"

"Um-hmm. Work it . . ."

"Risk it, Jason. Any goal you go after in a tentative manner, in life or in a game, you will not achieve."

Jason's forehead wrinkled.

"Take the gamble," McMillian whispered. His words accelerated, intensified, yet his volume remained low. "Commit yourself completely. Attack forcefully, with passion, with perseverance. Mass your forces. Mass your physical and mental forces on your objective. You've got nothing to lose. Play smart, not angry. Anger blocks your brain and saps your energy. Don't seek revenge. Seek your goals."

"Yeah," Jason answered.

McMillian sensed he'd said too much, that he'd thrown out too many ideas to be assimilated, internalized. "Jason! Just take charge."

From the moment the whistle sounded, starting the second half, violence on the field escalated. Still the referees made no calls. "Work it," McMillian yelled to his team. "Keep-away!"

The Elks attempted to play wide, to play across. Panuzio, at center mid, was key. He sent balls to the touchlines, lofted balls to the corners, directed play as much as possible by distributing to undefended space.

Drapins, the Kennedy coach, became more and more frustrated. "Settle it, Brian. You gotta settle it," he shouted at his far side half. "Step back," he yelled at his fulls. "Fall back!" Then, in rage, "You gotta step up. What the . . . Brian! Brian! Step up! Settle the goddamn ball! What the hell's the matter with you?! My grandmother coulda played that ball! What are you guys doin ta me?! Ted! Don't you dare let him by. If he gets by you . . ." Ted, Kennedy's wild-haired, goateed stopper, stopped in midplay. He planted his fists on his hips, sneered at Drapins. Drapins ignored him.

The Kodiaks adjusted, understood the change in Elk tactics, played East Lake's passing lanes with greater depth, covered the wide men with greater certainty. The momentum shifted. Again the Kodiaks took the initiative and Elk play became reactive, Sarrazin, Miller, Burke and Compari making desperation play after desperation play, running, chasing, catching breakaway wings or overlapping halves at the last second. They became exhausted from the streaks, the sprints. Exhaustion led to demoralization, which caused them to react slower, anticipate less. No one would say it, just as no one had said it during the past month, but all knew it, thought it, had thought it for a month. *If Aaron were in the middle, we'd be in control. The game would be different.*

"Jason!"

Panuzio's eyes flicked to McMillian. Immediately he realized he'd come nearly to the sideline while chasing the last play.

"Balance the field. Play the angles."

The ball sailed to the near-side Kodiak corner, in Kodiak control. As Jason turned he huffed out in exasperation, "These guys *are* fast."

"Not as fast as the ball," McMillian called. "Mass your forces. Seek goals."

At midfield Jason was knocked to the ground by the Kodiak sweeper who overlapped his stopper. No call. Panuzio rose, spat. "That's fuckin it!" he seethed. He took up chase. The Kodiak center forward shielded the ball from Compari, knocked it back to his unmarked sweeper. The big man collected it, started to the left, pulled it back, continued left, cocked his leg to shoot. Jason slid under his foot, knocked the ball to Miller who banged it up to Crnecki. Both refs, eyes on the ball, moved upfield with the play. Panuzio popped up, upended the Kodiak, did not look back. The playing was furious. Samadhi killed the ball in the middle of the Kodiak box, dumped it to London who brought it toward the corner but was flattened. No call. The defender played the ball to the touchline, then as Panuzio swiped, missed, then flattened the defender with a forearm to the chin. Jason leaped up, chased, made space, got open. Zinsser knocked one on the carpet to him. Panuzio one-touch flicked it to Crnecki who shot. A defender banged Panuzio in the back. Jason elbowed him in the ribs, spun on him, drove him into the ground, fell on him, hissed, "I got a bayonet goin stick through yer throat." The Kodiak keeper clutched the ball, punted it beyond midfield.

"I know what he doin out there," Martina said to Kim. "He gone mental. He snapped. Happen to me in lotsa games. He flyin. Refs aint callin shit. Look at this. He beatin that jerk who punched him. Look it. He beatin im everah time now. And that Jay-boy a yours, he enjoyin it. He ain't carin bout nothin cept toastin that toad. Cept takin his revenge. Oooo! He a nasty. I been there. You best watch yourself with that boy. He goin be another bad-ass. Like his old man in your old man's store, huh? Maybe goin be another Aaron."

"Martina!" Kim was shocked at Jason's play but somehow, with the game out of control, it seemed necessary. "Martina, you're remorseless! And I don't really know what happened in the store—"

"What I got to be sorry bout?"

"I didn't mean it that way," Kim said.

"Well, girl. I ain't sorry. Shee-it! I'd knock their heads off, too, they doin that ta me."

"Well, I . . . You still didn't answer me."

"You think I should, huh?"

"Yes," Kim said. "I do. I think you should tell them."

"Maybe I will."

"Aliena *will* be their grandchild."

"You don't say nothin, girl. If I want, when I want, I'll do my own talkin."

Again the play is back and forth and hard, and people are down. Again the Elks push it into the Kodiak box. A Kennedy fullback whacks the ball hard, a clearing shot. It does not rise but comes out low like a ground-hugging missile skimming the grass past the eighteen, then touching, skipping up. Jason, his eyes focused on the ball, planted his left foot to the side of the trajectory, his right foot, leg behind, cocked like a trigger, then firing, catching the ball six inches above the turf, his eyes still on the sweet spot, the ball exploding back as if shot from a howitzer, spinning, swerving up left, then like a baseball pitch, breaking, dropping right, down, around the Kodiak keeper, rippling the net.

"No way!" Drapins screamed. "No friggin way. Offsides."

The refs ignored the screams, the cheers, indicated an Elk goal. Santarelli was first to Panuzio, lifted him. Others converged, high-fived him, each other, then trotted into position for the kickoff. There was ten minutes playing time left. The score was tied 1–1.

Now both teams settled into concentrated attacks, possession play, counterattacks. Play oscillated from fast, hard and frenzied to slow and methodical; from numbers-up surges and fast breaks to keep-away play. There was no oscillation of the pushing, shoving, tripping; the half dozen players who had been throwing cheap shots all game continued to do so. There were no calls. Now Jason exalted in the escalation of violence. He got hit, hit back harder. He was cussed, he cussed back viciously. He added invective, threats.

With only a minute to go a deep pass bananaed to the Kodiak right wing and both teams rushed into the Elk defensive third, the sweeper again overlapping, advancing, blasting a cross from the wing. Kurjiaka extended one arm, the ball smacked his glove, seemed to stick to that one outstretched hand. He curled the arm down, pulled the ball in, crashed to the ground as a Kodiak player attempted to kick it from his grasp. Voices: "Whoa! Great save! Yeah!" Immediately Kurjiaka rebounded, sensed the shape of the field, the Kodiak overload in close, three of his Elk teammates alone by midfield. Kurjiaka launched a long punt beyond London on the right touchline as other Elks sprinted to take advantage of the numbers-up and Kodiaks sprinted to recover and defend. London brought the ball to the corner, crossed it just before the Kodiak sweeper took him down. No call. The ball sailed high, beyond the far post. Crnecki leaped, attempted to head it in behind the keeper, misplayed it. The ball bounded up, out toward the center of the box where Panuzio was racing forward. Jason leaped high, his head above the ball, eyes locked on the sphere, banging it down with his forehead into the near corner as the keeper attempted to recover from chasing the cross and missed header.

The Kodiaks were stunned. They had expected the game to be easy. Coach Drapins furiously shoved one of his own players. As the whistle blew signaling the game's end, he stormed from the sideline, shoved McMillian, refused to shake his hand. Bickering and more shoving erupted on the field, and one ref finally stepped in to separate two opposing players. The air seemed foul. Then the player who'd talked to Zinsser in the first half found him, grasped his arms, congratulated him. Zinsser grasped, squeezed back. "You played a really good game, man," Zinsser said.

"You too. We thought you gonna be pushovers. Who's that dude?"

"Him? Panuzio. He used ta be a fullback."

"Shit, man, he's bad. One crazy fucker. Bad as Drapins' hatchet men."

"I've never seen him play like that. He did go kinda crazy."

"Yer refs, man, they suck."

"Yeah. I thought so, too. You guys have a good season."

"You too, man."

On the walk to the locker room the Elks were not loud, were not boisterous. They'd played so hard—had elevated their game to a level it had never reached before, even with Aaron Williams, because with Aaron Williams the team had not needed to play so hard, so well, so much together, to win—they were in a new zone, assimilating a new identity.

For Jason, the game was a new experience. He had never been the hero before. He grinned wildly, uncontrollably—a smile that refused to be subdued. He felt an elation in his heart he had never before known, comparable only to the first time he'd kissed Kim, and this feeling, in some indescribable way, was beyond that, different anyway, a feeling of power, or accomplishment, a feeling of having achieved the impossible.

Johnny Panuzio sat in his car, in the parking lot overlooking the field. He had arrived with only a few minutes to play, in time to catch the pushing and shoving, the Elks' second goal, the spectators breaking into cheers. From the angle and distance he did not realize that it was Jason who'd scored. But then he did see Jason being mobbed by his teammates, being high-fived and low-fived and slapped silly, and he realized they'd won, that Jason had just scored the winning goal, and he too felt elated, yet he felt confused. He heard the receding spectators talking about the "ugly win" for the Elks, about Jason having been fouled and his fouling in return; about retaliation and counterretaliation and poor officiating. Jason, amid a group of Elks, passed his father's car without seeing Johnny, and Johnny, tentative, unsure, did not get out, did not go to his son. Instead he sat hunched, deflated, his left hand kneading his right. Jason, he thought, but the thought would not congeal. Jason had won without . . . unlike me . . . or Mitch . . . All the years . . . Johnny-panni confused . . . falling . . . miserable . . . tumbling . . .

He sees him. Outside it is crisp, cold, bright. Inside it is hot, stuffy; the lights are subdued; the fragrances from tiers and heaps of arrangements are overpowering. Johnny is nauseated. The funeral director—he is the same man who buried Richard seven months earlier, a friend of the family's—has been calling people to their cars, by name for nearly half an hour, yet rows and rows are still occupied.

Johnny is uncomfortable. His suit is tight, too tight. He's grown, added muscle. He is very strong. The muscles of his arms tax the wool fabric of the sleeves and he can barely flex. He feels sporadic droplets of sweat run from his armpits, trickle down until they hit his shirt where the suit presses it to his side. The sensation simultaneously tickles, annoys.

"Mr. and Mrs. James Allegrezza," the director says piously.

An old couple rises, shuffles to the open coffin. She kneels, crosses herself; he stands behind, looks upon his friend of these many years. The woman stands and the couple comes to where Nonna sits in the front row. To one side of her is Uncle John, her oldest son; to the other, Aunt Santina, Tina, the crazy one, the only unmarried daughter. It is the sixty-fifth year of her marriage. Nonna has seven children, twenty-three grandchildren. All are in attendance with the exception of Uncle Carlo and cousin Richard.

Mrs. Allegrezza puts her hands together, brings them to her lips, bows, cries, addresses Nonna by her first name, "Ercola . . . il bèllo è . . . Il Padrone è . . ." She cannot continue and Nonna grabs her hands to comfort her, but Nonna does not look at the woman, nor at her husband behind her. Johnny can tell she is aware that the funeral is behind schedule because of the near thousand people in attendance, is aware that the business of burying Il Padrone must proceed in a timely fashion for the ceremony to be dignified.

Johnny stands at the back of the viewing room with cousins Louis, Jimmy, Tony, Santo and Henry. They are the pallbearers; are dressed in dark suits, white shirts, black ties, gray cotton gloves. Except Louis. He is clothed in an army dress uniform with first sergeant insignias. He stands ramrod-straight. The others are more relaxed. Except Johnny. Johnny-panni cannot relax. He . . . He is thinking, feeling . . . I don't want to be in a funeral parlour. I want to be outside on this beautiful day, this Saturday after Thanksgiving; this morning when I should be on the field with Mitch Williams and our teammates. How badly he wants to play in this game, this last game of his senior year, this last game of his football career. Yet to be a pallbearer for Grandpa, for Il Padrone, it is not a request but a family order, and Johnny has complied.

Finally there is only Ercola, her children and their spouses, the funeral director and his assistants, and the pallbearers. The director motions the pallbearers forward. As they advance he gently tells John and Rocco, who are *holding, guiding their mother, "It is time." An assistant takes the flower arrangement with the wide white ribbon and golden word* PAPA *from the foot of the casket. He prepares to close the top half but John wants to touch his father's hand one last time and now Ercola shrieks, wails. She is shaking uncontrollably and her grief touches off Johnny's grief and tears come to his eyes, and Rocco and John, with Sal and Carmela, guide their mother to the door, to the long black limousine awaiting the family.*

A frenzy of activity erupts within the parlour as the director and his assistants close the casket, direct the pallbearers to form a line to pass the flower baskets, hangings, wreaths, out the back to the men and the truck that will bring them to the cemetery and arrange them about the gravesite while Giovanni Panuzio's body is blessed during a mass of Christian burial at Holy Rosary.

The stone stairs to the old church are steep, worn, slippery. Johnny is at the left rear of the casket. The box is matte-finished silver or pewter; the handles are subdued brushed brass. He had expected the handle to feel cold even through the gray gloves, but the handle feels warm, almost hot, and very smooth which makes it difficult to get a good grip. The box is heavier than he'd expected, or, he thinks, perhaps Henry or Jimmy is not carrying his share. In his leather-soled shoes Johnny finds the footing tricky and he, as strong as he is, as strong as he has become, he is afraid he might drop his grandfather.

Very quickly they are in the vestibule and the casket is placed on rollers and covered with a white and gold cloth with a red cross, which reminds him . . . reminds me of drawings I've seen in Ivanhoe, *or* Canterbury Tales, *or . . . A middle-aged priest in purple vestments greets the procession. "The grace and peace of God our Father and the Lord Jesus Christ be with you."*

The funeral director leads the response and the pallbearers chime in, "And also with you."

"Praise be to God, the Father of our Lord Jesus Christ, the Father of mercies . . ."

Johnny's mind wanders. Behind them the doors are still open and a cold wind circles the back of his neck and dries his earlier perspiration and makes him cold. The sun behind is bright, the interior is dim; the contrast makes it difficult to see beyond the priest.

". . . enables us to comfort those who are in trouble, with the same consolation we have received from Him.

"Blessed be God . . ."

From a small gold pail the priest pulls what to Johnny looks like a golden drumstick, like a baked and basted Thanksgiving turkey leg. The priest flicks it over the casket and sprinkles of holy water fly. A drop hits Johnny's fore-

head. "I bless the body of Giovanni Baptiste Michelangelo Panuzio, with the holy water that recalls his baptism . . ."

Me?! Oh . . . him. Nonno is dead. He . . . I . . . What a year, I am thinking. What a season. Nine en Oh! Nine en Oh because of the Dynamic Scoring Duo, Williams and Panuzio, Salt and Pepper, and their Lakeport High Laker teammates. All culminating in the Class LL Championship game 10:30 A.M., Thanksgiving weekend Saturday, 1965. In ninety goddamned minutes!

Immediately Johnny feels guilty for thinking goddamn *in church and he . . . I reconstruct the thought:* goll-dang minutes!

But what a year! Panuzio from his left back slot rushing for ten TDs, receiving for three, adding six points-after; and Mitch Williams from the right having run for twelve, caught one. The coach had put in three new plays for each, two each passes from Butch Capotte, and one each pitches from Capotte to the half and passes from the half to the weakside half streaking—Johnny to Mitch, Mitch to Johnny. What a game it was going to be! What a game! Even better than last week's.

". . . Lord hear our prayer and be merciful to Your son Giovanni, whom You have called from this life. Welcome him into the company of Your saints, in the kingdom . . ." Call me from my damn life, too! This is my life! This! Today! Why do you have to be buried today?

The procession moves into the cavernous, dank belly of the church. Johnny feels the eyes of all the people on him and on his cousins and he stands straight, attempts to emulate Louis as they bring the casket to the altar and the pallbearers take their seats in the second pew on the left and Zi Carmela's voice comes from the choir, "O God, our help in ages past, Our hope for years to come, Safe shelter while our life shall last. And our eternal home."

For Johnny, a mass is a mass. He does not see where this mass varies from the standard Sunday rite except that Zi Carmela is singing alone, and the homily is a recount of his grandfather's life, his wonderful accomplishments from little boy in a mountain village to soldier, to immigrant, to the camps, to shovel man, to ferryman, to businessman, to pillar of the community. Johnny's mind continuously skips to football. As the priest recites, "In Your mercy keep us free from sin, and protect us from all anxiety, as we wait in joyful hope . . ." Johnny is thinking of the last game.

It is third and two on the Roosevelt seventeen; 1:14 remains in the fourth quarter; Lakeport trails Roosevelt 16–20. Butch calls a fake pitch right, left back dive over right guard, on two. "Hut-wahn! Hut . . . !" Johnny explodes, clamps his arms about the ball as Butch slaps it into his stomach and the Roosevelt linebacker shoots the gap created by his nose tackle and defensive guard. Jimmy, who has been beaten by the defensive lineman, grabs the blitzing linebacker's ankle, staggers him. Still, the linebacker is intent on Johnny, expands his arms like giant pincers to tackle. Johnny straightens enough to bring his left knee up hard, high, into the falling player, punishing him for his attempt. Johnny spins on him, steps on him as he escapes the line pileup, lunges, twirls as the safety hits him at the twelve. Johnny refuses to go down. He breaks away to be caught by three pursuing linemen, tackled, pummeled on the Roosevelt four. On the next play from scrimmage—Zi Carmela is singing the "Ave Maria"; her voice is strong and beautiful and for a moment Johnny is back in church, back with the communal emotions, tears fall from his eye—Mitch takes a pitch, outsprints everyone to the corner for a 22–20 lead. Johnny adds two on the point-after. Only Wilson also remains undefeated. They will play for the championship on . . .

There is a police escort as the long line of cars makes its way from the church up Williams Street to Arctic where they pass by the elegant home that has been Giovanni Panuzio's pride for decades, then around the block and through Misty Bottom and out the boulevard that parallels Lincoln River and will bring them to St. Michael's Cemetery, which was once "in the country" but is now surrounded by homes, by stores, by machine shops and the interstate. Behind the escort car is the hearse, then the family limo and the sedan with the pallbearers. "Go ahead. See if it's started," Louis says to Johnny. Johnny looks from his older cousin to the driver, who shrugs. Johnny turns on the radio, adjusts the tuner. WLAK is carrying the game, live, but it has not yet started. They hear commercials, teasers, a news clip about Viet-Nam.

"Hey," Santo says, "d'ja hear the one about the old lady whose husband died and she cut off his dick and put it in a pot of boiling water?"

Tony feigns. "Ouch!"

Jimmy and Henry chuckle, and Johnny, in spite of himself, in spite of his feeling that this is inappropriate, laughs too. "So?" Henry asks.

"She says, I tasted it so many times raw, I wanted to try it cooked!"

"Oh, geez," Tony groans.

Santo's rolling. "How bout the one—"

"Shh!" Johnny turns up the radio volume.

". . . an absolutely beautiful day here at Veteran's Park," the WLAK announcer says. "During the pregame routine Williams has looked as crisp as the day, but I don't see Panuzio down there. Wilson quarterback Brian—"

"Of course you don't," Tony interrupts. Santo and Henry laugh.

"Hey." Jimmy changes the subject. "Why do they swing that incense thing over the coffin? It's like some pagan ritual or something, isn't it?"

"The holy smell—" Santo begins.

He is interrupted by Louis. "It's an old sanitary custom," he says, "dating back to before there were sealed caskets. They still do that in Viet-Nam."

"Who?" Santo blurts.

"The Viet-Namese," Louis says. "When you don't have a casket, you burn

incense to cover the smell. It's probably been going on for five thousand years. It's the sealed casket that's new."

"Still seems pagan to me," Jimmy says.

The others become quiet. Even though Johnny, Henry and Santo are seventeen, are seniors in high school, and their eldest cousin has been killed in Viet-Nam and their second oldest, Louis, who is there with them, has served a tour in Viet-Nam, the three are nearly oblivious to the war. Johnny does not follow the front page but follows the sports page; he does not read editorials but reads box scores and statistics. He has worked harder on his forearms, his grip, his explosion from a three-point stance, his stiff-arm, and his spin moves than he has on any subject in school. His grades have not suffered terribly, though they are not spectacular. His teachers have been mildly surprised by his combined SAT score of 1237. He is sure he is going to college, some college—hopefully with the assistance of a football scholarship. Screw it, Santina! Lady Satan! Your little nephew wasn't a retard. Ha!

"Sanitary," Louis repeats.

From the radio, "Looks like we're about set for the opening kickoff. Williams is back for Lakeport—" The sedan stops behind the hearse and the driver turns off the motor and the radio dies.

Again the footing is slippery as the pallbearers carry the casket from the curb in past four rows of stones, then uphill to the base of a monstrous marble monument holding a statue of a saint, or perhaps Jesus Himself, standing, gazing down, hands spread. The cousins wrestle the casket onto the framework and the thick green straps that will be used to lower the box after the mourners have left. An assistant replaces the flower arrangement that had been on the coffin at the parlour. Johnny notices that the ribbon has been removed.

". . . Our brother Giovanni has gone to his rest in the peace of Christ. With faith and hope in eternal life, let us commend him to the loving mercy . . ."

Johnny and the bearers stand behind the priest, behind Ercola, who is seated in a folding chair, behind her sons and daughters and their spouses, who are also seated. He looks at his grandmother, at his father and his mother, at the coffin, the mound of flower arrangements, the sea of people who are still arriving, making their way up the slight hill.

". . . May we who mourn be reunited one day with our brother . . ."

"Little Johnny-panni. Little Johnny-panni. Little Johnny-pa . . ." It's Mitch's voice and Johnny is really pissed. They are in the locker room, after practice, 1963. Johnny's told Mitch . . . Why in hell he ever told Mitch, he doesn't know, but he's told Mitch maybe a week earlier that Tessa still calls him Little Johnny-panni, and now Mitch is telling everyone and is teasing him, and he is on Mitch in the locker room wrestling him to the cold marble floor, holding his head in a hammerlock and trying to stuff a sock in his

mouth. Mitch is trying to throw him off, is punching him in the back, is still laughing and sputtering out, "Little Johnny-panni." "Knock that shit off!" *Coach Riccio is more pissed than Johnny. "Get the hell outta here and don't come back." Then, the next day, "Augh, please, Coach. Please." "Yer both suspended for two games. You make practice, but you can't play. You don't make practice, don't ever come back." They made every practice, and after two games they played every game for the rest of their sophomore year, all through their junior, and every game in their senior year—the Salt and Pepper Backs—until today.*

"Father . . ." I can see the priest as he prays over the casket, "into your hands we commend our brother. We are confident that with all who have died in Christ, he will be raised to life on the last day and live with Christ forever. We thank you . . ."

The funeral assistants are passing out flowers to the mourners. Johnny looks at his, studies his, is disappointed that his flower is broken, the petals on one side squished flat. How can he pay proper tribute to his grandfather with a broken, squished flower?! He does not want to go first, isn't sure if the pallbearers go before the general masses, if the family goes last as in the parlour, if . . . if . . . if . . . He looks to Louis. Louis' eyes are closed and suddenly Johnny feels a pang of true grief and he sniffs and can't hold back and his face contorts and his eyes water as he thinks not of his grandfather but of his cousin Richard, Louis' brother, thinks of how badly this must hurt Louis, thinks of Richard saying, "I was shy like that, too." Fuck you, Satan. Lady Devil who only Nonno, only *Il Padrone*, can control.

". . . but by Your glorious power, give him light, joy and peace in heaven, where You live forever and ever."

"Amen."

"Give him eternal rest, O Lord."

"And may Your light shine on him forever."

In ones, in twos, as families, people come forward, kiss their flower, place or drop or toss it on the coffin, then turn away; and away from the coffin, on the grass by the curb there is light banter and Tessa is saying to Mrs. Allegrezza, "Everyone is invited back to the house. Ma (she is referring to Ercola) expects everyone." And Mr. Allegrezza is holding Uncle John's hand. "Padrone," *he says to John, "you now must watch over the family."*

Johnny rides with Rocco and Tessa and his brother and sisters back to Nonno's house but he does not ask his father to turn on the radio. Sylvia, who is nineteen and in her second year at Columbia, is livid. "I think it's stupid and immoral."

"That's because you're stupid and immoral," Nick counters.

"What would you know?!" Sylvia snaps.

"I know what Louis told me. He said they're trying to reestablish a pattern of humane civic order."

"By killing people. He even wore—"

"Á," Rocco halts her. "Nòn è stuná. Not today, you know."

"It's happening today," Sylvia says in disgust. "Read The New York Times."

Nick sneers. "Louis says that someday that paper's going to be exposed for the liars they are."

Johnny is miserable. He isn't interested in Sylvia's concerns; is surprised that Nick seems to know something about it. He is thinking of the game; is sure it is over; knows that he can't go to the dance tonight. If they've won, he'll be embarrassed; if they've lost, he'll be ashamed. He has not called Barbara Finch; isn't certain he'll be able to from Nonna's. How long will they . . . he is thinking, but even as he thinks they he knows he means I . . . be stuck in the house with all those people? Tessa will insist on being the last to leave; will insist that every pot and pan—she'd already brought over the twenty-two-pound bird she'd purchased before Giovanni's sudden (expected but not quite yet) death—be cleaned and put away and the floors swept and . . . and . . . and . . .

The rooms were hot, stuffy, the light subdued. But Johnny-panni has escaped, perhaps only momentarily, to Rocco's car. He takes the keys from behind the visor, turns on the electrics, turns on the radio, listens to WLAK, to chatter and songs, to news bits and weather. He lays his head on the seatback, closes his eyes, wishes . . .

There are two announcers who have interviewed Johnny several times during the year. They are now chatting about the day, about the morning, about the game. "Williams was brilliant," Johnny hears one say. "Really brilliant. An incredible game." Johnny begins to smile. At least, he thinks, but before the thought solidifies the other announcer cuts in, "Certainly was. But without Panuzio the Lakers didn't have their balanced attack, and the Presidents defense was able to key on Williams."

Aw shit! Johnny thinks.

"He couldn't do it all by himself any more than Panuzio could have carried the Lakers this far without Williams. The Wilson Presidents thirty-one; Lakeport thirteen."

All the years . . . tumbling . . . Death evokes death, evokes thoughts of death, of past death, of death to come . . .

Captain Richard's death in March of 1965 . . . How severely maimed the Panuzio family was, is . . . Then with the death . . . by the death of Il Padrone, of Giovanni Baptiste Michelangelo Panuzio . . . of . . . me . . . not *me . . . how it somehow brought the family together . . .* could mine . . . ? *somehow healed the wounds . . . only to be followed by the death of First Sergeant Louis Panuzio in April 1966, in the coastal jungles northwest of Phan Rang. Dear God! How could this happen to my cousin? To my two cousins? A fatal blow; one from which—despite Tessa's "God works in mysterious ways. He has a multitude of reasons. Perhaps He needed Ricky; perhaps He needed Louis; perhaps He wanted us to examine ourselves"—the spirit of the extended Panuzio family ripped . . . a fabric shredded like the tattered ends of an old flag . . .* Nonno, how should we handle it? Nonno, how did you handle all . . . ?

Then the years that followed . . . more confusion for Little Johnny-panni. He matriculates at Colgate University in the fall of 1966. He does not play football. He holds a 2-S student deferment until 1968 when he drops out of school. Though he is exposed to the draft until 1970—a high draft lottery number puts him out of reach—he is never called up.

Mitch Williams is. He is drafted in the summer of 1966, serves two years in the army, one year in Viet-Nam with the 1st Infantry Division (the Big Red One). He is honorably discharged in August 1968; attends the University of Connecticut using GI Bill benefits. By 1974 he has earned an undergraduate degree in chemical engineering and a masters in engineering management.

And Johnny-panni . . . deep into the drug culture—spending much of those years stoned, protesting drug laws and crashing at various pads. In 1973 he returns to school, not to Colgate but to a small upstate campus, finally receiving . . . earning? . . . a degree in marketing in 1975 . . . meeting Julia Barnum in '76 . . . not even seeing Mitch in all those years . . . not a duo . . . not doing it by himself but thinking he is . . . not until 1983, when they are thirty-five years old and Johnny has brought his five-year-old son, Todd, to an East Lake Little Tyke soccer practice. Mitch's son, Aaron, is already a star, a tiny whirling dervish. And Mitch is the coach.

Seneca Falls Indian Casino, Heartwood, Saturday, 22 October, 9:18 P.M.

JOHNNY SWIRLED THE ice cubes in the last of his scotch, sipped the diluted booze, put the glass down on the small shelf to the right of the slot machine. A lovely young woman in a casino uniform—a short, mock-deerskin Indian-maiden dress—immediately removed the glass, asked sweetly, "May I bring you another, sir?"

"Ah . . ." Johnny hesitated. "Yeah. Sure. Johnny Walker Black Label. Make it neat." The girl smiled, turned, strode across the roulette-table carpet. He watched her go, ogled her back, her shapely legs, her feet in the casino uniform high-top moccasins. He sucked in his breath, grinned, bit his tongue. "Ooo-la-la!" he whispered to himself. He did not want to play the slots any longer, had only wanted to warm up with the machines, but now felt he had to stay there at least until the girl returned. He fed the machine, pulled its arm, fed, pulled, fed, pulled as mechanically as the mechanism spinning the fruits and stars and number 7s. Bells and flashing lights in the next aisle signaled a winner. A number of casino employees surrounded an older woman at the machine, applauded, congratulated her. Johnny glanced over, his brow furrowed. The occasion was festive; the room large, bright, airy, full of a communal energy he had never before associated with gaming. He fed his machine a little more quickly, hoping he might win just as the pretty girl brought him another drink.

His eyes roamed from the Slot Shack to the Tables Tepee where Nick, Mitch, Vernon and Brian DuPratt, an engineer in Mitch's department, were playing blackjack. Johnny could not see through the masses of people. Again bells and flashing lights and applauding employees erupted about the same fat old woman. Johnny slid off his stool, stood. The additional inches gave him a different perspective of the rows upon rows of chrome and brass machines, his own aisle tapering to an end point where small people on tiny stools yanked little levers on miniature machines. He closed his eyes, shook his head, reopened his eyes. The aisle changed, no longer tapered.

Earlier, at seven, when Mitch Williams had arrived at Johnny's, the house had seemed abandoned. Jenny and Rocco had been in the darkened living room quietly watching TV; Jason had been in his attic room preparing to go out; and Julia, who had gone to Lakeport at midday to shop, had not yet returned. "He's not ready yet," Jenny had whispered to Mitch. "Come in and sit down. Can I get you something to—"

"Thanks. No." Mitch had gone to the base of the stairs. "Hey, Johnny," he'd called, "you ready?"

"One minn-nit!" had come the returned shout.

Rocco heard, came to the hallway, nudged Mitch, smiled conspiratorially, shook a thumb toward the second floor. "He's late, eh? Always late." Without waiting for a response, he shuffled back to the living room.

"Hey, *Padrone*." Mitch followed him. "You hear the one about the guy waking up from a prostate operation?" Mitch turned to Jenny, winked. She screwed up her eyes.

"Who had a prostate operation?" Rocco asked.

"No. Nobody. This is a joke."

"Oh. What?"

"This guy's waking up from his prostate operation and his doctor says to him, 'I've got good news for you and bad news for you.' "

"Okay." Rocco laughed as if the joke were over.

Again Mitch glanced to Jenny, to the old man, back to Jenny. He did not want to make a big deal about Rocco not following the joke, but Rocco's confusion worried him. "Anyway . . ." He reached out, put his hands over Jenny's ears, went on. "The doc says, 'The good news is, we were able to save your penis and testicles.' " Again Rocco nodded, and Mitch continued. " 'The bad news is, they're under your pillow!' "

Rocco smiled, turned his attention to the television. Mitch was not sure if he'd heard him, heard the punch line, but he let it go, went back to the stairs. "Hey, old man," he called to Johnny, "let's move it. We gotta pick up Brian and Vern."

"Comin. Comin."

At the base of the stairs Rocco cornered Johnny in front of Mitch. "You got enough money?"

"Yeah."

"Take this." Rocco handed him a folded wad. "Enjoy yourself."

"I don't need it, Pop."

"Bet it for me." He let out a small—to Johnny, condescending—laugh. "Make me a rich man. If you win a million, I'll give you half."

Johnny's voice dropped. "Okay, Pop," he conceded, took the bills. "We gotta go." To Jenny he said, "Take care of your grandfather tonight, okay, sunshine?"

"Sure thing, Popsters. If you win a million, can I have some, too?"

"All of it. As long as you—" he sang the end of the line " '—don't take mah sun-shine a-way.' "

"Johnny," Rocco interrupted, "I don't like what's happening to him."

"To him? To who, Pop?" Johnny shook his head, bewildered, glanced over at Mitch.

"To Jason," Rocco said.

Johnny sighed. "What?!"

"He's upset. I see it. You and your wife aren't home enough."

"Pop, he's doin fine. He's almost eighteen. He doesn't need us to be home." Then to Mitch, "They won all three games this week."

Mitch nodded. Immediately Johnny felt guilty he'd brought it up. This was to be Mitch's first night out since the death, the murder of his son. Johnny had wanted to stay away from any topic that would evoke Aaron; had imagined a night in which they'd stay away from all seriousness; a night of frivolity, gaming, boozing, ogling the broads.

In the car, before they picked up the others, Mitch and Johnny's conversation immediately became serious, though it avoided all mention of Aaron. "You know what that's really about?" Johnny began. "That needs-you-home stuff?"

"He doesn't look very good to me," Mitch answered.

"Yeah. But that 'be home' stuff . . . What he's really saying is, stay home with me. Don't go out. Don't go to work. Don't go anywhere. It's like he wants me there all the time. He's getting so damn paranoid. Ya say to him, 'Hey Pop, how ya doin this mornin?' He answers, 'Goin downhill. It won't be long now.' Or like this mornin he says, 'If you don't clear the forest of the old trees, the young grow crooked.' Can you imagine? I tell ya . . ." Johnny caught himself.

"Is it paranoia," Mitch challenged, "or is it insecurity . . . brought on by dependency?"

"Or is it," Johnny retorted, "his focus on that dependency?"

"I feel sorry for him," Mitch interjected.

"I feel like a Zany Bird." Johnny stuck his arms straight out, his wrists cocked down, fingers extended; he bulged his eyes, bounced his head like the head of a cheap doll on a spring; set his arms aflail. "Ooogalaa-ooogalaa-ooogalaa!" he yodeled.

Mitch laughed and Johnny repeated his Zany Bird antics and they both laughed. "He still goin' into the basement?" Mitch asked through his laughter.

"Ah, not this week. He says he doesn't feel safe on the stairs. Which is what I've been telling him for months. I'm glad he's not goin down. It's mostly finished, anyway."

"Good for him. He's absolutely right about those shitty foundations. If they'd had a town engineer back when—"

"Shit. I don't want to talk about it. I'm really tired of . . . I don't want to talk about him. I don't want to talk about Julia, or Jason or the deli—"

"Yeah," Mitch interrupted. "What's happenin with that?"

"I don't want to talk about it. I really fucked up. God, did I fuck up."

"So . . . ?"

"Nothin's settled. I don't want to talk about it."

"Are they goina press charges?" Johnny just eyed Mitch. Mitch changed the topic. "Well," he said, "I got some good news for ya."

"You saved my nuts," Johnny gushed, "but they're under my pillow."

Mitch chuckled. "Naw," he said. Though they were making the attempt, they could not stay away from the topics that were paramount in their lives. "There's goina be another round of layoffs at GenChem."

"Shit! That's good?!"

"You're covered."

"Huh?"

"I talked to old man Tripps. I didn't let on . . . you know . . . but I kinda directed the conversation and he said the departments, like marketing, which have been . . . how'd he say it? . . . 'closely trimmed,' won't be involved."

"Christ! I gotta finish gettin my résumé together. I got five hundred bucks here. Plus Pop's twenty-five. I really gotta . . . If I could roll this into five grand—" Johnny changed voices to a Scottish burr/Irish brogue mix "—I wouldn't be so a-hurtin ta pay me bills, laddie. Gotta find me a potta gold."

"Johnny." Mitch didn't go along with Johnny's scheme. "Let's just go to get out. Like you said. Just for entertainment. I hate betting my money. I mean . . . You know, I've got a hundred I'm willing to drop to have a good time, but . . . I don't want to lose it. I'd never put my bill money . . ."

"Aigh, laddie," Johnny only half joked, "I've been a-gamin with me credit cards; takin em up on their fine offers tah advance me cash . . ."

"Oh, Jesus!"

"Juss fer six months, lad. And aht the best ah rates, too!"

As they wound through the streets of Lakeport to pick up Vernon, Mitch shook his head, said, "You gotta do something else, Johnny. You gotta get something else going." "Yeah—" Johnny began, but Mitch cut in, asked, "You remember the time your grandfather got arrested for gambling?"

"My grandfather?!"

"Yeah. Remember? We were . . . I don't know, eight, ten. At the Boys'

Club. One summer. All the old guineas used to gather in that little woods at the side of the club and they'd play penny-ante poker or somethin."

"Oh, yeah; that's right! They used to hide their, ah . . . They used milk crates. They'd pull them from the bushes each day so they didn't have to carry stools."

"Yeah. And the cops were playing 'Get the Guineas,' and they arrested all those old men for having maybe fifty cents in the pot."

"Yeah. McBaine. I forgot all about that. McBaine was chief of police, and he and his goon squad used to play 'Get the Guinea.' "

"Yeah. And 'Get the Nigger.' Course, then, most everybody's played that."

"Umm." Johnny hummed. "Hey, did I tell ya, I've been lookin more into the ferries?"

"For the lake?"

"Yeah," Johnny said. "I've been putting together a plan . . . a proposal. There's a manufacturer in Virginia, a shipbuilder who's made ferries for some Chesapeake Bay municipalities . . ."

"That right?!"

"Yeah. I got a bunch of data. Speeds. Capacities. Wake heights. I was doing some drawings, too. Thinking about the old terminal, about refurbishing it. Think of it with restaurants, boutiques. It's feasible. It really could be made to carry itself."

"You think . . . ?"

"Commuters, students, shoppers, sightseers . . . A change back, but better than before."

"Hmm! Sure," Mitch had said. "A change back. The more things change . . . *Á!* Maybe not with the gambling part."

Johnny looked back down the aisle of the casino. He thought of the earlier conversation, thought, chuckled to himself, Sure has changed! He licked his lips. They felt dry. He wished the good-looking girl in the Indian outfit would bring his scotch. As if on command, she appeared, smiled, dazzled him with her eyes, her perfect features, beautiful teeth. For a moment he simply stared, then he shook slightly, flicked a ten-dollar bill onto her tray. She bowed. He nodded. She left. He thought, Goddamn! That's a hell of a way to get tips.

Johnny downed the scotch, meandered through the slots looking at first one woman then another. Many of the machines were occupied by women he judged to be in their late fifties and sixties but some had younger women pulling their arms. Some of the women were pretty, a few quite attractive. In the Tables Tepee the women were generally younger, flashier. Johnny found it enjoyable to just let his eyes linger on this one's legs, on that one's butt. He found it odd that there were many more nice bodies and nice legs than nice faces. There were not a lot of nice faces.

"How ya doin?" Nick joined him in ogling the ass of one particularly shapely brunette.

"Good. You?"

"I'm up nearly two hundred. They just switched dealers, so I thought I'd cool it. This guy Brian . . . do you know him?"

"A little."

"He's hard-core. I ken feel it. I could feel him staring at my chips when I won. Worse than Vern." The brunette turned around, and Johnny and Nick turned to each other.

"How come you always win?" Johnny asked his brother.

"Just luck." Nick winked. "Boy." His eyes flicked toward the brunette. "What tits, huh?! Tonight I'm goina dream I'm breast-feeding right there."

Mitch and Vern came from the table with the new dealer. Vern seemed angry. "There's a club about a mile from here," he said. "You wanna listen to some music?"

"Ah . . ." Johnny began.

"Good food, too," Vern said. "Better'n the plastic shit in this place."

"Well, I guess . . ."

"If it aint happenin," Vern said, "we ken come back. Brian says they got a back room there fer real games."

AS JOHNNY, MITCH and the others were leaving the casino, Jason and Kim were pulling off Little Brook Road into a secluded parking area overlooking Finnegan's Pond. The night was Halloween-cold; a gusting wind blew blotches of clouds across the sliver of an ebbing moon. Kim left the motor running, the heat on. She pulled the release lever and the sedan's seat slid back to its extreme position. Gently Jason pulled her close; their burning bodies entwined; their mouths tenderly meshed. Kim tucked her head to his chest to slow him down but he wasn't into slowdown. He kissed her hair, her ears, her neck. His breathing became more rapid and she tucked down tighter, slid back a few inches, then knelt on the seat and pushed him back so she was on top and in control. He pulled her onto him but she resisted. He conceded; put his hands on her sides, let his fingers trace the curves of her breasts. She pushed on his shoulders, swayed her chest to his caress. He winced.

"What's wrong?" Kim whispered.

"Nothing. My back."

"It still hurts, doesn't it?"

"Only if I twist it like that."

"You should've seen a doctor."

"I don't believe in them."

"How can you not believe in doctors? Your uncle's a doctor!"

"If it were my knee or something, I'd go. But I think . . ."

"You're just afraid they'll tell you not to play."

"It's a lot better. It only hurts when you don't kiss me."

Kim giggled. "You're such a bullshitter." She kissed him on the lips. "I was really afraid for you yesterday. When you got hit . . ."

"That shitbird!" Jason adjusted his position, straightened his back. On Thursday they'd played Jefferson, making up the game that had been postponed the day after the fatal accident. On Friday they'd played Taftburg. Both days Jason had gone nuts on the field; in both games—which were properly called—he'd been yellow-carded for violent play, had been forced to sit out ten-minute suspensions as per scholastic league rules. In the first half against Taftburg he'd twice hit players in such a manner as to injure them and send them from the game. At the beginning of the second half the referee had specifically warned him about his slide tackles, which the man called "borderline from behind." Further, the ref had warned, "If you hit the man, whether you hit the ball or not, I'm gonna red-card ya and see to it it's a two-game suspension. Got it?" Jason had still played crazy but had made sure any hits he delivered were off the ball when the refs were looking elsewhere. He'd scored the lone goal in the Jefferson game; had assisted on both Elk goals in the shutout of Taftburg. The week had changed a mediocre season into something that was moving toward respectable. Their record was now 6–3–3.

"Everybody says you're playing really well."

"*Á.*" Short, harsh, yet subdued. "Pissed is more like it. I feel like I'm goina kill somebody. Like I want to hit my old man for—"

"But—" Kim had not anticipated his anger.

"What a dickhead. I can't believe he did that. I can't believe he went mental in your father's store and then turns it and blames it . . . However he did it."

"I still don't know if I got the story straight," Kim whispered. "My father wouldn't say . . . You know, he really does like you. And he knows I like—"

"I'm never goina talk to that jerk again," Jason said. His voice was hard.

"We don't know what really—" Kim began.

Jason cut her off. "I can't wait to move out."

"My cousin was in the store. That's how I heard part of it. Tía Carlena's son. He does the buying. I don't think you've met him."

Jason ignored what Kim was saying. "I might get pissed, but I'm not mental like him. I'm—"

"I know. I know you're not. I think my father probably went pretty mental, too. I still don't know why they were fighting."

"Maybe . . ." Jason stumbled with his words. "Maybe I am mental like him. Todd says I'm just—"

Kim stroked the side of his face. "No, you're not."

Jason slid his hands to Kim's waist. "You gotta be the most wonderful, the most perfect thing God's ever made," he whispered. "How can you . . . forgive . . . umm." Again they kissed passionately, petted each other, steamed up the windows, pushed back to cool down.

"Do you think God watches us?" Kim whispered.

"No," Jason said. "I don't think God's like that."

"Like what?"

"Like a person. Like a spirit. Maybe Aaron's spirit is watching us but I think God's much more than a spirit. God goes much further than . . . like Radkowski's 'the soul's high adventure.' "

"That's why we come here, isn't it?" Kim whispered. "You think Aaron's spirit is here."

"I don't know."

"I think Mr. and Mrs. Williams should be told about . . ."

"Does Martina want them to pay for like the doctor's bills? Or for support or something?"

"I don't think so. Her mom's working. She's covered under her mom's insurance but she won't even tell her mom. It's just that I . . . I mean, like . . . It is their grandchild. Like think how much you mean to your grandfather."

"Rocco?"

"Of course."

"I don't—"

"Jason! Don't say something dumb. He dotes on you. Every time I see him . . . I can just see it. You and Jenny keep him alive."

"Don't put that on me."

"It's not like a responsibility. It's a fact. His love is what keeps him going and that's what Mr. and Mrs. Williams will be cheated out of if they don't know they've got a grandchild."

"Well, I'm not goina tell em."

"Your father could. You could tell him and he could tell Mr. Williams."

"I . . . I don't know. I don't think so. He's a jerk."

"If Martina said it was okay . . . ?"

"What if I did and he, you know . . ."

"You know what I think God is like?" Kim said. "I think God is all loving relationships."

Jason attempted to make a joke to break the seriousness of their talk. "Chipheads can't say that," he said. "Not even computer closet chipheads."

"Yes, I can," Kim said seriously.

Jason shifted his tone to match her mood. "I think God is Time," he said. "Time gives purpose and design to existence."

"You're doing your poem on that, aren't you?"

"Kinda. Wanta hear it? I memorized it."

"Umm-hmm."

"It's called, 'If Time Stood Still.' "

"If time stood still," Kim whispered, "I'd make it stand still right here. Right now." Jason scrunched up his face, did not begin. "Well?" Kim prodded.

"I don't think you'll like it," he said.

"Try me."

"Okay. 'If Time Stood Still.' Here goes:

> Time gives organization to all things. If Time
> Stood Still, everything would be chaos.
> Without Time's sequential ordering
> Moving parts of the universe collide
> At random—
> There are no segments which might nicely repeat because
> segments assume sequentiality—of which
> there can be none.
> Complete vibrating craziness—
> Molecular destruction—
> Atomic frazzle—
> The Big Bang—
> THEN
> Expanding—expansion
> Expanding implies sequence
> Sequence implies time
> Time gives organization to all things
> Sequentiality
> Life
> Death
> Continuity
> Time
> God.

"I guess . . ." Jason paused, sighed. "It's not really like, you know . . . sophisticated. Not like the stuff Radkowski really likes. But it has, you know, like meaning to me."

"I think it's wonderful." Kim whispered. She was again lying against him. "I'm trying to understand it."

"It's not very 'poetic.' Like in the sense . . . you know."

"Maybe that's the problem with poetry. It's not written for chipheads. Most of it's written for meatballs. Chipheads have feelings, too. The meatballs just deny it. Deny we do. Because we express it differently from them."

"Tolerance for nothing but their own biases," Jason joked.

"But that's true, isn't it?" Kim said softly. "They are like that. They're like that because they're so defensive. It's really the chipheads and the scientists who are . . . ah, inclusive. Who believe in that egalitarian inclusiveness."

"I think Radko'll give me a C at best."

"If she does, I'll . . . I'll . . . I'll make her time stand still."

Jason chuckled, turned, gently guided Kim back, down, kissing, she pulling, both more passionate, more sensual than ever. He raised her sweater, kissed her stomach, licked her navel. His hands rubbed her sides as he ran his tongue up to her ribs, pulled her sweater up higher, undid her bra, kissed her breasts, licked her nipples, sucked in as much as he could. She lay back with her eyes closed; one arm hung below the seat, the other was behind her head. She wriggled to his kisses, panted. He moved down, kissed and licked her sides, moved his hands to her jeans, opened the belt, the buttons, exposed her cotton panties, worked his hands about her hips, inched the material down, slid a hand in behind, his fingers following the smooth curve of her ass, dipping between the cheeks. She stopped him as she always had, gently reaching, touching, holding his wrists, guiding them up. Again he kissed her stomach. As he worked his mouth up her torso, he opened his shirt, felt her warmth against the skin of his chest. He moved higher, undid his own pants, released his bent erection from the confinement of the cloth. He kissed her neck, slid higher, kissed her passionately, humped and rubbed against the velvet smoothness of her abdomen, humped quickly, panting, stiffening, ejaculating, shooting gobs of semen up between her breasts, collapsing.

"Oh!" Kim giggled. "Oh, Jason!" She squeezed him tightly. They had never gone so far.

"Kim." His voice was pale, spent. In his ears her name was the whisper of an angel. "I . . ."

She kissed the top of his head as it rested on her chest.

"Kim." Jason whispered the words. "Next time . . . I want all of you."

THE PULSATING MUSIC in the small club was loud, the air filled with smoke; the lights, unlike the casino, were dim. In the low light the faces of the women looked lovely. The men elbowed each other, joked, gestured. "Look at that one." "And at that one!" The food was outstanding, the drinks strong. After they ate and drank, listened and ogled, they moved through two sets of doors to a back room where there were two large round tables with two large, obese dealers. To sit, just to sit, cost fifty dollars. With the doors closed the music was subdued, yet the throbbing of the bass still vibrated the floor.

Johnny felt uncomfortable. Brian DuPratt sat to his left, Vernon Williams to his right, Nick to Vern's right. There were two men Johnny didn't know: one small, wiry, perhaps thirty, Filipino or South Asian or . . . Johnny wasn't sure, maybe Puerto Rican. He'd introduced himself, giving the incongruous name Scott. The other man, LeRoy, was big, white, maybe forty. His face was ruddy but not hale—perhaps the ruddiness of alcoholic decline. The dealer was immense, six by five, with thick yet pudgy tattooed arms, fat hands, fat fingers with eight grotesque rings, and eight rings or studs in his right ear. He smiled without looking at anyone; talked to Mitch who hadn't sat. "We got another chair." His voice was high, squeaky. "You might just as well."

"Nah," Mitch said. "This stuff's too rich fer my blood. I'll just watch."

"Suit yerself." The dealer snickered as if he were telling a joke. "Can't win, though, if ya don't play." Mitch didn't answer him. The dealer sniffed, cleared his throat, eyed Mitch nastily. "Can't stand there. You kin sit with Lily."

The second table was empty with the exception of a fat woman with heavy makeup. To Mitch the woman looked to be fifty-five, maybe sixty, but he guessed she was really in her forties, just heavily used. She sat, one arm down, hand cocked, bent back on the arm of her chair. The elbow of that arm pointed outward, looked like the stub of a branch someone had sawn off. Her other hand was perched loosely on a flopped wrist, her arm and elbow planted on the tabletop. She smiled, motioned Mitch toward her. "Augh . . ." Mitch hesitated, coughed into his hand, shrugged. "Maybe I will play." He sat between the dealer and Brian DuPratt, swung his head, taking in the room, the characters. Caricatures, he thought. Right out of a B movie. He chuckled, ponied up the ante, hid a scoffing laugh in another cough, thought further, *And we're all playin parts, too.*

"What'll it be, gentlemen?" the six-by-five dealer asked in his effeminate voice.

They began slow and easy, playing five-card draw for low stakes, gradually increasing the bets, chatting—mostly about sports and women, drinking, smoking, seldom having the pot top two hundred dollars. By eleven-thirty Johnny was feeling comfortable. A second, seemingly friendly game had begun at Lily's table.

"You see that letter in today's *Ledger*?" Nick tossed out the question between hands.

"Naw," Vern answered. "I can't read that right-wing crapola."

"Ha!" Brian erupted. He was in a good mood; was up by three hundred dollars. "I always thought the *Ledger* was a left-wing rag."

"It is." LeRoy's voice was a snarl. He was down five big ones.

"What letter?" Johnny asked. The dealer reshuffled the cards. The conversation had been sporadic, at times involving most of the men, though more often only a pair. Once or twice they had lightly touched on regional or national politics but generally the topics were avoided. The dealer, known as Large Larry, confined his speech to the cards, the pot, the house rules.

"Went kinda like this," Nick said. " 'Dear Mr. Superintendent of Schools: You are responsible for our children, on average, approximately three and a half hours per day.' In parentheses they had seven hours times one hundred and eighty days."

"Oh," Mitch said. "I see."

"It went on," Nick said, " 'We are responsible for our children, on average, approximately twenty and one half hours per day. If you raise our taxes, I'm sure you can do a better job for our children during your three and a half hours.' "

Mitch broke in. "Money won't necessarily—"

Nick held up a hand to stop him. He finished, " 'However,' this guy ended it, 'I am not so sure, if you take more money away from us, that we can do as good a job with our children in our twenty and a half hours.' I think," Nick added, "he said one hell of a lot right there."

Vern flipped a hand at Nick. "That's cause you doctors make a ton a money. You stuck down here where I am, we're dependent on tax dollars keepin our kids—"

"Wait a fucken minute," Brian erupted again. He pointed at Vern. "It's guys like you who are always claiming the government is a servant of the wealthy and the powerful. Same time, you say tax more. Make government bigger. And the bigger it gets, the worse off you are."

"I see you aint starvin ta death," Vern snapped.

"Agh . . ." Nick held both hands out high over the table, fluttered them. "I wouldn't a brought it up if I thought it'd cause an argument."

"Well," Brian snapped, "every time there's a tax increase, it increases the pressure on everybody. You escalate that pressure, you escalate people's frustrations. That's what leads ta violence."

"I wasn't talking anything about violence." Nick's voice was loud. "Actually, I was thinking about HMOs. What I see happenin in my practice is just nuts. I thought this guy's point about the problem in the schools was kinda parallel . . ."

"I don't see it," LeRoy said.

"Just play yer fucken cards." Scott dropped his hand in disgust. "I fold."

Nick dropped two, asked for two. "The government's become the overseer of the new health care system," he said. "It's their legislations that's created . . . Aaah! The whole goddamn system's outta whack but nobody's willing to analyze—"

"Whole fucken world's outta whack, man," Scott injected.

"But there's always a reason," Brian insisted. "Things aren't *just* fucked. There's a reason."

"Umm. Augh . . . I don't . . ." Mitch moaned tentatively.

No one wanted the argument. The conversation waned. Another round of drinks was brought. Brian left for a few hands, returned with cigars for the table.

"You hear the one," LeRoy began, "about the guy who comes home and finds his girl on the porch with her bags packed?"

"No," Johnny answered for the table.

"He looks at her and says, 'Honey, where ya goin? When I left this mornin I thought everything was fine.' She looks up at him and she says, 'The police called. They said you were a pedophile.' He pulls back like he's horrified, and he blurts, 'A pedophile! That's an awfully big word fer a ten-year-old.' "

There were laughs, snickers, chortles. Brian seemed to think the joke was in poor taste. Again the laughter and the conversation ebbed; the amount in the pots slowly increased.

"You see in the paper about those kids being arrested?" Nick asked.

"What kids?" Johnny responded.

"Three kids at Lakeport High. I think one was on the football team. Arrested right durin school. They'd stolen twenty grand in merchandise . . . computers, a couple of guns, jewelry . . . right out of some guy's house. But they arrested em in school. One kid put up a fight in the cafeteria."

"Is that right?" Vern seemed miffed.

Johnny wanted to kick Nick under the table like he'd done when they were little; kick him, make him shut up.

"This whole fucken world is just fucken fallin apart," Scott said.

"Am I the only guy who reads the paper?" Nick chuckled.

"Yer full a news," LeRoy said contemptuously.

"You see the court decision on integration?" Nick asked. "And city lines? In this state it is now unconstitutional for school districts to be drawn along municipal lines."

"Á." Mitch flicked his hand as if he were Rocco. "I don't know." His voice was thick, tired. "These things, when you read them in the papers, they remind me of Viet-Nam."

"Viet-Nam?!" Brian disparaged.

"I know what ya mean," Nick said.

"Yeah," Mitch said. "I don't mean what happened there. I mean *how* we approached what happened there. This is like Viet-Nam all over again. Like a domestic Viet-Nam."

"What the fuck you talkin about?" LeRoy sneered. "Nobody here's killin eighteen-year-olds."

Johnny glanced at Mitch. Mitch kept his head down. Vernon was about to say something but Johnny nudged Vern's leg with his knee. Vern bit his lip.

"That's not what he means." Nick banged his cards down on the table, added, "Jerk!"

"Well, what the fuck does he mean?" LeRoy shot back. "Asshole!"

"Gentlemen!" Large Larry interrupted. "House Rule—"

"He means," Nick blurted, "the coverage of issues is lopsided. Despite the rhetoric, there's almost no serious knowledge. It's political, not practical. No nonpartisan analysis. Right?" Nick looked at Mitch. Mitch barely nodded. Nick continued. "And there's no will to deal with the real problem because the real problem's been obscured by political bullshit. You can't solve a problem if you can't see it."

"Who put a quarter in you?" LeRoy tried to break the tension, guffawed at his own joke.

"These two guys were there." Johnny indicated Mitch and Nick.

LeRoy stiffled a laugh. Then let it out. "Smokin dope." Again he guffawed. "Rape, pillage and plunder. I seen *Platoon* four tim—"

"Fuck you!" Mitch pushed away from the table, paused, shot up. "Johnny," he said, "I'm goina take a leak. Then it's time to hit the road."

"Yeah," Johnny began. Before he could say more, LeRoy's renewed guffaw drowned him out. The men at the other table sensed trouble, hunkered closer together.

"Imagine . . ." Mitch focused in on LeRoy, bent forward, stared at his eyes. Mitch's voice was thick, controlled anger. "Imagine a TV program. A cop show. One like that one with Don Johnson. Imagine that it's edited to show the police apprehending people; breaking down doors; killing people. Now imagine they edited it, too, to cut out all the scenes where these criminals that Johnson's after . . . cut out all the scenes where they do their nasty crimes; their standard TV list—extortion, torture, murder of innocents, rape. Imagine a show that gave you no antecedents as to why the police were chasing the criminals. What do you think your opinion of the police would be?"

"Same as now." LeRoy leaned forward, met Mitch's challenge. "A bunch a Nazi control freaks."

Mitch leaned in further, became more intense. "Except when they're stoppin some guy from killing your kid." The words came from him like high-pressure but cold magma spewing onto the table.

"That's different." LeRoy shrank back. Suddenly he seemed afraid that Mitch was going to jump him. He wanted out of the topic.

"Gentlemen!" Large Larry huffed.

Mitch continued erupting. "That police example is what happened between America, its veterans and the goddamn press. You're the viewer; we're the police; they're the editors. We destroyed homes. We shot people. We killed people. That they were communist soldiers became like saying, 'Don Johnson killed some person because he was a used-car salesman.' Consider this, asshole! Two-point-two million Asians were killed by the communists after we withdrew. How do you think you'd feel about the police if the salesman was shown to be a brutal rapist, a murderer, a molester of children, a crack dealer who extorted cruel payment from his addicts, forced them to decapitate their nonaddicted brothers—like the communists forced their neophytes to do to their own families if they didn't join up? You'd probably see the police as heroes, wouldn't you? You'd see their violence as justified. Wouldn't you?"

"Hey." LeRoy threw up his hands. "Fine. You're right. I don't know nothin."

"That's right, asshole!"

"I said, okay!" LeRoy began to rise, began to leave, muttered under his breath, "I don't fucken need this shit."

"Fuck you," Mitch shouted. "Sit down! Play yer goddamn cards!" With that Mitch left the room. Johnny followed him. Vern followed Johnny. Both left their hands facedown on the table.

"Holy fuck," LeRoy said. "What's with him?!"

In the hall between the back room and the club Mitch was seething, angry at himself for his explosion, for disrupting the game. He turned his anger on himself, mumbled, choked out, "I lost it. Just fucken lost it. I just shouldn't a come. I shouldn't . . . This fucken country lost . . . It's just too fucken soon!"

Johnny put his arm over Mitch's shoulder. "Yeah. Yeah. Maybe. But the guy's a jerk. The guy's—"

"Fer us," Vern said to his brother, "we aint ever been found."

"Á." Mitch slapped the wall. "Maybe it's not the country. Maybe it's us."

"Let me go back in for my—" Johnny started to say.

"No." Mitch straightened. "I'll sit out here. I'm goina go. I just wanta go by myself."

"Nick can drop us . . ." Vern said.

"I could crash at Nick's," Johnny offered. He checked his watch. It was 1:20. "He's comin over tomorrow . . . today . . . anyway. Sunday dinner with Rocco."

"You sure?" Mitch did not look at his friend or his brother. "You better ask Nick."

In the back room Johnny found Nick glaring alternately at Brian DuPratt and LeRoy. "Personally," Nick was saying, "I find I've got a hell of a lot more in common with the average black Viet-Nam veteran than I do with the average white nonveteran. The reason you guys can't object to that jerk in office is because you didn't go, either. So you let him get away with all his shit . . ."

Johnny clenched his teeth. He didn't want to hear it. For nearly two decades he'd felt a twinge of guilt anytime Mitch and Nick talked about the war.

"House Rule Number One, gentlemen," Large Larry interrupted again. "Cards here, politics outside."

"Yeah. Right!" Nick snapped. Then he laughed. "This is 'merica," he said in a low voice. "We got rights here. We got freedoms."

After Mitch left, the game became more serious and the pots grew to four, five, six hundred dollars. At two o'clock the players took a break. A waitress brought in Reuben, egg salad and BLT sandwiches. The band played their last set. The kitchen closed. The players and dealer from the second table rose, left. The bar remained open.

"That's illegal," Nick said, pointing to LeRoy's sandwich.

"What's illegal?" LeRoy asked. He was still wary, though he was no longer overtly upset. He had climbed back to even.

"That sandwich," Nick said.

"It's fucken egg salad," LeRoy countered as if Nick were nuts.

"Yep." Nick said. "Lotsa mayo. Even buttered the toast."

"Oh, shit. Not yer—"

"Amount of fat and cholesterol . . . Skyrocket your serum cholest—"

LeRoy shook his head. "That's not illegal."

"Well. Not yet," Nick said.

LeRoy turned to Large Larry. "Next time I come here . . ." he began.

"How you figure that?" Scott spurted.

"*Á*. Just look at it," Nick said. "Look at what they've made illegal and the justifications they've come up with to pass those laws."

"You talkin about guns, man?"

"Naw." Nick drew out the word. "I was thinkin more like bicycle helmets. Makin it illegal for kids to ride without helmets. Sounds good, doesn't it?"

"I make Jenny wear one," Johnny said.

"I agree," Nick said. "I make my boys wear em. But we've made it illegal to ride without helmets. Same thing with motorcycles. The state says riders must wear helmets. We have a helmet law. The justification for the laws is that when someone is in one of these accidents and they're not protected, the injuries are usually severe and extensive and the cost to the public is astronomical. There's medical costs—emergency transportation and care, short-term intensive care, long-term healing and rehabilitation. Very often those bills are paid from the public coffers."

"What the hell's that gotta do with my sandwich?"

Nick smiled. "Just follow me." He chuckled. "If we get universal health care in which all costs are essentially public costs, shouldn't we control the highest medical costs to our society?"

"Okay," Johnny said. "Yeah."

"Except for places like this," Nick continued, "as a society we've virtually eliminated smoking, right?"

"Yeah." Johnny wanted to push him along. He'd finished his sandwich, had a thousand dollars on the table, wanted the chance to increase his winnings.

"Public-area bans, regulations, laws on secondary smoke. There's a four hundred percent tax on tobacco products."

"Yeah. Yeah. Yeah. Yeah." LeRoy also prodded him. "So what?"

"Why shouldn't it be against the law to have a high-fat intake?" Again Nick chuckled. "Why shouldn't there be a four hundred percent tax on Big Macs? Or egg salad? A fat-intake tax. Heart attacks, high blood pressure and strokes kill more people in the U.S. than any other ailment. Or any other cause for that matter. Just under a million people a year. Forty-two percent of all U.S. deaths. The cost in health care and loss of productivity is around a hundred and forty billion a year. Twice that of cancer. Twenty times that of AIDS. Ten thousand times that of bicycles. And eating that shit is like a self-inflicted wound."

"Yer nuts," LeRoy sputtered. "Yer . . . Just play."

"Maybe," Nick said. "Yer kinda overweight, though, huh? Few years in jail might do you good."

"Ante up, gentlemen," Large Larry whined.

"I'm tellin ya," Nick persisted, "in ten years they'll declare anybody, oh, maybe thirty percent overweight to be a criminal. Then we can add the Fat Police to the Smoking Police and the Thought Police."

"Maybe—" Larry smiled, entered the chatter for the first time "—they'll incarcerate me at a spa in Barbados. I'd like that. Someplace nice and warm."

"Naw." Nick laughed. "You'd burn more calories in North Dakota."

Involuntarily Larry's arms clinched to his sides. He shivered.

"What we're really talkin about is freedom," Nick said. "Personal freedom versus government control. Vern, you're always talkin about personal empowerment. Isn't that—"

Vern chuckled. "Nicky boy, you leave me outta yer babblin bullshit."

"What about if they said, 'You must lose that extra weight and must exercise, or we'll restrict your medical benefits; we'll fine you some monetary amount'? Why is that different from banning smoking?"

Vern ignored the question. "I'll see, and raise ya ten."

"I wonder," Nick muttered, his voice petering out, "how much a hundred thousand Fat Police would . . ."

The intensity of the game fluctuated. For the first time that evening the pot grew to fifteen hundred dollars. LeRoy seemed to be down the most; Vernon the second most. Nick, too, was down. Scott and Johnny were sliding back and forth, several hundred to the plus, several hundred to the minus. Brian DuPratt hid his status.

"Woo!" Scott blew out the word as he won the next hand.

"Shit!" LeRoy spit. "Fag fucken cards."

Large Larry gave LeRoy a dirty look. "A few more, gentlemen?" He accentuated the nasal quality of his tone.

The waitress who'd served the sandwiches came in. "Last round, guys," she said. "Should I bring doubles?"

"Sounds good," Brian said. The waitress left and he added, "I think I'm out. I'm goina just contemplate that babe's navel."

"Can't quit yet," Vernon objected. "Gimme a chance ta get even."

"Sure." Brian smiled.

"You ever wonder why people contemplate their navels?" Johnny asked. Although he had been pacing himself, he was now feeling the liquor. "Why not some other body part?"

"Yeah," Nick nearly shouted. "Like my dick. I like to contem—"

"Nah," Johnny said. "I mean, like, why not their heel? Or their nipple? Right now I'm contemplating my asshole." That brought on groans and chuckles. Johnny rocked back in his chair. "Think of it! It's like the portal of a spaceship. Where do you think those air-lock designs come from?"

"Yeah," Scott said. "Out yer ass." He looked up at LeRoy. "This is the weirdest bunch a . . ."

LeRoy quieted him with a nasty stare.

"Well . . ." Johnny paid no heed, chuckled, continued. "Certainly not from one's deep reverence over one's lint collector. No way, Jack. It's the asshole. The perfect sphincter. That cute little button winking at you from the back end of your dog. Or, if you're a lucky man, from your wife!"

"I'd be lucky if yer wife's was winkin at me," Vern blurted.

Johnny laughed. "Through this portal passes all the processed ingestion of your entire life on its way to perfect ecological recycling as nutrients and support for the flora kingdom, which will in turn produce new ingestibles to be recycled to the fauna kingdom, of which we are part."

Nick nudged Vern. "I think I know what Jenny's doin in school and who's helpin her with her homework."

"The perfect circle." Johnny smiled broadly. He was finally enjoying the evening. "Contemplate your asshole," he said. "It is that pink cherub's kiss which is even hidden by a thong bikini. The last place on earth you'd expect to find answers to existence, yet that is exactly why we should look there first. After all, haven't the assholes of the world taken over? Isn't it the assholes who have all the power? Look at ContGenChem. Isn't it the assholes who are trying to re-create us all in their own image?"

"Oh, man." Nick laughed at his brother. "What are you drinkin? I want one a them."

"Wasn't it an asshole at Gallina that got Julie fucked over? Seein an asshole bein fucked?"

"Humph!" Large Larry sneered at Johnny. "You men like to imagine things," he said. "I've got something for you to imagine."

"What?" Johnny slurred, stared at the dealer.

"I want you to imagine the most beautiful woman in the world." Large Larry directed his words at Johnny. "Just the most gorgeous, absolutely most beautiful woman."

"Umm." Johnny grinned.

"The nicest skin," Larry continued. "The most beautiful face. A great fucken body. I mean outstanding. She's so good-lookin, men shield their eyes in her presence. And not only does she look good, she feels good, she smells good, she tastes good. She even agrees with your opinions." Larry tittered. "There's nothin about her that's not top shelf—right from God's bar. She's perfect. She's yours. She loves you. She only has eyes for you. She's your love slave."

Nick looked suspiciously at the dealer. "What's this shit?"

"Nah. Nah. I just want to ask Johnny a question."

"Yer pullin some kinda crap," Nick said.

"Ask what question?" Johnny said. "Go ahead."

"This woman—" Larry smiled as he spoke "—sucks you every night of the week. And every morning, if you want it. Now, here's the question."

Johnny thrust his hip as if he were humping under the table. "Doesn't sound like there's any question to me."

"It's a proposition," Large Larry said. "Just hypothetical. A hypothetical proposition. Suppose you could have this most beautiful woman in the world, any way you wanted her. But there was a condition to it. And that was, you had to let her old boyfriend fuck you in the ass."

"What!" Johnny found the condition preposterous.

"Yeah. Seriously. I mean, just hypothetical. But suppose you could have her any way you wanted her. You could fuck her. She'd suck you off. You could tie her up or have her tie you up. Whatever you like. She'd be your sex slave for a month. AIDS, shit like that isn't part of the equation. Don't even consider it. She's clean; she's gorgeous; a perfect doll. You're not married. Everything's neutral, except, for you to have her, you have to agree to let her ex fuck you in the ass. Just once. Would you do it?"

"No!" Johnny was adamant.

"Come on, now. I'm serious. Think what you're getting here. The most perfect sex partner on the planet. The most beautiful woman God ever created. Wouldn't you do it?"

Johnny squirmed. "You're the one who's nuts," he said.

"How about for ten years?" Larry asked. "Wouldn't you agree to let this guy put his prick up that cherub kiss of yours just once?"

"Goddamn it, Larry." Nick held his glass as if he were about to throw his drink in Larry's face. "Shut the fuck up."

"He doesn't have to answer," Larry said sweetly. "Not now, anyway. Not to me. You all can answer it to yourselves later."

"Just deal," Brian said. He did not look at the dealer.

Now no one spoke. The play was serious, quiet, at times stupid because of the amount of alcohol they'd consumed. They shifted from five card to seven, bet on each new card as it was dealt. The pots rose to three thousand. Johnny lost several hands, won one, was up over twelve hundred bucks.

Larry dealt two facedown to each player. Johnny checked. Two queens. He received a trey, bet the first round exactly as did the other players. He was dealt a king; stayed the course; was dealt another trey, giving him a pair showing. LeRoy had a pair of fours; led the betting; pushed the pot to over a thousand. All players remained in. The last round dealt to show gave Johnny a queen, LeRoy a third four. Scott and Nick folded. Brian reviewed his cards. He could see that LeRoy had three of a kind showing, Johnny a pair of treys. Johnny, he reasoned, would not stay in if he had either another three down or a pair down. Neither would beat LeRoy's three fours. Therefore, Brian figured, Johnny had a full house. He too had a full house, kings and fives, only a pair of fives showing. He studied LeRoy's cards, calculated the chance of him having the last four, thought Vernon had had it showing when he'd folded. Brian raised the pot by $250. LeRoy and Johnny saw the raise; the last card was dealt down.

Johnny raised the edge of his card; hid his delight. It was the king of diamonds. His full house was now kings and queens. "I'll go, ah, two-seventy. You need seven hundred in there to stay in."

"See that, go another five bills," Brian said. That pushed the pot to over four thousand. The three remaining players were in for twelve hundred each.

"Make it fifteen hundred," LeRoy said. He counted out his bills, slid them to the center of the table.

Brian swallowed. He knew, was now certain, LeRoy had four of a kind. To remain in meant losing more. Still, to fold now meant losing seventeen hundred. He sat quietly contemplating his move, secretly pissed he'd gone this far.

Johnny put his hand in his pocket, pulled out his wallet, dug out his new platinum Visa card. He tossed the card into the pot. "That's my chit," he said. "Make it twenty-five hundred."

"I'm out," Brian said.

Large Larry scribbled a few numbers on a pad. "Should be ninety-one fifty in there, twenty-five hundred on that chit. You don't have to accept that."

"Nah," LeRoy said. "It's okay." He added another thousand in bills, peered at Johnny, slowly turned over the fourth four.

Johnny's face sagged but he hid it.

"Shit!" Nick said for him. "Shit."

The others stood, stretched, twisted.

"Hey," LeRoy said. He tossed the credit card back to Johnny, pulled in the cash. "You wanta go double or nothin on that chit?"

"No," Johnny said. "I'll, ah . . . I'll get it to ya."

"Look," LeRoy said. "I'm tryin to get ya outta this. You can go double or nothin twice. You gotta win one time. Trust me."

"What if I don't?" Johnny said.

"Then ya owe me a lot a money." LeRoy laughed. "We'll cut cards, flip a coin. Whatever you want."

"Let him go three times," Brian said. He winked at Johnny.

"Fuck im, man," Nick said. "Don't get inta that shit."

"Yeah. Okay. Three," LeRoy said.

Johnny reached over in front of the dealer, grabbed the deck of cards, cut, turned up a ten of hearts.

LeRoy cut, turned over a jack of clubs. He chuckled. "That's once," he said. "Five grand."

Nick grabbed his brother. Johnny parried Nick's grasp. He was intent on the deck, tunnel-focused. Again he cut, this time turning up a three of spades. LeRoy's card was a nine of hearts. "Ten grand." LeRoy laughed. "Once more?"

Johnny's heart was pounding. His hands were cold, damp; his mind numb. As if driven, he quickly cut the deck, turned up a queen of hearts. He looked up, blew out a heavy sigh. "Thank God."

"Hey." LeRoy tapped Johnny's shoulder. "Good for you. Let me see what I get." Without looking he placed his hand, wriggled his fingers over the deck. "I feel a five comin," he said. He turned over a king.

Johnny gasped.

"Let him go again," Brian blurted.

"Deal's a deal, man," LeRoy said. "Twenty grand. I know ya got money. I'll give ya thirty days. I know where ta find ya."

IT WAS NEARLY four in the morning when Nick dropped Johnny off. That had not been the plan, but after bringing Brian and Vern home, being more than halfway to East Lake, Johnny had insisted. He'd been quiet in the car, ashamed, embarrassed, in shock. His life had just gone not simply from bad to worse, but from bad to irretrievable. He'd made the others swear a vow of silence.

Johnny's mind raced, feverish-afraid-inebriated. His thoughts, even to himself, made no sense. I've been bilked. It was a scam, a setup. Cont-GenChem did this to me. They made me do it, made me gamble to make up for the loss in income. Gullible jerk. Kids are jerks. That's why . . .

He did not go in but watched until he could no longer see the tail-lights of Nick's car, then crossed the street, stumbled down the rocky beach to the edge of the water, kicked a rock which didn't budge. Fucked, he thought. I oughta just end this miserable existence right now. Fucked. His thoughts rolled, tumbled from his mind, not in linear strings of words but splotches of words and images and feelings inter-meshed with alcohol and adrenaline, now building a picture of Julia and Meloblatt, seeing, more disturbing, transforming, not Meloblatt and Hickel but Julia having an affair with Marvin . . . he, big Marvin . . . the image, romantic, strong as he'd been at twenty, rich enough to give her anything she could ever want, a ten-million-dollar bank account, a ten-inch dick . . . Big Marvin . . . his competition . . . butt-fucking . . . her story a cover for . . . Dreaming, convoluting, not Hickel . . . not Julia . . . he, Johnny, is bent over Marvin's desk . . . the one condition . . . fucking Marvin . . . being fucked by Big Marvin . . . being fucked by everyone . . . Fuck the woman! I'd let him fuck me up the ass for my twenty grand. Oh God! Oh God! Holy shit! How did I do this? Why did I do this?! What did I do? What . . . ? I gotta . . .

Johnny tiptoed in. Quietly he removed one shoe, stumbled, banged the wall as he attempted to remove the other. Dog Corleone came to greet him. His nails clicked on the hardwood. Johnny tried to stop him, put a hand on his back. The dog pushed against Johnny's hand, nuzzled his nose between Johnny's legs. "Go!" Johnny ordered; a harsh whisper.

He placed a foot on the bottom stair, listened to it creak as he shifted his weight. Shit, he thought. His thoughts were bleak, muted, jumbled, crazy. There was a seam of light under their bedroom door. Julia was up. As he reached for the knob he thought, Your fault. You needed a career. If I didn't cover back here, take care of the kids back here . . . You wanted me to be Mr. Mom . . . I could of been big . . . I could of . . . when it was NSC . . . then I'd . . .

Slowly he opened the door. On the bed there were a half dozen piles; letters, résumés, handwritten notes. The bathroom light was on, the door open. "You still up?" Johnny called quietly.

Her voice came softly. "I've been studying some of the responses I've gotten," she said. "And I was drafting a few thoughts . . . for a harassment suit against Meloblatt and Gallina."

Johnny bumped the bed, straightened. He removed his shirt, sat, undid his pants.

"Are you okay?" Julia asked. She appeared in the doorway to the bathroom. Her bottom half was covered by a pair of crushed-cotton pajama trousers with a Wisconsin Badger on one leg. Above she was naked.

Johnny gasped, smiled broadly.

"Oh, stop it." Julia chuckled. "You're drunk."

Johnny stood. He was in only his shorts and socks. "No, I'm not."

"Yes, you are." Julia laughed again. "I can tell."

"Umm!" Johnny hummed.

"Unt-uh." Julia covered her breasts, turned, retreated into the bath.

Johnny whipped off his socks, followed her in. One last time, he thought. One last time. *When you find out . . . you'll . . .*

She kept her back to him as she shook out the pajama top, aligned it so she could slide in her arms. He leered at her back. To him Julia's back looked like the young woman in the Indian-maiden dress; her ass looked like the blonde's with the great legs; her breasts—as she bent he could see the side and top of one, see both in the mirror—were better than the brunette's with the knockout tits. "Unt-uh, you," Johnny said.

Julia's arms were in the arms of the loose top but she hadn't yet flipped it over her head. "Don't look at me," she said.

"You've got to show em," Johnny said. He stood behind her, put his hands on her shoulders, blocked her from donning the top. He kissed her shoulder.

"Get out of here," Julia said. She laughed, wriggled her shoulders to his touch.

Lightly he ran his hands down from the top of her breasts, pulling the pajama top away, exposing her to the mirror where he ogled her image. "Come on now," Johnny whispered. "They're a work of art." He pressed his groin against her backside.

"Johnny," Julia said without conviction, "go away." Halfheartedly she attempted to raise the top.

"They're like a Rembrandt." He kissed her neck.

Julia laughed sweetly. "Stop it," she said.

"Unt-uh," Johnny uttered. He rubbed his chest on her back, his hands over her hips. "You wouldn't put a Rembrandt in the closet, would you?" Now they both laughed and he pushed his erection hard against her and she pushed back. "These should be on display," he said. "In public."

She let the pajama top fall to the floor. "Oh! Johnny!" In the bedroom the phone rang. They ignored it, Johnny pulling Julia's pajama bottoms down her thighs. The phone continued to ring. "Oh!" Julia panted. "What is that?"

"A wrong number," Johnny mumbled. He pushed his shorts to his ankles, stepped out of them. The phone continued to ring.

"That's going to wake the whole house," Julia said. She bent to pull her bottoms up. Johnny held her hips, slid himself back and forth over her smooth skin. Still the phone continued ringing. Julia heard Jenny stir in her room. "I've got to get it," she said. She pulled up her pants.

Johnny caught her as she answered the phone by the bed, again held her hips; again he pressed and rubbed and caressed.

"Hello?"

"Julia!" The voice was fast, hard, furious, frightened.

"Yes?" She was about to turn to Johnny, about to say, "It's Mitch."

"I need help. I need help right now. You gotta help me."

"Mitch, what is—"

"Where's Johnny?"

"He's right here."

"He's gotta come here. He's gotta take Whitney and Diana. Hide em."

"Wha . . . ?"

"They just shot the shit outta my house. They just shot—"

Johnny grabbed the phone. He'd heard the last line. "Mitch, what's going on there? Did you call . . . ?"

"They're comin. The police are comin. Johnny—" Mitch was nearly hysterical "—they shot my house! They set a fire on my lawn and shot—"

Through the phone Johnny could hear sirens. "I'll be right there."

The fourth of Johnny-Panni's last thoughts—9 December

I see him. He is n'gazz. *Crazy. He is bitter, angry, baffled. His mind can no longer work a thought; can no longer grab it, turn it, analyze it. Instead thoughts come, flow, flee as if they are independent of their processor, independent of my mind.*

Why should winter begin . . . ? This thought materializes at 10:14:27 P.M. on this ninth day of December while I stare, no I don't, I glance, that's all, I glance at my watch, as I walk . . . Why should winter begin on the shortest day of the year?! Why isn't the solstice exactly midwinter? Or midwinter the solstice? What stupid fool . . . Little Johnny-panni is angry . . . What fool made this rule? If I designed the world . . . I . . . he thinks . . . I . . .

I have added a dozen more pages to his report on reestablishing ferry service to the lake—details—a proposed shuttle schedule, a calculation of capital expenditures and operating costs and projected fares and the necessary volume of passengers . . . potential shoreline damage from wakes . . .

I have donned his heavy flannel-lined cotton trousers, his old quilted cotton shirt, leather boots, long coat—all as I have planned. We have set out into the darkness to accomplish our task.

It is dark, quiet, frigid. After twelve clear hours the sky has clouded, the temperature fallen. Sporadic flakes have fluttered all afternoon, have become steady. I see him move. Slowly he trudges to the water's edge. He stares into the harsh, amorphous dark. No light from Lakeport infiltrates to the east shore. He takes no joy being at my lake. His face is slack. He turns, lowers his head, steps in the direction of the pier. It is winter . . . the ninth of . . . not . . . fools . . . If the solstice fell midwinter, winter began six . . . five weeks ago . . . but . . . fool . . . He holds his head, his forehead, he cannot calculate . . . his head bent down, his . . . There on the ground before him there is a dark smudge, a darkness on the dark shore. He bends, brushes away a thin coating of fluff, uncovers a broken piece of branch in the now frozen slush. Johnny grasps, dislodges the stick, picks it up. It is a nice stick. What a nice stick! Despite clinging crystals of ice, it is light for its size. He hefts it, turns it. It is twenty inches long, an inch and a half in diameter. A giant . . . he thinks. Bigger than Harry's. Dead. He laughs. Trimmed by the wind. He laughs, looks up. There are no trees from which it could have fallen. Johnny lets the stick fall from his hands, steps on it, over it, stops. Again he picks it up. He climbs to the road, thinks to toss the stick, it is a stick, thinks to toss it across into his yard under a tree where it belongs, yet he holds it. There are lights in the house—in the living room, in the attic.

A deep bitterness, a deep sadness, envelopes . . . He thinks of LeRoy yet he . . . I bear him no malice . . . I . . . He has not told Julia. How could I? He has not told Mitch. Nor Rocco. How could . . . ? He has told Nick that LeRoy has settled for less.

I feel the corners of my mouth, feel the weight of . . . feel the sagging skin, cold, miserable . . . Something happens to a man when he can't support his fam . . . when . . . Trying to live in the lap of luxury without paying the dues . . . without . . . Mitch knows . . . overexten . . . This country doesn't need a good five-cent cigar; it needs Benjamin Franklin reincarnate; it needs . . . That's not it . . . That's not what it's about. Even if I had the money . . . Even . . . It'll be here soon enough. Not soon enough . . . but it's not about money. It is not . . . God! How did I do this? It's not money. It's not . . . It's . . . everythi . . . It's me. N'gazz.

A car speeds by. He turns from the house, from the road, back to the lake. He still holds the stick. His mind shuffles his feet but his feet do not move. His eyes shift to the pier yet in the blackness he cannot see the pier. Maybe if I'd done something else, he thinks, like he's thought for too long. Something meaningful, something . . . but . . . too late! Almost fifty. If I started school now, if I could get in, I'd graduate . . . I'd be competing against kids like Todd . . . like Aaron if . . . I could never compete . . . not with his mind . . . not . . . with Todd. With Jason. For the same entry-level slot. Cheating them . . . taking away a slot . . . Impossible!

I see Johnny-panni turn back to the road, step into the gutter. The surface is wet, gritty from the salt-and-sand mix the town's crews have spread. His legs move. With his leather boots it is easier to walk on the shoulder than it has been to walk on the rocks of The Point. I can see him, me, us . . . clearly. Very clearly. He shuffles south, away from the pier, moves in the direction of traffic, traffic at his back, walks toward Adam's Inn, toward The Bastille restaurant, toward South Lake Village, the dam. Why does he go toward . . . ?

A big mistake, he thinks. Not the joining NSC . . . it was good before . . . wasn't it? But . . . but . . . Tripps laughs at me. ContGenChem. Now ContGen . . .

So I made a mistake . . . but . . . Advertising. A life mistake. The wrong direction. The wrong life . . .

Stop. I make him stop. He is going in the wrong direction but I can't turn him back. Back, too, is the wrong direction. The wrong spot. The wrong . . . It's always been the wrong location. It's always . . . I . . . I would besmirch my lake!

At the intersection of Lake Shore and Fourth, rays from the streetlight bounce in the enveloping cloud, frolic amid the sparse descending crystals. Advertiser's words. Our crystals will make you everything you want to be. Be everything you can be. Join . . .

Though the night is frigid, the ambience I feel here, at the corner . . . warm, almost cozy . . . like a Christmas card drawing. I turn his head up, stare into the glow. Advertising, he thinks. And marketing . . . I will make him think. I will make him repent. I . . . because I thought advertising and marketing were where the chicks and money were. Where the . . . What a naive young doped-out dipstick! I could have . . . How much more I would have loved to be a producer; design a product. How positive my contribution could have been. Had I been an engineer . . . had I been a chemist . . . had I followed Mitch's route . . . developed a new process, something that advanced technology, something I could have looked back on and said, "I helped advance civilization." Instead of saying, "I helped civilization deteriorate!" Instead of saying, "I wasn't there for . . ." I could have developed a skid-proof . . . The car would know it had left the road. Katie Fitzpatrick would . . . Automatic braking. It would have known he'd stomped on the wrong . . .

Tears on his cheeks. I lower his head, feel the tears roll down as he walks from the glow of the intersection into the dark. A car speeds by, swerves at the last moment. The driver blasts its horn. Johnny smiles menacingly. He angles a foot farther from the gutter, a foot closer to the lane, continues south, snickers! In the cold his knees ache, his left knee cramps, catches. He stumbles, pushes on, not the least bit careful, proud of being not the least bit careful. Another car approaches, swerves, rushes by. He tries not to think but finds himself calculating the approximate traffic flow, a car every two minutes. Some drivers see him at a distance, give him a wide berth, some see him at the last moment, swerve to miss him, one does not see him at all, the side mirror hits the fabric of his coat. One will not see him at all, will not be . . .

Get hit by a car. If I get . . . If I let him get hit . . . I . . . Johnny . . . I let him . . . He thinks of himself, visualizes himself; thinks, visualizes, a mixture of words, images . . . not wearing a helmet . . . sees him being hit, his feet, knees, trapped beneath the onrushing skidding car driving, whipping his body forward, his head whacking the road, the curb. Task complete. The filthiness . . . the shame . . . the squalor of his mind . . . ended.

A car descends upon us. He steps into the lane. The horn blares, the car swerves. Involuntarily he shrinks back; simultaneously he swings his stick, hits the vehicle. It accelerates, horn blaring, driver gesticulating angrily. N'gazz! *he swears.* N'gazz! *He begins to shake, to vibrate, to cry. "Why won't you hit me?" He drops to the ground. His nose runs, his eyes flood. He urinates. I feel the wetness spread through the flannel lining; I feel it down his leg.*

"I'm sorry, Mitch. I tried. I tried. I couldn't . . . Oh . . . Pop! You . . . I'm . . . I didn't mean . . . I didn't mean for any of it . . . I'm . . . I'm so ashamed. Julia. Dear Julia . . . Jason, Todd. I have no answers. Oh my Sunshine. Don't hate me. I'm . . . useless . . . oh my sweet Sunshine . . ."

Johnny-panni crawls from the road. Sit. He does not know where to go. He crawls into the shrubs, through the shrubs, away from the road. It's right there, he thinks. The lake is right . . .

He stands. His tears stop. He feels cool, cold, numb. Lord, make me an element of Your peace. Make me an . . . If only You had. Lord, make me an element of Your lake.

Johnny-panni stumbles down the slope toward the water. His vision is blurred by the light snow, hampered by the darkness. He feels water at his ankles. He looks straight forward. To him the snow seems frail, seems strange. He feels it on his face as he feels the icy water fill his boots, freeze his knees, rise, yet it seems not a feeling, not he feeling it but some vessel he . . . we inhabit. He can't feel if I can't feel. His hands tremble, his entire body shivers not from cold but from below, from within, as if the vessel is fighting a virus. His vision darkens. The seventh polarization, I think. The words do not come from him but come to him from the darkness over the water. From outside. The seventh . . . BODY FROM SOUL.

I have a hole in my heart. As hard as I've been with you while you were with me, as hardened as my heart has become, I have a hole there, now, that can never be filled. Body from soul. I do understand. I . . .

"Finish."

The word comes to him not from his mind but from the darkness over the water.

"Seek answers."

I step back. "Pop?" He stares into the snow. "Pop?" The snow swirls.

"Before you can finish you must finish."

The Panuzio Home, East Lake, Wednesday, 26 October, 6:33 A.M.

"GOOD MORNIN," JOHNNY said with a softness he did not feel.

Jason didn't answer. He was at the kitchen table; the morning paper was spread before him. One hand held three toaster waffles; the other was wrapped around a glass of milk.

"You had a good game yesterday," Johnny said.

No response.

"How's school going? Your classroom work and . . . ?"

"Fine." Jason did not look up, did not raise his arms off the paper. On the front page there was a four-column-by-twelve-inch photograph of Jason and a player from Plymouth High. The photo was clear, the grass green, the white of the touchline distinct, the ball spinning yet nearly sharp enough for subscribers to read its logo lettering. In the picture Jason was crouched, his legs in a wide fighter's stance, the ball behind him. The Plymouth player was two feet off the ground, nearly horizontal, flying, sprawling, a look of agony on his face. Jason's knee was in his groin. The caption read: CAUGHT IN THE ACT, and the cutline said: "East Lake's Jason Panuzio (6) uses his knee to take down Plymouth's Alex Shaker during yesterday's game at Plymouth High. Panuzio was carded on the play for unsportsmanlike conduct. East Lake won the game, 4–1."

Jason studied the image of his face. He looked determined, fearsome, mean. He liked the look. He studied his legs, his arms. He looked strong. He looked at Shaker. To Jason his opponent looked foolish; stupid; victimized. Still, what had Compari said to him after the game? Something like, "If yer goina do that shit, at least don't get caught." There he was, caught in the act!

Jason turned the page before Johnny came to the table with his coffee. He pushed his foot into Dog Corleone's shoulder. "Go away."

"Don't give him any of your waffles." Johnny sat. "They're not good for him."

"I'm not," Jason said. He rose. "I need the paper. For history. Okay?"

"Sure." Johnny too put his foot on the dog, pushed him, snapped, "What are ya doin under the table?" The dog didn't move but rolled over, sighed loudly.

"I'm outta here," Jason said.

"Anything good in the paper?" Johnny called.

"Picture of our game." Jason's voice was flat. "A story sayin six kids were arrested on weapons charges."

Instant anger: "Where? Who? What weapons?"

"At the high school. After school. Yesterday. They weren't doin anything. Kid named Terry Whitman . . . It says he displayed a gun . . ."

Johnny flicked his hand. "Jerk."

"He just *showed* it to some other kids in the parking lot," Jason said defensively. "But that's school property, so they arrested him, and it said they'll probably expel him for the rest of the year. Even the kids just lookin at it are going to be expelled."

"Jerks!" Johnny repeated loudly. He tried to bite his tongue. Jason's comment seemed like the longest burst of words Johnny'd heard from him all fall. He didn't want to stop Jason from talking, wanted to warn him again about saying anything about . . .

"I'm gone." Jason slammed the door.

Again Johnny shoved Dog Corleone. "Do you gotta be right there?" he muttered. Johnny checked the clock, 6:42, forty minutes before sunrise. He thought to walk to The Point, to stand, to watch the water, the sky lighten. But the morning was cold; he felt chilled, sick.

For three days he'd hidden Diana and Whitney for Mitch, hidden them in Jenny's room. For three days the twins had not left that room with the exception of using the upstairs bathroom. They had eaten in Jenny's room while Jenny ate in the kitchen so that anyone surveilling the house would not notice a change in pattern. They slept in Jenny's room, studied from Jenny's books, listened to Jenny's music, read, chatted, danced—but not near Jenny's windows. No one phoned them. They phoned no one. Neither Mitch nor Laurie visited. Not even Vern or Elisse were told the whereabouts of their nieces. Jenny kept to her regular routine. When Tara asked if she knew anything, Jenny just shrugged her shoulders. When Kristin prodded, Jenny attacked, "Why does everyone think I would know?!" Though she kept the secret, she was bursting to tell Lena. Still, for two school days she'd successfully suppressed the urge. Even the school administration had not been informed; had been told only that the girls had been removed for their own safety.

Johnny poured a second cup of coffee, rummaged through yesterday's paper for something he hadn't yet read. His eyes fell to the middle of a letter to the editor. "I don't know why," the man had written, "any woman would support him. He's been shown to be a philanderer and a womanizer, and his record on affirmative action for women is the worst of any president in twenty years. Perhaps that's good for most men, but most men think he's sleazy. Men dislike him. Women love him. Please, explain this to me."

Johnny wanted to smile at the strange attack but he did not smile. He had problems and his problems had become much larger than his capacity to handle them. Julia thought his anxiety was because of the shooting at Mitch's; perhaps also because of Rocco's seeming sudden and drastic decline; plus their job situations and the general angst of the town, which had been increasing alarmingly ever since the auto accident in September. He had not told Julia about the card game, had not explained to her what had happened at Sanchez' Grocery. Nor had he told her about yesterday's call from LeRoy.

"You got twenty-eight days, man," LeRoy had said. "Get me my money or I'm gonna have ta take some action."

Weakly Johnny had whispered, "What action?"

"Action like I sell your chit to the highest bidder."

"Sell it?! What's that mean? Who buys . . . ?"

"Disciples of Hell, maybe." LeRoy named a well-known Puerto Rican gang which controlled much of Lakeport's South Street Projects. "Or the Immortal Pharaohs. Hell," LeRoy laughed, "even B-SIN and that skinhead group . . ."

"I'll see what I can—"

"LASH-OUT," LeRoy cut in. "That's the name. Lake Area—"

"Yeah," Johnny mumbled. "You don't gotta tell me . . ."

"Twenty-eight days, man," LeRoy warned.

"I'm . . . gettin a second mortgage," Johnny had lied. "But it's goina take at least forty-five . . ."

Julia descended from the second floor, entered the kitchen. She was wearing a soft, plush, teal-colored velour robe. "Shit," she seethed.

"What?" Johnny responded. To him Julia looked very tired.

"I don't like this," Julia whispered.

"What?"

"This . . . this putting us in danger."

"The twins?!"

Julia's whisper rose. "What the hell do you think I'm talking about?"

"It's the least we can do." Johnny's volume remained subdued.

Julia huffed, sneered. She poured herself a cup of coffee, came to the table. "Maybe I . . ." She had been thinking about it for two days; had been thinking about it but had not let it surface, had not allowed it to be defined within her own thoughts, for months. "Maybe Jenny and I should move out."

"What?"

Julia lowered her head, didn't look at Johnny, didn't answer.

Johnny stared at her. "Don't do something crazy."

"Like this isn't?" Julia retorted.

"It isn't," Johnny snapped. He stood. "I'll call you," he said. "Stay here."

Again Julia huffed, sneered.

Jenny jumped to the table. "Boo!" she shouted. Johnny started. Neither he nor Julia had seen Jenny approach. She threw her arms up high, opened her hands, screeched, *"Mama mía!"* She looked to see if Julia was in the mood for a hug, instantly decided she wasn't, turned to Johnny. "An Popsters, lob-sters!" She pirouetted, giggled, collapsed to the floor, hugged the dog.

As Julia scolded, "You're getting dog hair all over your clothes," Rocco shuffled into the kitchen. He was hunched, his head hung, his face sagged. He did not seem to notice the others.

Johnny hid his feelings, called loudly, "How ya doin this mornin, Pop?"

"Lousy," Rocco answered.

Jenny knelt, put her interlaced fingers on the table, elbows spread, chin on her hands. To Julia she said, "I've got band after school, and CCD tonight. Who's goina take—"

"What's the matter?" Johnny's question overpowered Jenny's voice.

"I'm dizzy. I'm . . ." Rocco opened the refrigerator door, stood looking in.

"Aaahh!" Johnny groaned. "There's Mitch." He looked at Julia. "I'll call you. Don't . . ." His voice tapered off. To Jenny he said, "And you, Sweetums, you remember . . ."

"I'm not a dolt, Popsters." Jenny laughed. "Get it?"

"It's set for twelve forty-five." Mitch fidgeted. "This is killin me, Johnny."

"Yeah. I would think." Johnny, too, was antsy. They made their way quickly to the highway, did not stop for gas, coffee or lotto tickets. "I would think," he repeated.

"How are you holdin up?" Mitch asked.

"Fine." Johnny shifted in the seat.

"I mean about the money. How much did . . . ?"

"A bunch," Johnny answered before Mitch could finish, purposefully halting the line of questioning.

"If you're in trouble, let me help."

"No. You got enough—"

"You're helping me. Let me help . . ."

"Not this time. I'll work something—"

"I can't do it without you, Johnny. You can't do it without me! You got troubles, I got troubles. Incredible, huh?"

"Yeah. I'll . . . I'll let ya know. Tell me the rest."

"Hilman," Mitch said. "You remember him."

"Yeah. From the state police."

"Yeah. Tom Hilman. It's going to happen today. He's going to be at your house at exactly twelve forty-five. He'll be in a dark blue Chevy sedan with the marker plate SPI-007. It's his own car."

Johnny chuckled, "Spy, double-oh-seven, huh?"

"Yeah. Except he says it stands for state police investigator. Anyway, tell Julia to expect that sedan and nothing else. There'll be a woman with Hilman, from child services—Heidi Gibson."

"You're not going to tell me where you're sending them, are you?"

"It's better for you if you don't know."

"Um." Johnny stared straight forward. "How long do you think?"

"When . . . I don't know," Mitch answered. "When this blows over."

Again Johnny shifted. "The articles won't make it worse, will they?"

"I don't see how they can," Mitch said.

"I could get the *Ledger* to postpone . . ."

"Nah. You finish em?"

"Mostly. With the way things have been . . . let's just say I'm better than halfway through. And Liz Callipano's agreed—"

Mitch cut Johnny off. "If they ever find who murdered . . ." He didn't finish the sentence but shifted the topic. "Did you read past the front page? About last night's town meeting?"

"No. I didn't see the paper. Jason took it . . ."

"Didn't see it?!"

"What?"

"Jason's picture."

"Oh. He said something."

"Biggest damn soccer picture they've ever put on the front page."

"On the front page?! Really?"

"Ah . . ." Mitch laughed. "You might want to see it before you go in. He really nailed . . . *Á*. You'll see! And inside, at the town meeting last night, they passed the teen curfew. Eleven P.M. Kids out after that hour will be brought to the police station and their parents will have to come pick em up."

"Your police state at work," Johnny said.

"Maybe," Mitch answered coolly. For a few moments they rode in silence. Johnny bounced his right leg nervously. Mitch rocked forward and back. "I've been thinking so much lately," Mitch said, "my head's like a speeding locomotive. We're in a time like a hundred years ago: major social shifts; general economic expansion; great moral crises. We're seeing astronomical profits going to a tiny elite. The bottom of the pyramid's exploding, the peak's getting higher and thinner." Mitch braced the wheel with his knee, used his hands to define a shape. "Kind of like a candy kiss but with the top becoming as fine as a blond hair.

"Johnny," he continued, "it's like the reestablishment of the feudal nobility. And we're seeing extreme reactions to extreme situations."

"Time," Johnny attempted to joke, "for the revolution."

Mitch said nothing, rocked forward and back. Then he blurted, "There's so much ta do. Somebody's got me labeled as an Uncle Tom. As a sellout. And they're attacking me and my family because they think we're anti-diversity. They look at me and say, 'Oh, he's got his; now he's one of em. He thinks, the hell with us.' I want to say to them, 'Who's really selling out? Those who are cheerleading your economic disadvantages, or those who are at the forefront of leading black America out of economic disenfranchisement?' Johnny, we gotta grab this issue, make sure it gets solved in a way that doesn't increase the mass at the bottom of the pyramid."

"Um." Johnny had not expected Mitch's verbosity, had expected Mitch to be as subdued as he'd been for most of the past six weeks. Instead it was as if Mitch were on speed. Johnny, too, felt as if he were speeding, but his reaction was internal, self-consumptive, buried beneath an avalanche. Right now he couldn't talk to Mitch about the deli, about money, about LeRoy's threat, about Julia. He wanted to listen. Instead he said, "It's hard for a middle-class white guy to talk about the politics of race. Because of where we start from. Because of the perception of where we're starting from."

"No shit." Mitch laughed.

"No shit." Johnny laughed too. "I might believe some of their policies are disadvantageous to . . . um . . . like to the poorer parts of the black community. Like in Aaron's thesis."

"Um," Mitch hummed. " 'To be assisted because of their blackness instead of their penury . . .' "

"Yeah. Those were his words. But if I say that," Johnny said, "I sound like a racist. I know I'll be criticized as a racist. But I can say it through Aaron's paper. It takes a lot of courage, Mitch, and a lot of commitment to expose yourself like that."

"Because you're not a racist," Mitch said. "And I'm not an Uncle Tom."

"Right," Johnny said.

"Even—" Mitch hesitated "—if you believe the policy they're attempting to institute is going to be bad for the people they say it's going to help?"

"Um. Huh?"

Mitch glanced over. "That, my friend, *is* racist."

"Whoa . . . I don't follow."

"Not having the courage to stand up and protect people who are being cemented into the status quo by programs which kill their mobility. Truly chickenshit!"

"Yeah . . . I . . ." Johnny's leg bounced. He was itching all over, itching to tell Mitch how excited he was about the upcoming articles; how he thought it would break the spell that seemed to have been cast upon them, upon the entire region; how the articles might even send him, Johnny, in a new direction; save him; maybe lead to a new career. But he could not say those things. He could not because he could not profit from Aaron's murder; could not yet even tell Mitch the content of the articles, not before they were published. He wanted to surprise Mitch. The articles would begin in four days.

"If you don't speak up," Mitch said, "even though you believe . . . like, some enablement programs . . . good for business because they trap people in, limit the competition. That's why so many huge corporations back liberal programs. Not because they're humanitarian but because the greedy bastards at the top know who keeps em in power."

"I should be taking notes," Johnny said. "I could use this . . ."

Mitch rocked. "If you don't speak out, you're chickenshit."

Johnny smiled. "Um. I think Aaron's death is making me realize that. His death and his papers."

"At first I thought it was drugs," Mitch said. "Now I think, maybe, he was killed because I'm seen as an Uncle Tom. Maybe he was killed . . . I don't know. I don't know if he was killed by whites who didn't like his blackness or by blacks who didn't like his whiteness. Or didn't like mine."

"That's the reason you said to go ahead with the articles."

"We've got to . . ." Mitch began, changed midsentence. "This hasn't made me more afraid. It's made me more determined. I'm goina protect the girls but I'm not goina let this issue die. I'm not goina let people say, 'Don't get me involved.' No matter their color. That'd be chickenshit. Saying that gives the *perceived* moral high ground to those who have been economically and morally disastrous for the people they're claiming to assist. We *hold* the true moral high ground. But if we don't speak up, if we don't assist, don't defend, then we're chickenshit. If you know that it's tough love that's the best way to help, you've got to have the courage to stand up and be counted. To do otherwise *is* racist. To do otherwise is chickenshit."

THE CORRIDOR WAS empty, the lights subdued. Classroom doors, by new policy, were closed, locked. Jason stood, stared at Joanie Mitterand's locker. He had asked Marcia Radkowski for a boys' room pass, which she'd gladly given; had meandered to the bank of lockers. He stood alone, bounced on the balls of his feet, clenched, unclenched his fists, gritted his teeth.

That's it! Jason thought angrily. Joanie was an acquaintance, on the field hockey team, the student council, catcher on the girls' softball team. Her friends called her Mitts. She was tall, strong, hefty but not fat. "That's fucken it!" Jason muttered to himself.

On Tuesday Mitts had been upset by graffiti someone had put on her locker. The letters had been made with a broad-stroke black marker in a flourishing stylistic sweep typical of the wall art Jason had seen in South Lakeport. *Joanie Mitts has nice Tits! Ask me. I know.* Before school started, several of her friends had helped her scrub off the offensive words. Now Joanie was in tears. There was a new message: *The Best of Clits, is Joanie Mitts. We know it, too!*

Vice Principal Michelle Dutchussy had not allowed her to wash the words away. She'd wanted Charlene Rosenwald, the principal, and John Schoemer, the superintendent of schools, to first see the writing. And she'd wanted photographs.

In this second incident, Kim Sanchez' locker, in the same bank on the same wall, had been similarly defaced: *Kim San-chez is a great lay. Ask us.*

Jason ground his teeth. That is fucking it! he thought. He thought each word deliberately, distinctly, as he stared from one locker to the other. Verdeen's gone too far. Too fucken far.

Kim had been even more upset than Joanie, had been worried the school would call her father, worried her father would make a scene.

How much of his shit are we goina take? Jason thought. There comes a time . . . there comes a time . . . Jason had heard the line but he could recall only part of it. There comes a time when the most humble . . . if he keeps his eyes open . . . can take his revenge . . . It was something from the *Godfather,* something he'd heard Uncle Nick say months earlier. Time, fucker! Jason thought. It's just a matter of time. Why wait?

Jason walked quietly past the boys' room to the janitor's closet. He tried the door. It was locked. He grasped the knob, squeezed, twisted. Still it was locked. His eyes shifted to the crack between the door and the jamb, to the cylindrical shank of the lock bolt. With a credit card . . . he thought, but immediately gave up the thought. He grasped the knob with both hands, squeezed until he was crushing his fingers against the ball, twisted with all his might, thought, *Fuck you and your goddamn photos,* yanked. The door shot toward him, almost whacked him in the head.

Jason ducked in, turned on the light, shut the door. The janitorial closet was larger then he'd expected but no different from others he'd seen—a set of shelves with cleaning supplies, a basin, brooms, mops, mop buckets on casters. The walls were brick, the floor concrete. The small room was quiet, quieter than the empty corridors with their humming fluorescent lights. With the door shut it felt to Jason as if it were nearly soundproof. He scanned the top shelf, then the middle shelves. He wasn't certain which cleaner took off permanent marker. He knelt, one knee to the floor; scanned the bottom shelf; noticed a floor drain; ran his hand over the drain cover. He bent closer. The strainer was held to the drain by two screws. Jason pulled a dime from his pocket, loosened one screw, the other; removed the perforated disk. He peered into the drain. The pipe was nearly four inches in diameter, went straight down for eighteen inches then curved toward the left, toward the boys' room. For a moment Jason remained perfectly still.

No more shit! he thought. We take no more shit. I can . . . I've got the power to hurt . . . I've got the power to hide . . . I've got the power to kill. "That motherfucker," Jason whispered. He replaced the strainer, the screws. He did not tighten the screws. First he did Aaron, Jason thought. I don't know how, but I know Verdeen did it . . . was behind it. That little fucker's always late coming from third . . . always has a pass to fourth. Unfucken-believable. He talks shit about everybody. Stirs up incidents. He was behind the house shooting. I just know it. It's his graffiti. I just fucken know it. Now he's got a lawyer suing McMillian over *him* being a racist! He . . . That's fucken it. I could do him. It's just a matter of time. He'll never lead me to who really did Aaron. I'll do him. A matter of sequence. Come to the closet. Put the bayonet in the drain. Get the right sequence. The right sequentiality. Clean up. A matter of biding one's time. First set the door so I can open it . . . Jason turned his attention to the lock.

"YOU PREGNANT, GIRL?" Martina asked.

"No!" Kim said emphatically.

"I heard you pregnant." They were by the double doors in the corridor just outside the cafeteria. Inside and out were bustling, noisy.

"Martina!" Kim's voice was a raspy, harsh, demanding whisper. "I am not pregnant. We haven't even gone—"

"Who you jivin?" Martina laughed good-naturedly.

Kim's face burned. Her eyes darted to see who might be listening. "I can't help it if you don't believe me!"

"Hey, girl." Martina swayed. "You actin like there somethin wrong with doin it. I done it." Martina ran a hand over her abdomen as if smoothing her shirt, again laughed. "I'd do it again. If he wasn't dead. Now you tell me; rumor say you doin it all a time with that Jay-boy."

"Never," Kim said. She turned from Martina and walked away.

"Well, aint you bein Miss Goodie Two-shoes," Martina called after her. Martina curled her lip, rocked her head side to side, sneered, muttered, "En I s'pose them shoes is tied together so's yer—"

At that moment Marcia Radkowski, who had come from the center of the cafeteria to the door to the main corridor, placed her hand on the door's opening lever and pushed. Martina spotted Marcia's face through the small window in the door. As the door reached about eight inches open, Marcia stepped forward with it. Suddenly there was a loud, explosive bang and the door jolted back. "Oh!" Marcia gasped. She looked through the window, didn't seen anyone, again began opening it. Again the smashing bang, the door jolting back into her.

"You bitch!" Martina screamed. "You fucken bitch!" From the corridor Martina pulled the door open. An instantaneous hush surrounded them. "You fucken hit me with the door! Twice!"

Marcia stood stunned, mouth agape.

Martina crashed into her, chest to chest. "You fucken bitch!" she raged. "You fucken bitch! I'm . . . You hit me with the fucken door!"

"I STRONGLY ENCOURAGE you to make the call," Charlene Rosenwald said.

"I . . ." Marcia hung her head. She sat in the principal's office, on a student's chair, before Rosenwald's desk. Her hands were on her lap, fingers entwined.

"Miss Radkowski," Rosenwald addressed the young teacher, "the decision is yours. I'm not going to make you do this, though my first concern is for the image of this school. If you'd like a few moments to think about it, please take the time."

"I . . ." Marcia began again but no words came out. She looked up, nodded her head.

Dr. Rosenwald stood. "The number's here," she said, indicating a sheet of paper on her desk. "Feel free to use my phone. I won't stay in here."

"Thank you," Marcia whispered.

Alone in the office Marcia Radkowski put a hand to her head. She was shaking. She was not sure how she'd gotten into the incident; didn't remember shoving the door into anyone; couldn't imagine anyone interpreting the incident as if she'd assaulted Martina Watts. Martina's explosive violence had scared her, had shocked her. Now Principal Rosenwald was "strongly suggesting" she call Mrs. Watts, report the incident to her; tell Martina's mother how wrong her own behavior had been; apologize to her for hitting her daughter.

Marcia looked at the phone. Her hands trembled as she lifted the receiver, pushed the numbers.

"Who's this?" the phone was answered.

Marcia was taken aback by the directness. "Ah . . . My name is Marcia Radkowski. Is this Mrs. Watts?"

"What she done this time?"

"E-excuse me?"

"You the English teacher, right? What she done this time? She done somethin?"

"Ah . . . no. Mrs. Watts, I just wanted to report an incident—"

"I know. She a'ways doin somethin. I thought gettin herself in her way, she might settle down. But no! She jus as bad as evah."

"No," Marcia said. "It was my fault. I hit her with a . . . a door. Is she . . . ?"

"You done what?!"

"I was coming out of the cafeteria. I wasn't looking through the window and I accidentally opened the door into her and—"

"She okay?"

"Oh. Yes. She wasn't hurt. She became very angry, but she wasn't—"

"That damn school! How many time she been hurt there!"

"I called to apologize to you and to her for—"

"I had it. I a'ready got the name of an attorney. I'll hear it when she get home."

"Yes . . ." Marcia began but was immediately cut off.

MITCH SLOWED, STOPPED on the road, let Johnny off across from his house, drove off. It was dusk, cool, autumn pleasant. During the day, by phone, they'd verified the transfer of Diana and Whitney, yet had agreed to still maintain the ruse until the girls were settled at their new destination. Johnny walked down toward the water, breathed the moist air. With all the problems, all the anxieties, the lake let him feel, at least momentarily, relaxed. He did not want to go in, did not want to be confronted by Julia, did not want to deal with Rocco's depression, did not want to feel Jason's estrangement. What a picture! he thought. God, I bet that hurt! He chuckled to himself that Jason thought he could keep him from seeing it. He thought to take the copy he'd cut out and put it on the refrigerator with a smiley face drawn on it.

Johnny lingered, finally turned. There was a red Econoline van parked in the driveway of the neighbor's house. Johnny's brow furrowed. He knew the McGraths did not own a van. He did not think they were home. There were no lights on in their house. Johnny stepped forward a few paces, stopped. Geez, he thought. Maybe I should call the police. Are they robbing the house? Again he started forward, stopped. Or maybe, he thought, maybe they're smarter than that. Maybe they've parked over there and they're in *my* house. Maybe they're after . . .

Johnny bit his lip. He was filled with indecision. He turned, looked back at the lake. They could have Julia hostage, he thought. He sucked in a breath, paced deliberately toward his house. God! Maybe she was right. Maybe she and Jenny should have moved . . . He did not go up the front walk but up the driveway toward the garage. As he reached the side of the house he glanced in the dining room window. He saw no one, began to tremble, continued pacing as if he were going to the garbage cans. He did not stare at the house but focused on it with his peripheral vision. Then, through the kitchen window, he saw Julia at the sink. He turned, faced the house. He saw Rocco at the table, saw Jenny fly into the room with Jason chasing her. "You little snot," he heard Jason yell.

Johnny chuckled, laughed. His face contorted. His laugh became a side-splitting shriek. Tears came to his eyes.

The Panuzio Home, East Lake, Monday, 30 October, 9:17 A.M.

JOHNNY MOVED HIS coffee cup farther toward the center of the table, spread the thick slab of newsprint, flattened the sheets, searched the front page. His heart was racing; his mind was on fire. In the bottom right-hand corner there was a small picture of Aaron Williams, his dreadlocks flying. Below the photo were three lines:

When Atlas Can No Longer Shrug
Area Youth Lectures from Beyond the Grave

The first in a series: see Page D-1

Johnny grinned. He felt satisfied. Despite the distraction of the deli incident, as he now thought of it, and the card game incident, as he thought of that, he'd been able to complete the series. On Friday he'd given the final section to Elizabeth Callipano of the *Ledger*. It had been, for him, a herculean task—not simply the reorganizing, editing and refining of Aaron's notes, but forcing himself to concentrate, to temporarily suspend from mind all the concerns and disasters that were driving him mad. Yet he'd done it! He'd done it for Aaron and for Mitch, for East Lake and for Lakeport. And he'd done it for himself.

He leaned back, closed his eyes, momentarily felt at peace. It'll break the spell, he thought. People will sit up, take notice. "Panuzio really wrote that," they'll say. "Panuzio is a man who bears watching." In his mind he humbly shook his head. "No. No, not me. Thank you, but the thoughts are really Aaron's." Still he smiled. I'll include copies with my résumés, he thought. Who knows where this could lead? Mitch'll love it. Aaron would have. Maybe I'll write a book. I should write a book. *How to Redesign America.* It'd be a best-seller. Screw that *Contract with America*! That *Bridge to the*

Next Century! Toll bridge to . . . Johnny chuckled; his thoughts accelerated. And screw Tripps! They'll celebrate our redesign; talk of proper cultural story, of ramifications . . . But I wouldn't let Gallina have it! They'll make the first offer, Johnny fantasized. They'll start the bidding war. They'll even be the highest bidder but I'll tell Meloblatt to shove it . . . shove it up Hickel's . . . ! Ha! There'll be enough money without Gallina. Here, LeRoy, here's an extra thou for you, for your troubles. I'll be able to afford Julia, afford to give her all the things she deserves. And she'll love me again. She'll love me like she once . . . "That's my husband," she'll say. She'll be at the mall, out in front of one of the electronic stores. There'll be twenty TVs: thirteen-inch, nineteen-inch, all the way up to a fifty-two-inch home entertainment center. "That's my husband with Charlie Rose. That's my husband with Ted Koppel. That's my husband . . ."

Johnny opened his eyes, leaned forward, lifted the first three sections, shoved them beneath the stack. He had told Mitch to check out the paper, that maybe there'd be a surprise in Sunday's; maybe more surprises all week. Before him there was a much larger picture of Aaron, plus a sidebar that told the story of Aaron's murder in the context of regional youth violence. The sidebar mentioned the futility of the six-week-old murder investigation; expounded on Aaron's life up to his final day. The paper had chosen to emphasize Aaron's stellar athletic career, but it also mentioned that he'd been an honors student, involved in student government and had interned as a legislative assistant for State Assemblywoman Cynthia Dyer the previous summer.

A second sidebar contained a review of the state court's decision regarding the racial isolation of inner-city minority students; a note on how John Panuzio had obtained and edited Aaron's thesis; and a critique by a Lakeport Common Council member of Aaron's theoretical framework. There was also a series of disclaimers by the paper itself, and an editorial by Elizabeth Callipano, daughter of the owner of the *Ledger*, and Johnny's advertising contact for ContGenChem. Callipano began by calling Aaron's work "thoughtful yet controversial . . . an example of suburban thinking," yet finished with "No high school student writes this well. Much in these articles is certainly the work of John Panuzio—" at this Johnny grinned, his eyes twinkled "—director of marketing for Continental General Chemical. The articles smack of the conservative ideology which is certainly a trait of that corporation. This commentator believes that Panuzio is attempting to pass off these ideas—in order to preempt criticism—as the work of an 18-year-old murder victim. The *Ledger* requests comments and rebuttals."

Johnny's mouth fell open. He reread the lines. Twice he'd met with Liz Callipano. She'd seemed so open, so sincere, so supportive of his position. How could she . . . ? he thought. Smacks of conservative ideology . . . ?!

Johnny was baffled, stunned. Request rebuttals! He became angry, gritted his teeth, inhaled, huffed. As he began reading he grumbled, "Bitch!"

The Lakeport Ledger

Section D-1 Copyright–The Lakeport Ledger–A Callipano Corporation Sunday, October 30, 19—

Area Youth Lectures from Beyond the Grave

"When Atlas Can No Longer Shrug—Freedom Is an Illusion"

The first in a series of essays by
Aaron Williams
with John Panuzio

RACE, CULTURE & PUBLIC POLICY: We stand at a critical time in the Lake Region, in this state, and in this nation, with regard to racial isolation and imbalances, and with regard to the equality of education for all, and to the legitimate role of government in our lives. It is now time for us to analyze not simply where we are, how we arrived here and where we are going, but also to understand what vehicle and what propulsion system has brought us to this point, and what vehicle and system is most suited for taking us into the future.

A Family Story

My father was born in Lakeport nearly half a century ago, in a house on Sixth Street near Glenn Avenue, right next to the Wampahwaug Northern Railroad's northbound tracks. He was the oldest of two sons of Allen Williams and Geraldine Sims Williams. Grandpa Williams was a day laborer and a night watchman; Grandma worked in the laundry at St. Luke's Hospital. After school and during the summer, my father, Mitch, and his brother, Vernon, were children of the streets—at least until Grandma came home at about seven o'clock. So goes my family's story.

At that time their neighborhood, Misty Bottom to across Center Street, was racially and ethnically mixed—more Italian and Eastern European than African. My father's closest friend, from then to this day, was and is an Italian-American. My father often told his children that it was his exposure to his friend's family, particularly to his friend's parents, that allowed him, as a black child, to believe in, and to aspire to, a higher calling in life.

My father sometimes put it this way. "I internalized elements of their stories, and of the stories of the neighborhood. These things were beyond the common lore of the small, more closely knit black community that was coming into the region because of the postwar industrial boom."

When I questioned my father about this, he said, "It was not a matter of optimism. Both the black and white communities of the midfifties believed things were getting better. Especially the black community—because the Supreme Court, in 1954, struck down the separate-but-equal doctrine of 1896, a doctrine that had reversed many gains made by blacks after the Civil War.

"It was more a matter of belief," my father said, "and of determination. Belief in the way things ought to be, in the way life should be lived, in what individuals and the community should be willing to sacrifice for a better future. My mother and father sacrificed greatly for their children, but their eyes were focused on the here and now, not on some distant future. In the home of Rocco and Tessa Panuzio there was more willingness to save and to invest, more willingness to pressure their children to study and to demand high grades, than there was in my household. The Italian families I knew had a strategy for the future; our black family had but a tactical plan for the present."

This, of course, is but a small piece of my father's story. But for him it was an essential piece. He was a scholar-athlete in high school, served in the armed forces, went to college, earned an advanced degree, became a successful industrial management engineer. Why? How?

Those questions demand analysis. And they evoke other questions. What is *Cultural Story*? Does Story determine physical, emotional and economic well-being? What stories are we telling ourselves today? How is Story told or conveyed?

In this paper I would like first to establish a framework for the importance and the effect of story; then briefly examine how race has entered the American consciousness; where and why the story of race is skewed; and finally look at the ramifications on education caused by the distortions, omissions and/or purposeful permutations of ambient cultural story. I will propose a regional solution to the problems of racial isolation and imbalance in inner-city schools, which have, according to pending court decisions, caused those schools to fail to provide equal education as is required by the state constitution. I believe this solution is viable for areas like the Lake Wampahwaug Region; that it is in line with the intentions of the State Supreme Court; and that it will effectively disrupt cultural isolation without institutionalizing politically correct racism.*

Johnny read the words he'd written. He beamed at the inclusion of his mother and father, of the reference to himself. Yes! he thought. Yes! This is good. This will help. This . . . His mind raced as his eyes skimmed the more technical meat of Aaron's thesis.

The Framework

The following framework . . . basic element of our approach . . .

The story we tell ourselves of ourselves, individually or culturally, creates our self-image and our world view. Behavior, individually and culturally, is consistent with self-image and world view. Story determines behavior.

As story changes, self-image and world view change; as these change, behavior changes; as behavior changes, so, too, change the results of behavior. That is, personal and cultural story have ramifications . . .

Ambient cultural story is complex, fluid and subject to external pressures, yet it also tends to be homeostatic. By **ambient** I mean . . .

By **fluid** I mean . . .

By **homeostatic** I mean . . .

Story is not always complete—there are omissions and gaps, both expedient and purposeful. Story is not always accurate—there are extrapolations, embellishments and fabrications. Story is not static—it is always growing, dying, being revised and reinvented . . .

. . . My father tells the story of a cold autumn evening when he was fourteen years old. He'd just left football practice and he was alone in Lakeport's west end. His friend had been sick that day and absent from school. As my father crossed through the park that night, perhaps 500 or 600 feet from where he walked, in a circle of light at the far side, he witnessed a group of boys younger than he, stoning, or perhaps ''apple-ing,'' an old woman. There were perhaps ten boys. The woman could not defend herself other than shuffling on, trying to protect her head with her upraised arm. My father says he did not believe the boys were physically damaging the old woman. Soon she and they disappeared into the darkness. Still, he relates, at that time he did nothing—

*Portions of these articles, as carried by the *Lakeport Ledger,* have been included in an appendix to this story. Here one will find only a summary—enough for the reader to understand the intense emotional investment Johnny Panuzio had in this work, and the effects upon Johnny of the reactions these articles engendered.

did not yell, did not go for help, did not intercede—fearful, he claims, that he might have gotten himself badly beaten. "I was frozen into inaction, into noninvolvement," he said. "I have thought about that incident many times. For me, that night was a defining moment. I vowed I would never allow the defenseless to stand alone."

Story can pass from person to person, from friend to friend, from father to son. My father's story of inaction and his vow of protection have been given to me and I have internalized them. It is one of the reasons why I believe that the cities cannot be abandoned . . .

Principles of Application

Long-term or cultural ramifications of public programs, policies . . .

Policy cannot be only a matter of aims and goals, but also must be a matter of manners and means. If there is one thing apparent from the government programs of the sixties, seventies and eighties, it is that even with the best intentions, *and* with a high degree of success in reaching stated goals, there have been numerous and disastrous side effects. The housing projects of Lakeport . . . concentrated economically disadvantaged minorities, and have isolated them from the surrounding, more affluent culture. **(This is the very essence of the lawsuit and court decisions we are now facing!)**

. . . If only negative elements of a people's story are reinforced, and positive elements are denied or dismissed, that culture will have no positive role models, and its macro behavior will reflect the negative self-image.

Tomorrow: Atlas Can No Longer Shrug

AT 3:55 P.M. ON Tuesday, November 1, Johnny's secretary, Lisa Crawford, buzzed his speaker. "Mr. Tripps wants to see you in his office," she said when he clicked on. "As soon as possible."

"Um," Johnny stalled. "Lisa, do you know what he . . . ?"

"No, Mr. Panuzio." There was no warmth in her voice.

"Okay," Johnny said into the intercom. "Shit," he muttered as he released the button. The Elks were playing the Lakers in East Lake and he wanted to leave quickly, get out of the office, catch the second half. He buzzed Lisa back. "Which Mr. Tripps?" he asked. "Is senior back up, or is Mr. Impec—"

"Mr. Nelson Tripps," Lisa answered curtly. "Perhaps about Mr. Williams."

On Sunday morning Johnny had spoken only briefly with Mitch because Mitch had been running late, had wanted to keep it short. "I got a chuckle outta that first part," Mitch had said. "Did he really write that stuff about me?"

"Sure did," Johnny answered. "The family history stuff was in a separate file. I thought it was a good way to lead off."

"I gotta tell ya," Mitch responded, "until I read that—and about that time in the park—I never knew he ever heard a word I said. You might want to think about that with Jason."

"Um. I guess," Johnny said. "What about . . . ?"

"I haven't read it all. Laurie's still packing. One o'clock flight. I'll read it on the plane."

"Um," Johnny repeated. He'd been disappointed; the most momentous accomplishment of his life, and Mitch hadn't even read it all!

"Cut em out for me, okay?" Mitch had asked.

"Sure will," Johnny agreed. "I'll get a few extra copies. Some of this stuff . . . It's really as much about me and my family as it is about you and yours. As much about whites as blacks."

"Yeah. I'd think so. About all of us together."

"Um. We can't do it without—"

Mitch's chuckle had cut Johnny short. "Hey, swing by the house just to check on things, okay?"

"Sure. You'll be back Saturday?"

"Probably Sunday night."

Johnny knew that Mitch and Laurie were being flown to ContGenChem's headquarters in Atlanta; that Mitch purposefully had arranged it so he and Laurie would be out of town during the time the articles were scheduled to appear. Johnny did not know, but suspected, that they were also going to visit their daughters. Mitch had told him that he'd enrolled Whitney and Diana in a new school. He had not told him where, not even in what state. And Johnny had known better than to ask. "Hey," Johnny had said, "call anytime and check in. I'll let you know how—"

"Sure will," Mitch had said. "Sure will."

Johnny entered Nelson Tripps' large office. "Sit down," the CEO said, directing him to a chair set before the desk.

"Thank you." Johnny sat, faced the ContGenChem CEO. Brad Tripps stood behind and slightly to one side of his father.

"You understand—" Nelson's voice was smooth, unemotional, efficient "—that you've put us in a difficult position."

"I . . . uh . . . No, sir. I don't understand."

"With these articles." Nelson Tripps reached, opened a dark manila folder that had been carefully positioned at the center of his desk. Orange highlighter made the words "with John Panuzio" and the line ". . . smack of the conservative ideology which is certainly a trait of that corporation," leap from the page.

"Oh." Johnny's tone was dismissive. "I don't know why she wrote that. I talked to her a number of—"

Nelson Tripps waved him to silence. "This is very serious," the older man said. "You, of all people, in your position, should have realized that the *Ledger* would insinuate, would publicly indict this company . . ."

"No, sir." Johnny's interruption was crisp. His brow furrowed; he could not fathom why the CEO was interpreting Elizabeth Callipano's words as an indictment of ContGenChem. He looked Nelson Tripps directly in the eyes. "Sir, I was shocked when I read that line. I did edit Aaron's files. I did reorganize them. But most of it . . . they *are* his words. His ideas. Mitch has got a copy of the original files on—"

"Stop right there," Nelson said harshly. "I'm not interested. Call this Callipano. Tell her you are faxing her a letter." Brad Tripps stepped forward, removed a sheet from a second folder. "This letter," Nelson continued. "Tell her you want to see this in tomorrow's *Ledger* alongside whatever additional cockamamy articles of yours they run." Nelson rose. "That will be all," he said.

Outside the office Johnny scanned the neat print on the ContGenChem executive letterhead.

> . . . with regard to the series of articles by Aaron Williams and John Panuzio that is being published in the *Ledger*; I would like to clarify a few points.
>
> First: The content of these articles is not in any manner the product of Continental General Chemical Corporation.
>
> Second: John Panuzio is not director of marketing for ContGenChem, but is coordinator of local, outsourced advertising. If he has used his position at ContGenChem in any way to influence the *Ledger* to publish his articles, this was, is and always will be without authorization. It is against this company's policy to be involved in local politics. Mr. Panuzio's use of unauthorized influence is under internal corporate review.
>
> Third: Continental General Chemical specifically disassociates itself from this issue. We are now, and always will be, an equal opportunity employer.
>
> Nelson Tripps, CEO,
> Continental General Chemical Corp., Inc.

AT 5:52 P.M. JOHNNY pulled into the East Lake High parking lot. He was angry, disappointed, again in shock. He had no idea what "under internal corporate review" entailed. Even worse, Liz Callipano had laughed at him; had happily agreed to publish Nelson's letter; knew immediately that it made for a bigger story.

The lot was dark, nearly vacant. Quickly Johnny maneuvered toward the field overlook. The field, too, was vacant, though there were two cars parked at the overlook, two women chatting. Johnny opened his window. "Hi," he called. "How'd they make out?"

"Oh, John. Is that you?"

"Um-hmm. I couldn't get away. Rose?"

"It's me," Rose Santarelli, Chris' mom, said. "Dark, isn't it?"

"Yeah. How'd . . . ?" Johnny again began but stopped to let the two women finish the sentences he'd interrupted.

"They won again, of course," Rose Santarelli said to him as she stepped over to his car. The other woman drove off. Rose leaned down to his window. "Two-nothing," she said. "Jason almost got carded again but I think it was the referee's fault."

Johnny sighed. "Well, at least—"

Suddenly Rose Santarelli slipped an arm, then her head, through his open window. She hugged him; gave him a second squeeze.

"Oooo!" Johnny laughed. "What was . . . ?"

"I just want to tell you how much we all admire you. You and your family for all you've done for the Williamses."

"Oh! Well . . . not really." He felt embarrassed. "Actually, a lot of it's been the other way around."

"You must be a saint," Rose Santarelli whispered. "A true saint." She turned, got in her car, left.

Now Johnny felt even more confused. A saint, he thought. A saint under internal review! His fantasies, his enthusiasm, his euphoria over the publication of the first "Atlas" article, had peaked on Sunday. As he stared at the field he bit his lower lip and wondered if he could weather the coming storm, the inexplicable controversy. Certainly, he thought, it can't get any worse. He shook his head, chased the thought away, wondered instead what it was like to be out there on the field, what it would be like to be out there just one more time—like he'd once been out there on a field so long ago. He closed his eyes. He imagined the feeling of again winning a game. He wrapped his arms about his chest, grasped his biceps, squeezed. So badly he needed a victory, any victory, even the vicarious victory of his son's team. So badly, he thought, he'd needed to see it, to see them win. And it had again been stolen from him, this time by Nelson Tripps.

Slowly Johnny drove back through East Lake, swung by Mitch's home to insure that everything appeared normal, meandered toward The Point. All the while, under his breath, he muttered a string of invectives while he pictured himself as Saint George the Powerful, his sword held over the cowering heads of his adversaries. Above him, above his subjugates, storm clouds gathered.

"HE'S AN ASSHOLE." Jason's voice was thick, subdued. He and Kim Sanchez had split from the library, had driven directly to Finnegan's Pond. "And so am I."

"No, you're not," Kim whispered. The night was cold. She'd left the car engine running. She did not know how to cope with Jason's moodiness; had expected him to be in good spirits after the win.

"I'm goina tell him it, too," Jason said. They were not touching. Jason sat slumped in the seat, his chin almost on his chest, his arms limp, his hands flaccid on the upholstery.

Kim stroked his left forearm.

"I coulda killed him." The words came from Jason like a poison fog seeping from a toxic dump. "I can't—"

"Don't," Kim said softly. "He's still your father."

"Not him," Jason said. "Juarez."

"I thought you were talking about your father."

"I was. The asshole stuff. He's such a hypocrite. Like . . . like he thinks these articles he's written are going to make him a million dollars. All last week, once the *Ledger* agreed to print em, he was going around with a shit-eating grin."

"Then . . . who's Juarez?"

"From Lakeport. From their team. The guy who—"

"Oh! The one who was knocked unconscious when you all collided? I don't think you can blame yourself . . ." Kim was referring to a play late in the game when Jason again had charged too hard, had smashed through Juarez, intent on getting the ball from a second Laker. All three players had gone down. Juarez had not gotten up.

"He wasn't knocked . . . Kim! He wasn't knocked unconscious."

"He seemed uncon—"

"I did it."

"You?"

"Yeah. When I was on top of him."

"I don't understand."

"He was under me. That big goon was on top of me but Juarez was on the bottom. He had his head right here." Jason held his right hand like a claw, a clamp, at the middle of his abdomen. "His head was like cocked and he couldn't move it so I grabbed his throat. I grabbed it and I began squeezing." Jason closed his fist. "With all my might. I could see his face. His neck was like mush and I pushed my fingers and thumb in so deep . . . I could see his eyes bulge. Do you understand? My fingers and thumb almost touched. His eyes like exploded out of his head and his tongue started coming out and then he went limp. I don't think it took three seconds."

"Jason!" Kim slid away from him.

"I know." Jason was morose. "I . . . I . . . I almost killed him. Kim, I almost killed . . ."

Kim gripped the steering wheel; her head shook back and forth; she was unable to speak.

"I'm never goina do that again," Jason said. "Never. I don't know what's come over me. *That* outta control! I coulda killed . . . I can still see his eyes just before they went out. That's why I said, 'So am I.' "

Kim turned, moved to him, put a hand on his head, pushed her fingers through his hair.

"That's not me," Jason whispered. "I don't want ta hurt . . . I wanna win, but not like that. I don't want ta kill anybody. I don't . . ."

"Jason," Kim said forcefully, "you are under control. From now on you'll always be . . ."

"I . . . I've been planning to . . . making plans . . . practicing to . . ."

"What?" Kim said softly. She caressed his face.

Jason pulled away, pulled his arms in tight to his torso, tucked forward. "Don't!" He spit the word out. "I'm not worth it. I gotta think."

JOHNNY COULD NOT concentrate. He sat on the sofa, sections of the day's paper beside him, the day's article folded out, on his lap. Jason was in the attic; Julia and Jenny in their bedrooms; Rocco asleep before the TV. Johnny glanced at his father, watched the old man's chest. His breathing was so shallow it was nearly imperceptible. Johnny took a deep breath, let it seep out, attempted to refocus on the paper. Even with the criticism, it was still a thrill to see the articles in print. Johnny skimmed Aaron's words, his words; attempted to pick out a few choice snippets:

Atlas Can No Longer Shrug

. . . Our society must still protect individuals from bigotry and prejudice. Discrimination in housing, education, employment and voting access must still be criminal acts. But saying this does not mean that reverse discrimination is the solution. Additionally, no society will ever be successful in controlling racism (or drug abuse, violence, gambling or corruption) by treating individuals, *unless* that society also maintains an ambient cultural story that leads to the desirable behavior. A society cannot make laws or pass policies that will make people rich. The opposite, however, is true. Policies can be made that will hinder the long-range advancement of subgroups or minorities. The much-maligned "welfare system" . . .

. . . not a matter of promoting forced regional integration or of promoting programs that will assist inner-city minorities to mingle with the middle class in the surrounding suburbs . . . These are Band-Aids . . . It is a matter of dilution not of people but of services and of programs of assistance . . . If these programs created equal attractiveness throughout the region . . .

Enablement programs may signal, or may create within, an individual or a segment of society an ambient story that says, "You are weak. You are disabled. You are not deserving of more than a subsistence existence. Because you are black, or Hispanic, or a woman or a veteran, you cannot do for yourself what nonblacks/Hispanics/women/veterans can do for themselves." If that story is internalized, it becomes true. Behavior is consistent . . .

. . . It is this ossification, this destruction of social mobility, of will, that can enslave even the strongest. Fighting this ossification presents a dilemma for minority advocacy organizations. They need to have their constituency concentrated, to be the majority in one area—this is their source of power. Simultaneously they recognize the need of the people to be diverse, to be part of the mainstream culture—this decreases their power . . .

Tomorrow: Williams' Plan for Regional Desegregation

BY THURSDAY, NOVEMBER 3, Johnny's emotional roller coaster was cresting higher peaks, diving faster, hitting deeper valleys. Julia, too, was moody. She was being sucked into a conflagration not of her making. Friends, co-workers, strangers were approaching him, approaching them both, asking them for their opinion on the state's desegregation plan, expressing their own—sometimes very forcefully. Letters to the *Ledger* had become more critical, more personal.

. . . Mr. Panuzio's attack on African-American culture is without merit, and his words damage the work of those of us who strive daily to increase feelings of self-worth and self-esteem among inner-city youth. What else do these children have? Destroying their culture and language destroys their identity . . .

. . . Whites have stripped us of our language, of our religion, of our culture. Mr. Panuzio . . .

. . . Mr. Panuzio's denial that Ebonics is a separate dialect of English is typical of his class prejudice . . .

. . . Mr. Panuzio doesn't live in the inner city. What does he know? He doesn't know anything. We are not a bunch of jungle bunnies . . .

During the day Johnny read and responded to each letter. Again he felt stunned, baffled, confused. "I didn't say," he mumbled to himself, "one single word about language or Ebonics. Where'd that come from? Why'd they acknowledge it by printing it? And jungle bunnies!" Woefully he shook his head. "How are they interpreting our words?!"

Johnny sat alone at his desk. His door was shut. His hands covered his eyes. "How are they . . . ?" he repeated. "I was very specific about how I defined culture. Aaron was specific about culture. Not art! Not language! Attitudes toward savings. Toward entrepreneurship. Not religion. Not ethnic African culture, but . . . but . . . Goddamn it. We're talking attitudes toward savings, toward scrimping now in order to save for something more durable in the future. All the goddamn things Julia and I have forgotten . . . all the . . . What do they mean? Do they want to preserve the ambient cultural attitudes of the inner-city street? Doesn't that say they want to keep young black men in those ghettos? Keep the gangs? Isn't that exactly what the court decision is all about? Damn!"

At 2:50 P.M. Johnny skipped out from work, drove to East Lake High for the makeup game against Roosevelt that had been rained out two weeks earlier. It was the last league game of the season and Johnny had been determined that nothing would stop him from seeing it. Still, because of the articles and reactions, he shunned most of the East Lake parents, stood alone far downfield across from the Rough Riders' penalty box. It was a good spot to watch the game, and Johnny's cheering was animated. It also was a good spot to avoid Rose Santarelli. In the last minute of play the Elks won on a through ball from Jason to Masad Samadhi. The win raised their season record to 10–3–3, qualified them for the LRIAC tournament semifinals. Johnny cheered, smiled, lagged behind in conversation with Eric London, Tim's father, talked about the slim possibilities of the team actually winning the league.

After the game Johnny again drove by Mitch's home. It was dusk as he swung up Red Apple Hill Road. Lights were on in the kitchen, in the living room, on the back porch, turned on, Johnny knew, by preset electronic switches. Johnny followed the meandering road to the end of the tract where he began a U-turn by a small, semiwooded glade. Jason's win had elevated his mood, had given him something to focus on other than his deteriorating situation. Suddenly Johnny startled. In the grass at the edge of the wood he saw a flock of huge, dark, slate-gray and purple birds with plump and rounded breasts—wild turkeys. Johnny had seen reports about the state's program to reestablish them in areas where they'd been absent for seventy-five years, but he'd never seen one in the wild. For some minutes he watched the birds graze. Their seeming fearlessness to his presence inspired him.

Slowly Johnny pulled from the side of the road. It was now quite dark. He turned on the Infiniti's headlights, saw a girl of perhaps fourteen or fifteen walking toward him along the edge of the pavement. Johnny rolled his car until he was beside her, pressed the button to lower the passenger-side window. "Hey," he called. "Did ya—"

The girl jumped back, jogged away, crossed the street behind him. "Augh, come on," he muttered to himself. He lowered the window on the driver's side, leaned out. "I'm not going to hurt you," he said. "I just wanted to—" at that the girl bolted up the road, sprinting toward the closest house "—to point out the turkeys . . ." His voice faded. I just wanted to share the experience, he thought. He was not sure if he should drive on, if that might scare her even more, or if he should just sit for a moment. Perhaps, he thought, he might drive to the house, knock on the door, tell the people who he was, what he'd just seen. Reassure them, and ask them to reassure the girl, that he meant no harm.

Probably scare them twice as much, he thought. What with Mitch's house being shot up . . . Probably get myself . . . I'd better just go. Johnny edged the car forward, stopped. He backed up to where he'd seen the turkeys, angled his car so as to focus the headlights on the small field. The birds were gone. As he drove home he thought, Man, something is wrong. Something's wrong with me. With us. All of us. But me . . . I used to be one of the good guys. I'm becoming a bitter old jerk . . .

ON FRIDAY MORNING, in his office with his door closed, Johnny quietly cut the articles from the papers he'd collected. He placed one set, in order, in a file folder for Mitch; kept two sets for himself. He had not read the day's article or the accompanying letters. Maybe, he thought, after to-day's . . . He bit his lip. He thought instead about this afternoon's game, the LRIAC semifinals against Lakeport . . . Lakeport again . . . His thoughts bounced back to the articles, and he determined he would dismiss every remark, every criticism, with, "Read today's. It's the last of the series and it ties it all together."

Transforming Story: Transforming the Region: A Proposal for Redistricting

There has not been a black person in my grandparents' or my parents' generation who has not suffered an indignity at the hands of a white person in a position of authority over him or her. Their distrust is understandable. However, I am speaking for my generation and urging *all* people of my generation to maximize our attitudes and actions for our own future benefits.

It is time for leaders of the black community to stop blaming the white community for all black problems. It is equally time for the white community to stop looking at the black community as though it were the root and source of all evil, all crime, all drug abuse—or if not the root, the most willing participants. Let us transform and transcend. Let us envision a future not simply in which black children and white children can sit together, but one in which all Americans of all races and all ethnicities truly have equal opportunities. Treating each other as adversaries makes problems worse.

Instead of a Diversity Plan designed to unite us through tolerance, let us change our perspective and propose a Unity Plan which also celebrates our differences . . . The difference is not simply rhetorical, nor is it one of emphasis. The objectives are the same, but one creates an ambient cultural story that will bring us together, while the other creates a story that tears us apart.

The following proposal . . .

. . . [S]ome of the plans under consideration are either ill-conceived Band-Aids or are so severe and coercive that Atlas can no longer shrug. Under the latter category, there is no freedom. When Atlas can no longer shrug, when governmental decrees are so overpowering that individuals have no choices, freedom is an illusion. When freedom is lost, ensuing macro social behaviors deteriorate . . .

. . . The ultimate failure of the plan could occur if the negative cultural attributes that have been concentrated in poverty pockets were celebrated and spread across the region . . .

We are now at a time, because of the court order, when the people in areas where education is working have the wonderful opportunity to dictate to the people in areas where education is not working—to dictate how programs should be run; what should be the academic standards; what should be the standards of student behavior; what should be the standards for teachers and administrators.

As long as the people of the City of Lakeport have been willing to assign, or willing to allow the court to assign, to the people of the surrounding communities the responsibility . . .

Disband the School District That Has Failed
Redraw All District Lines

The disbanding of old school districts that have failed does not eliminate local control over the newly realigned, regional school districts. This has been a major failure of various experimental programs that have ceded power to either commercial companies or to higher and more removed governmental entities.

The people of the district that has been disbanded become part of the new, regional district. They are not disenfranchised . . .

Far more important than cost-effectiveness, however, is the dilution of inner-city students into the population of suburban and exurban students. Once again, this *is* the court decree; and it is a desirable decree. The ramifications on both minority and majority subgroup cultural story, self-image, world view and macro behavior, if natural assimilation is allowed to flow, should be positive.

Johnny worked all day, worked his job. He did not go out for lunch, worked through that half hour, only stopping for a cup of coffee. He deflected inquiries and comments about the articles, even from those people who'd said they'd read today's and wanted to assure him they were on his side.

At three-thirty, in the can, Johnny finally scanned the *Ledger*. Accompanying Friday's article were an even dozen letters. Two were highly supportive of Johnny and Aaron's perspective; most were thoughtful; several went off on wild tangents; four were negative, hateful, the most severe criticisms to date, personal attacks on John Panuzio. It was obvious from the content of several that the writers had had advance copies of the last article.

. . . Mr. Panuzio presents the familiar case that the largely successful assimilation of past ethnic groups—particularly the Italians—into the American melting pot was made easier by a shared work ethic among tightly knit families; values, Mr. Panuzio states, which are not held by American blacks and Hispanics.

This standard neoconservative argument—much like the writings of George Will, William Bennett and Dinesh D'Souza—essentially rests on the presumption that *niggers* and *spics*, because of their alleged smaller brain size, are stupid and shiftless. It claims that blacks and Hispanics must be denied social safety nets and forced to work.

This is an ugly racist argument, one this reader cannot understand why the *Ledger* even chose to run, unless, of course—the disclaimer by Nelson Tripps, CEO of ContGenChem, notwithstanding—it was

> because ContGenChen is one of the *Ledger's* largest advertising accounts.
>
> . . . the notion that a high school student, black, white or otherwise, could have written this essay is absurd. Aaron Williams' essay is Mr. Panuzio's thinly disguised polemic for Mr. Panuzio's fascist beliefs . . .
>
> Luis Puebla, M . . .

"Fucking son of a bitch," Johnny shouted. He left work without saying a word, was in his car on the way to the game. "Teach me . . . I'm supposed to be one of the fucken good guys! Fuck! Teach me to stick my neck out! What the fuck! 'Niggers and spics.' I never said . . . never implied . . . never would . . . never came close . . ." Again Johnny banged the steering wheel. "He . . . on purpose . . . He misinterpreted it on purpose. Vindictive jerk. Afraid he'd . . ."

Johnny was livid. He drove down the interstate like a madman, exited for the dam, wove between cars, trucks, blasted into South Lake Village. Then it hit him. The game was in Lakeport. Again he screamed. But he did not turn around; thought he could not go to the game; could not go back to Lakeport; not after that letter—"fascist beliefs!"—not after the letter of Luis Puebla, mayor of Lakeport.

Johnny parked but did not go into his house. He left his briefcase in the car, left his keys, his coat. In his best suit he walked to The Point, sat upon the rocks, stared into the water. Everything, he thought. Absolutely everything I touch turns to . . .

"Dad." Jenny dragged herself up behind him.

"Oh! Hiya, Sweet-ums. I didn't hear . . ."

Jenny did not look at her father. She seemed ready to cry.

"What's up, Sunshine? You look—"

"Why did you have to . . ." Jenny stopped.

"What?" Johnny asked.

"My . . ." Jenny sniffed, then blurted, "My teacher says you're a racist. I heard her talking to the principal. Most of my friends think you want to bus the project kids to our school. And Lena says her mom doesn't want her hanging with me. She says we Panuzios, we're like poison."

East Lake High School, Thursday, 10 November, 2:07 P.M.

DEEP WITHIN THE school's corridors the steady drone of heavy rains could be heard.

"Coach." Jason Panuzio and Kim Sanchez stood outside the doorway of the history department office. They were side by side, holding hands. They did not look at each other but bent and peered into the small, cramped room. Bob Carsden, a world history teacher, came to the door, slid by the students without acknowledging them. "Coach," Jason called a little louder.

Within the office McMillian was at his cluttered desk, reading glasses on, head bowed, lost in thoughts and projections. Reggie Milanese, a civics and U.S. history teacher, rose from another small desk. She raised and clutched a stack of books. "Mr. McMillian," she said softly, "I think one of your players wants to see you."

"Hmm?" McMillian glanced over the rims. "Oh. Thanks, Reg." He removed his glasses. "Do you want me?" he called to the door.

"Do you have a few moments, Coach?" Timidly Jason and Kim advanced into the room.

"Umm. What's on your mind?"

"Ah . . . Can we . . . talk?"

"I've got a meeting," Mrs. Milanese injected. "If . . . Mr. McMillian, if Dr. Dutchussy calls for me, would you tell her I'm in D-seventeen?"

"Sure." McMillian scribbled "D-17" on a scrap of paper. "Panuzio." He pushed back from the desk. "What's on your mind?"

"Coach, you know the way you're always saying, 'Strategy begins with a question'?"

McMillian cocked his head. A smile curled his lips. "Yep."

"We've got a question."

"Um-hmm."

"More than a question," Kim said.

McMillian eyed her.

"Coach." Jason hesitated. "I think . . . I think I know where I'm going. I know where we have to go."

"Good—" McMillian began but Jason immediately cut him off.

"What can we do to help implement Aaron's plan?"

"Oh!" McMillian pushed farther back from the desk, gestured for the students to pull up chairs and be seated. "I thought you were going to ask me about tomorrow's game."

"Unt-uh," Jason uttered.

"Well, I assume, then," the teacher teased Jason, "Miss Sanchez is behind your sudden social consciousness." He used the French pronunciation of her last name.

Kim bowed her head slightly, then raised it, looked F.X. in the eyes. "It's Sanchez," she said. "It's Spanish. Sanchez. That's the way my father pronounces it."

"Oh. Okay," McMillian said. Again he smiled. "What do you—"

"You've read Aaron's articles?" Jason cut in.

"Yes," McMillian said. "I—"

Again Jason cut him off. "My father redid a lot of it."

"I know."

"And he's being dissed for it."

"I read the letters . . ."

"But I know most of it's Aaron's," Jason said. "I don't want my dad involved in this. Most of it *is* Aaron's words, and we think it's got a lot of merit."

"I do, too," McMillian said. "I gave him an A-plus on . . ." McMillian stopped, turned away from the students. He sniffed, swallowed, covered his mouth with a hand. "Where'd that come from?" he tried to joke. With the fingers of one hand he wiped his cheeks.

"We'd like to establish an integration panel," Kim said. "Here at the school. We'd like to work on the practical aspects of Aaron's plan."

"To explore the practical aspects . . ." Jason fumbled for the right words. "The feasibility . . ."

"You have Mr. Carsden for history?" F.X. began.

"He's a doofus," Jason blurted.

"Mr. Cars—"

"I mean . . ." Immediately Jason began to apologize, then stopped. "Coach." Rapidly Jason shook his head. "Mr. Carsden isn't capable of doing this. We want to establish a serious working group that can meet with other groups from other schools. We want to make recommendations to local school boards . . . and to the state legislature. Mr. Carsden . . . his idea of history is showing *Dances with Wolves.* We might like it, but it's . . . it's not really history. It's more like virtual reality."

McMillian chuckled. "Ah yes," he whispered. "How many times I've told Bob it would behoove us all to remember that virtual reality is fake."

Jason and Kim both laughed. For the next twenty minutes the three talked about Aaron's work, about how it had affected them, about who would have to be involved and who would be allowed to be involved. Kim produced a graphic representation of the region with municipal lines which she and Jason had developed on his computer. They overlaid the graphic with an acetate representation of proposed new education districts. Essentially Lakeport was the center of a divided pie. Each piece of the city had been combined with a suburban district. They talked about strategies, tactics and techniques, about taking the risk, committing completely, going forward without hesitation.

"It's sometimes . . ." Jason again stumbled. "It's sometimes like I can hear him. I hear him telling me, 'We don't have to treat others as adversaries.' Sometimes I think I can feel his presence. In the paper he told me, 'You don't have to—' " Jason froze, remained rigid for a long moment, thawed " '—have to attack.' Coach, I'd like . . . Are you goina be here a little bit longer?"

"Um-hmm. I'd expected us to have a practice today." He raised a hand toward the ceiling, shrugged.

"I've got . . . Let me go to my locker." Jason stood up. "I've got something I brought in . . . I want to give you."

"What?" Kim asked. She began to rise.

"I'll be back in a sec." Jason trotted from the office.

"Well . . ." F.X. rippled his brow. He was not sure if the graphics and the panel idea were Kim's or Jason's; if she'd just come because of him, or if she'd instigated it. "I used to work for a colonel when I was in the service," F.X. said to fill the quietness.

"Yes," Kim answered.

"Aaron's paper reminded me of him. He had a saying . . . He was a black guy. Brigade commander. Went on to become a general. Anyway, he used to say, 'When you see polarization build to the extent that group peer pressure keeps men who would move across races for friendship from doing so, then you've got trouble. When hard-core polarization arrives, it isn't long before violence erupts.' "

"You'll help us, then!" Kim beamed. "Won't you?"

F.X. smiled broadly. He sincerely liked these students, sincerely respected them. "With all the time I'll have once the season ends . . ."

"We'll need Principal Rosenwald's and Superintendent Schoemer's approval."

"I think I can sell them on it."

"And you and Mrs. DeLauro as—"

At that Jason popped back into the office. Quickly his eyes darted to each corner to insure they were still alone. In his hands he had a black wooden box. He sat, shoved the box toward Coach McMillian. "I was going to give it to my uncle," Jason said. "It's a bayonet from Viet-Nam."

F.X. started. He reached out, took the display box from Jason's hand, opened it, pursed his lips.

"My uncle Nick is a Viet-Nam vet," Jason said quickly. "He's a doctor now, but he was . . . But I want to give it to you. I . . . I bought it about a month ago."

"Umm." F.X. studied the weapon. "Yes. It is a communist bayonet."

"I bought it from a guy in Lakeport. In a shop there." Jason's words came quickly. "I'd really like you to have it. I think it'll mean more to you than to my uncle or me."

McMillian grabbed, rubbed his chin. "You shouldn't have brought this . . ."

"I . . . I thought of that . . . after. I've had it in my locker for a . . . ah . . . I was kind of afraid to take it back out . . . to bring it home. After what happened to those kids . . . Terry and all. But it's not really a weapon. I mean it was, but now it's a history piece . . . isn't it? Anyway, I'd like you to have it."

"Are you sure?" McMillian asked. He was no longer smiling.

Jason nodded but did not speak.

"If I take it—" McMillian rubbed the box with his hands "—I'd like to give it to the military museum in South Lakeport. If that's all right with you?"

"Yeah. Yes. It'd be great. Can you take it now?"

McMillian nodded. His eyes were hard on Jason's face. A pocketknife, even a butter knife, was a serious infraction of school rules. A twelve-inch bayonet, in a display case or not, would certainly bring down the wrath of the administration.

"I . . ." Jason looked down. Kim reached, grasped his forearm. She didn't know what he was doing. Jason's voice was very low. "I really didn't know where I was goin, Coach. Really," he confessed, "I . . . I bought it to kill Verdeen. I . . ." Jason kept his eyes down. Kim squeezed his arm. McMillian stared. "But I know I can't do that. I . . . I know I can't. I realized it a week ago. More. In that Lakeport game when Juarez . . ."

McMillian thought to interrupt, thought to tell this student that his admission would have to be revealed to Dr. Rosenwald. And to his parents. Then he thought of Victor Santoro saying to him, "Do a good job for this kid." And he thought, What would best serve doing a good job? He said nothing, listened.

"I can be just as effective without being violent," Jason said. "There's a difference, isn't there?"

McMillian nodded.

"Coach, I want Mike Verdeen to be on this panel. I . . . I do know where we're going."

AS JASON'S SPIRIT surmounted the tragedies of the fall and his own need for violence and revenge, Johnny's behaviors and thoughts continued to plummet. He sat in his parked Infiniti. He had arranged for a man from South Lake Village to take over his lease, to take "his" car, the only compensation being that the buyer would now make the monthly payments. In five days, on the fifteenth, the Infiniti would no longer be his. Johnny rested back against the leather seat, tried to let its contours massage him, comfort him. A relentless, torrential rain beat on the windshield, pounded the roof, the hood. A harsh, gusting wind jolted and rocked the vehicle. Still, inside it was comfortable, relatively quiet.

Johnny sighed. The clock glowed: 5:07 P.M. It was less than half an hour after sunset, yet dark, nearly pitch black. Before him he could make out very little. He thought to turn on the headlights but didn't move. Had it all, he thought, but I've blown it. Blown it all. Job, car, probably the house, maybe our marriage. Imperceptibly he shook his head. God, I hate this. I hate my life. I don't want to live like this anymore. I don't . . . I'm just goddamned sandwiched between everything. Between generations. Between town and city. Between . . . trying to span the moral abyss between corporate economics and family values. With all I've done for . . . or what I tried to do, anyway . . . fucken betrayed and abandoned . . . God! Lisa! Lisa, of all people. Going around telling people I cut her job. Like I had any goddamn choice. Like . . . How does he handle it? How do they all handle it? The Fitzpatricks? The Meades? Mayberrys? Espositos? Willises? And Mitch . . . His son's killed. His house is shot up. And this latest thing. He handles it. In comparison I've got no problems. I can't handle it anymore.

Johnny stared out the window. He was parked in the high school lot at the edge of the hill overlooking the varsity soccer fields, but he could not see the fields because of the darkness and the rain. There were no cars nearby, only a few near the school's main entrance. In the rearview mirror he could see lights in two of the building's wings. He looked back to the field, thought, Twelve days. Twelve days! He wants at least another three thou in twelve . . . I'll never raise it. Never! Not in that time. *Cuico faccia.* Jerk.

Johnny slapped his forehead, slapped it again, harder. Tears came to his eyes. He pictured Rocco shaking a partially closed hand, saying, *Nòn è stuná!* Don't be a jerk! Pictured Rocco as Rocco had been forty years earlier, big, strong, hard, standing over Little Johnny-panni, cuffing him, not hard, just enough to get his attention. *Nòn è stuná! You know?* Johnny sniffed, wiped the wet from beneath his eyes with his fingers. He crushed his teeth together, pictured Rocco as Rocco had been last night.

"Johnny, you gotta rake the leaves."

"Sure, Pop. Of course."

Pictured Rocco as he'd spoken, the old man's hands shaking—a new palsy. "You gotta get em away from the house."

"Yeah, Pop. Maybe on Sunday."

"They scare me. If a spark lands, it'll burn down your house."

"Huh?"

"Jason could rake em. Have Jason rake em."

"Yeah. In his spare time. I'll get to it—"

"You want me to hire somebody? I can hire some neighborhood kid."

Johnny pictured his own hands flaring, heard his voice exploding. "You want to hire somebody?! Hire somebody! I don't give a good goddamn about the leaves! I don't give a goddamn about the foundation! The goddamn foundation's been there for a century. It'll be there for another century. *Capisce?*"

Johnny leaned back, pushed himself back. He checked the rearview mirror to see if any new activity had developed nearer the school. He did not want to go home, did not want to face Rocco, did not want to see Rocco's sadness, hurt. Johnny moaned. Was it possible he had really said those horrible words? He did not want to go home, did not want to go anywhere. He wished there were a game to watch, to be absorbed by, to be . . . He'd watch it incognito! Keep his mouth shut. No one would . . . He pictured Aaron on the field with the ball. He saw himself picturing Mitch's son and not his own and he shook his head.

"That was quite a series of articles," Mitch had said to him on Monday morning. They had driven in separately, had met unexpectedly in a corridor.

"Yeah, huh? How was the trip?"

"Great," Mitch had responded. "How you doin?"

"Recovering." Johnny laughed. "I really got beat up in the paper. You'll see. I've got copies for—"

"I read em," Mitch said. "Nelson had the paper sent down every day."

"Oh. He didn't . . . What'd you think?"

"In retrospect?"

"Ah . . ." Johnny stumbled. "Yeah. I guess."

"Maybe you went a little too far," Mitch said. He checked his watch, letting Johnny know he only had a little time. "Aaron didn't formulate the plan quite like that, did he?"

"Pretty much . . ." Johnny answered.

Mitch changed the subject. "Hey, I see the team's won a few more games. They're going to make the league tournament, aren't they?"

"They did," Johnny answered. "Beat Lakeport again. In the semis. Hell of a game." Johnny did not tell Mitch that he'd missed it, that he'd driven across the dam before he'd realized . . . "Kurjiaka's really come into his own," Johnny said. "He's gotta be the best high school keeper in the state."

"Yeah." Mitch smiled. The two friends were barely making eye contact. "Jason's really come on this year, too."

"Umm. I guess. He's always bustin my *coglions.*" Johnny laughed. "He's got an attitude . . ."

"Kids!" Mitch chuckled.

"Yeah."

"You know what they did to Laurie the night we got back from Atlanta?"

"What? No. What?"

"I went in with the bags. She was still taking something from the trunk. I don't even remember what. Three kids jumped out from the bushes, pushed her down, then ran away."

"What?!" Johnny was surprised at the report, surprised that Mitch hadn't called him when it happened.

"Yeah. She's bruised. A cracked rib. Broken nose. They never said a word. Didn't call any names. Nothing. Just pushed her down, two quick kicks, and ran. We're not going to report it. Not officially."

"Why? Black? White?"

"Don't know. They had on hoods. Maybe gloves. Laurie never really got a good look. Hilman's got some new ideas. He's been goin over the autopsy."

"God! That pisses me off."

"Yeah, well, we'll handle it," Mitch had said. "Look, I gotta git. We'll talk later, okay?"

Pisses me off, Johnny thought. Again he checked the rearview mirror. No one had come. No one had left. It all pisses me off. It all . . . It . . . What the hell do I do now? Where do we go from here? Huh? Where, Julia? Huh? Where? What? Where? Johnny closed his eyes, journeyed into the darkness of his mind. He was on the field with the ball, controlling the ball, kneeing players in the groin, kneeing Brad Tripps and Nelson Tripps and Meloblatt and LeRoy and Emilio Sanchez and . . . He was on Red Apple Hill Road, in his Infiniti, making believe he was watching the flock of wild turkeys, staking out Mitch's house unseen, unnoticed, seeing all, vigilant, pouncing on the perpetrators, exposing . . . He was in Lakeport, in a phone booth, chuckling to himself, laughing, then dialing the ContGenChem main line, the switchboard, his pulse racing, "*Á! Cuic!* There ees a bomb." His accent is heavy, stupid, fake. It makes no difference. "There ees a bomb in the tower and eet will make Oklahoma look like a firecracker. You got thirty minutes to git eev-ree-one out." No. Not the switchboard. WLAK. McNichols. Or Folders. That asshole Folders. That . . .

Johnny shifted in the seat. He felt sick, felt the acid rising, burning, tasted the rancid sourness. Still he did not open his eyes. Inwardly he felt manic, outwardly torpid. *Fancul,* he thought. *Che pouzze schiatta.* He directed it at himself, thought of himself, looked at himself, reviewed himself. In two months he'd gone from fit to flaccid. His skin had gone from smooth to wrinkled; below his eyes the skin sagged, had become dark. His abs—his pride—were sheathed by a layer of flab, were distended by continuous intestinal distress.

"Win the goddamn game!" he blurted. His voice roused him. He shook, looked into the darkness that shrouded the field. *I need you,* he thought, and he imagined himself talking to Jason, saying to Jason something he could never say. *I need you to win this game. I, me, I need this victory. Just one more game and you're league champions. Just one more, damn it! Just . . . I don't . . .* Johnny put his hands to his head, held his temples. *I don't want to get old. I don't want to get old like you, Pop.* I don't want to be old. I don't want to sit and ache and be bored and be depressed and be scared that a spark is going to burn down the house. I don't want to be incontinent. I don't want to grow paranoid, to live in fear that every day might be the day my heart bursts or my brain ruptures or my kidneys back up and poison me. I don't want to live in a society that is deteriorating. I don't know where I am. I don't know where to go. I'm a drain on my family. I should just drive toward home. I should just drive right into the abutment of Route 86.

The Panuzio Home, East Lake, Friday, 11 November, 6:26 A.M.

JOHNNY WATCHED THE black liquid stream into the glass pot. There was a song he liked to recall now and again about coffee but his mind would not retrieve the words or the tune. Instead he angrily seethed, "Come on! Come on! What the fuck! Why is it taking so goddamn long?" He grasped the plastic cone with the filter and grinds, lifted it, stuck his cup beneath. That still was not fast enough. He raised the cone high, poured from the pot into the cup while the cone continued running. Eleven days, he thought. Eleven goddamn days. Maybe we could sell the lawn tractor. Maybe . . .

"Can I take the car to the game tonight?" Jason did not look at him.

Johnny looked up. He hadn't heard Jason come in. His son was dressed in a white shirt and tie but the shirt was open at the collar, the tie askew. His pants were baggy denim. Johnny eyed him. "Maybe. Let me think about it."

"I wanted ta tell . . . ah . . . Jeff and Miro, during school . . ."

"Maybe. I . . . Did your mother say if she was going? You look like a *cafone*."

Jason shrugged at the remark, turned his back. "I think she is," he answered. "It's the league championship. There'll be a lot—"

"Pop-sters lob-sters," Jenny burst into the kitchen, seemingly back to her smiling self. "I need ten dollars to go to the mall with Tara and Lena after—"

"Excuse me!" Jason sneered at his little sister. "We're talking here."

"Well!" She stuck her tongue out.

"Under the lights?" Johnny asked. "At Jefferson?"

Jason nodded. "It's a neutral field."

"I still want to think . . . No bus?"

"Ten bucks, most awesome Daddy-oh-man-god!" Jenny smiled.

"What mall?"

"In South L—"

"I gotta go," Jason cut his sister off. "Can you give—"

Johnny raised both hands. "One minute," he said emphatically. To Jenny he said, *"È necessario?"*

"Huh?" Jenny scrunched up her face.

Johnny scoffed. "Is it necessary? *Both* of you! We've got to make some cuts . . ."

"Where's . . ." Rocco shuffled into the room, hunched, frantic. "Where's Tessa?" His left shoulder was against the wall, his left hand patting the wall as if he expected to find an opening. "Where's Tessa?!" he bellowed as loudly as his frail body would allow.

"Pop?" Johnny cringed.

"Where is she?" Rocco searched the kitchen table, peered at the sink, at the doorway to the hall and living room, at Jason and at Jenny. His hands were shaking, his movements were fidgety, panicky. "She didn't come to bed. Is she out here? Is she on the couch?"

Jenny stared at her grandfather. His face seemed contorted. Jason too stood still. "Pop?" Johnny said again. He wasn't sure how to respond.

"Where is she?" Rocco demanded.

"Pop, Mom's gone."

"Where?"

"I think you're still asleep, Pop."

Rocco moved to the table, placed his left hand on it, rested but did not sit. He hung his head, closed his eyes, began crying, sobbing uncontrollably.

"Sit down, Pop." Johnny laid his hands on Rocco's shoulders to guide him into a chair.

"She's a good woman," Rocco said.

"Yep," Johnny agreed. "She was a great mom."

"How long has she been . . . ?"

"A couple a years, Pop."

Again there were tears, now weak sobbing. "I . . . I guess . . . I dreamed . . . last night. We wah-arre marrahrr-eed . . ."

"Pop? You Okay?"

". . . fif-t-th-ee . . . yaar . . ."

"Popsters," Jenny whispered. "Something's happening."

"Oh geez!" Johnny knelt, grabbed Rocco. "Pop!" he shouted. "Pop!" He squeezed Rocco's right hand. "Can you feel this?"

"Aaa-aahh . . ." Rocco's mouth hung open.

"Oh geez! Oh geez!" Johnny's arms began to tremble. "Jenny, get your mother. Jason, call nine-one-one. Oh shit! Then call Uncle Nick. Have him call Katzenbaum."

THEY STOOD TOGETHER, Kim leaning against Jason, Jason leaning back against the wall in Marcia Radkowski's classroom. Sunlight streamed through the windows, illuminated Kim's face, made her skin glow, her hair shine. "What did your mother say?" Kim whispered.

"They don't know anything yet. They took him to St. Luke's. My father's there with him. What did Rosenwald say?"

"She just put me off. She wants me to give a deposition on what happened."

"A deposition? On what? What does that mean?"

"You know. That thing that happened between Martina and Miss Radkowski? She wants me to give like a sworn statement. Like I know anything about it."

"I thought Martina dropped it."

"She did. It's not her. Rosenwald wants to make like a federal case out of it. She's more interested in finding people to blame than in us putting together a panel."

"What are you going to tell her?"

"Her?! I wouldn't tell her anything. I wouldn't trust her with . . . Besides, I really didn't see anything. That was when Martina said . . . you know . . . that Goodie Two-shoes . . ." The bell rang, beginning the period. Kim squeezed Jason. "Are you going to be able to play?"

"Yeah. My mom said that my dad said I should play no matter what."

"TELL TRIPPS HE can stick it up his ass," Johnny muttered. He was in the waiting room at St. Luke's Hospital in Lakeport, sitting in an uncomfortable chrome-and-Naugahyde chair, his feet firmly planted on the floor, his elbows on his knees, his face on the backs of his half-closed hands. He had checked his watch only a moment before, resisted the urge to check it again, knew that it couldn't be much later than nine-thirty, maybe nine thirty-five. All morning he'd waited with Nick; then alternately through the afternoon and early evening. They'd called Sylvia in Albany and Angie in Seattle to alert their sisters to the potential; only to be told, first by Katzenbaum, then in more detail by Alan Pollan, the hospital's head of neurology, that Rocco's condition was stable. Rocco had had a CAT scan, had been put nearly immediately on various clot busters and blood thinners which the emergency stroke team explained to Nick in great detail but not to Johnny at all. "The next twenty-four hours," Pollan had said, "are critical. The damage does not seem to be that extensive, but at his age it's difficult to predict . . ."

Johnny had called Mitch after the EMTs had left with Rocco. "Tell that micromanaging motherfucker Tripps to stick it up his ass," he'd said. "Tell him I don't give a rat's ass—"

"Johnny," Mitch had said, "I'll take care of it. You just stay cool. And don't call in. I'll take care of it. I'll come by . . ."

All day long people had come by. Mitch came twice. Laurie came. Nick, of course, and Julia, but also Dana and Zi Carmela and Donato Altieri, Tessa's last living sibling. Somehow word spread. Two priests from Holy Rosary came; men who had known Rocco during his days as a contractor came, and old neighbors from Center Street and Catherine Street and Fourth Street. People Johnny didn't know, had never heard of, had no idea of; people to whom Rocco had been a friend, a mentor, a fellow parishioner. Some cried, some prayed. Most had stories to tell—"We played bocci. He was a good bocci player. He always beat me."—or short anecdotes that illuminated Rocco and Tessa's life in a way Johnny had never seen.

By nine they had all left and Johnny had sat, had muttered, had watched some TV on the small screen in the waiting room, had muttered some more. He got up, went to the phone, called Julia.

"How's he doing?" Julia asked.

"No change, really. It's all on his right side. Partial, I think is the way they described it. More than a TIA but certainly not a full-blown thing."

"Ischemic," Julia said.

"Um. I guess. I was in there a bit ago. He was looking around, moving some, he was trying to talk. Something about that box. That damn box he's been looking for. He looked terrified. Pollan said to imagine it like you've got the worst headache possible, like . . . Ah, I don't understand all the stuff they're doing. Warafin drip . . . something. He's resting. Pollan said he might be home in a week. Maybe less. Or . . . It could be . . . *Á!*"

"Are you coming home?"

"I'm going to stay a little longer," Johnny said. Then he chuckled. "There's a rerun of a Phil Donahue program on Jeffrey Dalmer."

"The murderer?"

"Yeah. I don't know who's sicker, the guy who did it or the guy who publicizes it and then reruns it. Him and all the execs, the sponsors, the viewers . . ."

"Just change the channel," Julia said.

"Popular culture," Johnny snickered. "We ask for all the problems we . . . God! Shut me up. Shut me up! Hey, is Jason back yet? How'd they make out?"

"They lost," Julia said. "Three to two."

"Augh . . . Too bad. Was it a good game?"

"I guess. He didn't say. There was another incident in the stands but

I'm not sure what. His coach called earlier today, too. Not about soccer. And Kim's here. They're up in his room listening to music."

"Umm. Well . . . they've still got . . . ah . . . I . . . You think that's okay?"

"Kim? Yes, I do. I really like her and I think she's good for him."

"Um. Well . . . they've still got the state tournament, right?"

"Um-hmm. Next week."

CALLED TOO, JULIA thought. Not about soccer. Maybe I should have told him. But how? With all this . . . ?

Earlier: "Mrs. Panuzio?"

"Yes."

"F.X. McMillian. Jason's coach."

"Oh! Yes. Is everything . . ."

"Everything's fine. I just wanted to ask a few questions. Is . . . ah, your husband there?" Julia had explained the situation. "Oh. If this isn't—"

"Ask me," Julia said.

"Okay. Do you . . . Does your husband have a brother? And, ah . . . is he a veteran of the Viet-Nam War?"

"Yes," Julia answered. "Yes to both." She sensed the concern in McMillian's tone. "Is there . . . ? Did Jason . . . ?"

"Well. Look. I'm going to tell you something. I want to alert you to . . . ah . . . a situation. But I don't want it to go any further. Jason came to school with a Chinese communist bayonet fastened into a display box. He brought it in as a historical artifact, but bringing in a weapon like that without prior consent is against district rules. I don't want to see him get into trouble for this. I believe he knows he's done wrong. As a matter of fact, he came to me with the weapon and asked that I take it as a gift for the military museum in South Lakeport. Did you know anything about this?"

"No," Julia answered. "Where'd he get a bayon . . . ? Did his uncle Nick give it to him? I'll speak to—"

"No. No. He bought it, originally, he said, as a birthday present for his uncle. Look. I have it now. If it's all right with you, I'll donate it. He's a good kid. I really like him. I think he's maturing quickly . . . beyond his years. If nothing else happens, I'd like everyone to bury this. He's going to do some volunteer work for me—on an interscholastic panel he and Kim Sanchez are putting together. That'll be his restitution, okay?"

"Oh. Hmm. Of course. Thanks. Really." Julia had hung up the phone, concerned, confused.

FOUR DAYS LATER, on the afternoon of Tuesday, November 15, Charlene Rosenwald began her own inquisition. "There's something going on in this school," she told Victor Santoro and Michelle Dutchussy, "and we're going to get to the bottom of it. We're going to get to the bottom of it if we have to clamp a lid on every activity of every student here. We will proactively uproot every seed of violence . . . I want to know everything that goes on in this school. I want to know everything everyone says, or does or thinks."

"Mr. Anzo," Michelle Dutchussy reported, "has contacted two firms that have agreed to survey the school and make recommendations and proposals for surveillance systems for the corridors and—"

"I know. I've spoken with him. Dr. Schoemer also has spoken with him. Victor, I want you to oversee Mr. Anzo's work. He's not the most professional employee . . ."

"Yes, Dr. Rosenwald," Mr. Santoro said.

The principal studied the vice principal's face. "You're not in agreement with this plan, are you, Victor?"

"If this is what you believe it will take to make this school secure," Victor Santoro said, "I will carry out that assignment."

"Don't you believe a camera surveillance system will increase the safety of everyone in this building?"

"I'm sure it will." Santoro nodded.

"It will," Rosenwald said. She waved a hand to dismiss her assistants. "Who's out there to see me?"

"Marcia Radkowski," Dutchussy said. "English. And drama club adviser."

"Hmm. Send her in and shut the door."

Marcia entered. At five-ten, even in flats, Marcia towered over Dr. Rosenwald. Still the principal did not ask her to be seated. "Miss Radkowski, are you aware of the negligent manslaughter suit the Fitzpatricks have filed?"

"No," Marcia said. She stood before the principal's desk, gaunt, her shoulders slumped, her hands hanging, her right hand grasping her left thumb.

"Two-point-six million dollars," Rosenwald said. "They've named the school, the town, the Willises."

"Oh," Marcia said sheepishly.

"What do you know about them?"

"About whom?"

"The Fitzpatricks! Are you following what I'm telling you?"

"Yes. I think. Katie Fitzpatrick was one of my students."

"Miss Radkowski, I want a full written report from you, on my desk, tonight."

"On the Fitzpatricks?!"

"On anything you know about the violence which has been occurring . . . Were you at the game down in Jefferson on Friday?"

"No."

"You didn't see Ellen Darsey get pushed from the bleachers?"

"I wasn't there."

"Have any of your students said anything about it?"

"Not to me."

"Miss Radkowski, don't be obstinate. Have you overheard anything?"

Meekly, Marcia whispered, "I don't make a habit of listening in on other people's conversations."

"Well, it's time that you do." Dr. Rosenwald cleared a small work area on her desk. "That is part of your job," she said, not looking at the teacher. "Do you understand me? From now on, that is part of your job." She looked up. "Particularly at rehearsals. You are the adviser to the drama club, aren't you?"

"Yes, Dr. Rosenwald. We'll be presenting *Othello* the third week of March."

"Umm." Dr. Rosenwald paused. "Do you have anything to ask me?"

"No. Ah, well, yes."

"Yes?"

"Did you read the *Ledger* articles by Aaron Williams?"

"Yes."

"Weren't they wonderful?"

Charlene Rosenwald tapped a perfectly manicured fingernail on her desk. "The statute of limitations," she said, "on that incident in the cafeteria is one year. Mrs. Watts can file a suit any time up until one year."

"Yes, Dr. Rosenwald. I'm aware of that."

"I will consider that period probationary."

"PROBATIONARY?!" CIARA CLUCKED her tongue. "Probationary?" she repeated.

"Ciara." Marcia covered her face. Her breaths were shallow, her words quivering. "I'm so afraid."

"She's a scary woman," Ciara said gently. "The two of them. And Victor's just going along with it. He's less than a year from retirement. He doesn't want to jeopardize—"

"If the Fitzpatricks can—"

"Marcia." Ciara pulled the thin young woman to her, hugged her, held her. They were in Ciara's office sitting side by side. As Ciara held her she felt Marcia's tension drain, felt her breathing return to normal. Lightly Ciara caressed Marcia's head.

"You read his articles, didn't you?" Marcia whispered.

"Yes."

"They really were quite good, weren't they?"

"He was a brilliant student."

"I cut them out and put them in a notebook. I cut them all out and put each piece in order in a notebook with his words on the left and my notes and comments on the right. I read it so many times."

"You know that Jason Panuzio and Kim Sanchez have proposed forming a committee to—"

"I wish I could have discussed it with Aaron," Marcia said. She sat up, smiled weakly. "How I wish I could talk to him."

Ciara sighed. "Yes. I guess many of us feel that way."

"I read them to him. At his grave. Sometimes I go out there. At night. I've been reading him our play. He should have been my Othello."

Ciara's hurt for the young teacher came through in her voice. "Oh, Marcia. You poor . . ."

"If I tell you something, do you promise to keep it confidential?"

"Of course. If I didn't, no one would come to me."

"But it's not something . . . good. I mean, it's something . . . No one can ever know. I've prayed for guidance. I keep praying . . . I've got to tell someone. But if Rosenwald ever found out . . . I'd kill myself."

"Don't say—"

"I loved him," Marcia said. All tension drained from her face, her shoulders. She sat in perfect calmness, completely detached.

"I know. You've shown me by the way you talk, the way you—"

"No." Marcia's voice was spiritless. "I mean I . . . I made love to him."

"Oh, Marcia! I don't believe that."

"I did."

"Marcia, you did not!"

"Four times. The first time was on the beach at The Cove in South Lake Village. That was in the middle of July. In a secluded spot just above the beach. Then twice we drove out toward Taftburg and made love on a blanket in a cornfield. And once up by The Falls. That was in August, and we decided we shouldn't do it anymore. Not until after he graduated. It wasn't wrong. Not really. He was eighteen. He was already eighteen. I wasn't that much older. I'm only twenty-three now, so I was—"

Marcia was not looking at Ciara but was looking straight forward; her eyes were hazed, her look as if she were in a dream. Ciara's face was a stunned mask of disbelief.

"—still twenty-two. I was ten pounds heavier, so my breasts were fuller. And he had such a huge penis. I loved his penis. He was circumcised and the head of his penis was like a golden bell. It was like—"

"Marcia! Stop this right now!"

East Lake High School, Room 127, Thursday, 17 November, 8:40 P.M.

"... THUSLY WE ACHIEVE the economic and efficient delivery of public services without the Byzantine labyrinth of bureaucratic regulatory agencies," Town Councilman Norm Hume concluded.

Julia sighed. She, Jason and Kim had sat through more than an hour of seemingly inane policy discussion and debate. The classroom was hot, packed with more than a hundred people. Before Jason sat Dan Crnecki, Jeff Kurjiaka and Paul Compari. Scattered about the room were players and parents from all the high school's fall and winter teams. F.X. McMillian, Ciara DeLauro and physics teacher James Hawkins sat together in the front row facing a makeshift conference table. Seated on folding chairs at the table were Hume, Superintendent John Schoemer, Dr. Charlene Rosenwald, Police Chief Bruce Flanagan and high school Security Chief Gene Anzo. Behind them sat Michelle Dutchussy, Victor Santoro and East Lake Youth Officer Greg Ledbetter. In the hallway another two hundred parents and students milled around, sat at the base of the walls, attempted to peer in or listen. Dr. Rosenwald had resisted moving the meeting to the auditorium, ostensibly because that room was being set up for a band concert. If it also restricted the number who could voice their opinions, so be it.

"There's no way," Jason whispered to Kim. "No way they're going to cancel the season."

"This could go on all night," Kim responded. "They're doing the other business first. On purpose. They want everybody to go home."

Crnecki turned. "Way, dude!" he said loudly. "You listenin to these people? They talk a different language, man."

"Shh!" a man behind Jason hissed. Crnecki gave him a dirty look, turned around, muttered loudly enough for everyone to hear, "They aren't talking now, fool. They're in transition."

"How'd your grandfather look?" Kim whispered to Jason.

"Pretty good," Jason whispered back. "My father thought he should stay with him tonight because it's his first night home."

Kim glanced at Julia, whispered so only Jason could hear, "You haven't told your father yet, have you?"

"It . . . ah . . ." Jason whispered back. "I haven't found the right time to . . . I couldn't . . . you know, with my grandfather. I can't talk to him anyway."

Again the man behind hissed, "Shh!"

Julia spun, pointed her finger at the man. "If you don't like it, go sit somewhere else!"

"Who's talking to y—" the man began.

Julia cut him off. "Shut up! They'll be quiet when the proceedings restart. Some of you people in this town!"

Jason slid a bit lower in his seat; stifled a laugh.

"Next order of business . . ." Dr. Schoemer called.

The proceedings at the table were orderly, biting at times, but always orderly. The question of canceling all high school athletic activities, including the Elks' participation in the first round of the state soccer tournament scheduled for the next evening, came up, was discussed by the panel, then was temporarily tabled.

"Hey! Wait a minute!" Angelo Compari stood up next to his son. "We came to talk, too. Not just to listen."

"Yeah," at least two dozen students and parents blared.

"We will return . . ." Dr. Schoemer banged a gavel on the table. "We will return to the topic of interscholastic athletic—" again he banged the gavel "—competition after we've discussed the related AND perhaps more important topic of controlling teen behavior. We will now review the file on requesting town approval of an expenditure of one hundred seventy-four thousand dollars for a camera surveillance and recording system for the high school."

"You people are nuts," Angelo Compari muttered loudly.

Dr. Schoemer banged his gavel. "You may listen to this discussion politely or I will have the room cleared. Is that," Schoemer barked, "understood!" He glared at the standing man. Angelo Compari glared back in silence. Schoemer added, "After you've heard our discussion, we will open the floor to public comment."

Again the discussion became pointed. Police Chief Flanagan and Officer Ledbetter both offered objections to the surveillance system. Principal Rosenwald and Vice Principal Dutchussy stated it was necessary if rape, assault, murder and smoking were to be prevented. In the end the discussion was inconclusive. "Now—" Dr. Schoemer's eyes flicked about the room, came to rest on his gavel "—we will hear public comment. I will ask you to restrict your comments to three minutes."

"Enough time—" Mr. Hawkins rose as he spoke out unrecognized "—to insure zero understanding."

"Order." Dr. Schoemer rapped his gavel. "Mr. Hawkins, if the comments are pertinent and progress the point, I will allow the speaker to continue."

For nearly an hour, speaker after speaker rose, advanced to the floor microphone. Nearly half either expressed their concerns for their own children's safety, denounced other town youth as irresponsible, pleaded for a stronger security system and pledged their support for a town special budget request, or denounced the expenditure as unnecessary, as a waste of taxpayer money. More than half had no comment with regard to the security issue, were there solely to plead with the board to allow the games to continue. Finally Ciara DeLauro reached the mike.

She identified herself, then began, "Mr. Chairman, Chief Flanagan, members of the school board, East Lakers. Shame on you. Shame on you for thinking what you think of your sons and daughters. Shame on you for thinking what you think of your students. Shame on you for proposing—out of your fear—a policy, a procedure or a system of control. Yes, tragedies have happened here. Yes, there is the potential for additional tragedy. Yet only a few short weeks ago, one of our brightest students—the victim of the most abhorrent and ultimate crime—spoke to us, and gave us a format for examining problems and projecting policy ramifications—before they are decreed into existence."

In the seats Julia nudged Jason. "She's talking about Aaron," Julia whispered. "She's such a smart woman."

"Shame on us," Ciara DeLauro continued. Her voice was calm, yet she radiated a tremendous energy. "If we turn our school into a prison, should we be surprised if our students act like inmates? If we replace student accountability with surveillance, should we not expect more irresponsibility? We have only to look across beautiful Lake Wampahwaug. Has violence within the city school system abated since that system instituted prisonlike policies? Or has it increased? Or has it simply moved off campus to other areas? Has the quality of education risen, stayed the same, or fallen? Is better behavior produced by creating an educational environment which treats all students as untrustworthy individuals, or by creating one in which every student is presumed innocent and only individual students who have proven themselves untrustworthy are so treated?

"My Dear East Lakers—" Schoemer was about to bang that her time was up, but Police Chief Flanagan gently grabbed his wrist. Ciara continued.

"The problem with increased security is that it sows the seeds of an enclave mentality; of an us-versus-them perception; of sanctioned polarization—whether it be men from women, blacks from whites, cities from towns, the wealthy from the needy, workers from employers, citizens from their government or students from their community. The perceptions of polarization created by surveillance, valid or invalid, may create new, or accentuate existing, polarizations. When polarization increases, there is a corresponding increase in violence. When violence increases, there is a corresponding increase in polarization. This is a cyclical process which may be propelled by an overzealous rush to protect; by a paranoia without malice. Yet in the long run, increased security may make our children more, not less, vulnerable to violence."

Julia popped up from her seat. "Here! Here!" she shouted. She clapped her hands three times, sat. In the chair next to her Jason slouched lower, covered his face with his hands. Under his hands he was smiling.

Ciara smiled at them. "If total-school surveillance and armed patrols are not the answer," she continued, "what is? How do we maintain a quality learning environment while insuring the safety of our children? Isn't that the primary question? I believe the course of action most likely to achieve our goals is one which builds on the strengths of our teachers and our students, not one which limits their interactions, denies their accountability or removes from them the need to discipline themselves—here, at school, or anywhere.

"Shame on us all. Have we forgotten not only the quality of mercy, but also the power of mercy? The power of forgiveness?

"A student, a product of this school system, who was murdered has told us, 'Behavior is consistent with self-image and world view.' What self-image will these students internalize if they must endure continuous surveillance? What self-image will these players internalize if they are punished by not being allowed to compete? How will they view the adult world that surrounds them? What will be their ensuing behaviors?" Ciara paused. She noted that Charlene Rosenwald was doodling; that Dr. Schoemer was jotting an occasional note; that Chief Flanagan was concentrating on her every word.

In the audience, heads that had been nodding all evening snapped up, jolted at the word "players." A murmur arose. Mrs. DeLauro could challenge the powers that be! She could lead the charge! Dr. Rosenwald eyed the audience with suspicion.

"All self-images," Ciara went on, "are comprised of positives and negatives. Punishment tends to increase one's identity with the negative. Because of this, punishment may actually increase the frequency of negative behavior.

Can you visualize this? We may punish until self-image, and thus behavior, is dominated by negative characteristics. Is this where we are heading?"

Again Ciara paused. Now she looked directly into Dr. Schoemer's eyes, then into Dr. Rosenwald's. "Every one of us exhibits a variety of excesses and extremes. Sometimes we are too strict with our children. Sometimes too lenient. Sometimes families and schools and teams demand so much that unseen stresses inside a student drive him or her to be sick, or drive him or her into aberrant or violent or illegal behavior. Other times we don't ask enough and our low expectations are met and the child is set on a life path of underachievement and nonfulfillment.

"We don't always know—" Ciara shook her head "—do we? We as adults, as teachers, as counselors, as administrators, don't always do the right thing. Sometimes we are less than exact. All we can do is have a set of guiding principles; the right intentions; an attitude and process in place which allows us, when we see an individual foundering, approaching an extreme, to make an adjustment and try again."

Ciara turned to the audience of mostly parents and students. "My belief in the process of contrition, confession, restitution, absolution and reconciliation is well known in this school, in my church and in this town. The reason why it works is that contrition and confession break one from identifying with the negative characteristics within one's self-image; one no longer needs to match the 'evil' behaviors dictated by a debased self-image. Restitution removes guilt and restores positive self-image. It produces absolution within the self, and when that is produced, the individual should be reconciled with his or her society. Nothing else has ever worked!"

Ciara returned to those seated at and behind the conference table. "For these reasons, Councilman Hume, Dr. Schoemer, Dr. Rosenwald, East Lakers, I would first like to see the proposal for this very expensive, ill-advised and invasive surveillance system tabled forever. Secondly, I would like to see our Elks beat the britches off Avon tomorrow night."

"YOU WANT TO try some soup, Pop?" Johnny asked.

Rocco looked at him, feebly nodded.

"Chicken noodle?" Johnny asked.

Again Rocco nodded.

"Pop," Johnny said, "you gotta try speaking. The more you try, the sooner your brain will recover. Will have that plastic recovery where one area takes over for the damaged area."

"Uhn," Rocco uttered. He stood, shuffled slowly toward the kitchen, paused, turned, pointed at the TV. "Au-ff."

"Augh, we might just as well leave it on. Hey, see, when you want to, you can get the words out."

Rocco looked at Johnny. There was no warmth in the look; no coolness. He'd had, according to his doctors, an amazing recovery. His mobility was barely worse than it had been before the stroke. His speech center had been affected yet there were signs that that, too, was minimal—that as the brain made adjustments, much of Rocco's speech would return. "Au-ff," Rocco repeated. "Pa . . ."

"Pay? Pay the bill?" Johnny asked. As he moved into the kitchen he glanced back to see if his father was still following him. "The cable bill?" Johnny said. "I paid it." To himself he thought, I paid it. I paid him. Another grand. Another . . . Thank God for . . . The very thought of the phone conversation with LeRoy disgusted him. He'd even thanked him. "That'll be yer Christmas present, man," LeRoy had said. "I'll give ya till the end of the year." And Johnny had said, "Thanks. Thanks. I'll have it by then . . ."

"Pa . . . uhn," Rocco repeated. "Pa . . . uhn."

"Umm." Johnny pretended he understood what Rocco meant. He took a can of Progresso Chickarina from the cabinet, opened it, put half in each bowl, microwaved the two. He did not look at his father because it was painful to look at him. Rocco's face was slack, his eyes lifeless. He had slept most of the day since returning home. His face was stubbled, his clothes disheveled. "I hope," Johnny said to fill the quietness, "they don't stop the season. I'd be pretty disappointed if Jason couldn't play in the tournament."

"So . . . oh," Rocco said.

"Yeah. They're at a meeting at the high *skoo-ol.* I can't believe they're still there. Jenny's at Tara's. Tara's mother is going on their field trip tomorrow with them. She's goina drive."

Rocco shook his head. "Unh," he uttered emphatically. "Unh. So . . . oh. Ja . . . ss."

"Jason," Johnny said. "Yeah."

Rocco nodded. "Hou . . . p Ja . . . ss."

"Help? Jason?" Johnny attempted.

Again Rocco nodded.

"You want Jason to help you?"

Rocco shook his head. His hand moved slowly. He pointed at Johnny, then away.

Johnny nodded, took the bowls from the microwave, placed them on the table. Damn it, he thought. Damn it, damn it, damn it. How in hell are we going to do this? He ate slowly, purposefully trying to slow himself to Rocco's pace; found the silence and the pace exasperating, unbearable;

tried to think of something to say. "I was down in the basement yesterday. The walls look great."

"Unh," Rocco said. He pushed his soup away. "Bahk. Pa . . . uhn."

"Bank payment?" Johnny asked.

Rocco formed a square with his hands. To Johnny the skin of those hands looked like old parchment, like wrinkled old wax paper. "Unh." Rocco's face held no expression.

Johnny shrugged, indicated he did not understand.

Suddenly Rocco's right hand flew up in frustration. "Unh. Bahk." Then he flipped both hands angrily as if to say, "Forget it."

Johnny looked at his soup. He had no appetite. He swallowed. The doorbell rang. Johnny's head snapped up. He wasn't expecting . . . "Oh," he said. Rocco continued eating. He had not heard the bell. "Julia musta fergot her key. I'll let em in."

At the door Johnny was again surprised. Tom Hilman, the state police investigator, smiled sheepishly. "I know it's late, John, but I've had some . . . ah . . . thoughts."

"The girls are okay, aren't they?" Johnny asked.

"The . . . ?"

"Whitney and Diana. Mitch Williams' daughters!"

"Oh! Of course . . . Last time we . . ." Hilman shuffled. "This isn't about them. Not directly. I haven't heard . . . No news is good . . . and all of that."

"Tom, come in. Is everything okay?"

As he entered Tom Hilman muttered, "Umm. Yeah. You know. I just wanted to ask a few questions. Maybe ask the Missus a few questions. Wow! Lotta pictures."

"Oh. Our wall! Want some soup? My—"

"Who's this guy with the sword?"

"Ha! That's my grandfather. About a hundred years ago. In Italy. He was a cavalry . . . ah . . . He wasn't an officer. Just a soldier, I guess. I always think, in that uniform, he was an officer. He came over in 1898, went back to serve his time, came back in 1900."

Hilman's eyes shifted from picture to picture. "Lotta nice ones," he said. "Hey, you've become quite a celebrity with those articles."

"Not on purpose," Johnny said. "I just wanted to get Aaron's theory out. You know, I think he had some pretty valid points."

"Most of my colleagues agree."

"I thought it would be good for everyone," Johnny said. "I didn't anticipate the fallout. The . . . like hitting a bee's nest with a baseball bat. Were they the reason . . . ah . . . for Laurie?"

"Hmm?"

"When she got attacked. Broken rib . . ."

"Oh. I don't know. We haven't found anyone . . ."

"God! That made me feel like shit. Those articles . . . They were supposed—"

Hilman interrupted Johnny. "I liked em. But what do I know?"

"Coffee? Julia's not . . . She and Jason are still over at the high school. At that meeting . . ."

"Ah . . . It's a little too late. If I drink coffee this late, I'm up every hour, going . . . you know, to the bathroom."

Johnny chuckled in sympathy. "Somethin else?"

"No. Just a few questions."

"Let's sit in here." Johnny indicated the sofa in the living room. "Mitch said you're re . . . How did he put it? Reexamining the autopsy."

"Yeah. Not really. But I asked the examiner to give me extended parameters. We've been going on the theory that Aaron was killed sometime after five o'clock. But if you think back to those few days . . . those cold rains . . . I asked him, what if the rains cooled the body more quickly than you'd expect, maybe slowed the deterioration process which is used to establish the actual time of death? Particularly with how heavy that rain was. If it had pooled around his body, he'd be more like a drowning victim. You know, sometimes when we get a body from the bottom of the lake, it's amazingly well preserved."

"Uh! What'd he . . . What did the examiner . . . ?"

"He said he took it into consideration. It wouldn't affect the ballistics or the blood coagulation patterns inside . . . ah . . ." Hilman put his fingertips together, looked up toward the top of the far wall. "We're sure he was killed right there. But I think it could have been earlier. Maybe three o'clock. They don't like to admit it but they aren't always as precise as they like everyone to believe."

"Sure. Must be . . ." From the kitchen came the noise of a dish being upset on the table. "Excuse me. My father . . ." Johnny stood. "I just brought him home from the hospital this morning. Let me check on him."

"Of course. My father lives with me, too. I know . . ."

Johnny was out and back in a minute. Hilman was standing. He'd rebuttoned his coat. "He's okay," Johnny said.

"Can you remember back to last summer? Probably a Sunday in July."

"Yeah. Well. Kinda."

"I really wanted ta ask the Missus. She mighta been down in South Lake Village."

"Julia? In . . . Oh, she was working on her *big* project then. Let's see . . ."

"Maybe Sunday the seventeenth. She might of seen Aaron Williams down there."

"Julia and Aaron?"

"He mighta been with a girlfriend. Maybe you could ask her for me."

"The seventeenth?! That was my father's eighty-fifth. We had a big party here. Aaron came and picked up Jason. They had a pickup scrimmage . . . ah, let me think."

"Umm-mm." Hilman nodded excessively. "Maybe just ask her. She mighta seen something from Nightingale's."

Johnny-panni crouches. He places a hand on the ground, shifts his weight, kneels. He reaches into the hole, smooths the soil. The dirt feels cool, contrasts sharply with the hot summer sun on his back. It is already eighty-five degrees. It is Rocco's 85th birthday—Sunday, July 17. Johnny tamps the soil flat, rocks back, glances at his father who is seated on the weathered picnic bench in the shade beneath the maples. In an hour the others will begin arriving and Johnny wants the yard to look nice—or Julia wants it to look nice and he is willing to do the planting.

He grasps the plastic pot, splits the side with a utility knife, gently removes the last shrub being careful not to knock off the small pink flowers. The day is lovely. There is a slight breeze from the lake. He feels wonderful. He likes having his hands in the dirt. He hears Rocco sniff, again glances over. "What is it, Pop?" Rocco is sobbing, his chest heaving. "Pop?"

"I can't get there." Rocco pulls a handkerchief from his belt, blows his nose.

"Where?" He . . . "Where?" I ask.

"My father's grave," Rocco says. "I plant there every—"

"Flowers?" I interrupt. I'm not feeling sympathetic. There's goina be fifty, maybe more, people here in an hour. My cousin Henry Bragiotti, Zi Carmela's son, is flying in all the way from Phoenix. And Julia's working! Is still at work! Something "hot," she'd said. "On my big . . ." I haven't even showered or shaved. I haven't started the grill. I haven't . . .

"And my mother's." Rocco's sobbing is louder. "And Tessa's. Poor Tessa," Rocco blubbers.

"We'll get there," I say. I think, God! Now I've got to take him there, too? When? When the hell can I? When? Aloud Johnny says, "We'll get down there, Pop. Maybe next Sunday. These look pretty good, don't they?" He sweeps a hand across, indicating the long, new bed bordering the hedge. "Happy birthday, Pop," I say.

From the driveway at the side of the house comes the loud mechanical clankiness of a poorly tuned diesel. The motor chugs, lugs, backfires, dies. "Boom Ba doomba doomba doom Ba; Boom Ba doomba doomba Do! Hey, anybody home?"

I rise, see Nick disembark from his high 4 × 4 pickup. "Doom Ba doomba doomba doo-Dah . . ." I laugh, gather up the garden tools, glance at Pop. His crying jag has ended.

Jason makes the first greeting. "Hey, Uncle Nick."

"I've got three coolers of ice and drinks," Nick says. He opens the tailgate. "And a hot box, the table and chairs . . . You and Todd get em out, okay?"

"Sure," Jason says.

"How ya doin?" Nick slides one of the coolers to the edge of the tailgate, leaves it. He grabs Jason's right hand with his right, hugs him with his left arm, squeezes hard. "You get any taller and I'll be lookin up yer nose."

I chuckle. I flash on looking up Aunt Tina's nose when I was small. Jason says, "I'm fine." He tries to squirm loose but Nick's grasp is like an iron manacle. Nick turns him, wraps both his arms around him, lifts him from the ground, shakes him. "Hey . . . oh . . . whoa . . . I'm not much hea—"

"A hundred and seventy-five pounds," Nick says.

"One seventy-two," Jason answers.

"That's without yer shoes," Nick says. "Where's yer old man?"

"Right here," I chuckle between words, "watching you make a fool of yourself."

"Hey, bro?"

I hold up my hands. "If you hug me," I blurt, "I'm goina kiss ya."

"Uhh! Yuk!" Nick fakes spitting, laughs. His laugh is easy. It's good to see him. I don't see enough of my brother. It's good to see him on a happy occasion and not at a funeral. "Phase one of Op-plan Panuzio completed, sir." Nick salutes me but his hand is a fist with pinky and index finger extended, the mano cornuta. *Like giving me the finger. But playfully.*

"You bring enough stuff? Geez! Look at—"

"Enough to feed a division," Nick says. He winks at Jason. "You know, eat, drink and touch Mary." Jason hadn't heard that before. He stifles a snicker. Nick sees Rocco approaching. "Oh, hey!" He raises a hand, waves. "Hey, Pop! Happy eighty-fifth. You're lookin good. How's the foundation goin?"

"Thank you." Rocco smiles. There is no remnant of his depression. "Just starting. These boys . . . I wish these boys . . . Á."

"I brought a few bags a cement, some sand. After they get the food off, they can bring it downstairs."

"They don't do much around here." Rocco smiles but he is serious. "I don't know . . ."

"Um, well . . ." Nick's eyes dart to me, back to Pop. "Dana and the kids'll be here in a bit. She made the pasta just like Mom used to make. En I made the meatballs . . . Um-ummh . . ." Nick kisses his fingertips. "En braciola.

Ummm-umh. With raisins in the meatballs, pignoli *in the* braciola. *I think you're goina love it."*

"I gotta go in and wash up," I say. "Why don't you grab a beer? Get the boys to . . . Jason, you and Todd unload the coolers. Put em in the shade. Arrange the picnic tables an—"

Nick looks around. "Where's yer good-looking other half?"

"Á!" I say like I'm angry but also like I don't care. "Down in the village. Working on some blockbuster. Should be back pretty soon, too."

"Ha!" Nick laughs. "She's got worse hours than I do."

"Yeah," I laugh back. "But she makes more money than you do."

Two hours later the grill is smoking with sausage and peppers, hot dogs and hamburgers. The clank of horseshoes and the clack of bocci balls come from the game area in the farthest corner of the yard. Cans of beer are being popped open; wine bottles sweat on the picnic tables. Everywhere there is chatter, gabbing, stories, agreement and dissension. What a family! The afternoon is hot but relatively dry. There is still a breeze coming off the lake.

At the table closest to the barbecue Rocco sits with his little sister, Carmela, eighty-one, and with his brother-in-law, Lenny DiMassi, eighty-seven. With the exception of Donato Altieri, Tessa's brother, who has not come because of a flare-up of the gout, they are the last of their generation. With them are Father Bennedetto from the old parish; Dana, Nick's wife; cousin Tony, Sal's son; Tony's wife, Rosie; and cousin Henry, Carmela's son in from Phoenix.

"She played in the orchestra," Rocco says. He is smiling broadly.

"I didn't know what I was playing," Carmela laughs.

"I remember Papa used to make you play." Rocco dips a peach slice into his wine, eats half. He is in a wonderful mood. "When we would have company—" Rocco cannot help but laugh "—Papa used to call and you'd come out with your violin. Tina, bless her, she used to run away."

Lenny too is dipping fruit in his wine. The brightness of the peach is accentuated by the near red-black of the liquid. "Sure," he says. "When I was first going with your sister, your father made you play. I remember that."

"I don't remember," Carmela says.

Rocco laughs. He turns to the priest. "I'm surprised she didn't run away from home. Every time we had company, Papa'd make her play. And John. Remember how John used to play the piano? Remember that?"

"Uncle John?" Tony asks.

"Oh, yeah," Rocco says. "We were the only ones in the neighborhood with a piano."

"And," Carmela adds, "at that time we were the poorest."

"We were never poor," Rocco says.

"During the depression we—"

"Á." Rocco waves his hand. "I don't remember."

"I remember," Tony says. "I mean, I remember cousin Richard . . . He used to play." To his wife he explains, "Ricky was the oldest of the cousins. Uncle John's oldest. We all looked up to him. He used to play up a storm."

"I never met him," Rosie intones, "did I?"

"Oh, he was killed . . . Geez, that's . . ."

Henry finishes for Tony. "Thirty, thirty-two years ago."

Rocco indicates Carmela. "I used to love it. I used to love it when Papa had you play." Rocco laughs again. "I didn't have to do nothin."

I approach the table, carrying a platter. The talk of Ricky has made me uncomfortable. I don't know why. "More sausages? Hamburgers? There's lots more. Padre, mangia! Let's eat it up."

Tony reaches for another hamburger. "You remember when Ricky used to play the piano?" he asks me.

"On holidays," I say. "He used to sing, too. We'd all sing."

"Those were the days," Tony says to his wife. "At Il Padrone's."

"Ha," I laugh, stop. Jenny, Nicco and Jessie Minton, Angie and Tom's daughter, are in the middle of the yard trying to keep a soccer ball away from Dog Corleone. I eye them, think if they miskick the ball they might hurt one of the old folk. "Farther away," I yell at Jenny. She gives me her disgruntled look, her "don't rain on me" look. The octogenarians are indifferent.

"They don't go to church," Rocco whispers. Lenny cups a hand behind his ear, shakes his head, puts his finger to the adjusting knob on his hearing aid, turns it up. "They don't go to church," Rocco says louder. He nods to the priest, then points to Dana, then Tony. "You go, don't you?"

"Usually," Dana says. She begins to stack the dirty plates. Tony doesn't answer.

"We had that little church," Rocco says. "Remember our little church? Everybody went. I don't know what's the matter with them. They got this big church. Beautiful. They're making it even bigger. We had a little church. Everybody went. Their church, nobody goes."

At the center of the yard, I try to interest the kids in more food but only Dog Corleone wants to eat. I toss him a piece of sausage. He catches it and makes it vanish. I yell at him. Scold him. I'm not angry at him. Why am I pushing him away? "That's all!" I . . . Johnny pushes him again. The dog pushes Johnny back, with his nose. "That's . . . All!" Johnny says emphatically. "Capisce?"

Jason and Nick are playing bocci, tossing the target ball, attempting to just kiss it with the bowlers. I approach with the platter, overhear them.

"I think he's slime," Nick says.

"Because of his foreign policy?" Jason asks.

"No. Because he's slime," Nick says. "Someday—"

"One of the teachers at school, I think, dislikes him, too. He's—"

"What's he teach?"

"History. Contemporary Issues."

"Sounds like a liberal . . . a finòcchio *. . ."*

"He's our soccer coach. He's a vet. I'm pretty sure he's a vet, too."

"Ah, well . . ." They retrieved the balls, retossed the target ball. "Well . . ." Nick spots me. He raises his voice. "You know what the Godfather says?"

"What?" Johnny and Jason say simultaneously.

"He says, 'There comes a time,' something like this, 'There comes a time when the lowest man on the totem pole, if he keeps his eyes and ears open, can take his revenge on the man on top.' "

I've no idea what they're talking about. "How bout a hot dog?"

Nick laughs. "Do you have any idea what goes into those things?"

"You brought em," Johnny says.

"That doesn't mean I'd eat one," Nick says. "Hey, Pop looks good."

"Yeah," I say. "There's a hundred things wrong with im, but he's coping. Kinda grouchy. Katzenbaum's got him on a new diuretic and he's constipated."

"Is he using his Metamucil?"

I shrug.

"Julia's not back?" Nick asks.

"Guess not," I say. I pass it off. But . . .

Dana has gathered the young children and bribed them to stand near the old folks' table by telling them she'll bring out the cake when they're all around. The older children, Todd, John and Sara Minton, Peter Nittolo and his wife, Cailyn, with their nineteen-month-old, Francis, form up in a circle of chairs. Rocco's eyes are bright, his face is beaming. ". . . all twenty-three of the children in your father's generation," he is telling Jenny, Nicco and Jessica, "successful. Two doctors, four teachers, a college professor, a nurse, big bosses in business . . ."

"Even a lawyer," Carmela says.

"Dio benedica." *Father Bennedetto taps his chest, laughs.*

"And an army captain," Tony chimes in.

"God bless his soul and his brothers," the priest says sadly, makes the sign of the cross.

Carmela immediately changes the tone. "And no divorces," she says. "Who could ever divorce a Panuzio? Who could ever make a better husband or wife?"

"That's because of respect," Rocco says. "The man respects the woman. The woman respects the man. Each takes care of each. My mother and father started a dynasty—"

"Grandpa," Jenny says, "you've told us this."

"Did I tell you they started with nothing? They didn't have a pot—"

"I know," Jenny says. "To pee in." Everybody laughs.

"And my brother John went to college. Santina went to normal school to be a teacher but she got sick and didn't finish. All my brothers and sisters finished high school. Today you'd say, È fissaria. *'No big thing.' Ah, but when I was in high school . . . And then one year college."*

Angie Minton interrupts her father. "I didn't know that, Pop."

"Sure. To CCNY. City College of New York. But those were depression years and Carlo was in his third year and only had one year to go. Il Padrone *said to me, 'Rocco, you can't finish for three years. Carlo can finish in eight months. When he finishes, we can send you back.' But I went to work. Everybody tried to work but I had a job with Mr. Fusci." Rocco turns to Rosie. "Your grandfather," he says. Then he pauses, looks at Carmela. "Carlo graduated?"*

"Sure, don't you remember?"

"John graduated. No Italians went to college. Sal graduated. I don't remember . . ."

"Well, Grandpa," Jenny speaks up, "I'm going to graduate from college."

Rocco nods. "You'll be even better. You'll be a doctor. Like Nicky. He served . . . he went to school and medical school. How proud your grandmother was."

"What about my Popsters?" Jenny asks.

"Á. Johnny . . . He did okay. He finally did okay."

*"*Èh, *Pop." I force a chuckle. "What are you tellin her?" Then to Jenny, "Whatever he says, Sunshine, you take it with a grain of salt."*

"Ooo!" Nick calls from near the grill. He is tipsy. "Here comes that good-lookin honey."

Julia is breathless, flushed. "Oh, I'm sorry I'm so late," she calls out to everyone. "I didn't think it would take so long."

"Com'ere, gorgeous." Nick grasps Julia about the waist, hugs her. "God," he says loud enough for me to hear, "I don't know what the hell you're doing with my brother." More quietly, a stage whisper, he says, "If it was you and me, I'd keep you chained to my bed—"

"Nicky!" Julia pushes him away, laughs. She does not take it as an advance but as her brother-in-law complimenting his brother on his wife. I understand this, would have liked to respond similarly when Dana arrived but felt that Julia would not understand. "We waited and waited," Julia says, "for this call from L.A. From a really major producer—"

Nick cuts in. "When I grow up," he says, "I hope I can go to work dressed like that."

Again Julia laughs. She has made it to the table where she is kissing the old folk, shakes hands with the priest, hugs Dana, Sylvia and Angie. "Has everybody eaten?"

"We saved you a plate," Angie says. "In the oven."

Rocco is now holding Robbie on his lap. At eight, Robbie is too heavy for his grandfather but he is the youngest and Rocco knows he's not going to get lighter. "That's who we are," Rocco is saying to the children. "That's what's behind every Panuzio. My father risked everything. He used to say, there is nothing we can't achieve if we have the courage to try, the commitment to preserve and the faith to believe."

"Hey." A new voice comes from the driveway. It is deep, loud. "Padrone. Happy, happy birthday." Mitch Williams comes into the backyard.

Angie comes over, kisses him. "My hero," she says. To her husband she says, "When we were kids, I always had a secret crush on him."

Tom laughs. He does not know Mitch but has heard of his exploits when he was a high school football player. They shake hands as Nick blurts, "Holy cow! It's Mitch and Joe and Phil Rizzuto! Just in time for cake. How's that good-lookin boy from southern Italy doin?"

"Great." Mitch laughs. "Couldn't be better. How's my doctor from northern Africa?"

"Join me in a toot." Nick laughs.

"In a minute. Padrone, here," Mitch says. He holds out a present.

"Wha-at?" Rocco says.

"It's nothin, Mr. Panuzio. Just a little happy birthday and thank you. Actually, it's all the silverware I stole from your house when I was a boy."

Those nearby chuckle. Rocco unwraps the box, pulls out a sweatshirt with an Elk's head on the front. On the back is the slogan LIFE IS A CONTACT SPORT: LIVE WITH INTENSITY. "Welcome to the country," Mitch says. "Welcome to East Lake."

After the song is sung, the cake eaten and the children dispersed, the older cousins gather about the table with the elders. "Hey, next year, huh?" Tony cups a hand over Nick's shoulder. "Next year we'll have an even bigger party."

"Yeah," Johnny says from behind them, "why not, huh?"

Tony turns. "No, Johnny, don't you get it."

"Get what?" Henry asks. "It'll be Uncle Rocky's eighty-sixth."

"One hundred years," Tony says.

"What's one hundred years?" Brian DiMassi and his sister Lena DiMassi-Taylor join them.

"One hundred years of Panuzios in America," Tony says. "We gotta have a really big celebration." He opens his hands before his face as if he's spreading out a panorama. "One Hundred Years in America—A Panuzio Family Odyss—"

"That's a great idea," Henry interrupts. "I never thought of that. We oughta do a giant family tree. Johnny, you goina have it here?"

"I . . ." I'm baffled. I . . . baffl . . . No. He is pissed at Julia. Baffled at Henry's question. He shrugs. "I gotta check with Julia first." He doesn't know why he said that. He can make the decision. "Make sure she doesn't have something planned."

"A year from now?!" Henry says.

"Yeah," Johnny answers. "She does that. Trips, vacations. Like that."

"We'll get all the cousins . . ." Tony glances up at the sky. "How many would we be if it were just the cousins and their spouses?"

At that Aaron Williams walks into the backyard. He flicks his dreadlocks, smiles. "Hi, Mr. Panuzio." Four heads turn. "Ah . . ." Aaron smiles shyly. "I mean . . ." He waves to Jason. "Captain's practice," he calls. "You comin? Pickup scrimmage against Lakeport."

"Yeah. Give me a minute to get my cleats." Jason trots to the back door. His cousin Sara, sixteen, Angie and Tom's daughter, involuntarily stares at Aaron. He is the most handsome boy she has ever seen.

As Jason goes in, Julia comes out. Johnny notices, for a split second . . . Sure he sees it. Sure it is there . . . Julia and Aaron locking eyes. Then Aaron looking down, Julia turning to the table. "Coffee's ready," she says. Johnny grits his teeth.

The boys leave for practice. Mitch leaves for home. Peter and his wife depart with little Francis, who is now fussy, crying. Father Bennedetto blesses Rocco, the other old folk. He, too, leaves. Tony reopens the conversation. "Uncle Rocky, whatever happened to Uncle John, anyway? He moved to Chicago, didn't he?"

Carmela is terse. "So be it," she answers.

"Huh?" Tony utters.

"I gotta pee." Rocco rises. "Ow! Fa Napoli!*"*

"You okay?" Carmela asks.

"Oooh. I just banged my leg on this damn table. Che pouzze *. . ."*

Beside Tony, Henry says in an undertone, "You don't know?"

"No," Tony says. "My father never talked about—"

"After Aunt Fran killed herself?" Henry says.

"Did she?" Tony asks. "See, that's what I never really knew."

"She slit her wrists in the bathtub," Henry says.

"Aah," Tony moans. "My mother and father would never tell us. I remember the funerals. Not hers. I think I was in Florida when Aunt Fran died. But I remember Ricky's and Louis'. And Il Padrone*'s. God, do I remember those. But Fran's . . ."*

Jenny comes to the table and the conversation ceases. "Is the cake all gone?" she asks.

Zi Carmela pulls her close. Jenny partially resists, then surrenders. Carmela smooths her grandniece's hair, makes a sign of the cross on her forehead. "How old are you?"

"Twelve," Jenny says.

"Um-hmm." Carmela nods. "This Christmas," Carmela whispers, "this Christmas I teach you to make mal occhio*."*

Jenny scrunches up her nose. "I don't like to cook," she says.

Carmela laughs. "The cake and cookies are inside," she says. She lets Jenny go.

"Yeah," Henry continues. "They say she got into the tub. Fully dressed. She'd completely cleaned the house. By then Uncle John was an alcoholic and I guess it was pretty messy. She cleaned everything, climbed into the tub with a bunch of towels. She wrapped the towels around her arms so she wouldn't make a mess. Then she pulled a razor blade up her wrists to her elbows. Or . . . just one, I guess. You probably couldn't do—"

"Oh, God!" Tony squirms as if he feels his own flesh being cut. "Because . . ."

"Because she was pretty unbalanced," Johnny says. He sits across from Zi Carmela, beside Tony. He, too, now is tipsy, but it is not a nice tipsy like Nick's but an angry tipsy, a . . .

"Fran had those great sadnesses," Zi Carmela says.

"I guess," Johnny says.

Tony hums for a moment, nods. "I don't know why my mom and dad didn't tell us. I don't think any of us knew. Maybe Cecilia, but she never said . . ."

"A mother tries to protect her children," Zi Carmela says. She looks directly at Johnny. "And a father. You don't know how he tries to protect you. How he always protected you."

"Pop?!" Johnny says. He doesn't know what she is talking about. The foundation! The what?

"Why Fran was so angry to kill herself . . ." Zi Carmela shakes her head, is talking as much to herself as to her son and nephews. "Because John didn't protect Richard and Louis the way Rocco protected his own."

"What do you mean?" Johnny asks.

"Á." Zi Carmela turns away.

"I DON'T KNOW how we're going to do this," Johnny said to Julia when Julia finally returned home. Jason had gone immediately to his room. Rocco was already asleep. Johnny pondered telling her about Hilman's visit, asking her his questions, but he held off.

"Are you going to have to bathe him?" Julia asked.

"I don't think so," Johnny said. As he eyed his wife he realized he had not thought through that situation.

"Well, I'm not," Julia said. "I'm not a nurse. Maybe we can have the Visiting Nurses come in."

"Yeah. Maybe. Ah, do they . . . Is that covered under insurance?"

"You'd better find out."

"Yeah," Johnny said quietly. "Yeah. Our outgo's so much higher, right now, than our income . . ." He paused.

"He could live with your sister," Julia said. "Or Nick could help out more. I don't know how you got us into—"

"I don't know . . . either." Johnny's voice tapered. He could not get it out of his head that she had spent that day, that exact day, with Rod Nightingale. "You goina tell me about the meeting?" he asked.

"If it had been a business," Julia scoffed, "it would have taken twenty minutes. We were there for three and a half . . ." She stopped, turned to him. "Did you know the Fitzpatricks are suing the Willises and the town for two-point-six million?"

"Two-point . . . For what?"

"Angelo Compari told me . . . I think he called it a wrongful death suit."

"Yeah? How's the town liable?"

"They let her miss her game. I think that's the claim."

"Umm? Well . . . I . . . *Á!* Are they going to play tomorrow? That's the—"

"They still haven't made a decision." Julia snickered. "They said they'd take it all under consideration and make an announcement in the morning. You know the counselor, DeLauro? Ciara De—"

"Yeah." Johnny kept his eyes on her face, his eyes on her eyes.

"I think . . ." Julia did not look at Johnny. His staring made her uncomfortable, made her think of things she had not told him: the revelation that Jason had brought a bayonet to school; the job offer from a publishing house in Washington, D.C. Had he taken a call while she was out? "Ciara made enough points to force them . . ." Julia continued, stumbled, recovered. "She said . . . like six polarizations. She's really a brilliant woman. I'm sure there'll be a copy of her remarks in tomorrow's paper."

Johnny just stared.

WHERE CHARLENE ROSENWALD failed, the autumn's near-continuous inclement weather succeeded. The East Lake–Avon game, along with all first-round games in the thirty-two-team state tournament, was postponed from Friday the eighteenth to Monday the twenty-first. Monday afternoon, all four Lake Region teams that had been selected, Roosevelt, Wilson, Lakeport and East Lake, advanced. In the Northwest quadrant, the seventh-seeded Elks scored on a first-minute penalty kick, then held on to defeat second-seeded Avon 1–0.

The second round was played the following day. Under an unseasonably warm drizzle, tired players, with less than twenty-four hours rest, played sloppily on wet, muddy fields. Lakeport defeated New Albany 5–3 in the Southeast; Wilson topped Brunswick 5–2 in the Northeast; and in the Northwest, East Lake beat league rival Roosevelt, after two ten-minute overtime periods with the score deadlocked 1–1, in the ensuing shootout, 5–4. Partly due to fatigue, partly due to field conditions and partly due to the intensity of the play, sloppy as it might have been, not a single team escaped without at least one serious injury. Round three, the quarter finals, was now scheduled for Saturday the twenty-sixth. Johnny Panuzio had not witnessed either East Lake victory. However, in the stands for the Roosevelt game was Mitch Williams. His heart was breaking.

The Panuzio Home, East Lake, Wednesday, 23 November, 6:11 A.M.

NO MILK, HE thought. Unbelievable. The day before Thanksgiving and there's no milk in the house. Johnny was up early, in the kitchen early, making coffee, searching the refrigerator for breakfast makings, banging around as if he were some sort of self-appointed alarm clock for the entire house. "No goddamn milk," he cussed. For a moment he glared at the dog. Dog Corleone laid his chin on the floor, looked up guiltily. Johnny snickered, pointed at the dog. "You drank it, didn't you?" The dog remained impassive, head down. "Com'ere," Johnny said. The dog did not move. Johnny went to him, knelt, scratched Dog Corleone behind the ears, then brought his coffee to the table, sat, stared mindlessly into the wet blackness. He thought to rise, to carry his cup to the front of the house, to go out to The Point, watch the lake, but he had no gumption.

At six-thirty Jason limped in. He was dressed in baggy jeans, a sweatshirt, one shoe on.

"Mornin," Johnny said. "How's the ankle?"

"Hurts."

"Maybe you should stay home."

"Naw." Jason did not want to talk to his father, but this was more like business, the business of the house. "If you do that, they won't let you play. Like on a Friday with a Saturday game. Besides, it's only a half day."

"Should you tape it? Or wrap it with an Ace?"

"I'm goina ice it till the bus comes." He opened the freezer, removed a tray, knocked the cubes into a plastic bag. He hobbled to the table, sat, put his swollen ankle on a second chair, covered it with the bag. "Aa-aah. Ooo!"

"Sore?"

"Cold."

"Umm."

"Pop?" There was something.

"Yeah."

"I was startin to tell Mom some stuff last night. After we dropped Kim off. Kim made me promise to tell."

"Tell what?!" There was instant anger in Johnny's eyes.

"It's . . . Oh, no!" Jason clammed up, shook his head in disbelief. Under his breath he snarled out, "Mr. Equality . . ." then louder, "It's nothin about me. Me an Kim. It's about Aaron."

"About that panel you're trying to—"

"No. We're going to do that. No matter what Rosenwald says. Coach has got a strategy. He's goina take our plan to an interdistrict meeting. He knows that if they like it . . . he's sure they'll jump at the idea . . . Rosenwald would look like a *bigot*—" Jason placed extra stress on the word "—if she tries to block it. If she does support it, then he says we should let it look like it was her idea."

"Hummph! Then what . . . ?"

"I want you to tell Mr. and Mrs. Williams . . . ah . . . something . . . from us."

"About the panel?"

"Ah . . . God! There's my bus!" Jason jumped up. "Ow!" he yelped. Quickly he hopped toward the door, grabbed his sneaker, sock, book bag.

"I can drive you," Johnny called after him.

Jason snickered. "Not in that old Chevy Bel Air thing."

"What about . . . ?"

"Mom'll tell ya." Jason let the door slam.

"Am I the only person to ever have slept with a student?" Marcia Radkowski was standing behind her desk. Third period, shortened because of the half-day schedule, was almost over. She had chosen to give a preprinted pop quiz so she would not have to interact with the class. "Am I the only one?" she said again. She enunciated very clearly yet spoke very quietly. None of her students heard her. She wanted to practice the words, let them form in her mouth so that her mouth would form them perfectly when she did speak them. "Am I the first? Am I the only teacher to ever have fallen in love with a student? Certainly not. You may think horrible things about me, but I am not a horrible person."

Marcia stood a little taller. She raised her chin. "Dr. Schoemer," she said. "I . . . uh . . . no . . . He was eighteen and I was . . ." Marcia's carriage sagged, her shoulders drooped. I can't tell them, she thought. I can't . . . I . . . Why are they doing this to Ciara? Why did I tell her? Rosenwald's going to put her on the rack. It's my fault. It's all been my fault. Everything that's happened . . . But . . . they can't make us stay today. Today's a holiday. I'm not going to. "I'm not!"

"Huh?" Jeff Kurjiaka asked.

Marcia looked at him. "Excuse me?"

"Did you just say somethin?" Jeff asked.

Marcia cocked her head, gave him a questioning glance. "No," she said. "I didn't say anything. Are you all done?"

Perhaps half the students in the class were now looking up. "Yeah," Jeff said. "This is kinda easy stuff. Didn't we have this quiz when we were freshmen?"

Marcia leaned far forward, smiled an odd smile. "Why, Jeff," she said, "when you were a freshman, I was still in school. How would I know?"

ROCCO SAT IN a rocking chair on the far corner of the front porch, looking every bit of his eight-and-a-half decades. He had on a coat, a hat, gloves, a small blanket tucked in about his legs. He sat alone, his eyes barely open. It was now midafternoon. The rain had ceased, the clouds had partially broken. In the sky sunbeams split the roiling black canyons, burst out, warmed the old man's legs, vanished.

Behind him, through the lace curtains of her Victorian sitting room window, Julia watched, pondered. She was hesitant to speak loudly for fear he might overhear her conversation even though she was pretty sure he couldn't hear her at all, and even if he could, she knew he couldn't tell anyone what she'd said.

"I don't know anything about those figures," Julia said into the cordless phone. "I wanted a first printing of one hundred thousand."

"Do you know Andy at the printing company?" Justin Robustelli asked.

"No."

"He was in charge of the press runs. They only printed eight thousand."

"Eight . . . ?!"

"Yeah. And they only shipped fifty-seven hundred."

"I had preliminary orders for sixty . . . sixty-seven thousand, if I remember correctly."

"That's what I thought. I had six stores order me copies. Every one of em came back and said the publisher was out. That's how they blocked it, by blocking the distribution. I had friends all over the country order it. Not available. That's how they forced it to fail."

"God," Julia apologized. "I'm sorry. I really am sorry. That was all done just to make me look bad."

"I know. I talked to one of Zerrelli's assistants, too. That fuck Meloblatt killed the deal."

"Marvin?!"

"You didn't know?"

"I thought, maybe, but not really. Not . . . I mean, Gallina still needs to make money."

"It was Marvin who called and told Zerrelli that the book was tainted," Justin said. "That I'd plagiarized the material. Supposedly Zerrelli said, 'You gotta be kiddin. Marvin, babe, I'm not about to put twenty million into this property if you can't guarantee the rights.' That's what this guy heard him say. He said Zerrelli said, 'Babe, some two-bit judge someplace can hold up the release. We can have it in the can, copied, ready for distribution, and some pip-squeak-yer-fucken-honor can't hold it up.' He, the assistant, called Nightingale for confirmation."

"Rod Nightin—"

"Yeah."

"Are you sure?"

"I've got a cousin who works at Disney who knows this guy pretty well. More than pretty well. Julia, I spent six years writing—"

"I know. It shows. It's a masterpiece—"

"I tried to get the rights back but that Melo-fuck refused. They even found a loophole in the contract so I don't get the rest of the advance."

"Shit," Julia said. She glanced back through the curtains to make sure her voice hadn't carried outside.

"You told me—" Justin Robustelli said; Julia's attention was distracted by seeing Jenny sitting, legs dangling off the porch, at her grandfather's feet "—so you have grounds, too. He killed my agreement to get to you, but that damaged me . . ." Julia could not understand what Jenny was saying but could hear her din and see her face working a mile a minute. ". . . sexual harassment. Both civil and criminal recourse . . ."

"Justin," Julia said. "The main problem is, I didn't let them make me resign. I wasn't fired. I flew off the handle and quit. Maybe I've been around you Italians too long. I exploded and quit. My attorney said, if I'd been fired, I'd have better grounds. But I got impulsive. That's what they've got to fall back on."

"So! Yer goina let that bastard get away with it, aren't you?"

"I . . . I don't know."

"You are."

"I guess . . . I guess I am."

"When it comes down, answer my subpoena."

The next day, Thanksgiving Day, Johnny said to Jason, "Seems like everybody in town's excited about you guys reaching the quarter finals." It was late afternoon. They had had no company; Todd had not come home, but had flown to St. Louis, then gone up to Eileen's for the holiday. They'd eaten but not feasted, had carved the small turkey, but had barely spoken. Even Jenny had been subdued. Finally Johnny, Jason and Rocco had moved to the living room, had sat before the TV. "Can you play on that ankle?"

"Yeah," Jason said. He felt uncomfortable. His father was edgy, his grandfather sullen. He wanted to be with Kim.

"Your mother never told me . . . You wanted me to tell Mr. Williams something?"

Jason slid down into the couch. "Yeah," he said. He did not look at his father but stared at the game on the set before them. "Ah . . . I think . . . Are they selling their house?"

"No." Johnny turned to Jason. "Least not that I've heard. Why?"

"There's a rumor in school that they're moving to Atlanta. That Mr. Williams is being transferred."

"I think he'd tell me . . ."

"They're . . ." Jason hesitated. "I don't know if I'm supposed to say it or not. They're—" quickly he spewed it out "—going to be grandparents."

"Who?"

"Mr. and Mrs. Williams."

"One of the twins?! I can't . . ."

Jason shook his head. He couldn't believe how stupid his father was. "No." The word steamed out of him. "Do you remember Martina? Aaron's girlfriend."

"Martina? Marti . . . Oh, ah . . . yeah."

"Martina Watts. She's pregnant."

"Aaron's old girlfriend?"

"Yes, Pop! Aaron's old girlfriend. She's like four and a half months. With Aaron's—"

"Aaa-ah!" Johnny slapped his forehead. "Does Mitch know?"

"That's what I've been tryin to say. I wanted Mom—I started to tell her—to tell you. To tell him."

"Oh! Oh, oh, oh. Good God! Are you sure? How long . . . ?"

"More than four months."

"No! I mean, how long have you know? How come you didn't tell me before? This is something—"

"I've been trying to tell you. I haven't known that long. Martina told Kim, but Kim thought Martina was going to have an abortion, so she didn't say anything, but then Martina decided to keep it. That's why I think . . . I mean . . . it'll be their grandchild. They might want to do something. I don't know."

"Pa . . ." Rocco blurted. Johnny and Jason both looked over. The interruption gave them a chance to break from the discomfort of talking to each other. "Pa . . . unh." The old man's face was expressionless; his eyes looked straight forward.

Again Johnny hit his forehead, this time lightly with the heal of his palm. "Payment?!" he said in exasperation. To Jason he said, "He's so goddamn worried about paying the cable bill. Or the electric." Loudly to Rocco, Johnny, his hands flaring, said, "They're paid, Pop!!"

"Finish," Rocco said. It was only one word but it was perfectly clear. He remained expressionless.

"Finish?" Johnny asked. Now he was intent on that one word; on Rocco's one perfect word. He stared at the old man. "Finish what, Pop?"

"Maybe he means the basement," Jason said.

"God!" The amazement at Rocco's word dissipated. Johnny gritted his teeth. Under his breath he growled, "Don't you ever give up, Pop?"

"Pa . . . unh. Pa . . . unh," Rocco said. "Bi . . . be." Very slightly his head shook back and forth.

"Come on, Pop." Johnny stood. "Why don't you go to bed? Let me have the nightmares about the bills."

"I'll help him," Jason said. He also stood. "Can you talk to Mr. Williams?"

"Ah . . . I . . . tomorrow. I can't call him tonight. I'll see him tomorrow. This is kinda somethin you don't tell people over the phone."

"Maybe . . ." Jason paused, sneered, said quietly, "You can see Mr. Sanchez, too!"

"About what?!"

"Like you don't know!" His voice rose. "Like maybe about an apology!"

"I didn't—"

"Yeah! Mr. Equality. Mr. Fairness. Mr. Bring Us All Together! You're a . . . You hate me and Kim together because you're bigoted."

"Is that what you think?! Is that why you've been so . . . pissy? Why you've been—"

"Why shouldn't I be?!" Now their volume was loud.

"I . . . I didn't plan that. It has nothin ta do with her . . ."

"Bein a spic?!"

"I didn't say . . ." Johnny clenched both fists, snapped them down. "I . . . It was a mistake. I thought there was a drug deal . . . You don't know what happened."

"That was her cousin! He's the store's buyer. Yer a jerk! You think yer such a good guy. You pat yerself on yer back cause you see yerself like some super dad cause you come to my games. Yer nothin but a hypocrite . . . a fucken racist jerk! That's why! Adults are jerks. That's why I didn't tell you! Who the hell can talk to you?"

HALF AN HOUR later Jenny came in to say good night. Johnny was still seething. "Good night, Sweet-ums." His words were curt.

Jenny ignored his tone. "Hey, Popsters, what's Grandpa writing?"

"He's writing?!"

"He's writing on the kitchen pad. In his room."

"I . . ." Johnny was shocked. He'd assumed, with Rocco's inability to speak, that he'd also been robbed of his ability to write.

"He wouldn't show it to me," Jenny said. "I think he's embarrassed because his handwriting is like really terrible to the extreme."

"Let's go see, Sunshine." Johnny rose. "Uh," he groaned. He straightened his back, flexed his left knee. "I hate this couch," he said.

"I heard that," Julia called from the dining room.

Johnny began to clamp his jaw, instead put a hand over his mouth, winked at Jenny, made a silly face, stage-whispered, "Ooops!"

Johnny and Jenny tiptoed back toward Rocco's room, making believe they were sneaking away from Julia's scrutiny. "Very funny," Julia said without humor.

Rocco's door was closed. Johnny tapped, opened it a crack. The lights were out. The faint sound of rales let the conspirators know their prey was already asleep.

"I TALKED TO Justin Robustelli yesterday," Julia said.

"Umm," Johnny uttered. They were in their bed, sitting up, reading lamps on, not reading. "Umm," Johnny hummed again. He knew she'd overheard his argument with Jason. He wanted her to bring it up so he could defend himself, so he could tell her about Martina. And maybe about Hilman.

"It reminded me . . . When we were waiting for his contract. For confirmation from Zerrelli in L.A. I remember I was down at Rod's cottage in South Lake Village. Out on his deck."

"Yeah. On Pop's birthday. When you got tied up," Johnny said.

"Um-hmm. I remember we were waiting for the call. We were overlooking the beach and the water. It's a beautiful spot. Rod was trying to come on to me."

"Um."

Julia turned, scrutinized Johnny's face. "You don't seem surprised," she said. He didn't respond. She shrugged, continued. "We'd had some wine. He tried to put his arms around me."

"I'd try that, too."

"What does that mean?!"

"I still think you're the most beautiful woman who's ever walked the face of the earth. I'd try to come on to you too."

Julia made a "tsk" sound, smiled, said, "You're blind."

Johnny moved close, ogled the little bit of exposed skin of his wife's shoulders and neck. She did not push him away. He slid his arm behind her back; she rested against him.

"It's good to talk like this," Julia said quietly. "I feel like we've grown so far apart."

"It's all that's happened," Johnny said. For a minute he just held her, felt her. He'd almost forgotten how good she felt, how good it felt to touch her, to squeeze her. He did not want to know about Rod. Not yet. He was sure he'd done more than put an arm around her. Maybe he'd literally tied her up. The thought was both titillating and repulsive. Her words, certainly, confirmed to him what he now thought of as Hilman's suspicions.

"That's when I saw Aaron down there with a woman," Julia said.

"Oh. His girlfriend. Jason told me . . . asked me to . . ."

Julia looked up askance, let her head come down slowly. "No," she said. "No, it wasn't his girlfriend. Tom Hilman called. He asked me about it. I don't know how he knew. I think I'd forgotten all about . . . It was a white woman. A tall white woman. Very pretty. I didn't know her . . . She kind of looked familiar but I don't think I knew her. I remember her skirt. It was a very colorful sarong-tie skirt that matched her bathing suit. When she got up she was tying it back on."

Johnny reared back, wiggled his eyebrows. "She didn't have it on!"

Julia pulled away. "She had a bathing suit on. You put those on over the suit. Men!" Julia moved farther away. "You don't know anything."

"Yeah," Johnny said. All thoughts of titillation vanished. "We're all just pieces of shit." He slid down, lay back, punched up his pillow.

"That's not what I said," Julia said.

"Um." Johnny turned on his side, his back to his wife. He wanted to ask her what she knew about Martina and the pregnancy, wanted to know more about this white woman, wanted to know if she knew that Hilman had come, had talked to him, too. But he was miffed at Julia's "Men!" tone.

"You know," Julia said to his back, "you're not the only one around here who's going through a crisis. Every place I turn, every time I think I've got something going, some offer coming, it falls through."

"Um." Johnny hummed. He was too angry, too hurt to answer.

"I hate living like this," Julia said. "I hate it."

The Panuzio Home, East Lake, Friday, 25 November, 7:19 A.M.

JOHNNY'S JAW WAS clamped. His teeth, molars ground. The muscles of his face were in such spasm his ears hurt. He rolled to the edge of the bed, squinted at the clock. He had not set the alarm, did not need to be up, felt more exhausted than he had when he'd gone to sleep. All night he'd dreamed—about Julia and Rod; about Rocco falling down the basement stairs; about LeRoy siccing goons on him; about Jason leading goons and internal reviewers against him; about Mitch leaving, moving to Atlanta, taking Jenny to protect her from LeRoy; about Todd coming home with his girlfriend only to find the girl was a guy and, as is only possible in a dream, he was pregnant; again about Jenny.

Most vividly Johnny remembered Jenny, his last dream of Jenny; of Jenny being killed in an automobile accident, of his sadness until later when a black-robed gentleman approached him, gave him a check for two-point-six-million dollars. He'd smiled shyly. He'd glanced to the check, to the figure: $2,600,000. His smile had broadened. He had wanted to feel guilty but had felt elated.

Johnny shifted, rolled back, took a deep breath. The room was just becoming light; the windows were gray, dotted and streaked with rain. He listened for the lake but there was no sound; listened for the drone of cars on Route 86 but, on this day after Thanksgiving, traffic had not yet picked up. He heard the attic stairs creak, heard Jason open, shut, latch the door, descend to the kitchen.

Again Johnny rolled. Beside him Julia moaned. He twisted, looked at her. She was stunning. In sleep she was an angel, the most beautiful woman he'd ever seen. Really, he thought, she is a wonderful woman, a wonderful mother, a wonderful person. If she weren't, he thought, if she had not been, it all might be so much easier, be so much . . .

He lay back, stared at the ceiling. He felt a terrible sadness, felt as if the muscles of his face were being pushed back, down, beaten from all directions. Punches coming from all directions, he thought. Punches he could no longer parry, deflect. For months he'd felt as if he were being pummeled but at least he'd intercepted some of the blows. Now the shots were landing full force. He felt sick, disgusted, horrified with himself for his dreams, for his dream of Jenny; terrified of rising, of facing Jason, Julia . . . If I hate this, he thought, and if she hates this, how much longer can it last?

There was a light knocking on the bedroom door. "Dad! Dad!" Jason interrupted his thoughts. The knocking became louder, the voice more insistent. "Dad! You should come quick."

Johnny rolled, propped himself up on an elbow. "What?" he whispered. It angered him that Jason would wake Julia.

Jason pushed the door open. "Dad! Grandpa . . . I think . . . He's not breathing."

In death Rocco seemed pained, uncomfortable. His eye sockets were hollow; his temples sunken; his open mouth dry, pasty; his skin tight, yellow, shriveled, splotched with blue-black webs.

Johnny sat on the edge of the bed beside the body, reached out, folded Rocco's hands over his chest. Tears flooded his eyes. Behind him Jason also cried. For a long time neither spoke, neither moved. Dog Corleone slunk into the room, quietly lay down. Julia held Jenny in the kitchen.

"There's a note here," Jason whispered. His voice came hoarse.

Johnny turned, tried to ask, "What?" but nothing came out.

"Is this what he was writing last night?" Jason lifted the kitchen pad. He turned on the small light on the desk beside Rocco's little TV.

Johnny only shrugged.

"Should I read it?" Jason asked.

Johnny nodded.

" 'When there are questions,' " Jason read, " 'help us seek answers.' " Jason moved the page closer to the light. "This isn't so unreadable," he said. " 'When a cloud descends, help us seek light.' It's a poem," Jason said. "Or maybe a prayer." He stared at the last few lines until he could decipher the words. " 'When darkness surrounds our family, help us reach inside, help us build on our solid foundation. Bring us to finish our tasks. Help us do right. You have believed in us, help us believe in each other.' "

Death events, burial events, crashed upon him, cascaded upon them all, fast, furious slow motion, blurring days into a murky, semicoherent collage of past present future sticking to him, to Johnny-panni, to them all . . . *to us like the oil spray, the oil tar they used to keep the dust from flying on dirt roads in the summers when Rocco would drive us out to East Lake and the dust would choke us and they'd come around with the truck . . . The Truck! . . . with the oil and we'd throw rocks to get the driver mad and the spray man mad and they'd stop and spray at us but it would miss but the mist would hang in the air after they left, or we'd get in it, or throw Nick in a puddle, a slick, so he'd get in trouble, and the oil would stick to us and to everything like slow-motion murky semicoherent days surrounding death. Surrounding dust to dust.*

The room was hot, the lights subdued. Like all funeral parlors, he thought, Hot. Stuffy. Johnny wanted to leave, to flee. Like the funeral of Katie Fitzpatrick, he thought. Like the funeral of the others, like Ricky's, like *Il Padrone*'s, like them all. Same faces. All the same faces staring, like staring into a fishbowl. All the same . . . All different yet all . . .

I am outside. Outside the fishbowl looking in and he is inside trying to look out at me except that he does not know that he is in there and only feels my eyes.

Like Aaron's. At Aaron's he . . . *he was* . . .

He was the bowl! The glass! They looked at it through him . . . through me without touching it, without it touching them, hurting them, without them hurting Mitch, and I could support Mitch and I could be the glass without even knowing it because looking through me did not hurt me.

"Oh, Johnny!" An old woman faced him, a face in a sea of faces. "I remember you when you were just this big." Johnny stared blankly. He did not want to kiss her but he kissed her. Her skin was fragile, covered with powder. She hugged him and he smelled the powder but hid his revulsion. "He loved you so much—" Johnny did not want to stand, to greet, to chat "—I always knew everything that happened with each of you." She indicated Sylvia to Johnny's left, Nick and Angie to his right. "From Tess," the old woman said. "Then from Rocky . . ."

"Who was that?" Johnny whispered.

"Mrs. Fusci," Nick said. "Cousin Tony's wife's mother."

"Who's that with Zi Carmela?"

"I don't know. Ask Sylvia. Or Angie."

"Syl. Who's that with Zi Carmela?"

"That's Mama's sister's husband's sister."

"Who?"

"Aunt Cara and Uncle Joe Romano. She's a Romano. I don't know what her . . . The others are our second cousins. Or third. I think Angie knows. I remember the faces but I can never remember the names."

"That," Nick whispered, "is because twenty or thirty years ago when we met them, we didn't care if we knew who they were."

Sylvia put her hands together, bowed to an old gentleman. "Thank you so much for coming."

"You remember me?"

"Of course I remember you. How are you?"

"Old. Old as Rocky." His voice was loud, expressive. "Boy, what a builder! Always building. He could fix anything. And could he shoot the shit. Nobody could outtalk Rocky. This is Johnny, eh?"

Sylvia turned to her brother. "You remember Mr. Romano?"

Gruffly the old man said, "No-ooh! You got me mixed up. I'm Santarelli. Chris' grandfather. From the high school."

Sylvia was baffled, didn't let on, was glad when Johnny greeted the old man.

"You gotta be here," Mr. Santarelli said to Johnny. "I'm only comin to say my good-bye. I remember when me en Rocky used to watch you and that colored play football."

"Oh . . ." Johnny's voice was respectful, subdued. "I don't think Pop came to too many—"

"What'da ya mean?" Mr. Santarelli was offended, very loud. "We always came. Boy, could Rocky shoot the shit. Usually about you. Now I go to my grandson's games. I usually see you there but you never shoot the shit with me. How come? *Á!*"

Johnny began to mumble but Mr. Santarelli surged on. "You gotta be here, but me, I'm goina go watch. When was the last time East Lake made the quarter finals, eh? You're lettin Jason play, eh?"

Johnny nodded. "He'll be at tomorrow's wake and the funeral on Monday. He and Todd are going to be pallbea—"

"Good," Mr. Santarelli interrupted. "Rocky always thought you shoulda played your last game. He always said . . ."

The next night, the second night of the wake, Sylvia's son Peter brought his nearly two-year-old son, Francis, into the parlor over the objection of Cailyn, Peter's wife. "Grandpa, my grandpa—" Peter tapped his chest "—was very ill and he died and is now in heaven with Baby Jesus."

"At Uncle Kevin's with Baby Jesus?" the little boy asked.

"Heaven, not Kevin," Peter said. "Heav-ven."

"Where's heaven?"

"It's all around us," Peter said patiently. "It's the moon and the stars and the night sky."

"I don't see heaven." Francis' voice was loud, happy. "I don't see heaven." Johnny felt embarrassed for Peter and for Cailyn and for Sylvia. The little boy's voice carried throughout the parlor. "Where's heaven?" Francis asked again. The question became a game. "Where's heaven?" again and again.

Good question, kid, Johnny thought. Then he thought . . . *Francis, when your son is two, I will be like Rocco. Will you bring him to my . . .*

"This is Sherwood." Julia presented her beautiful sixteen-year-old niece, whom Johnny had not seen in a decade. Julia was a rock. She pregreeted, postgreeted, handled Johnny's faux pas, foe paws, with grace, with charm, with dignity. She comforted the children, the elderly. She knew exactly what to say. She . . . *Johnny-panni knows nothing. He is slow. He is retarded. He is jealous. He founders . . .*

Flounders. A fish. A fish in the bowl without water stumbling his fish tongue unable to speak with a mouthful of stones, unable to speak in tongues, unable to speak in Italian or English yet she covers for me, him . . . So strong. So capable . . . She can handle anything . . . anybody . . . any body . . .

Johnny held Sherwood's hand. She had grown tall, was strikingly beautiful, looked like a young Julia. "I remember you—" the words splattered from his mouth "—when you were just this big."

"*Padrone,*" Sherwood said. She smiled, her eyes dazzling, her face radiant. "*Padrone,*" she addressed Johnny-panni, "it is an honor to be here, even if it is such a sad occasion."

Johnny was stunned. Who told her . . . he thought. Who told her to say that? Or, he thought, did I hear words that were not spoken? That came from . . . ?

SUNDAY NIGHT THE immediate family—brothers and sisters and Zi Carmela—met at Nick's, ate in the dining room, ate Nick's medallions of beef in cabernet and honey sauce while the spouses and children ate in the kitchen, ate, ate, ate. In the dining room they spoke of the business of death, of estates, of executors. They drank Strega, they shook their heads. "I think Julia would appreciate it if we cleaned out his room before Christmas," Johnny said. "The idea that he died there, in the house, gives her the heebie-jeebies." They all agreed.

"There's not much stuff," he said. He squirmed in the chair. Johnny had to pee. He did not want to get up. *If you pee in my fishbowl, I'll swim in your toilet!* N'gazz! *He cannot even say it to his brother and sisters. He is not retarded; he is a little* n'gazz. "Most of it was split up after Mom died, or when he moved." Again they all agreed.

After dinner they moved to the living room, sat, vegged out, watched TV. Except for Zi Carmela and Jenny.

"Shh." Carmela put a finger to her lips. She beckoned Jenny to follow. Johnny followed too, to pee, but he heard, saw, made believe he was not spying on them.

"What are we going to do?" Jenny whispered. She was bored. She wanted an adventure.

"I want to show you something."

"What?"

"Keep following."

"Into the kitchen?!" Jenny did not hide her disappointment. She had imagined her great-aunt bringing her to some secret passage, some mystical room. Johnny too was disappointed, but a spy cannot show disappointment.

Zi Carmela turns on only the one dim under-the-cabinet light. It is a dream, an image. He cannot tell if it is reality or fantasy. Carmela is the good witch, the witch of the East, not like the wicked Tina, Santina, the female Satan. Carmela pulls a plain wide-rimmed pie plate from one cabinet, a small juice glass from another. She fills the bowl with cold water from the tap, fills the glass one-third up with Uncle Nick's best olive oil. Then she dips her right index finger into the oil, drops three drops into the water, whispers, "In nòme del padre, del figlio, e dello spirito santo." *She pulls Jenny close, grasps her hand, straightens her finger, dips, drops the three drops of oil. "Repeat after me," Zi Carmela says.* "In nòme . . ."

Jenny repeats the words. It is mysterious, even if it is the kitchen.

"Umm!" Zi Carmela shakes her head. She is very serious. "I don't like this."

"What?" Jenny asks.

"The water. We'll try again." Zi Carmela empties, refills the bowl.

"It's city water, isn't it?" Jenny asks rhetorically. "Pop says city water isn't very good because of the plant, but Mr. Williams says the effluent from the plant is cleaner than our tap water, and he should know. He's an engineer."

"The water's fine," Zi Carmela says. The spy wants to scream, "We live in a fishbowl. I've peed in it. I've polluted . . ." "But—" Carmela's old eyes are intent on the bowl and she does not hear the thoughts of the spy, or if she does, she dismisses him as inconsequential "—the water and the oil want to jump apart."

"Of course," Jenny says. "Oil's lighter than water. And its surface tension keeps it in beads." Science, Johnny thinks. She knows everything. Jenny knows . . . Jenny . . .

"Watch more closely." Zi Carmela does not take her eyes from the plate. "Watch very close." With her thumb she makes the sign of the cross on her forehead nine times, repeats nine times, "In nòme del padre . . ." *She leads Jenny through the ritual. Again she drips the oil into the water. Again Carmela shakes her head. "He is unhappy," Carmela whispers.*

"Who?"

"Your grandpa."

"But why? How do you know?"

"I don't know why. You must learn these words. Then we will try again." Carmela takes a deep breath. "Occhi e contro occhi e perticelli agli occhi—Crèpa la invidia e schiattono gli occhi.* *Say it with me."*

Jenny attempts to repeat the words, stutters. Carmela is strict. She corrects, repeatedly points to her eyes, leads Jenny through the words again and again, and Johnny memorizes the words and sees the motions, the movements, the magic incantation over the fishbowl of the spirit.

"What do they mean?" Jenny asks.

"It means," Carmela says, " 'Eyes and contrary eyes and the pupil's opening to the mind's eye—envy splits or dies, and eyes rupture.' "

"Uck!" Jenny shudders. "Why would we say that?"

"It is how we make mal occhio. *How we restore the spirit and make the soul once again whole. When someone curses you, or if they envy you, or if they are fascinated with you, it steals a piece of your soul. When the oil stays together, the soul is whole. When you learn to do it, you can do it for anyone. Living or dead." And Johnny thinks it is not for Rocco that the oil splatters,* shpritzes *on the water, but it is for Jenny because he has dreamed, he has envied . . . has for two-point-six . . .*

Johnny-panni coughed. "What are you guys doin?" he asked. He turned on the main kitchen light. He tried not to let it show but he did not like this . . . this witchcraft. He was determined to break the spell. *He will break this . . . this coven! He will make them* schiatta, *burst. He does not like the word* schiattono. *Does not want to know whose soul . . .*

"Making *mal occhio."* Jenny smiled.

"You're doing what?" He acted surprised, choked on the words.

"You don't need to tell him," Zi Carmela said. "This is only for the women of the family."

Men! Johnny thought.

ON MONDAY MORNING the police escort was followed by the hearse with the casket and the flowers, then by the limousine with the pallbearers—Sylvia's sons, Peter and Kevin, Nick's son, Nicco, Angie's oldest, John, plus Todd and Jason—then by the limos with Zi Carmela and the immediate family, and finally by the cars, a few Cadillacs, mostly small, imported sedans.

"God always said . . ." Father Bennedetto went on and on. Johnny's thoughts wandered. The church was cold, the day miserable. Though it was his father's funeral, though Johnny had been at this funeral, this exact funeral

---

*Di Stasi, Lawrence. *Mal Occhio.* North Point Press. San Francisco, 1981.

a thousand times . . . *the singing . . . the beauty . . . Al-le-lu-ia! Al-le-lu-ia!* . . . instead of it becoming clearer it . . . what? it . . . life? death? souls? God? . . . it became murkier. Dust to dust. Ever living, ever loving . . .

Sylvia delivered the eulogy. "Life wants to keep living." Her voice wavered. "There was something at his core, at Rocco's core, at my father's very heart, which kept him going. Something at the core of his being which was always searching for meaning. He is a life fulfilled—" she paused, sniffed "—in self, in country, in marriage, in family, in friends, in God . . ."

From the funeral parlor they rode to the church, from the church to the cemetery where Rocco was laid to everlasting rest beside Tessa, where everyone cried because Zi Carmela's pain was so raw it ripped to the very core. *And still he, Johnny-panni, thinks, feels, sees the murk of death events colliding . . . Al-le-lu-ia! Al-le-lu-ia! . . . he, detached in the bowl from what is happening there as much as I am detached here from him . . . Al-le-lu-ia! . . . here now watching him, disliking him.*

"Did you invite them back to the house?" Julia asked.

"I think I invited everybody."

"What about Mitch?"

"He's gotta go to work. He said he wants to talk to me about something. Maybe next week."

"Did you tell him . . . ?"

"I didn't think the time was right. I'll . . . I'll talk to him . . . We'll talk later."

"Us, too." Julia looked away.

Everyone left. Johnny collapsed on the couch. He and Julia had had words.

"A bayonet to school! How could you not tell me? A bayonet! I can't believe it. What a jerk! Kids are jerks. What the hell was he thinking? I oughta . . ." Johnny had felt as if he were coming apart. Then Julia dropped her second bomb, told him of her job offer. "It's something I'm really considering," she said. "What about my job?" he countered. "Your job?!" She almost laughed. "You don't really have a job anymore. Don't you realize that?"

Johnny felt numb. He sprawled on the couch, stared blankly at the black screen of the TV. Julia retired to their bedroom, Jenny to hers. Jason drove Todd to the airport.

When Jason returned, he returned to the quietness of a family estranged, a household dissipated. He was disappointed about having missed school; about having missed the morning announcements during which he knew old man Santoro would have said, "Elks two, New Ireland one. Goals by

Crnecki and Panuzio. Semifinals this Wednesday, the thirtieth . . ." Jason did not know who or where they would be playing. He thought to look in the paper, thought to call Kim. Yet he did not. As with the others, an anxious and distracted lethargy seemed to suck him dry. In the kitchen he got a glass of milk, some pastries that remained from earlier. He headed for the hall, the stairs up. He did not want to walk by his father. He hesitated, went into the back hall, again hesitated, went into Rocco's room.

For a long moment Jason just stood in the small room. It had been tidied, the bed had been made, soiled clothing removed, but otherwise it was exactly as it had been four days earlier. Jason sat on the bed, looked at the small desk, the TV where his grandfather watched the morning mass every day. He looked at the ceiling, the walls, out the window into the backyard. It all felt impersonal and the feeling came over Jason that this was just a room, that Rocco's presence had been little more than that of a guest in a hotel, that he needed to grasp something more real. He patted the bed, rested his elbows on his knees, stared at the floor between his feet. He dropped his torso flat to his lap, let his arms dangle, barely took a breath. With his hands on the floor his fingers scratched the carpet, the bed leg, something dry and hollow. Jason tapped his fingers on the surface beneath the bed. "What the hell . . . ?" he thought. He slid from the bed, knelt, looked under. Jason reached under, pulled out a brown corrugated cardboard box perhaps ten inches by twelve inches by eight inches high. The top was not sealed but the flaps were interlocked. "Grandpa's box," he whispered to himself. "Grandpa's box! Under his bed?!" Jason chuckled. He thought to bring it to his father but he did not want to speak to his father. Again he sat on the bed. He placed the box on his knees, read the yellowed mailing label—Mr. John Panuzio, 4346 Zhalineski Street, Chicago, IL.

"What the heck!" Jason whispered. He undid the flaps. On top there was a military garrison cap from World War II; the cap, Jason recognized, that Rocco was wearing in the old picture on the family picture wall. "Ha! How about that," he said quietly. He removed the hat, picked up a manila folder, opened it. Inside there were articles from more than half a century earlier, a citation to Rocco Panuzio, a photo of Tessa Altieri at perhaps twenty-five. Jason thought to read the articles but was intrigued by the box, by the neatly striated, if not chronological layers of family history. He removed a diary, glanced through the first few pages. It made no sense to him, nor did he know who was Francesca DeLuccio. He laid the book on top of the folder, pulled out another military citation. "Award of the Silver Star. Captain Richard Panuzio . . ." Oh, Jason thought. Sure, Dad's cousin who was killed . . . He dug further. "The Purple Heart . . . Louis Panuzio . . ." Then he found the official death notifications for both Richard and Louis Panuzio, found more citations, found ribbons and medals and an old, oddly cut picture of Richard and Louis with Nick when Nick was perhaps fifteen. Someone had been cut out.

Carefully Jason repacked the box. Quietly he stood, turned out the light. He carried the box to his attic hideaway.

By Wednesday, November 30, in the house, at ContGenChem, at East Lake High, the final unraveling of the fabric had begun.

Johnny had not returned to work. He'd spent much of each day alone. Walking. Standing out on The Point. Watching the lake. Terrified of the future. Julia had sequestered herself in bed, said she had a cold or the flu, begged everyone to stay away. Jenny busied herself by playing with water in her room, slopping it all over the upstairs hall floor, not wiping it up. Jason felt the tension, had papers and projects due, had worked particularly hard on a report, a plan for a fusion-powered automobile, had ignored everyone.

"We've got to talk," Kim whispered. They were in third-period English. The bell was about to dismiss them. Marcia Radkowski had not been in since the previous Wednesday. The substitute teacher was clueless as to their topic, their procedures, the state of the school.

"Yeah. I'll walk ya . . ." The bell sounded. Students jumped up, mobbed the door, pushed to get out. "What's up?"

"I know you have the semifinals today, but . . . Jason, there's a rumor going around . . ." Kim looked over her shoulder, pulled Jason's ear closer to her mouth. "Martina told me she heard that Miss Radkowski resigned."

"Why? Why would she? She's probably just got a cold like everybody else."

"Over an affair with a student."

Jason pursed his lips, shook his head. "Martina's just saying that cause she hates her. Who'd she hear it from?"

"I . . . I think she might know . . ."

"Bullshit!"

"Do you know?"

"What?"

"With Aaron? Last summer? Did you know about it?"

"No way."

"The rumor says that Miss Radkowski told Mrs. DeLauro and that Mrs. DeLauro's going to be fired for keeping it a secret. That the police—"

"They can't do that! They . . . Can they?!"

"I think. Has your father told Mr. Williams about Martina?"

"Shit if I know. I told im. But, you know, with my grandfather . . . I'll ask. After tonight's game. You comin?"

"Of course."

JASON LOOKED UP into the bright lights surrounding the stadium at Piedmont. A seventh seed from one quadrant, in reality the twenty-eighth seed in the tournament, had never before beaten a one-seed from another quadrant. The smile on his face could not have been broader. East Lake had just upset Gasden 1–0. Jason looked into the stands, spotted Kim. His face nearly split. God, what a feeling, he thought. Thank you, God.

He felt a tug, a squeeze on his shoulders. He looked. F.X. McMillian squeezed him again. "Congratulations. Great game, Panuzio. Great control. You've come a long way."

"Thanks, Coach."

"I'm really proud of you. Of all you guys. And you, Jason. I'm proud of what you've become."

GOD, JASON THOUGHT. I'm really proud a this. He rapped the cover of the book, thought to throw it across his room, thought to destroy it. Chickenshit, he thought. No wonder. Chickenshit. Fucking bribed em! Fucking paid em off! Jason did not know where to go, what to do. It was late night, Monday, December 5. On Saturday it had snowed and the championship game had been postponed. On Sunday it had snowed again and on Monday school was closed while town crews plowed, sanded and salted. Frazzled exhaustion jerked him up, dropped him back to his bed, tossed him. "*Goombah* and *Goommah!* Ha! Fermenting hate!"

Jason rose, descended the stairs to the second floor. The door to his father's room was closed. He thought to knock, thought his mother was still ill, wondered if she knew. He descended to the main floor. Under his arm was the box, Grandpa's box, Great-Uncle John's box, the box shipped from South Lake Village to Chicago, then back to Lakeport and finally brought to East Lake and pushed out of sight under Rocco's bed.

Jason spotted his father, asleep, in Rocco's chair, the TV on but the volume muted. He noted his father's breathing, noted the shallowness, the almost imperceptible rising and falling of his chest. Johnny had not shaved since the day of the burial. The dark stubble on his face was thick, uneven. His hair was unkempt—on one side it was crushed flat, on the other it was kinked and sticking out at odd angles. On top his deep balding intrusions surrounded a center copse that stuck up like a thicket of rush on a barren beach. He coughed, scratched his face, did not open his eyes.

"Dad," Jason said. He did not try to be gentle. "Dad, wake up."

"Huh! Oh." Johnny closed his lips, moved his jaw. His mouth was dry from sleeping with it open. His licked his lips yet still they felt pasty. He could barely form words.

"Have you read this?" Jason held out Francesca DeLuccio's diary.

"What is . . . ?" Johnny sat up, squeezed his eyes shut, reopened them.

"It was in Grandpa's box. I found his box. It was under his bed."

"Oh. Oh! What . . . ?"

"It's a diary. Your godmother's."

"Aunt Fran's?"

"It's all about Ricky and Louis and, uh . . . you and Uncle Nick and Grandpa."

"Um. About us." Johnny was finally becoming conscious.

"You better read it, Dad. It's about when your cousins were killed in Viet-Nam."

"Yeah. That. Geez . . ." Johnny pushed a hand through his hair. Again he coughed. Phlegm was thick in the back of his throat. "Yeah . . . that kinda tore the family apart. Then Nick went down and signed up . . . He just went down and signed up without telling . . . telling your grandmother or grandfather . . . I thought they'd . . ." Again he shook his head to clear it. "Well . . . that was after Fran died. After she . . ."

"Committed suicide," Jason said. He put the box on the sofa, said, "Read it."

"Um," Johnny mumbled. "Tomorrow. What the hell time is . . . ?"

"Ppph!" Jason blew out the sound. He turned, walked away.

The phone rings. "Hi," Johnny says.

"Johnny!" The voice is frantic.

"Yes."

"This is Uncle John. Get you father. I need him right away . . ."

"Ah . . . sure."

Now I am running. We are in the Village. In South Lake Village. Nick runs after me. We can hear sirens coming. I take the stairs to the brown shingled bungalow three at a time. "Stay out here," Rocco says. He goes in, does not come out for a long time. The sun is strong but clouds gather, roil, build into a thunderhead. The police and an ambulance come, go. Rocco emerges. Uncle John emerges. Johnny is looking at him, thinking of the games he always played with the kids, always played with Little Johnny-panni. "If you can open my hand, you can have it." Uncle John smiles, flashes a silvery quarter. Johnny-panni tries and tries. "Uncle John, why is your hand so hard?" "A man's hand must be hard to protect his family; to smash the bastards out there . . ." Uncle John's hands are shaking, are flaccid, are gray like the clouds. Are splotched with red.

The Panuzio House, East Lake, Tuesday, 6 December, 6:00 P.M.

"THAT BASTARD ROCCO!" Johnny read. He'd read the line, the passage, twice. He could not concentrate. He could not comprehend, could not . . . Again Johnny read, "That bastard Rocco!" He was in the dining room. Rocco's box was on one chair; much of the contents were spread about the table. Johnny had skimmed many of the earlier parts of Aunt Fran's diary, had settled in on her account of her feelings about Richard being killed, then about Louis being killed. Then about Rocco. Another punch. He did not think it but felt it. Another disruption destroying his world, destroying his mind.

An hour earlier he'd been elevated for the first time in . . . He could not recall. Mitch had swung by on the way home from work. He'd been concerned, worried. And he had a plan. "Think about it, Johnny." Mitch had bubbled with enthusiasm. "A consortium. I've already talked to twenty of the guys who commute. Every one of em is interested."

"Umm." Johnny's mind had been inert. His golden eyes had darkened from months in a downward spiral. "It's . . . I mean . . ." Slowly he became aroused. "You know that's my dream. It's always been my dream. All I ever wanted to do, Mitch, was to be out on the lake. Be part of the lake."

"I know." Mitch's excitement—to Johnny, seemingly Mitch's first excitement since Aaron's death—was contagious. "And you could do it," Mitch said. "We could put together the consortium for the seed capital, and you could do the general planning. Who knows more about the lake and the old ferry system than you?"

"Yeah," Johnny smiled. "Yeah! I've already been doing . . . You know. But I . . . It was like an academic exercise. But, Mitch, it *is* feasible. I know it is."

"Then do it." Mitch beamed. "Make it a formal presentation and we'll show it to—"

"Mitch." Johnny's smile suddenly waned and he again became morose. "I . . . ah . . . I got something to tell you, too. I . . . With all that's been . . ."

"What?"

"About Aaron. It's about Aaron. Jason told me . . ."

"What?" Mitch's spirit's were still high. "Spit it out, old man."

"Martina Watts—" Johnny looked at the floor "—is four and a half months pregnant with your grandchild."

"What?!" Quick. Terse. A mask of anger sliding over his face. "I don't believe this."

"I don't know if it's true," Johnny said. "Jason told me, ah . . . a while back . . . but ah . . . with all that's happened, I forgot . . ."

"You forgot?!"

"Yeah. I'm sorry. I . . ."

"Don't you think this is something Laurie and I need to know?!"

"I'm sorry. With all . . . Jason only told me . . ."

Mitch stood with his mouth open, his hands up, open, stunned, asking without uttering a sound, *How could you not tell me?*

"If you'd like me to contact Martina for you . . . I . . ." Johnny stumbled. "I know you don't like her . . ."

"LIKE HER!" Mitch erupted and Johnny flinched. "Like her?! Hilman thinks she's . . . She's still a suspect."

At first Johnny had not understood. Then he'd realized, and had said, "No. No way. She was at her game when it happened. Remember?" But Mitch had clamped his mouth shut, had turned, had stormed off.

"That bastard Rocco!" Johnny read the line in Aunt Fran's diary for a fourth time. Disruption upon disruption, he thought, felt without words. "That bastard!" Fran's words. "My beautiful, my lovely sons. I have cried every day for four years. I cry for you now. And that bastard bribed Mandanici to keep his sons out of the draft. After my two wonderful boys are murdered, that bastard bribes the board to lose their files. Like that little dolt Johnny-panni is more valuable than my Richard. Than my Louis! How can that bastard ever face his brother?! John should disown him. John should disown this horrible family. Kill my honest sons; cheat and connive to save his dishonest seed, his conniving, deceitful germ. I hate you, Rocco. I hate you, Tessa. Richard loved you so. He honored you and your damned service. General Mark Clark! *Fancul!* The big general! Monte Casino! *Va Fancul!* Don't you know they joined because of you! You might as well have killed them with a gun. 'God bless America!' 'America's the best land of all.' You're poison. 'America saved the world from Hitler.' Isn't that what you taught them? You could have shot them both and saved us all the nights of worrying while they were overseas.

"Never!" Johnny read on. "Never, Rocco. Never will you set foot in my house. Tessa, over my dead body, will I ever speak to you. But you, Rocco, you, you bastard. It is you, with that payment that has dishonored my sons. It is you I hate. Scinto told John. 'I'm sorry,' he said. 'If we'd all been a little smarter in '65 . . . in '66. If we'd been like your brother Rocco. I could have gotten the gratuity to the right man . . . to Mandanici. He knew how.' "

Johnny closed the book. He did not know . . . He did not know how . . . He closed his eyes. Saw an image of his uncle John on the porch of the bungalow on that day in 1969. It was the last time Johnny saw him. Uncle John moved. Johnny had thought, had he thought anything at all at the time, he thought, 'Uncle John moved. So. People move.' That's all.

Johnny pounded the table. He gritted his teeth. He socked his forehead with both hands. He saw an image of his uncle John's casket. It was 1975, early summer. Rocco had flown out, packed and shipped a few things, brought the body back. There was talk that it had all been in vain, that John had drunk himself to death. At that time, 1975, Johnny had been stoned; had found it humorous.

Johnny laid his head on the table. He did not want to be seen, did not want to be disturbed, wanted to withdraw into a shell, wanted to die. All . . . he thought. All of it. How could I have forgotten to tell him? *Mitch, I'm sorry. I'm so sorry. One sorry motherfuc . . .* And this. A bribe. *A bribe!* I didn't go because of a bribe! Zi Carmela knew. "How he protected you. You don't know how he always protected you." I'm a fake, Johnny thought. My whole life's been a veneer, a fraud, a façade. I'm not even who I always thought I was. I'm not even me!

A dream? "What the hell's this water?" His feet are heavy. He is in the living room. There is water halfway across the floor, soaking the carpet, flowing, spreading. It seems so real his feet are wet. He glances up toward a door but the door is closed. The water is coming from beneath the door. Damn it, he thinks. I hate this. I hate it. Gingerly he tiptoes, tries to keep his feet out of the puddles. He opens the door, sees the entire room is flooded, glances to the bath, immediately thinks, Broken pipe, but he does not go to the tub. He thinks he is thinking through the logical sequence of checks—the pipes, the valves, the sink, toilet, tub. He retreats, skips, stumbles down the basement stairs. It is no longer my house. The foundation is sand, hard-packed. It is a mess, worse than ever . . . worse than he's ever seen—dank, smelly, mildew, barely enough room between boxes and bikes and old clothes and stacks of newspapers and cardboard that haven't been recycled in years—hardly enough room to move. The water is four inches deep, rising. Everything is wet as if it has rained inside, rained all night long. There is daylight coming through the rear basement wall, gray light, twilight. The wall shifts, the top falls toward me a foot, eighteen inches. I am outside, looking into the basement from outside the door at the front of the house, a double wooden door like on a barn right there in the sand foundation just above the footings where the dirt has never been backfilled, and now the yard is gone, the front of the house shies back from the washed-out edge of the hill. Johnny-panni grabs the handle, thumbs the lever, pulls the door open. Dog Corleone leaps at me. I startle. Dog scampers away. There, there, big as a Clydesdale, lying on its side, a zebra. The animal lifts its head, looks apathetically at me, at me the intruder, lies back. The black is not deep black but charcoal. The white but soot gray. The animal does not seem to be wounded or ill. It makes no attempt to move.

I step in. The front wall quivers, the rear wall lists. Wooden posts—where are the lally columns?! the concrete slab floor?! the new bricks?!—sink in the mud, tilt askew.

"Sandwiches are ready." He hears her call. Actually hears the voice. Who?

The crack in the rear of the foundation widens, grows as he watches, as little Johnny-panni watches, as . . . Someone else is with him. Someone else is trying to remove items of value before the house collapses. Perhaps, he thinks, it is Nick. He wants Pop's tools. Or Mitch. Trying to rescue him before the entire weight of the structure buries everything forever and ever . . . Al-le-lu-ia! Al-le . . .

"They're going to get stale," she calls. There is irritation in the voice. "Why doesn't everybody come now?"

What the hell's she doing? he thinks. What . . . ? Who? It isn't Julia. Perhaps Sylvia. Perhaps Tessa. Perhaps Nonna . . . Zi Carmela . . .

Don't they realize what's going on down here?! Or Aunt Jo . . . Can't she see . . .

Can't she . . . he . . . see? The façade . . . falls . . . the . . .

the seed . . .

the germ . . .

the beginning . . .

Look.

Look back! to . . .

. . . falls away. There is darkness . . . darkness descending . . . a storm . . . descending.

He shook, looked up, rose. It was after 8:00 P.M. on the sixth of December. Johnny went to the closet under the stairway, removed his long wool coat, his heavy winter boots. Without a word to anyone, he moved to the family picture wall. He did not look. He placed a hand lightly on the heavy gold filigree frame. His eyes remained cast to the side. He did not glance at *Il Padrone*, could never again lay eyes upon him. Johnny-panni shuffled to the front door, walked to The Point. His mind was rigid, manic, anguished; his body tense, flaccid, spent. The first of his last thoughts . . . had begun.

The last of Johnny-Panni's last thoughts–10 December

the final convergence

The wind pushes. There is no wind. It drives me. I do not care.

I do not care, Johnny-panni thinks. I do not care if I die. I'm tired of this shit. I hate it. I'm not living the life I want . . . I'm not . . . I'm tired . . . So damn tired.

I turn. Look at me. It is me. I know it is me even if it is him. I am here watching him. He is there watching me. Dear God, help . . . please help . . .

I know what we are doing. I turn. One last time. Look. One last time. At the house, at my house, at the lights, at the dark grays and wet blacks of the land and the trees, at the ground and street and gutter all black and gray.

A chill. My shoulders pinch to my neck. My arms tighten to my sides. I feel dirty, itchy. I . . . He . . . unshaved . . . unshowered since . . . since . . . ? Look at him. Disheveled. Tired. Ill . . . his eyes moist as if from an infection or the flu . . . his breathing shallow as if . . . The night is clear, calm, cold. Lights from Lakeport stretch for miles on the surface. Stars reflects as if the lake is a mirror, as if I can submerge myself into heaven. Al-le-lu-ia. As if . . . There is no moon.

Thirty years. He shakes his head. His eyes, jowls, sag. The hangdog of gloom. Thirty years! Festering! Smoldering! Thirty years of lies, of bribes, of suicides, of drinking to death, of . . . That's what it's been all about. Thirty years. A festering decaying façade now rotten, now falling away.

Thoughts fragment, spurt, fall, fail. He approaches the pier, is driven to the pier by the wind. There is no wind. Is driven by a force that has gotten inside. Is behind the façade . . .

It was a good idea. He slips on the icy rocks, stumbles. A good idea but it'll never happen. If it was a good idea, why hasn't someone else thought of it? If it were viable, someone else would be doing it. It's the cost. Not just the shuttles but the piers, the terminals, the dredging. Prohibitive. And the regulations. Federal, state, local. A labyrinth. Permits alone would take decades. Maybe thirty years! And for what? A façade . . . another . . . If only . . .

Precursors. Johnny slips again, falls, winces. He stands. He does not brush himself off. Precursors, he thinks. Sins of the father, he thinks. All the good! All the hard work, the struggles that tempered their character in the camps, the World Wars, the depression. Immigrant values. Building, striving. From Giovanni Baptiste. Crushed. Crushed me like Raskolnikov. Like . . . He killed himself. How did he kill himself? Why? Why did Aaron die? Who . . . ? Questions without answers. Always without answers . . .

Wretched, vile, slovenly mind.

A zebra?! for God's sakes! A zebra! What the hell is a zebra doing in my basement?! Jo . . . Jenny . . . !

I mount the pier. Think of these few days. Of his days. His comings and goings. His reticence while he has moped . . . while he has faked . . . has worked on the proposal—The Reestablishment of Ferry Service . . . a façade . . . while he wrote letters—Dear Zi Carmela . . . a veneer . . .

The pier is slick but not as slick as the rocks, not as slick as life's . . .

It is dark. The pier reflects no light. He walks forward . . .

When he walked The Point. When he walked the road. When . . . stood in the wet, in the cold, in the snow dressed like a hick, like a shovel man ready to shovel shit or slop hogs or . . . "You look terrible," he'd heard Julia whisper. I can see her whispering to me. "I'm worried about you," she said. Why? he thinks. Why do you fret? You are too beautiful for me. You should have found someone better. He answered, "It's the flu." I see him answer. He does not look at her. Feels he is too disgusting to be looked upon. "Just like you had."

It's me. Why did he not say to her, "It's me. I am terrible. Me. Killer of Goombah and goommah. Instigator of death. Racist jerk. Broke . . . For two-point-six million you can have . . ."? "Mama . . ." Jenny screams. "It's okay, dear," Julia answers her. "It takes time for a man to come to terms with the death of his father. What are you doing with all this oil? What's all this water on the floor?"

"Chickenshit," Jason whispers to Kim. "Just plain chickenshit." "I know," she whispers back. "Maybe that's why he doesn't like himself."

Maybe, Little Johnny-panni thinks, maybe it's . . .

Ya gotta know when to show em—he blares out, blasts out the words into the darkness without sound—know when ta hold em; know when to fold . . . when to fold . . . How does it go? Know when to walk away, know when to . . . His thoughts are echoing from the lake. From my lake. Know when to sink . . .

No answer.

Jerk! People are jerks! People make people into jerks. How come they never found the weapon? The gun? What a bunch a jerks. Give me a fucken break, Hilman. You ask a million questions, you seek no . . . Did you question Nightingale? Did he tell you he . . . He . . . he tied her up. Had her tied up. I'll show you! And Aaron! Catting around! Jerk! Say it like it is! Womanizing! Whoring! Julia's seen him on the beach . . . Whoring! No. How's she put it? "Marcia . . . Marcia Radkowski?!" Julia's hand, long delicate fingers on her face, on smooth skin. "Oh! Of course that's who . . . ! That's what Hilman . . . Oh-oh!" So! Listen! A man is made to go a loving . . . A woman's made to weep and fret . . .

A man loves his wife. She doesn't love him. It's not the image . . . not the ambient cultural story. But it is the reality . . . the . . . gender be damned. A million stars reflect as if I can submerge myself into heaven.

"JULIA?"

"Oh! Mitch. I'm glad you called."

"How are you? And, ah, is Johnny there?"

"So-so, Mitch. He's out on The Point. Again." Julia squeezed the phone. "God! I wish he wouldn't do this. I don't even know where he goes. He . . . For five days. Mitch, he just keeps wandering around out in the snow. Or he's buried in those papers of his. I'm really worried about him. He's so . . . I don't know. Withdrawn. Or . . . I don't know. He hasn't been to bed in five days."

"Umm. Yeah, I could sense something. When I talked to him a few days ago. Wednesday, maybe."

"I'm really worried," Julia said. "I wanted to tell . . . For two days I tried to tell him I turned down that job offer. That I'm staying right here and working this out. But I can't talk to him. When he's here, it's like he's not. With the way things have gone wrong for him, for all of us, I guess, these past hundred days—"

Mitch interrupted. "That's why I wanted to talk to him. Look, I'm going to come over. Finally there's some . . . um . . . I'm not sure if 'good' is the right word, but some solid news. I talked to Hilman. Aaron's murderer confessed."

He drops from the pier. Drop to the floating dock. He . . . It is so much easier when I see him and don't see me, when I see him . . . I see him stare into the water, into the mirror of heaven. He kneels on the dock as if in prayer but he does not pray. He stares, loses himself in the water, in the smooth, beautiful, icy surface, asking the water . . . He does not know what to ask. Why are

there six polarizations? Why are . . . ? What possibilities . . . ? Alternatives . . . ? What will the seventh be like?

No answers.

He leans over. Thinks of possibilities, of could-have-beens.

Think . . . Imagine . . . Johnny-panni plops back, sits sideways on one cheek of his ass, his left hand on the dock, his legs askew, his eyes falling not to the surface of heaven but to the dull paint of the dock covered with clouded ice.

"Hi."

Johnny looks back, pulls back, shakes, spins.

"What are you doing down here?"

"Huh?"

She is in the ice. Beneath the ice. Clouded.

"The game's over," Jenny says. She seems wired. "They lost," Jenny says. "Jason called it a blowout. Four-nothing. But I thought they like played really okay, but I told him his play sucked anyway."

"Four . . . ?"

He is in the ice with her. I see him on the dock, propped on one elbow on the dock, seeing them, himself, me . . . in the drab ice coating the drab paint . . .

"Umm," Jenny hums. "He said it's okay. He said they had a great season. Then he called me a snot-head."

"You guys!" Seeing her there sets off in him an avalanche of pieces, of parts to the puzzle, of possibilities.

"He's up showering," Jenny says. "Kim and Mama are in the kitchen. Todd called. He said he's going to be cramming straight through to the twenty-first. Aren't you cold? What are you doing?"

"No. I'm . . . I'm . . ."

"Mr. and Mrs. Williams were at the game. Jason talked to him, and Mr. Williams told him to tell you, 'It don't mean nothing.' He said you'd understand."

It is not Jenny. It is Julia. I see her in the clouded ice.

She giggles like a teenager. "Do you remember . . ." She brings her fingers to her face. "Remember how we used to sit here? Together? What we've done here?! Oooo-oooo! I'll always love this spot."

"Me too . . ." Johnny laughs. He abruptly stops.

"You still haven't told me . . ." Julia begins.

Johnny stands. "I . . ." He glances to the house. "Oh God!"

"Johnny?!"

"I know . . . Come with me. We've got to . . . and . . . Jason. Get Jason. And Kim. I'm not chickenshit." He stands. He is sprinting. His mind is speeding. I'm not. I'm not. He is. I'm not. I'm not afraid. Be not afraid. Be not afraid of the possibilities. Come, follow . . . There is nothing we cannot

achieve . . . Rocco's words . . . The courage to try, the commitment to . . . Imagine. Possibilities. Imagine.

He looks at his hand on the dock on the ice. The wind forces him lower. There is no wind.

"THANKS FOR COMING over." Julia let Mitch in. "I'm worried about him." She led Mitch into the living room.

"Well," Mitch said quickly, "I wanted to come. I had to come."

"Are you going to tell me . . . ?" Julia put her hand to her face. "I mean . . . who . . . ? Or should we . . . Oh, Mitch, it's so cold tonight. You didn't have to . . . I mean, if Johnny were here you could have told him over the phone."

"Julia," Mitch said, "it's no big thing. Really. I wanted to tell you, tell both of you, in person. He's still out by the lake?"

Julia nodded. "You spoke with Hilman?"

"I was with him for two hours. You're not going to believe how it happened."

"Was it . . . ?"

"This . . . This'll . . . It's so odd. I talked to Johnny on the phone the other day, and he told me that Jason had found Rocco's box. That box he'd been looking for. He said Jason found it under Rocco's bed! Then I was talking to Hilman and I told him about that and Hilman just kind of lit up."

"Do you want to wait until Johnny comes back in?" Julia asked. "I'm not sure when that'll be. But at least you won't have to tell it twice."

"I don't mind. You think he's . . ."

"I don't know. I don't know where he is. Or how he can spend so much time out there in this weather."

"Yeah. Well, he always loved it out there. I'll tell you, then I'll go out and find him and tell him." Mitch settled back into the overstuffed chair. "It wasn't racism, Julia. It wasn't skinheads or angry black gang-bangers." Mitch seemed relaxed, his face animated by the release from ignorance of Aaron's death. "It wasn't even some random act or anything to do with drugs. It was Martina Watts. Because she was afraid. It wasn't even on purpose but was a stupid accident. It's tearing me up, but . . . I don't know how to explain this. Somehow . . . somehow, it's better." Mitch paused, took a deep breath.

"Tom Hilman," Mitch began again, "the police investigator?"

Julia nodded.

"He told me about going out to Martina's house . . . to the Wattses' house."

Again Julia nodded.

"He said it went like this. He knocked. Mrs. Watts answered, immediately said to him, 'I ain't buyin . . .' " Mitch chuckled. "So Hilman said, 'Hilman. State police. We met—' But Mrs. Watts cuts him off. 'What those kids done now? What you doin here this hour?' Hilman asked, 'Is Martina home?' And Watts snapped back, 'She in her room. She ain't done nothing.' "

Mitch shifted forward in the chair, eyed Julia, loosened his face with a series of quick stretches and wiggles. "Like this," he said. He assumed three different voices—rough and coarse for Mrs. Watts, slow and casual for Tom Hilman and flat yet sad for Martina—as he narrated the story:

> "Would it be possible for me to speak to her?" Hilman asked.
>
> "I guess. If she aint asleep. You might jus come in. You look like a hobo. How come you aint in uniform?"
>
> Inside the trailer Mrs. Watts disappeared into a back room, reemerged. Tom marched straight toward her. He didn't wait for her to beckon, or for Martina to come out. "Mr. Hilman," Mrs. Watts began.
>
> "I know im," Martina said. She was dressed in loose jeans, a loose, plum-colored sweatshirt; was sitting on the side of her bed. "He come ta all the games. Soccer junkie, aint . . . aren't you?" She did not get up.
>
> Tom ignored her question. "There's something you have that has to be brought out," he said.
>
> "Like what?" Martina asked.
>
> "I think you know what I'm talking about," he said. Then he remained silent. Martina didn't answer.
>
> Mrs. Watts moved between them. "She aint—"
>
> "Mama!" Martina broke in. "Leave us a minute."
>
> "Okay. Okay, baby. But if you need me, I'm . . ."
>
> Hilman shut the door, still didn't speak.
>
> "Who told you?" Martina asked.
>
> "No one."
>
> "You know what he done to me?"
>
> "I think so."
>
> "Stole my virginity. Knocked me up." She pulled the sweatshirt tight to expose the roundness of her belly. "Then he gone en . . . Stole my virginity. Got me pregnant. Then he dumped me for Miss . . ." Martina's face contorted.
>
> "But you two got back together," Tom said to her. "That stumped me."
>
> "He dump me again. He—"

"Martina, for quite a bit of time I couldn't figure out how you—"

"Because you dumb." Tom laughed when she said that. Martina smiled, but she was crying. "You figured it happen after four o'clock. Our game started at three-thirty, huh? And I pulled a hamstring in that game at four. But he was already dead . . . Don't take no time. You go down Hayestown Road to 86 an up Little Brook. I was there an back . . . I didn't mean ta do it. I loved him."

"I know," Hilman said.

"He . . ." Martina rocked; her tears came harder. "I only meant to scare him. I only meant . . ." She aimed her hand, pulled the trigger. "Like that. But he jump. He jump right into where I'm shootin. Then he fall. He jumpin and tremblin. He hurt so bad." Martina tried to hold her tears back but she couldn't. "So bad. I hurt him so bad. I'm thinking, *That's how I hurt. That's how you hurt me.* Then he ain't jumpin. Ain't twitchin. An I'm . . . I'm like . . . like . . . I'm like . . . freakin! Like, *Why did you jump?* Like, *Why didn't you love me like I loved you? Like I still love you?* I never ever held a gun before. Never even ever. And I know he's dead. I know he is. Like he died so fast. Then I'm thinkin, Shit! They goina get me. They goina get me. Then I'm thinkin, No. He done me. I'm goina make it look like someone else done him. So I shot up his . . . You know. You know, a girl don't go doin that to a boy, so they naturally think a boy did it."

At that, she stopped crying. She became like ice and said, "It didn't devastate me none. You know, I know it an accident. It just somethin that happen. An like I said, it wouldn't a if he hadn't jumped just when I—"

Hilman cut her off. "Under the bed, Martina?"

"Maybe," she said, but she didn't move.

"Please give it to me."

"What you goina do with it?"

"It's evidence, Martina. You know this. We're going to go to the police station. I believe you when you tell me it was an accident. When are you due?"

"Four months."

"You know Mr. and Mrs. Williams?"

"Yeah."

"You know they know you're carrying their grandchild."

"I don't need . . ." Her shoulders suddenly slumped. "Maybe I do," she said. Then she slid from the bed, pulled from beneath it some folded clothes, sighed. "In here. I'm not angry you came," she told him. She handed him the bundle. "Heavy, aint it?"

"Heavy . . ." Mitch said to Julia. There were tears on his cheeks. "But that's the story. It's odd; when Tom told Laurie and me . . . we just . . ."

"Oh, Mitch," Julia said. "I know Johnny needs to hear it. But you shouldn't have to tell it again."

"I want to tell it. It's . . . What's the word? Cathartic. Or . . . Anyway, he should hear it from me. It's not good but it is good . . . good to know . . . And maybe, you know, maybe she does. Maybe Martina does need . . ." Mitch stopped, swallowed.

"Over," Julia said.

"A beginning," Mitch said. "I . . . Laurie and I . . . we . . . If Laurie and I had raised her . . . ah . . ." Mitch shook his head. "It might have been different." He smiled weakly, winked. "Hey, let's go out and find Johnny. It'll be good for him to know, too."

He rubs the ice, thinks, Someone's going to commit suicide. His face is nearly on the dock.

" 'But half an hour!' " he hears her say, hears her quote the line. She is lying down. Her face is nearly on the dirt. She is going to kill herself as he watches. Her words are slow, heavy. Though she holds the play in her hands, she cannot see the words. She does not need the script. " 'Being done,' " she answers Desdemona with Othello's line, " 'there is no pause.' "

I am lying on the dock. I am seeing. I know but I don't. It is all possible, Johnny-panni thinks, thinks, his mind running fast . . . And when everyone knows, they will hail me. They will look at me. They will say, "That's Johnny-panni. He's a man to bear in mind. He's the one who solved the great issues tearing us apart. He's the one . . . Now that we've got a regional governor . . . He'd make a great governor." That's what they'll say. He'll . . . And he saved her, too. How did he know? A visionary.

A vision. In the drab ice on the dock.

"I don't know," Jason answers her. "I've never seen him like this."

"Everybody went to the Bastille. Aren't you hungry?"

Jason pulls Kim close, nips her ear. "For you," he says. "For all of you."

"I don't like being in here," Kim says. "It gives me the creeps. At night, anyway. I think he's . . . Why would he think she'd be here?"

"She didn't answer her phone," Jason says. "He eliminated the other possibilities, and Mrs. DeLauro thought maybe . . . I guess she comes here and reads to him . . ."

At the entrance to the cemetery Kim whispers to Jason, "How could he see this? Don't you think he's nuts?"

On Aaron's grave Marcia Radkowski whispers, " 'But while I say one prayer!' " She lies down, clutches the play close to her heart. The barbiturate overdose has diffused throughout her system, has decreased her sensitivity to outside pain. "My great Moor . . ." she moans. "My fault . . . All . . . carnivorous, lecherous self . . ."

"Let's just call out," Kim says. They have reached the last row, the one at the end where Aaron has been buried for two and a half months, has been cold for . . . "Miss Radkowski?" Kim calls. She feels silly calling out into the blackness of the night, into the dark corners of the cemetery. "I'm freezing." Kim shudders.

"It's only a couple hundred feet," Jason says.

" 'It is too-oo late.' " Marcia hears herself quote the great Moor as the Moor SMOTHERS!!! her.

"Holy shit!" Jason screams. "Holy shit!" He lifts the teacher.

"How could he possibly have known?" Kim trots beside Jason. "Oh, dear Lord. Oh. You drive." Kim is nearly hysterical. "Drive to the East Lake clinic."

Drive! It is me. Drive me to . . . NO! Look! TA-DAH! No one knows how, but Johnny-panni put it all together. He had a vision. He has vision. They only know . . . Oh, I would have the last laugh. Yes! Yes, that would save me. They only know that he has saved her life. That he is a hero. He is not chickenshit. He can see . . . see it right here in the ice. See . . .

He strokes his beard, turns the wheel about three degrees. It is a year, no, eighteen months. They have moved forward in record time. The sun reflects from the water, shimmers, refracts. He can see the crowd, maybe a hundred people, standing, waiting. His thoughts, too, shimmer, refract. Seek light. Help us reach inside. Help us believe in each other. He throttles back. How had Mitch put it? he thinks. A series of acts, each act a vector with magnitude, direction. The sum of life, our destiny, is the sum of how we place our vectors. Place our vectors . . . place our vec . . .

Behind him people begin clapping. How had he thought it, explained it? Think of the possibility. I would say, "In the killing there was life. Strange, terrible, tragic. That murder which has taken so much away from so many; which has ripped the very fabric of this culture, has given us back our lives, is the very thread that will mend this culture. Let us tell this as our cultural story . . . how in dying he has brought us together. How . . ."

In the crowd Eileen Panuzio whispers, "She's beautiful."

"I think you have to say, 'He's beautiful,' " Todd says to his wife.

"Boats are usually referred to as she," Eileen insists. Their eyes follow the shuttle as it approaches the new pier.

"This one's a he," Todd says. He tries to see under the tassel top. The day is clear, crisp, the sun sparkling in the craft's wake. "You can't call it a she if it's called the San Rocco."

"Is that your father?" Eileen begins.

Behind them a car skids to a halt in the new lot. Mitch Williams springs from one side. He does not wait for the girls. "Oh!" He throws his hands up. "Thank God we haven't missed—"

"About three minutes out," Julia says. She is the publicist, the public relations specialist for the new system. She is so beautiful. So happy. Her smile sparkles. She does not look at Mitch but keeps the San Rocco in the viewfinder, keeps the captain, her husband THE CAPTAIN, whom she adores . . .

"Is that for the commercials?" Mitch asks. He turns, motions for Diana and Whitney to hurry. Laurie stays in the car. "Come on," he calls excitedly to the twins. "Oh, excuse me," he says to Eileen. "You're . . ."

"This is Eileen," Todd says. To Eileen he says, "This is my uncle Mitch."

"Diana." Mitch spins. "Go back and get your mother. She's got to see this." He turns back, says apologetically, "She doesn't want the baby to get cold." He does not wait for an answer but asks Todd, "Are they all on the boat?"

"The shuttle?" Todd laughs. "I think," he says. "Pop and Jenny, anyway. Kim. And Uncle Nick, Aunt Dana . . . I don't . . . It holds a hundred and twenty . . ."

"Vern and Elisse, too," Julia says from behind the camera. "I know just how I'm going to do the commercials."

Very slowly Johnny guides the San Rocco into the slip. Mitch is surprised at the crowd on board. This is a test run, not a maiden voyage. "Laurie, look at this!" He smiles. He stares at the San Rocco. "I never thought I'd see the day." Mitch's chest is bursting.

When the shuttle is properly secured and the gangway is in place, the first passengers file down past Kim and Jenny, who are the stewards. "Jason's goina be like fried to the extreme missing this," Jenny says to Kim.

"Can't be in two places at once," Kim answers.

"Another stupid soccer game!" Jenny says.

Mr. and Mrs. Sanchez come down, kiss their daughter, follow the crowd to the small terminal where cocoa, coffee and zeppoli are being served.

"Wave to me," Julia calls. She zooms in on the stewards.

Kim and Jenny laugh. "Not just another game," Kim protests. It is hard not to laugh with the camera leering at them. "It's the entire Northeast tournament. Only state champs . . ."

Why? Why only Northeast? No. Johnny rubs the ice. He is flat on the ice

scrubbing it, erasing it. The national tournament, he says. Say it is the national championship.

"Popsters," Jenny booms. "I wanna drive back. Can I? Can I?"

Johnny laughs, tousles her head.

"Padrone," *Kim says. "It's great. Really, this is . . ."*

Mitch smothers Johnny with a bear hug. "Ya did it!" he explodes. "When can we start shuttling students? How long till we have three shuttles? Can you speed it up more?"

"I couldn't a done it without you," Johnny-panni says. "And, I guess . . ." He is smiling. He is so happy. So, ". . . you couldn't a done it . . ."

If he is so happy, why do my eyes tear?

". . . without me."

"I STILL CAN'T believe anyone can love this . . . in this weather!" Julia said to Mitch. "It's one thing in the summer . . ."

"Á." Mitch chuckles. "He always—"

"Cold and dark and slippery and . . ." Julia put her arm through Mitch's arm. "I don't see him. He could be anywhere."

They crossed the street, approached the water's edge, scanned the shoreline. "It is pretty out here," Mitch said. "Awfully cold. Are you okay?"

"Yeah. At least there's no wind." She cocked her head. "Is that . . . ?"

"Where? What?"

"Out on the . . . umm. Nothing. I thought I saw . . . Just a dark spot on the dock."

I turn, turn back, turn around, slide, edge over, stare into the lake. I . . . he leans . . . slips. "Wha . . . ?" He tries to stop. What? he thinks. Why? he thinks. He looks back, up to the pier. No one. At the shore. No one. No one has come. He is alone. Why . . . ? he thinks. Why am I . . . No possibilities.

Johnny's neck bends down. His torso lists. He strains. His abs tighten trying so hard to right him. His legs come up. He topples, slides, slow motion, a million years to splash. His face, head, into the icy water, his body, clothes, boots, pushing him down. He lets his body submerge. Frigid water rushes into seams, spreads, cools him, hurts him. He does not struggle. Does not move, lets his body sink, lets his heavy clothes pull him down. Hurts. Cold. Ice on skin lowering his temperature. He is free. Free of ContGenChem. Free of LeRoy. Free of Emilio. Free . . . He flashes: Hilman. Autopsy. The body of Little Johnny-panni will not decompose rapidly in the icy . . . Boots fill. Feet freezing. All I ever wished for . . . Free of pain. Free of self-disgust . . . disgust with Little

Johnny-panni . . . Teeth, eyes, stinging. Then dull. Submerged . . . Al-le-lu-ia! . . . in heaven . . . Clouded . . . to be a part of the lake . . . my lake . . .

"WHAT THE HELL was . . . ?" Mitch let Julia's arm drop. His head snapped toward the pier's end, to the floating dock. "What the hell . . . ?" He took a step toward the pier. Slipped. "You don't think . . . ?" He took another step. "Shit." Mitch ran. His feet slipped. He hopped, recovered, ran, reached the pier. Mitch ran/shuffled on the icy surface. Julia tried to follow him. Fell. Mitch reached the incline, searched the water, saw nothing. "Maybe not . . ." he muttered. Still he descended, slid, backed onto the floating dock, slid, knelt. "Shit!" He crawled to the edge, stared at the blackness. Lights reflected back. He stared deeper, beyond the sparkles, beyond the refracted starlight into the dark, saw a deeper darkness. "Shit!" he screamed. He splatted flat, rammed a hand into the water, recoiled at the cold, jammed it back in, hit something, grasped but could not grasp. He lowered his shoulder, his face on the surface, grasping the dock with his other hand with all his might, trying to keep from sliding off. Again his hand hit, grasped. He pulled. It came toward him. He slid toward it. "Shit-damn, shit-damn." He clutched, edged back, pulled, edged back, afraid his hand was too numb to hold on, edged back, pulled, lifted. "Julia!" he screamed.

"Here." Her voice broke. She was directly behind him.

"Hold my damn legs."

Epilogue

NEARLY HALF A decade has passed since Little Johnny-panni attempted to end his life by sliding into the icy darkness of the Wampahwaug, since Mitch Williams pulled him, comatose, back onto the dock.

East Lake has changed. It is larger now. There are more businesses. More traffic. Two new churches. A new school. Much remains the same; much is different. Victor Santoro, the vice principal at East Lake High, retired on schedule. Ciara DeLauro, the guidance counselor, retired early. The file on her involvement in the tragedy has been sealed. Her balancing influence at the school is deeply missed. In the fall F.X. McMillian still coaches the boys' soccer team; and now, in the winter, girls' basketball. Charlene Rosenwald and Michelle Dutchussy have been joined by a new vice principal.

Marcia Radkowski, amid scandal, left her classes that midyear. She quit teaching, moved out of state. No one knows how Johnny-panni knew some of the things he knew. He seemed to have a certain sensitivity. Three days before his plunge, he had told Julia that Marcia would attempt suicide; that the attempt would be made on Aaron's grave. Marcia did make that attempt. She was unsuccessful.

There is a sense of burden in this town: the burden of the teen deaths in the car accident up by The Falls; the burden of Aaron's death; the burden of Martina's fall. She seemed to feel no remorse; continued to maintain it was an accident; said she'd fired the additional rounds after he was dead so no one would suspect her. Even though the murder was not premeditated, the ensuing actions were deemed to have been designed specifically to deceive, to hide her involvement or complicity. Martina Watts is serving a seven-year prison term at the Groton Correctional Facility for Women. Laurie and Mitch visit her every other week. And they bring their granddaughter, Aliena. How much of this burden they blame on their son is not known. How much on themselves? How much should we, each of us carry?

More burdens: The regional lawsuit over racial isolation of minority students, the court decision, the panels, the multiple countersuits—will probably not be resolved in our lifetime. The Fitzpatricks' suit against the Willises and the town still has not come to court. And the outcome of Justin Robustelli's suit against Gallina has never been announced.

The burden of Johnny-panni's collapse and suicide attempt sits heavily upon him. Sometimes he tells himself that had Julia or Mitch, Jason or Jenny, intervened, Little Johnny-panni would not have let himself make that final slip into the Wampahwaug. Or had Mitch not been so short with him when Johnny told him about Martina's pregnancy. Or earlier, right after Mitch returned from Atlanta, right after the publication of Aaron's articles in the *Ledger*. Nelson Tripps, ContGenChem's CEO, knew, as did everyone, that the articles had been altered, edited and refined, by Johnny, and that Johnny had selectively chosen to emphasize only certain aspects of Aaron's rough notes. Tripps had warned Mitch Williams to distance himself from John Panuzio. At the same time, Tom Hilman, the state police investigator, had asked Mitch to keep quiet about the attack on Laurie. And he had purposely, with Mitch's knowledge and agreement, started the rumor that the Williamses were moving to Atlanta. It all served to create a polarization between Johnny and Mitch. At least in Johnny's mind. Johnny was hurt, felt that he had lost his closest friend.

Still, had they intervened more forcefully, Johnny-panni probably would not have listened. That is the way it is with depression. He was a man who was lost; who'd forgotten his roots; forgotten the audacity and grit of *Il Padrone*, of Rocco, of all his forebearers. Johnny was a man who'd lost his foundation. He could not, or would not, admit his thoughts, his fears to anyone. He was afraid of their disapproval. He'd lost the courage to persevere, to overcome obstacles. He believed it better to take solace in thoughts of suicide, believed it better to live in silence, to die with the hurts.

It was the cumulative weight of the hurts . . . the revelation of Rocco's bribe being the last but not the least . . . that led to the demise of Little Johnny-panni.

And thank goodness!

On that night, in those cold waters, Little Johnny-panni died. On that night, from those cold waters, by the eyes of Julia and the hands of Mitch, John Panuzio was reborn.

Changes: The one-quarter of Rocco's estate that John and Julia received covered their debts—his gambling debt, the overdue bills. There was even enough to supplement Todd's, Jason's and Jenny's tuition. Todd has graduated. He lives with his wife in Missouri. They are expecting. Jenny is a senior at East Lake High, an honors student, a basketball star. She still goes fishing. Sometimes Mitch's twins join her. She wants to be a marine biologist. Jason is a senior at the University of Virginia, a physics major. He has continued to play soccer, has expressed a desire to coach. Kim is a senior at Lehigh University. They see each other often.

Julia and John traveled a long road. They live a more frugal existence, more in line with those immigrant values of *Il Padrone* and of Rocco and Tessa. And they are more active in the town, the region—Julia as a publicist for Senator Sam Tonnelli.

As for John Panuzio, he is back, and it is he. Only he. He is back, stronger, wiser. John. Not Johnny. Not Johnny-panni. He knows who he is, who he was, where he is going. One might say, Johnny-panni finally grew up.

There is independence being out of the corporate structure. Independence and freedom. Perhaps there is a lack of security, though, too, there is a lack of false security. Daily John Panuzio busies himself writing—mostly articles on the lake or on the environment. He writes from behind the counter of his shop—Panuzio's Boats, Bait and Tackle.

The reestablishment of shuttle service on Lake Wampahwaug remains only a dream.

Appendix

The Lakeport Ledger

Section D-1 — Copyright–The Lakeport Ledger–A Callipano Corporation — Sunday, October 30, 19—

Area Youth Lectures from Beyond the Grave

"When Atlas Can No Longer Shrug—Freedom Is an Illusion"

The first in a series of essays by
Aaron Williams
with John Panuzio

RACE, CULTURE & PUBLIC POLICY: We stand at a critical time in the Lake Region, in this state, and in this nation, with regard to racial isolation and imbalances, and with regard to the equality of education for all, and to the legitimate role of government in our lives. It is now time for us to analyze not simply where we are, how we arrived here and where we are going, but also to understand what vehicle and what propulsion system has brought us to this point, and what vehicle and system is most suited for taking us into the future.

A Family Story

My father was born in Lakeport nearly half a century ago, in a house on Sixth Street near Glenn Avenue, right next to the Wampahwaug Northern Railroad's northbound tracks. He was the oldest of two sons of Allen Williams and Geraldine Sims Williams. Grandpa Williams was a day laborer and a night watchman; Grandma worked in the laundry at St. Luke's Hospital. After school and during the summer, my father, Mitch, and his brother, Vernon, were children of the streets—at least until Grandma came home at about seven o'clock. So goes my family's story.

At that time their neighborhood, Misty Bottom to across Center Street, was racially and ethnically mixed—more Italian and Eastern European than African. My father's closest friend, from then to this day, was and is an Italian-American. My father often told his children that it was his exposure to his friend's family, particularly to his friend's parents, that allowed him, as a black child, to believe in, and to aspire to, a higher calling in life.

My father sometimes put it this way. "I internalized elements of their stories, and of the stories of the neighborhood. These things were beyond the common lore of the small, more closely knit black community that was coming into the region because of the postwar industrial boom."

When I questioned my father about this, he said, "It was not a matter of optimism. Both the black and white communities of the mid-fifties believed things were getting better. Especially the black community—because the Supreme Court, in 1954, struck down the separate-but-equal doctrine of 1896, a doctrine that had reversed many gains made by blacks after the Civil War.

"It was more a matter of belief," my father continued, "and of determination. Belief in the way things ought to be, in the way life should be lived, in what individuals and the community should be willing to sacrifice for a better future. My mother and father sacrificed greatly for their children, but their eyes were focused on the here and now, not on some distant future. In the home of Rocco and Tessa Panuzio there was more willingness to save and to invest, more willingness to pressure their children to study and to demand high grades, than there was in my household. The Italian families I knew had a strategy for the future; our black family had but a tactical plan for the present."

This, of course, is but a small piece of my father's story. But for him it was an essential piece. He was a scholar-athlete in high school, served in the armed forces, went to college, earned an advanced degree, became a successful industrial management engineer. Why? How?

Those questions demand analysis. And they evoke other questions. What is *Cultural Story*? Does Story determine physical, emotional and economic well-being? What stories are we telling ourselves today? How is Story told or conveyed?

In this paper I would like first to establish a framework for the importance and the effect of story; then briefly examine how race has entered the American consciousness; where and why the story of race is skewed; and finally look at the ramifications on education caused by distortions, omissions and/or purposeful permutations of ambient cultural story. I will also propose a regional solution to the problems of racial isolation and imbalance in inner-city schools, which have, according to pending court decisions, caused those schools to fail to provide equal education as is required by the state constitution. I believe this solution is viable for areas like the Lake Wampahwaug Region; that it is in line with the intentions of the State Supreme Court; and that it will effectively disrupt cultural isolation without institutionalizing politically correct racism.

The Framework

The following framework draws on and is extrapolated from numerous works, including books and articles by Thomas Sowell, M. Scott Peck, M.D., Huey Newton, General Colin Powell, Hugh Pearson, James Baldwin, Louis Farrakhan, and Dr. Martin Luther King, Jr.; from interviews with F.X. McMillian, Ciara DeLauro and James Hawkins (all of East Lake High School), with State Senator Loren Bibbeton and Assemblywoman Cynthia Dyer, with General Harrison Dunney, and last but not least, with Mitch and Laurie Williams, my parents.

I have proposed the following theory of social behavior to explain the complexities of the phenomena herein examined—specifically race relations and racism in regard to equal education. I have attempted to construct a theory which is cohesive, simple, elegant, and capable of broad and accurate application. Perhaps this is only one student's perspective, but to me, *Story* must be the basic element of our approach.

The story we tell ourselves of ourselves, individually or culturally, creates our self-image and our world view. Behavior, individually and culturally, is consistent with self-image and world view. Story determines behavior.

As story changes, self-image and world view change; as these change, behavior changes; as behavior changes, so too change the results of behavior. That is, personal and cultural story have ramifications.

Because story has ramifications, it is necessary to analyze and to understand the current story we are telling ourselves of ourselves; the current story we hold individually, or as a subgroup, as a town, a region, a state or a nation. If one sees oneself as a scholar, one behaves in particular patterns. If one sees oneself as a writer or an engineer, as a soldier or a patriot, as a radical or an alternative person, one also behaves in particular patterns. One's behavior in the present is very different if one's story is of despair, of drugs and of violence, than if one's story is of striving, of betterment and of advancement; very different if one describes oneself as a victim, or if one's self-description is that of a proud, accountable citizen of his town and region; and very different if one tells oneself he is a follower of the Nation of Islam and a disciple of Louis Farrakhan than if one internalizes the story of General Colin Powell.

One's behavior, too, is different if one believes his goal is immediate, positive personal stimulation, or if one's focus is on the self as part of an ongoing community, as part of the continuity of humanity. For individuals one might make a matrix of all possibilities—story and behavior are tremendously complex. Yet it is possible to pinpoint beliefs, to pinpoint story. For a culture or subculture, the pin must be replaced with the brush—yet cultural belief and cultural story can be ascertained.

By the term *cultural story*, or more fully, **Ambient Cultural Story**, I mean our current *common knowledge*, our *collective national* or *ethnic* or *racial myth*, our *conventional wisdom*, our *popular memory*, our *folklore* in all its myriad manifestations.

The story we tell ourselves of ourselves, individually or culturally, creates our self-image and world view. Self-image consists of internalized, cumulative and weighted images, which create belief patterns, perceptual formats, understandings and conceptualizations. It is through this lens that we view the world. At the most fundamental level, self-image determines macro behavior.

Said another way, culture is built upon self-image and beliefs, and self-image and beliefs are based upon ambient story. Thus behavior is consistent with self-image and with story. Behavior includes actions in the present as well as plans and projections for the future.

Ambient cultural story is complex, fluid and subject to external pressures, yet it also tends to be homeostatic. By **ambient** I mean general consensus, the bulk of the story, the feeling and flavor we get from the news and from films, the data that become boilerplate in news stories, or that are distilled into high school textbooks. I mean clichés, stereotypes, biases and prejudices. I do not mean that denials, variations and/or opposing stories are totally absent.

By **fluid** I mean that alteration of ambient story is possible, and that such alteration changes self-image, and thereby alters macro behavior. There would be no issue of racial isolation and educational inequality for minority students if story were not fluid.

By **homeostatic** I mean that story tends to revert to prior general consensus. For example, if one has repeatedly heard, and been convinced, that the typical welfare recipient is an unemployed inner-city minority whose family has received public assistance for generations, and then one is told that most welfare recipients are white, live in suburban or rural areas, and will spend approximately one year on the dole, one will be reluctant to dismiss the bulk of the earlier ambient story—particularly if it is still being reinforced by story generators.

By **external pressures** I mean that individually or culturally we are influenced by the stories others tell us about ourselves. One might include here the written word, both fiction and nonfiction. In America today, however, the greatest external pressure on story comes from television—a medium from which more than half of all Americans derive 100 percent of their news; a story generator, or information gatekeeper, that the average American watches for more than six hours each day.

Behavior is consistent with self-image and world view. That is a basic tenet. There are individual deviations. Group self-image is necessarily more complex than individual self-image. Still self-image controls attitudes and actions.

For example, at the most base level: When we as a nation believed in Manifest Destiny, our policies and actions reflected that belief. When we viewed ourselves as an altruistic nation willing to go anywhere, to bear any burden in the defense of freedom, our actions and foreign policy tended to be in accord with those principles, with that idealism. And when our paradigm was the advancement of civil rights, great social strides were taken toward inclusiveness and equality.

Yet with the completion of the interstate highway system, which has allowed people to work in cities and live in suburbia, and which has enabled ''white flight'' from the inner cities; with the rolling economic recessions of the past twenty years; and with the passel of public programs that have produced unforeseen side effects, attitudes have changed. Stories have reverted to those of earlier decades. Ensuing social behaviors now reflect those changes. One author noted in the late eighties, ''We now exist in a time when we believe in looking out for number one, in getting our piece of the pie no matter whom we screw over or abandon. Once egalitarian inclusiveness was considered a virtue. Now it is equated with the political and economic misdeeds of insincere city, state, and national politicians and bureaucrats.''

In ancient Greece there was an adage, *Ethos anthropou daimon*, ''A man's story is his fate.'' A society's, or an ethnic group's myth—the story it tells itself of itself—too, is that society's or group's fate. What happens to a society if the people come to believe they are as morally bankrupt as their social commentators repeatedly tell them they are? Or to a group if the people come to view themselves as prone to violence, greed, racism, and bigotry? Of if they are shown that violent physical response is the best means of dealing with someone with opposing viewpoints? Are the thresholds for reacting in manners consistent with those images lower than if the self-view is of a people as accountable and disciplined citizens striving for a better tomorrow for themselves and future generations?

Macro behavior is consistent with self-image, and self-image always meshes with ambient story unless acted upon by a significant outer force. Yet the theory of cultural or ''macro'' behavior cannot be used to determine specific behaviors of individuals. It is, instead, analogous to quantum physics. One cannot predict the behavior of a particular individual from cultural myth any more than one can predict the path of a specific electron—but overall trends can be predicted, and accurately. And they can be directed by controlling ambient story.

Macro behavior can be manipulated by story control—as the founders of our nation so well recognized and feared. It was not coincidental that freedom of speech was included in the first article of the Bill of Rights. Newspaper magnate William Randolph Hearst's spreading of disinformation is an example of story control altering macro behavior—in this case instigating the Spanish-American War. Another example might be drawn from Cambodia's Maoist dictator of the mid-1970s, Pol Pot. His policy ''Year Zero'' was an extreme attempt to wipe out existing cultural story and supplant it with an alien ideology in order to alter macro behavior.

Other examples: One may infer fear of story control from recently expressed angst over the mergers of Disney/ABC and Westinghouse/CBS. Are America's image makers and information disseminators becoming too monopolistic? Will they control cultural story making via narrow, self-serving productions? The billions of dollars spent yearly on advertisements—a form of story telling and/or image making—is a primary form of cultural image manipulation and behavior control.

Story is not always complete—there are omissions and gaps, both expedient and purposeful. Story is not always accurate—there are extrapolations, embellishments and fabrications. Story is not static—it is always growing, dying, being revised and reinvented. What is consistent is that story forms self-image and world view, and behavior is consistent with self-image and world view.

People have learned many ways to describe themselves. Individuals might include age, gender, ethnicity, nationality, political tendencies, religious affiliations, region, race, height, color of eyes, size of nose, amount of facial hair. These tags represent characteristics. Every person whose career is in advertising knows that ethnicity has characteristics; so too, nationality, religion, and political affiliation. For the individual, we might call story-based cumulative characteristics *personality*. For a group, we use the term *culture*.

Some elements of personality or of culture are shaped by specific *defining moments*. My father tells the story of a cold autumn evening when he was fourteen years old. He'd just left football practice and he was alone in Lakeport's west end. His friend had been sick that day and absent from school. As my father crossed through the park that night, perhaps 500 or 600 feet from where he walked, in a circle of light at the far side, he witnessed a group of boys younger than he, stoning, or perhaps ''apple-ing,'' an old woman. There were perhaps ten boys. The woman could not defend herself other than shuffling on, trying to protect her head with her upraised arm. My father says he did not believe the boys were physically damaging the old woman. Soon she and they disappeared into the darkness. Still, he relates, at that time he did nothing—did not yell, did not go for help, did not intercede—fearful, he claims, that he might have gotten himself badly beaten. ''I was frozen into inaction, into noninvolvement,'' he said. ''I have thought about that incident many times. For me, that night was a defining moment. I vowed I would never allow the defenseless to stand alone.''

Story can pass from person to person, from friend to friend, from father to son. My father's story of inaction and his vow of protection have been given to me and I have internalized them. It is one of the reasons why I believe that the cities cannot be abandoned.

F.X. McMillian explains it thus: "If the countryside abandons the cities, it will be like a reverse Maoist tactic—but it won't make the cities or the countryside any safer. It is the same with the Third World. What will happen if we don't assist Mexico, if we do an 'Atlas Shrugs,' and EPR rebels gain significant footholds? Will we, here, be safer or less secure? You see, what goes on elsewhere may be our business."

What happens in the inner cities is the business of the suburbs. What happens in the suburbs is the business of the inner cities.

Principles of Application

Long-term or cultural ramifications of public programs, policies or laws, or of media projections, often differ from the intent of those programs, policies, laws or projections—because ***individual and cultural self-images thereby induced are more determinant to long-term, macro behaviors than are the direct effects of the policies or projections***.

For example: If one is working with youth, one must be very cautious in the manner programs are established to prevent unwanted behaviors—drug abuse, teenage pregnancy, suicide—least the program have the opposite long-term effect and actually increase the unwanted behavior by creating elements of self-image that would not otherwise be present.

The best of intentions notwithstanding, other examples of misfired policies might be drawn from the creation of poverty pockets while attempting to provide affordable housing; the accusation of racism leveled against America's Viet-Nam veterans by "antiwar" organizations attempting to disengage American military involvement; or the ascendancy of the violent image of black males over other elements of our personal and cultural story because of the romanticizing of black militancy by the media.

Policy cannot be only a matter of aims and goals, but also must be a matter of manners and means. If there is one thing apparent from the government programs of the sixties, seventies and eighties, it is that even with the best intentions, *and* with a high degree of success in reaching stated goals, there have been numerous and disastrous side effects. The housing projects of Lakeport, built to provide adequate shelter for an element of the population that was living in deplorable conditions, have indeed provided better housing conditions for thousands. The projects have also concentrated economically disadvantaged minorities, and have isolated them from the surrounding, more affluent culture. **(This is the very essence of the lawsuit and court decisions we are now facing!)**

The story of interracial violence within the American military of the 1960s and 1970s repeatedly has been portrayed in popular media projections, yet the ambient story we hold is distorted both in number and in emphasis. During the very worst year of inter-American violence, the total number of serious incident reports (SRI) with racist causation was approximately two hundred, for a force, including rotations, that numbered some 700,000 (Dunney). And what has very seldom been reported or told are the millions of close interracial friendships—that is, racial harmony—within an American military that had never before been so totally integrated. One might speculate that the skewing of this story has been to the detriment of race relations in America; that were our ambient cultural story one of racial harmony, and our self-image one of people getting along without regard to skin tone, macro behavior would follow story and image. The principles of harmony and tolerance are taught and fostered in our schools—yet, with respect to Americans in Southeast Asia, our schools continue to emphasize the worst and disregard the best. This is self-defeating.

As have been the most commonly publicized stories of black protest. Hugh Pearson wrote in *The Shadow of the Panther: Huey Newton and the Price of Black Power in America*, "The radical left and the left-liberal media continue to play a major role in elevating the rudest, most outlaw element of black America as the true keepers of the flame in all it means to be black." One must ask, has the media's forced ascendancy of this element of the story over all other elements of black protest and black life kept many African-Americans in a ghetto-culture mind set?

It is important to keep in mind that our cultural story, our mythos, includes not only the misjudgments, errors, crimes, atrocities and scandals of our past, but also the great accomplishments, the altruistic struggles, the valor and sacrifice earned and waged with tremendous effort, that have brought betterment of the human condition to millions. If only negative elements of a people's story are reinforced, and positive elements are denied or dismissed, that culture will have no positive role models, and its macro behavior will reflect the negative self-image.

Tomorrow: Atlas Can No Longer Shrug

Atlas Can No Longer Shrug

. . . Our society must still protect individuals from bigotry and prejudice. Discrimination in housing, education, employment and voting access must still be criminal acts. But saying this does not mean that reverse discrimination is the solution. Additionally, no society will ever be successful in controlling racism (or drug abuse, violence, gambling or corruption) by treating individuals, *unless* that society also maintains an ambient cultural story that leads to the desirable behavior. A society cannot make laws or pass policies that will make people rich. The opposite, however, is true. Policies can be made that will hinder the long-range advancement of subgroups or minorities. The much-maligned "welfare system" is perhaps an example. Some of the current criticism of these programs is baseless; however, some of these programs have had disastrous side effect, for many and varied reasons.

Let us first hypothesize a principle called *attractiveness*. Attractiveness pulls people with a particular predisposition to particular areas or programs. This in itself is not a problem. But when an allurement is, by public policy, so established as to virtually coerce a concentration of minorities, the attractiveness indeed becomes the problem.

Our local welfare programs—for housing, food, and medical treatment—are municipality-based rather than regionally, statewide, or nationally based. A municipal system creates poverty pockets; a universal system will weaken those pockets. A municipal system in which a central city offers greater services than surrounding towns creates pockets of poverty cultures; a universal system will weaken the attractiveness of pockets by allowing (not forcing) the dispersal of the poor throughout the region. The long-term effect, as it is expected to be with education, will be to provide the poor with positive role models—that is, to present to them role models with a different cultural story . . .

. . . not a matter of promoting forced regional integration or of promoting programs that will assist inner-city minorities to mingle with the middle class in the surrounding suburbs . . . These are Band-Aids . . . It is a matter of dilution not of people but of services and of programs of assistance . . . If these programs created equal attractiveness throughout the region, then individuals or families would make their moves of their own free will and choice . . .

Enablement programs may signal, or may create within, an individual or a segment of society, an ambient story that says, "You are weak. You are disabled. You are not deserving of more than a subsistence existence. Because you are black, or Hispanic, or a woman or a veteran, you cannot do for yourself what nonblacks/Hispanics/women/veterans can do for themselves." If that story is internalized, it becomes true. Behavior is consistent with self-image. Is that not why we cheer the person who screams, "Rubbish! I can do it!" or even the little train that says, "I think I can. I think I can"? Caution to those who seek empowerment programs—some create a loss of empowerment in the name of empowerment!

. . . the *cultural capital,* as Sowell defines it, includes attitudes toward entrepreneurship and education, toward specific skills, toward general work habits, toward saving, spending, and investing . . . (*Culture,* as here used, does not mean arts, music, language, dress, etc.)

Interestingly, when a family, no matter where their financial situation begins, learns to manage and control its cultural capital, it becomes upwardly mobile both socially and economically. The corollary is also true. When a family, no matter its starting point, forgets these basics, its economic trend is downward. This phenomenon transcends race and ethnicity, which is why there are rich and poor in all races and ethnicities. This does not mean that African-

Americans have not or do not face obstacles beyond those faced by European-Americans. Yet the most difficult obstacle to surmount is not outside prejudice but one's own subculture attitudes—particularly if those attitudes are being reinforced by enablement programs that concentrate those same attitudes in physical sites (poverty pockets), that have in turn ossified a portion of the community into that subculture and into those pockets, and that have destroyed the social mobility of those who wish to break free. It is this ossification, this destruction of social mobility, of will, that can enslave even the strongest. Fighting this ossification presents a dilemma for minority advocacy organizations. They need to have their constituency concentrated, to be the majority in one area—this is their source of power. Simultaneously they recognize the need of the people to be diverse, to be part of the mainstream culture—this decreases their power . . .

Tomorrow: Williams' Plan for Regional Desegregation

Transforming Story: Transforming the Region: A Proposal for Redistricting

There has not been a black person in my grandparents' or my parents' generation who has not suffered an indignity at the hands of a white person in a position of authority over him or her. Their distrust is understandable. However, I am speaking for my generation and urging *all* people of my generation to maximize our attitudes and actions for our own future benefits.

It is time for leaders of the black community to stop blaming the white community for all black problems. It is equally time for the white community to stop looking at the black community as though it were the root and source of all evil, all crime, all drug abuse—or if not the root, the most willing participants. Let us transform and transcend. Let us envision a future not simply in which black children and white children can sit together, but one in which all Americans of all races and all ethnicities truly have equal opportunities. Treating each other as adversaries makes problems worse.

Instead of a Diversity Plan designed to unite us through tolerance, let us change our perspective and propose a Unity Plan which also celebrates our differences, a plan that seeks to combine all the threads of this land into a single multipatterned and multicolored tapestry which we call America. The difference is not simply rhetorical, nor is it one of emphasis. The objectives are the same, but one creates an ambient cultural story that will bring us together, while the other creates a story that tears us apart.

The following proposal represents a strategy for the future. It was initially drawn to specifically represent the Lake Wampahwaug region; however, it is not specific to our region and may be used as a general paradigm for any region with a central, medium-sized city (50,000–250,000). This proposal cannot be applied to large metropolitan areas—New York, Chicago, Boston, St. Louis, Los Angeles, etc.—because of their much greater areas of dense population. Though the same principles and processes apply, modifications, not here addressed, would be necessary.

I have proposed this solution not only because I believe it is less invasive and less disruptive than other plans being considered, but also because I believe some of the plans under consideration are either ill conceived Band-Aids or are so severe and coercive that Atlas can no longer shrug. Under the latter category, there is no freedom. When Atlas can no longer shrug, when governmental decrees are so overpowering that individuals have no choices, freedom is an illusion. When freedom is lost, ensuing macro social behaviors deteriorate and the Land of the Free becomes the land of virtual slavery! No one benefits.

Some of the proposals of the first category—such as the national voucher system—will, I believe, result in unintended side effects similar to the side effects of the housing projects of the past forty years. With reference to voucher systems and magnet school systems, one must ask: Which students will take advantage? What will happen to those students who are left behind? What story, what self-image, and what world view will the ''remnant'' internalize? What cultural characteristics will concentrate in the ''left-out'' neighborhoods? Will these programs result in even greater disparity between the educational haves and the educational have-nots?

Ramifications of proposed programs and policies must be projected before legislation is passed. A plan to move even 100 students from District A to District B, and 100 from B to A, presents a logistical nightmare for those providing the transportation as well as for the students involved. However, this is of minimal consequence when compared to the nightmare produced by placing anyone in any district in which they do not have, and are not likely to develop, a vested interest.

Below I will present a solution *that maintains local parental control and that allows students and families to have a vested interest in their school and their school district*. For whatever policy or plan is adopted, we need the equivalent of an Environmental Impact Report—except this should be a Cultural Impact Report, a study on the projected effects of the statutes on ambient cultural story, and thus projected changes to cultural self-image, world view and macro behavior.

Not in the above terms, but in essence, the above is exactly what the state lawsuit and pending decision have decreed. This state is not unique in its rulings. A case in Kansas City, Missouri, stemming from a 1977 lawsuit in which parents claimed unequal educational opportunities was still in the courts in 1994, when White House attorneys filed briefs with the Supreme Court arguing that student achievement test scores should be a factor in determining whether a school system has eliminated segregation.

Our state's supreme court's pending desegregation order recognizes that segregation in the inner-city school districts, though unintentional, has increased dramatically in the past twenty years. It acknowledges the need for breaking certain aspects of inner-city culture, and the need to expose inner-city youth to suburban and exurban cultural norms. Whether the plaintiffs in the lawsuit wish to agree with that wording or not, this is the essence of their request. Said another way—those inner-city parents who pressed the lawsuit want their children to be, culturally (economic/work attitudes), more like suburban and exurban youth. Their sole goal may be economic opportunity, but those opportunities are most often created by specific cultural attitudes—not by government programs.

Whether the plaintiffs understood the essence of their request, I do not know; but that pith is essential to the social health of the Lake Region. The suit, the court decision, the recognition of the need to desegregate, all make ultimate sense. They will make ultimate sense, however, if and only if positive cultural attributes are assimilated in areas in which there is a paucity of these attributes. The ultimate failure of the plan could occur if the negative cultural attributes that have been concentrated in poverty pockets were celebrated and spread across the region.

No matter one's intentions—for good or for evil, from love or from hate, from fear or from pity—inner-city poverty pockets cannot be abandoned or be left to fester on their own. Suburbia and exurbia cannot look the other way. That would be the equivalent of one saying, "Well, the cancer is only in my lungs. The rest of me is healthy. I'll ignore it."

As a nation we are one body, and if any part of our body is ill, we are ill. Still, one does not attempt to raise the self-esteem of a cancer by celebrating its differences. One celebrates the healthy tissues with the hope their ascendancy will cause the cancerous cells to atrophy.

We are now at a time, because of the court order, when the people in areas where education is working have the wonderful opportunity to dictate to the people in areas where education is not working—to dictate how programs should be run; what should be the academic standards; what should be the standards of student behavior; what should be the standards for teachers and administrators.

As long as the people of the City of Lakeport have been willing to assign, or willing to allow the court to assign, to the people of the surrounding communities the responsibility for the education of the children of the city, then the people of Lakeport must be willing to live by their own *and* outside co-dictates.

If you are a resident of a school district where the system is working, it is now your duty to direct the boards of education in areas neighboring your district that have defective systems, in the ways and manners to run their business (which is now, by court decree, your business). But in doing so, you must become part of the neighboring system (see below).

Further, being that the court has ruled that town borderlines are no longer a valid or legal criterion to establish a school district, and seeing that 80 percent of the average local town's budget is their educational budget, one might conclude that a well-managed system in South Lake Village, or in Kansas, or in Simsbury, or in East Lake, has every right to direct a poorly managed system in Lakeport or in a neighboring defective system—*by combining with that system.*

Personally, I do not understand why the judge has chosen to further disempower the people of the cities when what would probably make more of a difference is to increase their empowerment by encouraging them to be, or making them, more accountable for the outcome of their own children's education.

One additional point before I present a plan that I believe maintains local or parental empowerment, meets all other criteria the court has established, is cost-effective, and for which the Lake Region may prove to be the perfect testing ground (Cultural Impact Study for the nation?).

Over the past several years, the *Ledger* has reported that schools of the "poor cities" in the state rank second to the schools of the "rich suburbs." It should be noted that Lakeport spends $7,922 per student per year. East Lake spends $7,068 per student per year. If you subtract the average cost per student for transportation, the figures become: Lakeport $7,685; East Lake $6,761. The idea that city schools are poor and suburban schools are rich, at least in the local area, must be matched against spending figures. Funds, of course, come disproportionately from the state to school districts—essentially the rich suburbs, via tax transfer payments, already support the cities.

It is not a matter of rich and poor as far as what the school districts have to spend, or as to what scores students within a district achieve on standardized tests. Other factors, such as ambient cultural story, determine outcome.

Disband the School District That Has Failed Redraw All District Lines

The disbanding of old school districts that have failed does not eliminate local control over the newly realigned, regional school districts. This has been a major failure of various experimental programs that have ceded power to either commercial companies or to higher and more removed governmental entities.

The people of the district that has been disbanded, become part of the new, regional district. They are not disenfranchised. The new district is not based on municipal lines, yet all people within the new district are local residents. Local control is not lost. The failed district no longer exists.

The redrawing of district lines and the dissolution of the failed district should be cost-effective because little has changed: No long-distance busing is required, and the least cost-effective district no longer exists . . . (No matter the expenditure, if students are not being educated, the system is cost-ineffective.)

Taxing for the new districts should be handled in a manner similar to taxing for the overlapping fire district that exists between Lakeport and South Lakeport. That is, for any property within a district, the portion of the tax collected that would have gone to the town's or city's school board will now simply go to the new public education entity.

Far more important than cost-effectiveness, however, is the dilution of inner-city students into the population of suburban and exurban students. Once again, this *is* the court decree; and it is a desirable decree. The ramifications on both minority and majority subgroup cultural story, self-image, world view and macro behavior, if natural assimilation is allowed to flow, should be positive.

FROM THE AUTHOR OF

First Things First

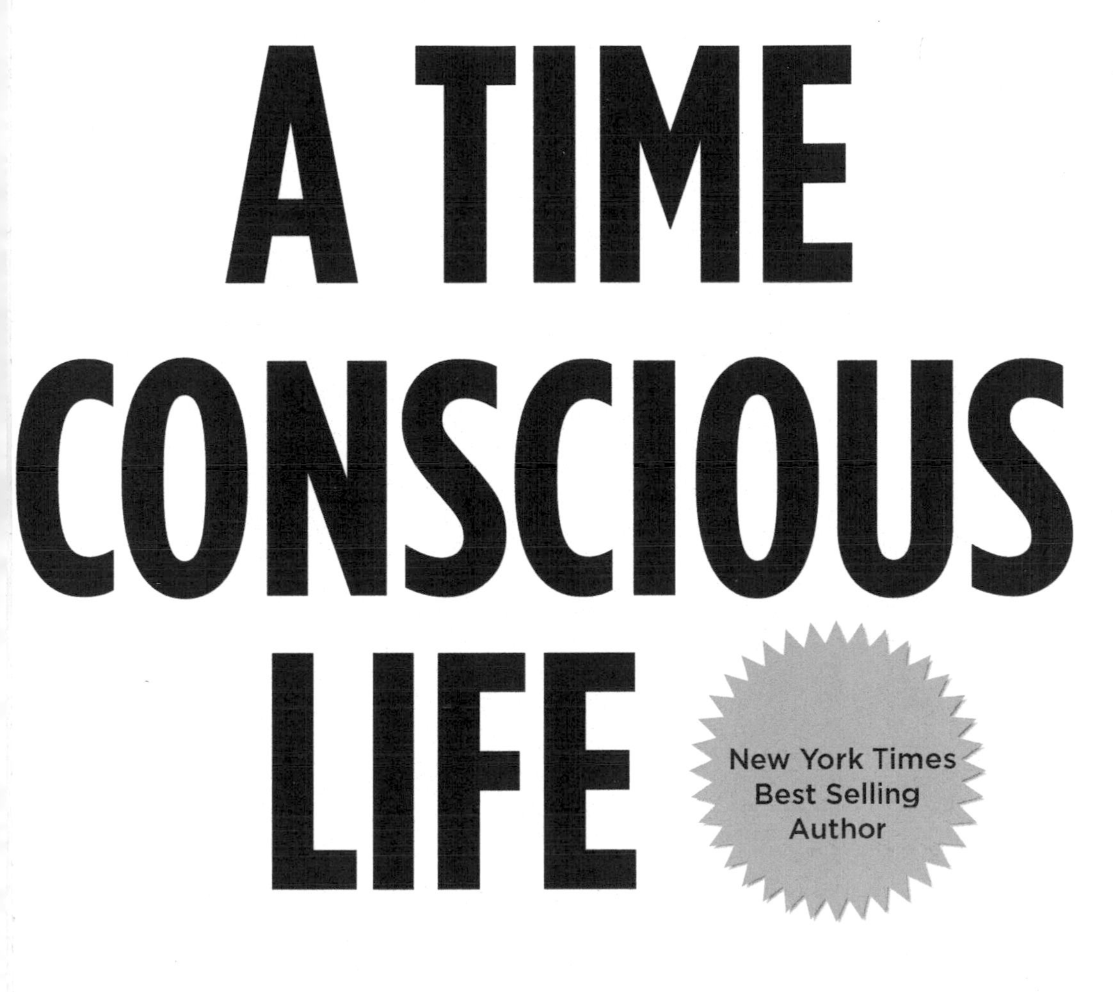

A COMPILATION OF QUOTES FROM

Stephen R. Covey

INSPIRATIONAL PHILOSOPHY FROM DR. COVEY'S LIFE